# *He held out his hand.*

"Your weapons, Miss Parker."

She didn't move.

"Don't make me have to search you."

She turned to follow the path up the hill leading to his cabin, obviously thinking if she did what she was told, he would not disarm her.

"Your weapons, Miss Parker."

Her back stiffened for a moment before she bent over. She turned and threw her knife toward him. She was so quick, he had no time to move. The knife landed point down, less than a half an inch from the toe of his boot.

Unable, momentarily, to move, he glanced down at his feet. Damn, the woman was a menace. "Was that skill or luck?"

She laughed aloud, surprising him. "I'd say it was a bit of both, Sheriff."

He bent over and drew the knife out of the ground. "Have you any more weapons, Miss Parker?"

"Indeed," she admitted. "But that's the only one I have any intention of parting with."

# Touch
# of
# Lace

## Margaret Brownley

A TOPAZ BOOK

TOPAZ
Published by the Penguin Group
Penguin Books USA Inc., 375 Hudson Street,
New York, New York 10014, U.S.A.
Penguin Books Ltd, 27 Wrights Lane,
London W8 5TZ, England
Penguin Books Australia Ltd, Ringwood,
Victoria, Australia
Penguin Books Canada Ltd, 10 Alcorn Avenue,
Toronto, Ontario, Canada M4V 3B2
Penguin Books (N.Z.) Ltd, 182–190 Wairau Road,
Auckland 10, New Zealand

Penguin Books Ltd, Registered Offices:
Harmondsworth, Middlesex, England

First published by Topaz, an imprint of Dutton Signet,
a division of Penguin Books USA Inc.

First Printing, February, 1996
10  9  8  7  6  5  4  3  2  1

*Topaz Man photo © Charles William Bush*

 REGISTERED TRADEMARK—MARCA REGISTRADA

Printed in the United States of America

To George, for giving
this "Traveling Lady" a place in his heart.

# Chapter 1

The old peddler lived on Brubaker Street in a part of Boston seldom mentioned by proper society except, perhaps, in hushed tones. Certainly no respectable woman would choose so much as to stroll past Thieves Corner, let alone venture along the confusing network of alleyways and dead-end streets that were but an anchor's throw away from the busy loading docks.

That's why the appearance of one Miss Abigail Parker caused such a stir that bleak gray day in January. Curiosity ran rampant among the many paupers and thieves who lined the gutters and huddled in the shadows. What would bring this formidable young woman to these parts? Hadn't she heard the tales?

Beggars peered over sandwich boards proclaiming them "blind," and blinked their eyes to get a better look. Tattooed youths loitered in doorways and whispered among themselves as to the identity of the brash young woman.

Ignoring them, Abby hurried with single-minded purpose through the narrow cobblestone maze toward the old peddler's house, never once stopping to look at street signs or to ask directions.

An old grizzled man wrapped in a threadbare blanket coughed and nudged the slumped body next to him. "That fool woman might be puttin' on airs, but she ain't pullin' the wool over my eyes. She ain't no stranger to these parts."

Abby smiled to herself as she hurried past him. A

fool, was she? Well, maybe so. In any case, he was right about her being no stranger.

Between the ages of ten and seventeen, she'd slept in each of its cold, drafty doorways and scrounged for food along every rat-infested alleyway. She sharpened her wits and, some said, her tongue on the raw edge of Thieves Corner.

The faces of the vagrants had changed, the thugs looked more menacing, but the street remained much the same in the five years since the uncle she'd not known existed had come to her rescue.

Thoughts of her beloved Uncle Randall spurred an urgency in her step. Never would she forget the day he'd found her. The things she said to him! The names she called him! She thought he'd invented the story about being her uncle; she was convinced he meant her harm, would do to her what she'd heard had been done to other women who had suddenly disappeared from these very streets. It wasn't until he'd returned with an old leather-bound Bible listing her father's name that she dared believe his startling tale of two brothers separated at birth.

Lord knew why he bothered with her. Any social mores she'd learned from her parents had long since been abandoned for the hard-edged deportment necessary for street survival. Yet, despite her ragamuffin appearance and unsociable behavior, her uncle treated her like a long-lost daughter and had patiently taught her what it meant to trust again.

He had rescued her in every sense of the word. Now, it was her turn to rescue him.

The flared flounce of her gray walking skirt flapped against her felt lace boots as she chased away the pigeons from the debris and trash strewn along the way. Head held high, she walked with brisk purposeful steps, a survival tactic she had learned in her youth. Given a choice between prey, a thief would unerringly target the one moving at a slower pace.

Her gray wool double-caped mackintosh fell below

her waist in graceful folds. Despite the cold damp air, she'd decided against the warmth of a muff or even gloves. Such amenities could be a hindrance should she need to defend herself.

Her honey-colored hair was caught in a perfect smooth bun and tucked beneath the brim of her jaunty felt hat. She had more fashionable hats at home, but preferred the anonymity provided by the double-mesh netting.

She held her umbrella like a weapon as she artfully dodged around wagons and horses. Ahead, she spotted a uniformed policeman taking a bribe from a man she recognized as a pickpocket. She grimaced in disgust and crossed to the other side of the street. Her homeless years had taught her that a man wearing a badge was often the worst of all thieves.

The dirt-streaked face of a street urchin caught her eye. The boy was probably twelve or thirteen, older than many street urchins and certainly older than she was in those first years on the street, but he still had the bewildered, frightened look that marked him as a stranger to the streets. He probably had no way of knowing that the vulnerability in his face would make him a target of every gang member in the area.

The innocence of the boy struck a strong enough chord to dangerously slow her step. She ached for the child, but knew if she slipped him money she would put his life in even more jeopardy. Instead, she purchased some fresh warm buns from a street vendor, hoping, perhaps, to strike up a conversation with the lad and find out the whereabouts of his family. But by the time she'd paid the vendor, the child had disappeared. After a futile search, she handed the buns to a blind beggar and hurried on her way.

Upon turning a corner, she spotted the boy again, his back pinned against the side of a brick building by three tormentors. Oblivious to the boy's plight, scores of homeless souls lined the various doorways, trying to catch snatches of sleep in the relative safety of daylight. Only a fool would close so much as an eyelid after dark.

Not one person paid the boy the least attention. The law of Thieves Corner was of necessity harsh; each man, each woman, each child stood alone. It was survival of the fittest and anyone interfering with one of the roaming gangs would pay with limb, if not life.

The boy's eyes were wide with fright. He had nothing of value and it sickened Abby to think what the gang members demanded of him.

Slowing her stride, she slipped the umbrella into her left hand and reached into her boot with her right. She pulled out her knife with more speed than care and inadvertently sliced the fabric of a perfectly good skirt.

"Holy blazes," she muttered under her breath, in deference to her uncle's patient tutelage. It was a fine time to discover her knife skills had grown rusty during these last five years of living a normal life.

The first time she'd drawn her knife in her uncle's presence, he'd almost had cardiac failure. Even now it was hard not to smile as she recalled the horror on his face the day he'd first set sight on her lethal knife, with its gleaming six-inch steel blade. Her dear uncle had tried in vain to discourage her from carrying such a weapon. "You're a lady, not a warrior," he'd said. As if one had anything to do with the other.

She was close enough to hear the boy's pitiful pleas. Judging her distance carefully, she eyed the stack of wooden crates next to the building and spotted her target. She prayed to high heaven her aim was better than her draw.

The most she could hope to accomplish was to scare the hoodlums away. But if they saw her throw the knife or otherwise suspected she had tried to distract them, she might find herself in a whole peck of trouble.

Keeping her eyes directly ahead as she walked, she gripped the blade between her fingers and thumb. To the right of her, dozens of people were tucked into every possible nook and cranny of a three-story brick building. She felt an old familiar anger well inside. Fewer people had been known to stage a revolt. Yet, experience told her these malingerers were not likely to jeopardize their own safety for the sake of another.

A quick glance confirmed that the bullies were too occupied to notice her. With a little luck, the gang members might take her knife as a warning and think they were under siege. Timing was essential. She stopped, turned, drew her hand over her head, and brought her arm forward in a quick sweeping arc, releasing her knife at shoulder level. It was done so quickly and smoothly, in barely a second or two, that by the time anyone turned to look for the knife thrower, she'd already distanced herself.

She allowed herself to look back when a commotion sounded behind her. Failing to do the natural thing would draw more attention to herself than was wise.

Much to her amazement, the entire stack of wooden crates had come crashing down. A tangle of arms and legs fought to be free of the crates. By the time the three bullies had crawled out from beneath the jumbled heap, the youth was gone.

The leader of the pack gave each doorway a cursory glance. His hard-steel gaze dismissed Abby as a possible suspect. After studying the blank faces across from him, he cursed angrily, kicked a crate, and took off down the street, the rest of his gang at his heels.

No sooner had they disappeared than laughter rang out from one of the recessed doorways across the way. A grizzly man with a huge mass of frizzy hair limped over to the fallen crates, found Abby's knife, and hobbled across the street. He was still laughing when he handed her the knife, handle first, and bowed at the waist.

"Only one woman I know can throw a knife like that," he said grinning. "And that's Traveling Lady."

Startled to hear her street name after all these years, she stared at the face of the man. Her habit of walking all night long, up and down the street, never stopping to huddle by the fires like the others, had earned her the moniker Traveling Lady.

"Cowhide? Is that you?" His face looked more like the ashes of a fire than anything likely to be found on a steer, but his laughter was unmistakable.

"So you remember. . . ."

"How could I not?" She tried to hug him, but he stepped aside.

"You're all prettied up now and looking like one of those fancy ladies who live on Bunker Hill. It ain't proper for you to go around huggin' the likes of me."

The reference to Bunker Hill made her laugh. No one outside of Thieves Corner would mistake her plain garb for that worn by Boston's upper class. "Since when have I ever been concerned with being proper?"

He gave her a toothless grin as he looked her up and down. "Not for as long as I've known you. My, if you haven't turned into a beauty. Always knew you would. What are you doin' back in these parts?"

"I'm here on business," she explained.

"Business, eh?" He lowered his voice. "Any business you have here can't be legal."

"It's legal, Cowhide," she assured him. She glanced around and, seeing no sign of the gang, leaned toward him. "The boy?"

Cowhide regarded her with the patient tolerance of a child-weary parent. "He's been here a week or so. Stays pretty much to himself."

"Has he no family to help him?"

Cowhide gave her a sharp look. "A person's entitled to his privacy." It was not the first time he'd reminded her of this unspoken code of the street that required everyone to assume a false name. Had the code been less rigid, and the others been more willing to reveal her whereabouts, her poor uncle might well have found her years earlier.

"I want to help him. Take him home with me—"

"That kid was so scared he ain't never gonna stop runnin'."

"But—"

"Go home, Traveling Lady. You don't belong here no more."

She lay a hand on his arm, aware of the thinness of his shirt and knowing it was probably the warmest attire he owned. Every Christmas, her uncle had arranged for a shipment of blankets and boots to be sent to the area. She felt a twinge of guilt. This year she'd been too distraught to continue the practice in her uncle's absence. She promised herself to correct the oversight at once. "Watch over him, please. Would you do that for me?" She was asking more of him than she had a right to do.

"You ain't changed much, have you, Traveling Lady?" He regarded her with rheumy eyes. "I'll watch over him. If I find him. For you I'd do anything. You once saved my life, and I won't eve' forgit it."

She'd almost forgotten the winter she'd nursed him back to health after his bout with pneumonia. Had she not persuaded a doctor to give her medicine, Cowhide would surely have died.

"Now git the hell outta here." With that he hobbled back across the street, cussing and raising a fist at the driver of a milk wagon.

Abby glanced around, then quickly slipped her knife back into her boot. She regarded the damage to her skirt with dismay. The slit traveled halfway up her leg. What a fine kettle of fish! She held the torn fabric together the best she could and continued on her way.

The tall brick tenement house stood at the end of the block. She walked past a long row of doors, checking the names on each dull metal plate. She'd occupied herself many nights by reciting the names on the doors from memory. She had once envied the people who lived in the row of grim brick houses. At the time, these modest, even lowly accommodations seemed as refined as a king's palace. Today, she saw them for what they were.

Finding the one she sought, she gave the weathered

wood door a brisk knock. Overhead, a lone seagull let out a wailing cry.

The door creaked on its rusty hinges as it opened, revealing a stooped little man with a bushy un-trimmed beard.

"Mr. Klein?"

The man peered over the metal frames of his specta-cles. "You must be Miss Parker. Come in. Come in." His voice crackled with age, but his eyes, though faded, were sharp and alert. She followed him through a small entryway into a sparsely furnished room. A log burned lazily in the fireplace, adding but a token of warmth to the shabby surroundings.

She set her umbrella down and lifted the veil away from her face, folding it back over her hat. "Have you any news of my uncle?" she asked impatiently, not wanting to wait another minute to hear what the ped-dler had to say.

"Sit down, sit down." He lowered himself on a chair and waited for her to make use of the only other chair in the room.

She remained on her feet. "Please don't hold any-thing back." Randall J. Parker had been missing for four months. The last letter she'd received from him had been posted from Denver, Colorado.

The old man pressed his gnarled fingers together. "After I received your letter, I wrote to the proprietors of every hotel or boardinghouse I know personally. I also contacted other peddlers who work in the area. I was able to determine your uncle was last seen heading for a little town called Dangling Rope. It's about twenty miles south of Cripple Creek. I'm afraid that's the ex-tent of my news."

In essence, he'd told her no more than she already knew. Disappointed, she lowered herself onto the hard-backed chair. Mr. Klein had been her last resort. There was simply no place else to turn. "I'm really afraid something may have happened to him."

"You don't know that for certain. Lots of men go

west and are never heard from again. Gold fever can make a man forget who and what he is. *Oy vay*. Your uncle would not be the first to neglect his family in the quest for gold."

"My uncle would never forget me!" she said hotly. "Something's happened to him. I'm sure of it." A clump of wood crackled and rolled from its fiery bed and the old peddler heaved himself to his feet to add another log.

Watching him, Abby made up her mind. "I have no choice but to travel to Colorado myself."

Mr. Klein straightened and turned. "I don't think that would be wise."

"Why not?" Never one to sit still for long, she stood and paced back and forth as the idea took hold. "I should have thought of this before. I have a list of my uncle's regular customers. One of them might know something that would explain his disappearance."

The old man looked horrified at the thought of her traveling alone. "The Colorado gold mines are no place for a lady." It was the second time that day someone had used the term *lady* in such a manner. Both men had meant to be complimentary, she supposed, but it only reminded her of the many and, in her opinion, unnecessary restrictions society placed on women. She wondered what the old peddler would think if he knew of the knife she kept with her at all times.

"Your uncle's disappearance could be the result of foul play," the peddler continued, his voice gentle.

She fought against the idea like a warrior fought an advancing army, but she knew the man didn't mean to alarm her; he was only trying to be practical. "If I go to Colorado, I can find out one way or the other."

The old man shook his head vigorously. "A lady has no business in those lawless gold towns."

"It seems to me a *lady* has business wherever she puts her mind to have business!" Because the peddler looked taken aback by her boldness, she tried to cover her outburst with a demure smile. "I know the names of all my uncle's customers, what they like. I can attend to my uncle's neglected business while I'm making inquiries. It only makes sense that I go."

Mr. Klein drew his fingers the length of his beard. "If you've got your fool heart set on rescuing him, then go to Colorado. But don't go fooling around with the peddling business!"

"It's my business, too," she said stubbornly. It was her responsibility to keep her uncle's books and answer his correspondence. If that didn't make it her business, then what in the name of heaven did? "In his absence, many orders have been delivered to the house. Surely his customers must be waiting for these goods. If they're not delivered soon, my uncle could lose everything he's worked for all these years."

Flames from the fire were reflected on his spectacles as he regarded her. "Even if I were to teach you everything I know—which I have no intention of doing—it won't make you a peddler. Peddling takes a certain instinct you're born with. You either have it or you don't and I've not heard of a woman having it."

Abby stood behind her chair and shook her head in disagreement. "There isn't any law that says a woman can't have anything she puts her mind to. Besides, I've worked with my uncle enough to know peddler ways. Why, I know all kinds of things about the business. I know I'm entitled to two hundred pounds free on the train, providing I can get it into a single drum." She used the popular term for a peddler's trunk. She could never manage the canvas pack old-timers still wore as a matter of pride on their backs. Such packs were known to weigh as much as a hundred and eighty pounds. "I know how to travel all the way to Colorado and back on a one-way train ticket . . ." On and on she continued, describing all the aspects of life on the road as described by her uncle.

Despite the chilled room, the old peddler drew out a handkerchief and mopped his forehead. The small square window faced a brick wall, letting in little in the way of light or air.

"I know all the ways a drummer might save money. I also know that peddlers must maintain proper hygiene," she continued. "My uncle never failed to wash his socks out every night." He often claimed that no peddler worth his salt would rest his head to pillow until his socks were hanging over the nearest branch or windowsill. Her now deceased aunt waged many an argument with her husband over his socks. He insisted upon washing his own, even between road trips, but poor Aunt Ida considered this an affront to her housekeeping skills.

"What about food?" Mr. Klein quizzed her.

"When in doubt, ask for an egg," she replied, reciting one of her uncle's favorite expressions. Most peddlers had to adhere to strict dietary restrictions due to religious beliefs. Though her uncle's religion offered no such restriction, he proclaimed the practice a healthy one and had laughed heartily upon learning that the Cherokees referred to peddlers as egg eaters.

Mr. Klein nodded, but the skepticism remained on his face. "You are most knowledgeable about our profession, but this does not make you a peddler. A woman could bring much shame and dishonor to our ranks."

Annoyed that the man had such a low regard for her abilities, she drew her netting back over her face. "I believe you give me more credit than I deserve."

The retired peddler looked taken aback. "Peddling is a very old and very noble profession—the world's oldest, I believe."

"Really, Mr. Klein? I thought it was . . ." She caught herself just in time.

"Go on, Miss Parker. You thought it was what?"

"Agriculture," she said, thinking quickly.

The old man stared at her for a moment, then surprised her by laughing aloud. " 'Tis a pity you're a woman. If you were a man, you'd make a fine peddler. Quick minds always do."

She gathered up her umbrella. "Since I can't do anything about my gender, I guess my mind will come in quite handy."

Shaking his head in disapproval, Mr. Klein walked her to the door. Unfortunately, she had forgotten about the scandalous slit in her skirt until she caught him staring down at her hem.

"May I ask what wares you will be peddling?" he asked.

Still irritated at herself for cutting her good skirt, Abby drew the fabric of her skirt together. "Cosmetics."

The old man looked incredulous. "You're trekking all the way to the gold mines to sell cosmetics? No one uses cosmetics in those towns but—"

"I know. My uncle has quite a thriving business. . . . He said the real gold mine was in those brothels. The women have money to spend and don't mind spending it. It's amazing that more peddlers haven't discovered the possibilities, don't you think? Why . . ." She stopped, suddenly aware that Mr. Klein appeared to be hyperventilating.

"Mr. Klein! Are you all right?"

"I'm fine," he insisted, though his face was red and his eyes were nearly popping out of his head. He practically pushed her out of the door. "Whatever you do, don't tell anyone you know me." With that he slammed the door in her somewhat startled face.

# Chapter 2

Moments after the Hundley stagecoach rolled into the deserted town of Dangling Rope, Colorado, Gunnar Kincaid stood in front of the fire-damaged Grand View Hotel and wondered what in the name of God he was doing there.

He was the only one of several passengers foolhardy enough to disembark at what was little more than a ghost town. The others, mainly bankers and investors, had continued their journey to the booming gold mining towns of Victor and Cripple Creek, some twenty miles away.

The driver tossed Gunnar's travel-worn valise into the hard-packed snow, then swung himself up to the driver's seat. "Gee-who!" he shouted with a snap of the whip. The eight sturdy horses rushed forward. The stagecoach rolled out of town almost as quickly as it had come, the sound of iron-tired wheels and horses' hooves fading in the distance.

A forlorn feeling washed over him. If he'd had an ounce of sense, he'd still be on that stage instead of this godforsaken town that amounted to little more than a few empty buildings.

Obviously, a stage taking the side trip to Dangling Rope was unusual enough to warrant the attention of what few residents remained, including his younger brother, Nathan. Among those present, five, amazingly enough, were women.

Nathan greeted him with a wary, almost sardonic look. At first Gunnar hadn't recognized him. He'd lost weight in the year since Gunnar had seen him last. At twenty-five, Nathan was two years younger, but his unkempt blond hair and unshaven face made him look years older.

Nathan swaggered toward him. "I was wondering when you would get here, big brother. Couldn't wait, could you?"

Gunnar bit back the angry retort that rose to his lips. He hadn't expected a brass band to greet his arrival, but he'd expected a warmer reception, especially from his own kin. The trip from Chicago had been a nightmare. High winds and snow had damaged a main trestle, forcing him to abandon the rails and journey to Denver by stagecoach. From there he'd traveled by train to Divide, where he was forced to bribe the stagecoach driver at great expense to go out of his way to Dangling Rope.

Not wanting to get into an argument, Gunnar let his brother's mocking remark go unchallenged. There would be enough time later for airing the family wash. He glanced at the charred shell of the hotel. Part of the downstairs and nearly all of the second story were gone. "Is there somewhere I can get some shut-eye?"

"Is that all you want, big brother? Just some shut-eye?" It was obvious by Nathan's slurred voice and wavering stance he'd been drinking. Gunnar's jaw tightened. Nothing had changed; not a damned thing. Though Gunnar would do the world for his brother, had practically chased around the country after him, they were not close, and hadn't been since that long-ago fateful day. . . .

Nathan addressed the curious onlookers. "This is my brother, Gunnar." He spoke with feigned heartiness. "Came to bail me out of trouble. Just like all the other times."

A dark-haired woman with tight corkscrew curls stepped forward. Her red velvet dress, plunging neckline, and painted face gave no doubt as to her occupation. The faded dress with its yellowed lace trim was living proof that no business was immune to hard times. "I'm Madam Rosie and these are my girls. This is Meg and Ginger and that's Ruby over there. She's a bit shy around strangers. Stop by and see us sometime. A brother of Nathan's deserves special attention."

The woman named Ruby held her head down, keeping her face hidden. But Meg and Ginger regarded him openly, their painted faces and garish sateen gowns almost grotesque in the late afternoon sun. The sight of their red painted lips, brightly colored cheeks, and startling blue eyelids threw him back momentarily in time. *Don't mess Mama's face,* echoed a voice from a distant past. Swallowing the wave of distaste that rose to his throat, he doffed his hat and nodded. "Much obliged, ladies."

"And this is Otis," Nathan slurred, placing an arm around the stooped shoulders of a thin man with a horseshoe mustache. "Owns the . . . the . . . whatever that is."

"The general store," Otis said, shaking Gunnar's hand. "So you're Nathan's brother, eh?" He eyed Gunnar with a look of surprise.

"You've heard of Mom Bull, big brother," Nathan continued, and all eyes swung to an enormously built woman smoking a cigar.

Mom Bull. Mother of the most notorious gunslinger in the West. Of course he'd heard of her. Gunnar leveled his gaze at her square homely face and decided then and there he never wanted to meet her son. At six feet tall, she matched him inch for inch, though widthwise she was twice as big. Shaking hands with her felt about as pleasant as putting his hand in a vise.

"That's my restaurant o'er yonder," she said. "I serve three meals a day, seven days a week."

"And not one meal fit to eat," Otis said beneath his breath. He quickly introduced the rest of the townsfolk, then pointed toward the hill that rose behind the town. "Maybe your brother can stay in one of those empty cabins up yonder."

Seeing the look of hostility on his brother's face, Gunnar picked up his worn valise and nodded. "I won't be staying more than a day or so."

Mom Bull blew smoke in Gunnar's face. "You ain't got a whole lot to say in the matter. It could be weeks, maybe months before the next stage returns." She gave Nathan a meaningful look. "I think it would be a good idea for you to take your brother up to the cabin." Turning to Gunnar, she added, "I serve supper from seven to nine, breakfast from six to eight, and lunch whenever I feel like it."

"Thank you, ma'am. I'll remember that."

"See that you do." Mom Bull stomped away, with Otis giving chase. Rosie herded her girls together and marched them down the street like an old mother hen.

Nathan produced a bottle of whiskey and lifted it to his mouth.

Disgusted, Gunnar tightened his hold on the worn leather handle of his suitcase and started up the hill. His heavy boots crunched against the hard frozen snow.

Nathan followed. "Big brother to the rescue."

Ignoring the bitterness in Nathan's voice, Gunnar trekked toward the first cabin and dropped the valise on the rough wooden steps. Guessing from the amount of leaves piled on the porch, he'd say the cabin was unoccupied. He turned to face Nathan.

"Your wire said you were in trouble again. What the hell did you expect me to do? Forget it?"

Nathan gave an ugly laugh and lifted the whiskey bottle to his lips once again. Gunnar angrily knocked the bottle out of Nathan's hands.

Nathan looked surprised and Gunnar could guess why. It wasn't like him to resort to violence, though heaven only knew Nathan had given him ample reason in the past to lose his temper. No matter. His anger today paid off and, judging from the look on his face, had either surprised or scared Nathan into sobriety. At least he looked less insolent.

"Now suppose you tell me what's going on."

Nathan wiped away the whiskey that had spilled on his chin. "A prospector told me this area had all the signs of a major gold vein." He nodded at the creek behind the cabin. "We even found some yellow. He was right about the gold. The only problem was, he was off by about twenty miles. That's the chance you take when you buy land on speculation. But Bull don't see it that way. He said that if his mother doesn't get a proper return on her dollar, I'm a goner."

Gunnar turned the collar up on his coat and gaped at his brother in disbelief. "Bull Crankshaw threatened you?" He glanced up at the sky. Dark clouds promised more snow; the cold air confirmed it.

"How do you always manage to get yourself mixed up in these kinds of things?" He was still furious about last year's Dodge City affair. Had he arrived in Dodge City a day later, he'd have found his brother buried with his boots on. The time before, he'd sprung his brother from a Texas gallows and the two had raced out of town with an angry mob at their heels.

Nathan glanced at what remained of the whiskey bottle. The last of the liquid trickled from the brown glass neck and the smell of whiskey permeated the air. "I could run. Change my name so Bull would never find me. So you could never find me."

Gunnar gritted his teeth. He'd gone through hell because of Nathan—and probably would again. "Why didn't you, dammit? It would have saved us both a headache."

Nathan scraped the toe of his scuffed black leather boot across a patch of snow, leaving a wavy line. "It wasn't just Bull's threat. A man gets tired of running, you know?"

Gunnar lifted his brow in surprise. Running? Is that what Nathan had been doing all these years? Traveling from state to state, territory to territory, building town sites that never amounted to much and bilking honest folks out of hard-earned money just so he'd have to keep running?

Feeling a bone-wrenching weariness, Gunnar climbed the wooden steps and walked into the dimly lit cabin. He glanced around, barely taking note of his surroundings. It was his brother who commanded his attention. Always, his brother.

Sometimes the span between them seemed as wide as the Grand Canyon.

"How much money have you cheated these folks out of?" Gunnar asked, referring to the odd assortment of people he'd met earlier. Why they'd remained in this ghost of a town after everyone else had left was a puzzle.

Nathan leaned against the doorjamb. The king-sized chip on his shoulder momentarily abandoned, he looked strangely lost. "It's different this time, I swear. I honestly thought I'd found the perfect place for my town."

The perfect place. How many times had Gunnar heard that? Nathan never stayed at any one thing long enough to make a success of it; he'd left a trail of rotting buildings and dying towns behind him. "It's high time you face up to a few facts. No place is perfect."

The chip appeared again and Nathan's face turned red with anger. "Why did you bother coming?"

Gunnar sucked in his breath. He was no stranger to his brother's rage and hatred. But it still hurt, dammit. He stepped past him and stood on the porch, inhaling the fresh, pine-scented air. He eyed the majestic view around him. Rugged mountain peaks rose around the little town, giving a sense of permanence to Dangling Rope that was deceiving. From what he saw, the town was no more permanent than the wind.

"Why?" Nathan asked again. "Why did you come?"

Gunnar's jaw tightened. He knew why; hell, it didn't take much brains to figure that out. It was guilt that brought him here. Guilt would keep him here. Each and every night of his life, he'd lain in bed and wondered how many times he'd have to save his fool brother's neck before the guilt would go away. It was times like today he doubted it ever would.

He leaned against the rough wood post that supported the porch. Drops of water trickled from the edge of the roof. He didn't want to talk about guilt. Not now. Not ever.

At the edge of the clearing, a deer stepped out of a grove of trees, lifted its head in the direction of the cabin, then foraged at the clump of greenery that poked through the snow. "I came because you're my brother. You know I'd do anything for you."

Nathan turned away and for several moments the brothers stood side by side, each lost in his own thoughts. "It could have been something, this town," Nathan said at last. "When we found flecks of yellow in that creek, I was so certain . . ."

Gunnar sighed; he'd heard variations of this story more times than he cared to remember. "So you sold these poor people a bill of goods."

"I honestly thought they'd get their money back." Nathan dipped the brim of his hat down over his face. The wind had started up. The sky had grown noticeably more gray, the air colder in the last twenty minutes or so. "You won't have to worry about me much longer, big brother. Old Bull said he was going to have my head on a platter if his mother loses her money."

Gunnar pushed his breath out between his lips. He still couldn't believe his brother had been messing around with the kin of the West's most notorious gunslinger. "Serves you right for promising things you can't deliver."

"Dammit, Gunnar! I'm going to save this town. Just you wait and see."

"What's to save? There's nothing here but a few empty buildings."

"Otis came up with an idea. He says there's talk about forming a county and having an election at the end of the year for county seat. Wouldn't that be the kicks? If we became the county seat? With your knowledge of the law . . ."

Gunnar shook his head in disbelief. Lord help him. He'd have a better chance of getting the moon named county seat. "I don't know anything about Colorado law, Nathan. Even if I did, do you honestly think we could get this hole-in-the-wall on the ballot?"

"What other choices do I have? Would you rather I change my name—hide out somewhere?"

Gunnar rubbed his chin. "No one gets away from Bull Crankshaw. He'll hunt you down to the ends of the earth. I'll talk to him."

Nathan kicked an empty bean can down the steps of the porch. "The hell you will."

Gunnar rubbed his aching head. He was too tired to argue. It had been a difficult journey from Divide. The road had not been repaired since a terrible blizzard hit the area in early December. The ruts were so deep in places, it was a miracle the stagecoach hadn't broken an axle.

Gunnar's gaze traveled down the slope to the two-story wooden buildings that made up the town of Dangling Rope. The hotel stood across from the boarded-up sheriff's office. The general merchandising store was bookended by two empty saloons. He supposed the saloons had been deserted like everything else the instant word had reached town that gold had been discovered in Cripple Creek.

Today, the doors swung in the stinging wind as if the owners had only moments earlier rushed from the building, picks in hand, to join the race for gold.

Gunnar leaned over the side of the railing and let his gaze follow the ragged line of mountains behind the cabin. Standing taller than the rest, Pikes Peak's dazzling white winter coat stood out against the ominous gray sky. As he watched, flurries of snow began to fall.

Dangling Rope with all its faults had a raw rugged

beauty that was pleasing to the soul and eye alike. Gunnar imagined that each season brought its own special beauty to the area. Still, no town flourished on beauty. A town needed gold or silver or some other economically feasible asset. It needed the railroad and investors. In essence, a town needed everything that Dangling Rope didn't have.

"Would you look into it?" Nathan asked. "Find out what we have to do to get this town on the ballot."

Gunnar couldn't believe his ears. "Do you honestly think we could get this town on the ballot?"

"Why did you bother coming?" Nathan's voice was filled with loathing. But there was a look in Nathan's eyes that surprised Gunnar. It was a look of a drowning man reaching for a sinking raft. There was frantic hope in that look—and maybe even desperation—however much they were hidden by contempt.

Gunnar gripped the rough-hewn railing with both hands. As much as he was tempted to feed that hope, he wasn't sure if he should. It would only postpone the inevitable, and maybe even make matters worse. Maybe he should just give Nathan the money to leave. Get him out of his hair once and for all. It was a tempting thought.

He and his brother were almost as different in appearances as they were in temperaments. Gunnar was the taller of the two. Standing six foot three, his body was hard and lean. Nathan stood two inches shorter; his stockier body was more compact, though less muscular.

Gunnar inherited his dark hair and eyes from his mother's side. Both contrasted sharply with Nathan's lighter eyes and blond hair, derived from their ne'er-do-well father. The two brothers were as different in looks and temperaments as it was possible for members of the same family to be.

Gunnar felt the weight of frustration settle on his shoulders. Despite all the problems Nathan had caused him through the years, despite all the bitterness, the

anger, the hatred and resentment, Gunnar's love for
his brother ran deep. He would do anything to right
the terrible wrong that had started Nathan on this terrible and self-destructive path, had, indeed, devoted
most of adolescence and all of his adult life to that
very cause. He'd gladly sell his soul if he thought it
would help Nathan put his life together and find some
measure of peace and contentment.

"All right, I'll look into it." Compared to what he'd
done in the past to save his brother's neck, this was
small beer.

Nathan looked surprised. "What?"

"I said I'll look into getting the town on the ballot."

Nathan brushed against his whiskers with the back
of his hand. "Do . . . do you think we have a chance?"

"A chance? Are you crazy? Do you honestly think we
can convince a bunch of politicians that an out-of-the-
way, no-nothing speck of a town is worthy of such
consideration?"

"Then why the hell bother?"

Gunnar stared down the hill toward town, at the
swinging doors of Sleazy's Saloon, and recalled the terrified tear-streaked face of a five-year-old boy screaming, *Don't go! Please don't go!* "Hell if I know."

# Chapter 3

It was early May and the last of the snow that had blanketed the town for nearly six months straight had finally melted. Wildflowers bloomed freely, and a vivid array of reds, blues, and yellows flamed across the meadows, spreading over the sides of the canyons and up the mountain slopes like a colorful patchwork quilt.

The Hundley stagecoach teetered dangerously, its bullwhip thoroughbraces worked to the limit, as it barreled toward Dangling Rope. The road resembled a strip of narrow ribbon tossed randomly across the mountain.

Abby gaped out the window, her eyes round in horror. She was convinced she'd not live to see Dangling Rope, or any of the other towns, for that matter.

The driver swerved to miss a dangerous rut, barely managing to escape the edge. Maintaining her rigid posture, Abby pressed her hands that much harder into her lap. Holy blazes! If she managed to survive the journey up the mountain, she would be tempted to stay there rather than endure another trip on this road.

The other passengers, all men, seemed oblivious to the alarming rocking motion of the stagecoach or the precarious strip of a road that was barely wide enough to accommodate the team of eight hefty horses. It was hard to determine what was worse: the jarring of the crowded stage, the oppressive heat and choking dust, or the annoying calm of the other passengers. It irritated her that she was the only one with sense enough to worry.

Abby leaned closer to the window, hoping to get

some air. Four of the men sat calmly discussing union problems up at the mines. Another man read the Denver newspaper as he mopped his forehead with a dusty handkerchief. Next to him a youth who looked to be no more than sixteen or seventeen slept, his chin on his chest and his head bopping around like a cork in water. Fanning herself furiously, Abby glared at the men. The stagecoach lurched and Abby cried out.

"It's all right, ma'am," one said kindly. "The driver ain't lost a passenger yet and, as far as I know, not more than three teams." He gave her a reassuring smile. "Now you just hold on. We'll be in Dangling Rope in less than an hour."

The man with the newspaper grumbled, "If we weren't forced out of our way on some feminine whim, we'd be in Victor in an hour and not some damned flyspeck town known as Dangling Rope."

"That's enough, Bruce. The woman's upset."

The men fell silent, for which Abby was grateful. This whole trip had been difficult and emotionally draining. She'd been on the road for weeks now and had followed her uncle's trail from Boston to Colorado. She'd delivered her uncle's orders and assured his customers that her uncle had not purposely neglected them. Mostly, she'd questioned everyone who might have known her uncle, no matter how remotely, in the hopes of gaining some clue as to her uncle's mysterious disappearance. To date, she'd learned nothing new.

Any hope she had of uncovering her uncle's whereabouts now appeared to depend entirely on what she learned in Dangling Rope, his last known destination.

The stage veered sharply to the right, then left. With an anxious glance at the red-rocked cliffs that rose on either side of the road, Abby was convinced anew she would never survive the trip.

It had taken months for Gunnar Kincaid to organize the town and prepare the scant number of residents for the visits from state officials.

He'd spent days in Denver, learning the legalities of forming a county and applying for the county seat. No one could tell him exactly what qualified a town for such a distinction. As far as Gunnar could determine, after a few requirements were met, the selections were made on little more than the whim of a few politicians.

An hour before the officials were due to arrive for their inspection, Gunnar stood in front of the few townsfolk who called Dangling Rope home. The number had dwindled to twelve during the last few weeks, thirteen counting himself. The main requirement for a county seat was a significant population. Thirteen residents was hardly significant by anyone's account. To make matters worse, he'd had a falling-out with Madam Rosie over the color of her brothel and she refused to let her girls help out, leaving him only nine people to work with. The damned pink building was an eyesore, but at least he'd managed to draw attention away from the shocking color by plastering a sign outside the building that read OPERA HOUSE.

He stood in the middle of the street where he'd told the others to meet him, and checked his notes. "All right, folks. Let me have your attention. Mom Bull . . ." He glanced at the hat she'd finally agreed to wear to hide her sheared locks. Unfortunately, on Mom Bull, the hat looked little larger than an inkwell and her hair stuck out from beneath the brim like needles on a pincushion.

Gunnar regretted making her give up her rawhide hat, but the high brim added inches to her already impressive height. She already towered over two-thirds of the townsfolk. The plain-cut blue dress gave her as much definition as a whiskey barrel, but it was infinitely better than the canvas overalls she generally wore.

One of Gunnar's biggest challenges was to talk her out of preparing the politicians a meal. Everything the woman cooked was charred, curdled, or tasted like sawdust.

"You make an impressive librarian." He only hoped no one would notice her mustache or the ever-present cigar that dangled from the side of her mouth.

Mom Bull pulled the cigar through the air and grinned, obviously pleased with herself. "Wait till my son hears that his mother is a librarian." She laughed. "To think I never so much as read a book. Don't that take the cake?"

"Yes, well, we don't want anyone to know you can't read."

"I won't say a word, Captain." She bit off the tip of her cigar and spit it onto the ground. "Not a word."

"That's sheriff, Mom Bull, not captain, and I'd appreciate it if you'd hold off on the cigars until after our guests have left." He ignored the face she made, and he went over his instructions. "As soon as you see us coming, step outside and make up some excuse for not inviting us in." The library consisted of three books total, and these could be seen quite plainly from the window.

"Don't you worry none, Sheriff. I'll just tell them about my son's influence and they'll change their mind about touring the library."

Gunnar looked up from his notes. The only influence Bull Crankshaw had was when he stood behind a six-shooter. "I think it would be better if you don't mention your son."

"I have a question." The man known as Clod Weinberger stepped forward, his ever-present fiddle in his hand. His dream was to become a good enough fiddle player that the instruments would one day bear his name. "Like that there Stradivari fellow," he liked to say.

As far as Gunnar was concerned, Clod's fiddles seemed to lack the dignified ring of Stradivari's violins, but he made no mention of it. Any man wise enough to have a dream earned the right to pursue it. Even if he couldn't play worth a knothole. Gunnar had heard better music coming from a colicky baby.

Despite the odds, Clod had a better chance of reaching his goal than Mom Bull, whose ambition was to earn recognition as a world-famous cook.

Gunnar tapped his pencil against his writing tablet. They had rehearsed everything for weeks. "So what's your question?"

"I'm supposed to be the hotel clerk, ring the church bells, and fiddle. What if I'm ringing the church bells or fiddling and a guest shows up? I can't be two places at one time."

"What makes you think a guest is going to show up?" Gunnar asked, biting back his impatience. He'd explained all this earlier. "Not one person has inquired about a room for the entire three months I've been here. If by some strange chance someone wants a room, you'll have to explain that the hotel has only been partially restored from the fire." Actually they'd done an amazing job in disguising the fact that the hotel consisted of only a lobby and an impressive staircase that went nowhere.

"How are you going to explain the church tower swaying?" Nathan asked.

All eyes turned toward the south where the white spire of a church steeple could be seen. The existing church had recently collapsed when a lost turkey farmer had trekked through town with his herd of turkeys. The turkeys tried to roost on the roof of the church, with disastrous results.

Since there was no time left to rebuild, what remained of the steeple had been attached to the top of a pine tree. It looked authentic as long as the wind didn't blow. Unfortunately, a spring storm was brewing and the steeple was about as steady as a drunk trying to walk a straight line.

"Let's hope the wind dies down," Gunnar said.

"Anything you say, big brother."

Gunnar raised an eyebrow, but held his tongue. Nathan looked impressive in his suit and derby. If only he'd get that damned chip off his shoulder. At least he was sober. That was something, but Gunnar wasn't foolish enough to think it would last. Still, he could hope, couldn't he?

"What do you think of our mayor?" Gunnar asked the others, trying to humor Nathan out of his ill temper.

"I think he looks mighty official," Mom Bull said, slapping Nathan on the back.

Unbalanced by the hearty blow, Nathan regained his usual cynical attitude. "Almost as official as our sheriff looks."

Gunnar polished the tin star pinned to his vest and adjusted his hat. His shiny new spurs jingled against his tooled-leather boots. He'd stayed up half the night filing the rowels until they were blunt.

Mom Bull looked him over from head to toe and laughed. "You look like a Monkey Ward sheriff," she jested. She'd found it amusing that the sheriff and mayor outfitted themselves by ordering everything through the mail-order catalogue. Since mail was no longer delivered to Dangling Rope, the order had been delivered to Cripple Creek.

Gunnar chuckled good-naturedly. With all the things that could go wrong, his clothes were the least of his worries.

"How come you and Nathan only have to play one part?" Clod grumbled. "I have to play three parts in addition to being deputy sheriff. Why, even that actor, Edwin Booth, never played more than one part at a time."

"Someone has to stay with the officials. How would it look if Nathan and I kept dashing about?" Gunnar tossed a key ring to the man named Mole, a bushy-headed, squinty-eyed old geezer who had been persuaded to join the effort with the promise of whiskey. "You can let yourself in jail."

Mole missed the keys and scrambled to the ground after them. "You said I could stay in jail the e'tire night if I did me job right."

"Mole, if you pull off the part of a model prisoner, you can stay in jail for as long as you want. Are there any questions?" Gunnar spun around at the sound of a horse racing into town. It was Reverend Patcher, the circuit preacher. "It's about time," he called. "You're three days late."

"I prefer to think of it as being four days early," the preacher replied. "Now what do you want me to do? You said it was important I be here."

"I said it was important for your horse to be here." Counting the preacher's horse, they now had four horses and a mule. "I want you to ride your horse up and down the street. Try to coordinate with the others so it sounds like this is an active and busy town."

The preacher looked indignant. "Are you saying you made me come all this way just so I can ride my horse up and down the street?"

Mom Bull clamped down on her cigar and glared at the man. "You're a traveling preacher, ain't you?"

"Hurumph!" The preacher was incensed.

"All right, everyone," Gunnar said. "Take your places. Mr. Mulpepper and the others are due any moment."

Everyone hastened to their assigned spots with a minimum of grumbling. Gunnar started for the office and when Nathan failed to follow, he stopped in his tracks to face him. "Are you coming?"

"I need a drink." Nathan's face grew alarmingly red. "Dammit! Don't look at me like that. All I'm asking is for one drink." He looked more desperate than arrogant. His hands were shaking and sweat beaded his brow. Any hope Gunnar had that his brother would lick his alcohol problems were dashed.

More frustrated than angry, Gunnar grabbed his brother by the collar. There was no time to argue. "Get the hell inside." He shoved Nathan in the direction of the sheriff's office. There'd been moments—not many, but some—when Gunnar thought they might actually succeed in making something of this town, something of Nathan. His brother had actually looked pleased when the townsfolk had gathered around to hear him take the oath of office as mayor. But for every step Nathan took forward, it seemed to Gunnar his brother took at least twice as many back.

Nathan stumbled inside with Gunnar close behind. Mole watched from his jail cell as Gunnar splashed water across Nathan's face.

"Now, ain't you done a job on this jail," Mole said conversationally. "Never saw one quite like it." Mole was referring to the oil painting of a naked woman that hung on the wall. It was the only picture big enough to hide the hole left by an escaped prisoner.

Gunnar tossed a clean towel at his brother. "Don't look too content, Mole. We don't want our guests to think you don't have proper respect for the law."

Mole's nose was practically in the woman's navel. "I never had so much respect in me life," he replied. "A man can git used to this *culture* stuff you're always talkin' about."

Nathan wiped his face and tossed the towel onto Gunnar's desk. "I can't do this." His voice shook. "Something's going to go wrong. I feel it in my bones."

Gunnar raked his fingers through his hair. Nathan was right, of course. Never for a moment did Gunnar think this harebrained scheme would work. But for a short period of time, he and Nathan had actually worked together like brothers instead of archenemies. "Would you stop worrying? Nothing's going to go wrong."

"I have every reason to worry. It's my neck on the line. Please, Gunnar. Just one swallow."

Gunnar felt concerned. If he gave in to his brother's wishes he'd be contributing to the problem. But he could hardly stand by and let Nathan fall apart, thus jeopardizing months of hard work and the last chance, no matter how slim, of making something of the town that meant so much to Nathan.

As ridiculous as the idea seemed, he meant to see it

through to the end if only to delay the moment when he would have to send Nathan packing. This time, perhaps, for good.

"I'm trying, Gunnar. Can't you see I'm trying? I haven't had a drop to drink in two days."

"I know." Gunnar squeezed Nathan's shoulder. God, he hated this, hated having to play nursemaid to his brother. All he ever wanted was for Nathan to be happy. Sighing, he unlocked the bottom drawer of his desk, reached for the half-filled bottle of whiskey he'd confiscated from Nathan days earlier, and shoved it into Nathan's shaking hand. Nathan fumbled with the cap and drank thirstily.

Angry and resentful that the bottle could do more for Nathan than he could, Gunnar turned to the open doorway. He glanced up and down Main Street. Every building had been freshly whitewashed, and the windows cleaned. Some of the shops had signs explaining the closures. The nonexistent clerks were at a nonexistent funeral. Lord, what he had to do to save his brother's neck.

Convinced Dangling Rope looked as good as it was ever going to look, he narrowed his eyes at the sound of horses. Seeing the three men round the curve and ride into town, he took the bottle away from Nathan and put it back into his desk.

Nathan wiped his mouth with the back of his hand. The arrogance and hostility had returned, but at least he was no longer sweating or trembling.

Gunnar adjusted his hat. "Let's go."

# Chapter 4

It was midafternoon when the stage carrying Abigail Parker arrived in town. Feeling beleaguered and eternally grateful she had survived the hair-raising ride, Abby craned her neck out the window of the stagecoach, hoping to find Dangling Rope a bit more civilized than the last twenty or thirty towns she'd traveled through since leaving Boston in search of her uncle.

She was pleasantly surprised at what she saw. The town looked almost perfect in comparison to what she expected. A church steeple gleamed from the distance. The wooden buildings had been recently whitewashed and there was even a library, the first she'd seen since leaving Boston.

A wooden sign reading OPERA HOUSE was attached to the back of a large building. The opera house was painted a shocking pink color, the likes of which she'd never seen.

"Dangling Rope," the driver bellowed, opening the door of the coach and glaring at her. The man had tried to talk her into going to Victor, but she stoutly refused. Her uncle was last seen heading for Dangling Rope. In any case, three of her uncle's customers lived here.

Ignoring the stares of the male passengers, Abigail lifted the hem of her skirt and disembarked. The driver set her wooden trunk on the boardwalk in front of the hotel, cussing and complaining the whole time about stubborn women who didn't know their place in the world.

Abigail slapped a coin in his palm. She was sorely tempted not to pay him one penny more than her original fare, but she had put the man out of his way. For all his ill humor, she was grateful to him.

The disgruntled man leaped into the driver's seat and, repeating the name of a few well-known religious symbols, including "bloody St. Joseph" and "Holy Mary," picked up the horses' reins. "Gid-up and good riddance," he shouted over the backs of his charging team.

"And good riddance to you, too," she bellowed back.

The vestibule of the hotel was empty, with not so much as a desk clerk in sight. Abigail leaned on the bell with the palm of her hand. After several minutes, a rather odd-looking man wearing wire spectacles without lenses came rushing breathlessly through the doorway behind the counter.

"May I have a room?" Abigail asked politely.

The man looked surprised, almost startled to see her. "Sheriff Kincaid sure does think of everything." He winked. "That was good. Real good. If I didn't know better, I'd think you were a real person, if you know what I mean."

Abby stared at the man. Perhaps he'd misunderstood. She placed her parasol on the counter and leaned toward him. "I asked for a room."

The man laughed. "Where did Kincaid find you? You're great." He glanced at his watch. "Oops, I've got to go. It's time for me to ring the church bell." He winked for a second time. "Course we don't have no church bells. We don't even have a church. But none of those fool politicians is gonna know that." He left the same way he'd come.

Completely baffled by the man, Abby tried to decide what to do next. Leaving her trunk where the driver had set it, she walked outside just as a horseman rode by, a Bible tucked beneath his arm. Upon seeing her, he lifted his hat. "God bless you, miss."

"God bless you, too," she called back. She hoped the

blessing had been given out of habit and not as an ominous warning. It did seem a bit odd that every business in town was draped in black, even the saloons. There were at least a dozen signs that read GONE TO FUNERAL. Someone important must have died to merit this much attention.

Spotting the library, she stopped. At least one business was open.

Inside the small wood-framed building, Abby was greeted by a mannish-looking woman with a cigar dangling out of her mouth. The woman rose, surprising Abby with her height. She had to be six feet tall, and was almost as wide.

"You can call me Ma Bull," she said. "Everyone else does. That's 'cause of my son, Bull. I don't suppose many mothers are named after their son."

"I don't suppose they are," Abigail agreed.

"Now, what can I do fer ya?"

Abigail glanced around the empty room in confusion. "I thought this was the library."

"It is, sorta," the woman said, pointing to the single shelf of books displayed in front of the window. "It's the only books we could round up on such short notice." She lowered one lashless lid, and Abby wondered if winking was an affliction unique to this particular town.

"Course we don't have no library," Mom Bull continued, "but Sheriff Kincaid insisted that we show those fool politicians some culture. Jus' between you and me, they won't recognize culture if it hits them betwixt the eyes."

Abigail was more confused than ever. The town didn't have a hotel—or, at least, one that was open to guests. And if she could believe what she'd heard in the short time since her arrival, Dangling Rope didn't even have a church or a library. What else did this town not have?

Abigail decided the sooner she conducted her business and left, the better. "Could you direct me to the residence of Madam Rosie?"

Ma Bull looked Abigail up and down. "So you're gonna be one of Rosie's girls, eh." She shook her head. "Personally, if I was a man, I'd want a woman with a bit more flesh on her bones. But don't you worry none. The men 'round these parts are so desperate, they'll settle for any ole thin'."

Abigail didn't know whether to take offense or to laugh. "I'd like to reach Rosie's before dark—"

"Don't you worry your head none. Rosie and her girls live in the big pink house on the next street over. The sheriff ordered the house painted white, but Rosie was so incensed, she made the girls stay up all night paintin' the house back to its original color. You should have heard the sheriff! He had a conniption fit, he did. I heard him carry on all the way to my place."

"It's a pink house, you say? Is it the same color as the Opera House?"

Mom Bull winked. "Don't tell a soul, but we don't have no opera house. That's Madam Rosie's place. Isn't that the kicks?"

"The kicks," Abby repeated. Yes, indeed, the sooner she finished her business in Dangling Rope, the better. She only wished she didn't have to spend the night.

She left the library and stopped to stare at the sheriff's office opposite the hotel. A horseman rode by, tipping his hat, and she realized it was the preacher again. "God bless you, miss!"

She watched him ride to the end of town, circle his horse, and gallop back, tipping his hat and calling out his blessing for a third time.

Shaking her head, she started for the pink house that wasn't an opera house and, for all she knew, wasn't even a brothel.

# Chapter 5

Gunnar Kincaid sat behind his desk facing the three state officials and tried to concentrate on Mr. Mulpepper's tediously dull diatribe on the ins and outs of forming a county and the responsibilities of a county seat.

His speech was momentarily interrupted when Mole's loud snores drifted from the jail cell and drowned him out. All three of Mr. Mulpepper's generous chins shook as he glared reproachfully at the sleeping man. "Good heavens! Does he always snore like that?"

Gunnar motioned to Nathan, who was sitting closest to the cell, to give Mole a shake. Once the deed had been accomplished and peace restored, Mr. Mulpepper continued. "You do realize, of course, the town will be required to build a courthouse?"

Gunnar handed him a map of the town and surrounding area. "As you can see, we've already picked out a site."

"Oh, dear, you haven't broken ground yet?"

"Well, of course." Gunnar remembered distinctly that Nathan had stuck his ax into the ground while they were trying to fell a tree. That was breaking ground, wasn't it? "You might want to keep the map for future reference."

Mr. Mulpepper slipped the map into his portfolio and scribbled something on his writing tablet. "Now, let's see, next . . ."

Gunnar sat back as the man droned on. Mole started

to snore again, requiring Nathan to reach through the bars and shake him a second time.

Trying to look interested in what Mr. Mulpepper was saying, Gunnar made a point to jot down a few notes on occasion. With any luck, the man would eventually tire of hearing himself talk.

Actually, Gunnar had no complaints. Discounting Mole's loud snores, everything else had gone like clockwork. Better than clockwork. Even Nathan had managed to be friendly and attentive to their guests.

But by Jove, no one could have predicted the stage would make an appearance after nearly a three-month absence! It was all Gunnar could do to keep from running outside to hug the driver. Now wouldn't that have been something? He'd like to have seen the faces of these intolerably stodgy men had he done anything so outrageous. Still, if he ever had occasion to meet the person responsible for the well-timed arrival of the stage, he intended to personally shake the man's hand.

The church bells pealed out the hour of four and the lawmaker named Philip Wrightwood pulled out his gold pocket watch to check the time. The man was obviously impressed.

"Can't even get the clock at the capitol building to maintain accuracy." Mr. Wrightwood drifted over to the window. "Good heavens!"

Gunnar exchanged a quick glance with his brother. "Is something wrong?"

Mr. Wrightwood turned. He looked shaken. "I could have sworn I saw the steeple move."

"Move, you say." Gunnar quickly joined him and peered out the window. The steeple wasn't just moving, it was swaying back and forth like the tail of an over-friendly dog. Acting quickly, Gunnar steered the dazed man away from the window and over to a chair. "Is this your first religious experience?"

"Eh . . . religious experience?" Mr. Wrightwood's face was a shocking white in color. "I can't say I've had a lot of religious experiences." He tugged on the collar of his shirt. While his companions wore the more conventional bowties, Mr. Wrightwood wore one of those new-style teck scarfs knotted at his neck and hanging like an arrow down his chest. "Can you, Horace?"

Horace Clayton was a white-haired man with a ruddy complexion. His white mustache swept upward, then turned down at the ends. "As far as I know, the only time you stepped into a church was when you were running behind in the election."

"I was only behind a few votes," Wrightwood protested, offended. "The church didn't move an inch then, but I won the election anyway."

"That's a miracle in itself," Gunnar said dryly, patting the man's hand. Under the guise of pouring the man a glass of water, Gunnar whispered in Nathan's ear. "Tell Clod to get rid of the steeple." The steeple idea was a bad one, but if he played his cards right, he might be able to turn the situation to his advantage.

After Nathan left, Gunnar handed Wrightwood a glass of water. "I think it's significant that you would have your first religious experience in Dangling Rope. I believe it's a sign."

"I quite agree with you." Mulpepper rose from his chair, presumably to take a look for himself at the church steeple. But Gunnar was too quick for him; He stayed him with a firm hand on the shoulder, and offered him a cigar.

When the immediate crisis was over, Gunnar took his place behind his desk. "As I explained to you earlier, this town is dedicated to providing the quality of life not found in the gold-mining towns. As you have no doubt observed, culture is important to us."

Mulpepper's eyes flickered over to the painting on the wall of Mole's cell. "Yes, yes, I can see that. That's why we gave you high marks for having a library."

Gunnar and Nathan had walked them through the town earlier, taking care to whisk the others past Madam Rosie's pink monstrosity. The garish three-story pink building had raised a few eyebrows, but the sign reading OPERA HOUSE satisfied their curiosity. As the men walked by, Clod hid in the bushes to give the impression a rehearsal was in progress; the wailing throb of his fiddle filled the air as Clod poured heart and soul into a rousing rendition of "Oh, Susanna." The men were duly impressed, which said more for their ignorance of music than Clod's playing.

Now Mr. Mulpepper sat forward, the smoke from his cigar forming a blue wreath around his head. He had the kind of short thick body that should never keep company with the checkered suit he wore. "Tell me how you managed to turn this town around. Why, it had the worst reputation in the county. Isn't that right, Clayton?"

Clayton nodded. "It was terrible. You wouldn't believe the fights that went on here."

Mulpepper gave a solemn nod. "We dubbed it Horizontal City."

Gunnar pressed his fingers together. He knew they'd have to discuss the town's past eventually. "Horizontal?"

"The citizens drank so much, they couldn't stand upright." Mulpepper laughed at his own joke.

"I've never seen art displayed in a jail cell before," Clayton remarked. "I say, sir, what are you in jail for?"

Mole looked appropriately repentant. "I got caught breaking curfew."

"You have a curfew in this town?" Mulpepper looked properly impressed.

"That we do," Gunnar said. "Can't have people running about all hours of the day and night." Nathan returned and Gunnar leaned toward him to see if everything had been taken care of. It was obvious by the smell of whiskey on his breath that Nathan had stopped for another drink en route.

"Well, I must say . . ." Mulpepper turned to the other officials. "This is the sort of mature town that deserves the county seat."

"I quite agree," Mr. Wrightwood said. Obviously still

shaken from his "religious" experience, he glanced anxiously at the window.

Not to be outdone by his colleagues, Clayton donned a pair of spectacles and nodded vigorously.

Sensing the lawmakers were about to make a decision in the town's favor, Gunnar leaned back in his chair and relaxed. "As long as I'm sheriff, I guarantee Dangling Rope will remain a law-abiding town."

Mr. Mulpepper held his cigar in front of him. "It will be more than that if I have anything to say about it. It will be the county seat!"

For the first time since the three men had arrived, the strained look left Nathan's face. "Gentlemen! That's music to my ears."

Abigail worked the brass knocker on the door of the building marked OPERA HOUSE. To say the house was pink was an understatement. It was more purple than pink, and as bright as the sun on newly polished brass. No wonder the sheriff objected to the color.

The door swung open. A thick-waisted woman stared at her, obviously surprised. The gaudy circle of red on her cheeks drew attention to her sagging features. Her face was made to look pudgy by an unfortunate array of sausage curls.

"I'm looking for Madam Rosie," Abby said warily, not knowing what to expect from anyone she met in this town.

"I'm Madam Rosie." The woman gave her a critical once-over. Abby got the distinct impression the woman gave her low marks for her plain, almost prudish, high-collared dress. "I'm afraid you've come to the wrong place. I barely have enough work for the girls I have. A few miners here and there. But most of them prefer to take their business to Cripple Creek and Victor." The woman's gaze lit on Abby's prim bodice. "You could try the mining towns, I suppose." She shrugged and started to back away.

"Wait." Abby pressed her hand hard against the door.

"I've no desire to work for you. I came to deliver your order." She checked her notes. "You ordered facial cream and French perfume from my uncle, Mr. Parker, and—"

"Well, mercy me." The door opened wide. "I was beginning to think we'd never hear from that man again." She looked Abby up and down, this time with more curiosity than censure. "Your uncle, you said?"

"Yes, that's right. My name is Abigail Parker."

"It's a pleasure to meet you, Miss Parker. Come in and I'll introduce you around." She turned and hurried down the short hall. She stopped at the bottom of the stairs and lifted her voice, "Girls, do hurry. We have a guest." Girlish squeals filtered from the second floor and feet scampered overhead. "Come," Madam Rosie said, beckoning.

Abigail followed Madam Rosie into a formal parlor. At first glance Abby thought the parlor looked elegant with its crystal chandeliers, marble-faced fireplace, and French tapestries. Only upon closer inspection did the worn carpet and frayed upholstery become noticeable.

Abby sat on the faded velvet divan at the madam's invitation and wondered, as she was prone to do on such occasions, if her uncle had once sat in this very same room, perhaps in this very same spot.

Running footsteps preceded the arrival of three young women. Suddenly the room was filled with the rustling sound of fancy taffeta gowns and the women's high-pitched tittering voices.

"Girls, this is Mr. Parker's niece. Miss Parker, please meet Meg, Ginger, and Ruby."

The two younger women squealed with delight, but the older one named Ginger sat on the arm of a chair and quietly filed her nails.

"W-we were b-beginning to think we'd never hear from your uncle again," the one named Meg stuttered, her face turning red.

Surprised that a woman in her profession still had the grace to blush, Abby took an instant liking to her.

"Uncle Randall disappeared several months ago. I've not heard from him since."

"Disappeared?" Ginger exclaimed, her file posed midair.

Meg looked so upset, her hands fluttered nervously. Ruby sank limply into a chair.

Madam Rosie tugged on a sausage curl. "This is all so perplexing. He didn't strike me as the kind of man who would just take off and not let anyone know his whereabouts. What do you suppose could have happened to him?"

"I have no idea. All I know is that I received my last letter from him in September."

"September?" The young woman named Ruby spoke for the first time. The right side of her face was badly scarred which probably explained why she kept her face lowered as she spoke. "He told me he heard of this miraculous product that would cover . . . my . . . my face." She fingered the ugly red mark on her cheek. "He was going to order it for me."

Abby lowered her eyes so as not to stare. She had the overwhelming urge to help this woman, but none of the cosmetics she brought with her would cover such a disfiguring scar.

"She was burned in a fire," Rosie explained. "She was only a rugbug at the time. Just two years old."

"How awful," Abby said.

"It *is* awful," Madam Rosie declared. "In fact, now that I think about it, I remember distinctly. He was going to have dinner with us before he left town."

Meg concurred. "I—I'd almost f-forgotten. It wasn't like Mr. P-p-p . . . your uncle not to keep an appointment."

"Not like him at all," Ruby concurred.

Abigail's heart raced. This was the first real clue she'd found in all the months she'd been on the road. "If he had made another appointment with you, then my uncle disappeared while he was here in Dangling

Rope. It's quite possible the four of you were among the last to see him."

Madam Rosie's tight curls bounced like tight springs. "Why, it does look like that, doesn't it?"

"Dear me," Ruby exclaimed. "Have you talked to the sheriff?"

"Then you do have a sheriff?" Abigail asked.

Madam Rosie sniffed down her nose. "We have a sheriff, all right! Or at least that's what he calls himself. That Gunnar Kincaid comes out of nowhere and starts telling us what to do."

"I'll s-say he does," Meg said.

Ruby defended him. "He did pretty up the town."

Rosie glowered at her. "Pretty up the town, my corset." As if reminded of the bone and steel stays around her middle, she tugged and pulled at her sides as if to seek relief. "We have a library that no one can use, a hotel not in operation, a church that doesn't exist, and a funeral that's nothing more than a figment of his imagination. Why, the only genuine article here is me and my girls."

Ruby giggled. "We're genuine, all right."

"Did you b-bring us some cosmetics?" Meg asked. Her eyes wistful, she gazed longingly at Abigail's pack.

"Yes, I did. But only the usual order. None of this will cover scars, I'm afraid." She gave Ruby an apologetic look and made a silent vow to search out whatever it was her uncle had promised her. Abigail unfastened the straps on her pack and spread a wide array of jars and vials on a satinwood drop-leaf table that Madam Rosie had cleared off.

Meg left the room momentarily and returned with a basket of fresh eggs. "Y-your uncle always l-liked our eggs," she explained. "Said they were the f-freshest in the West, and c-cooked up nice over his c-campfire."

Abby smiled. She didn't have a campfire, but perhaps she could persuade someone to boil them for her.

It was while she was sorting out the orders that the low strident sound of a male voice echoed through the house. A drunken miner staggered into the parlor, singing at the top of his lungs. The smell of alcohol and tobacco filled the room, blotting out the delicate fragrances of Abby's cosmetics and perfumes. "Well, now," he slurred, looking straight at Abigail. "What have we got here?"

"You're too early, Charley," Madam Rosie said. She pointed to a neatly printed sign hanging on the wall. "We're closed until six. Same as always. Come back later."

"I don't wanna come back l . . . later." Charley hiccupped. "I want her." He pointed straight at Abby.

Looking him square in the eye, Abby rose and, in a no-nonsense voice, informed him of his mistaken notion. "I'll have you know I'm a drummer."

Grinning, Charley leaned toward her, forcing her to back away. "Don't apologize," he said magnanimously. "I'll take it any way you want to dish it up."

Abby's eyes flashed. "I'm a businesswoman!"

He shrugged. "So what's the problem? I'm here on business. Name your price." He plunked down a bag of gold.

Madam Rosie pushed him away from Abigail. "Get out, Charley, or I'll toss you out and it won't be pretty."

"I'm not goin' anywhere till I git what I came fer." He lunged toward Abby, who barely managed to step aside in time. Charley kept going, landing headfirst into the dark fireplace.

Madam Rosie nodded to the girls. "You asked for it." At her command, the girls flew at the man, arms flailing.

The miner fought them off, grabbed his gold, and took off like a fox trying to escape a gun-toting chicken farmer. Ruby giggled and brushed her hands together. "I guess we showed him."

Smiling at the women, Abby returned to her wares.

Madam Rosie walked back into the parlor after checking to see that the man had left. Her curls bobbed up and down. "Damned fool. Can't take no for an answer. Now where were we?"

Meg dipped a finger into the lip rouge and rubbed it across her lips. "W-w-what do you think?" she asked, puckering her mouth for all to see.

"Gorgeous!" Ruby exclaimed, seeming less inclined to hide her face.

Ginger stopped filing her nails and glanced up, but made no comment.

"The color is excellent with your skin and dark hair," Abby said. "Unfortunately, not everyone can wear red."

Madam Rosie looked surprised. "You mean this comes in different colors?"

"I don't believe so," Abby said. "But it should, don't you think? Women don't look the same. So why should they all wear the same-colored lip rouge?"

Meg turned her head this way and that in the mirror. "I think l-lips should be r-red."

Ruby gave Meg a nudge with her elbow. "Don't argue with Miss Parker. She's an expert."

"Oh, I'm not really," Abigail said, feeling suddenly inadequate and remiss. All she'd thought about these last few months was tracking down her uncle. She had delivered his goods and carefully made note of any new orders, but she hadn't done much in the way of offering advice. "All I'm doing is delivering my uncle's merchandise so his customers don't think he's neglecting them."

"Well, if you ask me, your uncle's mighty lucky to have a niece like you," Ruby said.

A loud pounding came from the front door. "Now what?" Madam Rosie muttered. "Weeks go by and we don't see a soul. Now all of a sudden we're busy as a beehive." The pounding grew louder and more persistent. She left the room and scurried down the hall, her voice raised. Thinking there was an emergency, perhaps another dreaded fire, Meg, Ruby, and Ginger hurried to the hallway to see for themselves the source of all the racket. Not knowing what else to do, Abby followed.

Madam Rosie unlocked the door. "We're not open until six—"

The door was pushed open, and poor Rosie was pinned against the wall. The miner had returned and this time he was not alone.

# Chapter 6

Madam Rosie's curls shook angrily. "How dare you come into my house in this unseemly manner. I must insist that you leave at once!"

"I ain't leaving until I get what I came for!" the miner said gruffly. "I want the drummer!" He pointed at Abby, who stood huddled with the others at the end of the hall.

Abby sucked in her breath. It wasn't the first time a man had looked at her in such a lustful way. Not by any means. It had been an almost daily occurrence on the street. But Thieves Corner offered numerous escape routes and, being both small-boned and agile, she was able to dart in and out of alleys at great speed. Many times she'd slip through what was little more than a crack in the wall and make her escape. But here in this house she felt trapped.

"I told you, I'm not for . . ." What in the world was it called when a man paid a woman for sexual favors? "Hire."

The miner grinned, but there was nothing mirthful about his smile. "Did you hear that, boys? The little lady said she's not for hire."

The miners laughed and followed their leader down the hall. Abby had little choice but to back into the sitting room. Like a trapped animal, she searched the room frantically, hoping for some previously unnoticed means of escape.

All six of the men crowded into the room after her, giving Charley full rein. Meg was pinned to the wall by a short, balding man, and Ruby was pushed into a chair. Two men held Ginger by either arm. "One at a time, men," she complained. "I don't do threesomes."

Charley's red watery eyes were focused on Abigail. Clumsily, he advanced toward her, kicking a tapestry footstool out of the way. "If you don't want me to hire you out, maybe we can work out a more permanent arrangement."

Madam Rosie gave an impatient sigh. "Get the hell outta here, Charley."

Charley spun around to face Madam Rosie. "Don't worry. You'll get your money." He nodded to one of the other men, who handed the madam a bag filled with gold. Madam Rosie glanced around the room and seeing how she and the girls were outnumbered, shrugged and took the bag from him.

Abby reached for her knife, but Charley lunged at her and sent her flying back against the wall. Before she could regain her balance, he'd grabbed her by the arms. "Now let's see if this little wench is worth all that gold."

Abigail tried yanking herself free, but he was far too strong. He slid his other arm around her waist and pulled her close. His rough whiskered chin rubbed against her cheek with the coarse feel of sandpaper. Breath reeking of whiskey and tobacco, his foul lips pressed against hers. A wave of nausea began to rise.

He slipped one arm around her waist, freeing her left hand. Frantically, she reached for the table behind her in search of a vase or paperweight—anything—that could be used as a weapon. All she found was the basket of eggs.

Desperate, she wrapped her fingers around an egg and, with as much force as she could exert, slapped the shell hard against his forehead. The egg cracked open and, momentarily surprised, Charley drew back to wipe the runny yolk out of his eyes.

Using the brief reprieve to good advantage, she gave him a sound kick in the shins. Grunting, he released her and she quickly grabbed the knife from her boot. She straightened just in time to prevent the other miners from storming her.

Brandishing the knife, she slashed an invisible line in front of their startled faces. "If you know what's good for you, you'll stay right where you are."

The room was as rife with expectancy as a stage before a curtain call. Meg, Ruby, and Ginger gasped and the men, including Charley, froze. Madam Rosie looked about to faint.

Abby held the knife shoulder high, ready to plunge it into the first man who dared step into range. "Now, gentlemen, if you would be kind enough to walk back down that hall and out the front door, we'll pretend this unfortunate incident never happened."

For a moment it appeared as if the matter would be resolved to Abby's satisfaction. Unfortunately, one of the miners took it upon himself to take a flying leap and kick the knife out of Abby's hand. The knife flew up and hit the crystal chandelier before falling to the floor.

Abby grimaced in pain and grabbed her hand. Holy blazes, she hated having her knife kicked out of her hand. Furious, she dashed across the room after it, but just before she reached her weapon, Charley clamped down on the knife with the heel of his boot.

"Looks like we have a wildcat on our hands." His eyes gleamed in relish. "Well, now. I always wanted to tame me a cat. Get her, boys."

Charley's companions formed a circle around her. Bent at the waist, her arms poised for the fight of her life, she watched the men advance. Kicking her foot shoulder-high, she caught one of her attackers beneath the chin. He fell back, but the others charged forward, grabbing her from all sides until she was unable to move.

Physically trapped, she resorted to the only weapon left to her: her tongue. "Let me go, you scalawaging, pricking, good-for-nothing . . ."

The more she shouted out her fury, the more Charley seemed to enjoy himself. Running out of names to call him, she paused to catch her breath.

"Well, now." Charley was actually drooling. "Bring her to me, boys."

Abby felt the panic rise inside her. After surviving all those years in Thieves Corner, it was almost ironic that a town as innocuous in appearance as Dangling Rope would prove so much more dangerous.

Just as she thought there was no way out, Ruby surprised her by picking up a vase and bringing it down hard on Charley's head. This show of action by the most timid of the women inspired Meg to grab a wooden music box and heave it across the room. It caught one of the miners on the temple and he took a nosedive. Soon all the women were in the act, including Ginger and Rosie. The men were bombarded with glass vases, silver candlesticks, and even furniture.

Charley ducked and his companions dived for cover.

Encouraged by her earlier success, Ruby walloped one of the beefy miners over the head with a paperweight. When he turned on her, Abigail grabbed her knife off the floor, but she didn't dare throw it for fear of hurting one of the prostitutes. Instead, she caught his shirt with the tip of her knife and sliced it off his back. The man, thinking she'd skinned him alive, ran down the hall screaming.

Abby whirled about upon hearing Meg cry out behind her. One of the miners had her pinned to the floor. Knife raised, Abby rushed to Meg's defense.

The door to the sheriff's office burst open. Clod stuck his head inside and Gunnar feared he was going to report some trouble with removing the church steeple. "Trouble at the . . . eh . . . Opera House."

Gunnar jumped to his feet. "Damn!" he muttered. Trouble couldn't have come at a worse time. Why, he practically had the legislators eating out of his hand. "Sorry, gentlemen. Some of our . . . eh . . . entertainers tend to be a bit temperamental. It happens in the best of towns."

"Yes, yes, of course," Mulpepper said. "The best of towns."

Gunnar grabbed his hat and ran the short distance down the hill to the brothel. Nathan tried to persuade the government officials to stay, but they insisted upon going along.

"I want to see how the sheriff handles himself in action," Mulpepper explained, his short legs barely able to keep up with Gunnar's long even strides.

Action was the last thing Gunnar wanted to see. He was a lawyer by trade, and a sheriff by chance. Madam Rosie had done this on purpose. He was sure of it.

He led the others around the corner to Myers Street just as a chair came sailing through the window of the shocking pink brothel. He ducked in time, but Mr. Mulpepper's generous girth made him less agile. The chair hit him in the forehead, sending him wheeling about. "What in hell . . ."

His curses were drowned out by the sound of breaking glass. Gunnar barreled into the house, almost breaking his neck when his foot slipped on a raw egg.

Catching himself in time, he ran down the hall to the sitting room. He was aghast at the sight that greeted him. A full-fledged battle was being waged between the prostitutes and the miners.

Before Gunnar had time to evaluate the situation, he was attacked from behind. Swinging around, he caught a glimpse of a blue-eyed beauty just before she bashed him over the head with a picture frame.

Glass exploded around him. Stunned by the impact, he shook his head and, recovering quickly, grabbed the woman by the arm.

She glanced at his badge and shrank back in loathing. "What in devil's name took you so long?" she demanded. "Sin to Moses, you're lucky we weren't all dead before you bloody well got your ass over here!"

The woman said a few more choice words before he released her arm. "I'll deal with you later!"

"Like hell you will!" she shouted. Then, quicker than a striking rattler, she spun around and jumped on Mulpepper's back.

In no time flat, the three officials were mired in a tangle of flailing arms and legs, fighting for their lives. Nathan was on the bottom of the pile, and all that could be seen of Clod was one canvas-clad leg.

Gunnar pulled his Colt .45 from his holster and pointed the barrel toward the ceiling. He fired twice. The glass chandelier, already pulled loose from its moorings, came crashing to the floor, missing Mulpepper's head by a hair's breadth.

The heap of battling foes grew still, everyone too winded to move. Only an occasional groan broke the strained and awkward silence that followed.

Gunnar glanced across the room at Nathan, who was nursing a bloodied lip. Next to him, Clod wiped egg off his face.

Gunnar reached for the hand of the blue-eyed stranger who was sprawled on the floor amid an intriguing jumble of white laced petticoats. A tantalizing glimpse of white flesh showed above her black lisle hosiery.

Refusing his help, she lifted herself off the floor and quickly straightened her skirts.

The woman perplexed him; she fought like a man and talked like a guttersnipe, yet she had an air of vulnerability that made him want to protect her. As if she needed his protection, he thought. Even now, she carried herself like a warrior as she glared at him: head held high, chin jutting out, shoulders thrown back. Her proud demeanor was especially commendable given the sad condition of her clothes. The bodice of her otherwise prudish dress was ripped, revealing one creamy white shoulder. Her skirt was slit up the side.

He lifted his gaze to study her face. Her blue eyes flashed angrily. "If you are finished leering, Sheriff, perhaps you will kindly do your job and arrest that man, so we can all go back to work." She pointed to an unconscious miner. Out of all the people in that room, the man appeared the least likely to pose a problem.

The sheriff wished he could say the same for the man's blue-eyed accuser.

Mulpepper moaned aloud and rubbed his forehead. A nasty red bump was rising over his left eye. He lay flat on his back with Madam Rosie's gartered leg flung across his chest. "Madam, kindly remove yourself at once!" The man couldn't have sounded more righteously outraged had he been a priest.

Madam Rosie pressed her ample bosom into the poor man's face. "I don't mind at all, shorty."

His face a bright red, Mulpepper scrambled to his feet quicker than a man jumping out of the way of a rabid hound. His face turned blue with rage as he wagged his finger in Gunnar's face. "If this is how your hardworking officials are treated in your town, then I'll personally see to it that you never see the county seat— or anything else!" He picked up his flattened derby, stuck it on his head, and made a beeline down the hall and out the front door.

# Chapter 7

After marching the miners, along with Madam Rosie and her girls, to the sheriff's office, Gunnar summoned Mom Bull. "Check for injuries."

Mom Bull glanced at the disheveled group of people. "I said I would be the librarian and that's all I agreed to do. I ain't no nursemaid."

Gunnar was running out of patience. He had more prisoners than he had ever hoped to accommodate and they were making so much noise, he couldn't think, let alone get a word in edgewise.

As if this weren't enough, Mole took to rattling the bars of his cell and complaining to high heaven. "I ain't sharin' me cell with no one. And that's final!"

"Quiet!" Gunnar bellowed.

Mole retreated to the back of his cell and pouted like a spoiled child. Meanwhile, one of the miners was passed out on the floor. Another was draped over a chair like an old pair of pants.

Madam Rosie made her girls stand behind her, as far away from the miners as possible. "Do what you have to do, Sheriff, and be done with it. I've got a business to run and a corset that's killing me."

For two cents, Gunnar was tempted to tell her what she could do with her business *and* her corset! First there was the hassle over the color of her place. Now this. "No one is going anywhere until I know who started the trouble."

Madam Rosie quivered with rage. "And why should I tell you anything?"

"Because I'm the sheriff and I can make your life miserable if you don't."

One of the miners stepped forward. "She started it." He pointed to the blue-eyed beauty who had given the sheriff such a colorful piece of her mind.

Gunnar wondered why he'd not noticed her in town prior to that afternoon. Now that he noticed her, it was all he could do to take his eyes off her.

He stood directly in front of her, surprised to discover how small and delicate she actually was. She looked nothing like the hard-mouthed, hard-brawling woman of moments earlier. The top of her head barely reached his shoulders. "Is that true? Did you start it?"

A look of indignation clouded the delicate features of her face. She stood legs apart, unaware, he suspected, that her skirt was torn to her thigh. Hands on her hips, she glared at him. "I did no such thing!"

Trying to keep his gaze from wandering to the areas exposed by her torn apparel, he kept his eyes focused on her face. "And your name is?"

"Abigail Parker." She tossed her head and, in so doing, released the last of her hair from its confines. Untidy curls fell en masse to her shoulders. Funny, she didn't look like an adventuress. For one thing, the lovely pink of her satin-smooth cheeks and soft-pouted lips looked natural to him, and not the result of some paint bottle.

One of the miners peered from beneath a blood-stained bandage wrapped around his forehead. "She attacked Charley with a knife."

"And where is your knife now, Miss Parker?" Gunnar asked, curious.

She looked surprised by the question. "I keep my weapons in the usual places, Sheriff."

Weapons? How many did she have, for Pete's sake? And what did she mean by "usual" places? His gaze dropped down the length of her, but not wanting to be accused again of leering, of all things, he quickly abandoned the visual search. "Very well, Miss Parker.

Suppose you start from the beginning." It took enormous willpower not to stare at her bare shoulder. Sakes alive, maybe he did leer.

The woman's eyes flashed with blue fire. "I was showing these ladies my wares when this . . . this . . . despicable excuse for a man tried to hire me." She stopped and glared at Gunnar as if waiting for him to say something.

Gunnar cleared his voice. His eyes dropped down to her fast-heaving bosom. Wares? Is that how she saw herself? As nothing more than a business commodity?

"I'm not quite sure . . . eh . . . why are you so upset? Was it the way he approached you?" Perhaps brothels had rules for that kind of thing. "Was he rude to you?"

Miss Parker's eyes grew round. "Of course he was rude to me. Never have I been so offended in all my born days. Well, maybe once or twice before. But no more than that, mind you. It's a disgrace, that's what it is. If a woman can't even show her wares without being accosted. What in blazes' name kind of a town is this?"

"It's a cultural town," Mole chirped from his jail cell. He glared at the sheriff. "Or at least it was before you brought all this riffraff in here."

Gunnar scanned the short list of businesses requiring a license. Madam Rosie and her girls were the only ones listed. "I don't see your name, Miss Parker. Do you have a license to conduct business in this town?"

She leveled her blue eyes at him. "Of course I don't have a license, but that's no excuse for what this despicable man tried to do . . . I'm a traveling lady and I have never been required to have a license in any other town."

"A traveling lady?" Gunnar rubbed his chin. He recalled the shocking though nonetheless fetching way she'd swung at that boorish politician. A traveling wildcat would be a more apt description.

"A drummer," she explained.

"And a mighty good one at that," Madam Rosie said.

"From now on, I'm going to purchase all my cosmetics from you, even if you do carry a knife."

"Cosmetics?" Gunnar swung his head to stare at the traveling lady. "Your wares? You sell cosmetics?"

"That's what I've been trying to tell you!"

"She was. Heard it with me own ears," Mom Bull said, slapping a bandage on the forehead of a miner named Steamer.

Her hapless patient yelled out.

"Hold still," Mom Bull growled.

Gunnar leaned against his desk and crossed his arms in front of him. If he wasn't so damned mad, he'd be tempted to let the whole bunch go. But someone was going to pay for messing up the town's chances of becoming the county seat. "Deputy, throw them in the cell."

Clod grinned. These were his first official prisoners since taking the oath of office. "It'll be my pleasure." Clod made quite a to-do of the process, lining everyone up in a certain way and designating one cell for women and another for men.

"If you all behave yourselves," he told them, "I'll play my fiddle for you."

Everyone more or less cooperated, needing little more than a well-placed nudge here and there to fall into place. Everyone, that is, but Miss Parker, who pushed Clod away and placed herself boldly in front of Gunnar's desk.

Gunnar sat back in his chair. He should have known. "Do you have a problem, Miss Parker?"

"You bet I have a problem," she stormed at him. "You pompous son of a—"

"Miss Parker! I must insist you keep your personal opinion of me to yourself. Now what, exactly, is your problem?"

"I'll tell you what my problem is. This is a terrible miscarriage of justice. Madam Rosie and her girls were simply defending their property."

"And you, Miss Parker, were simply defending your

honor. I know." He stood. "Clod. Let Madam Rosie and her business associates go." He turned his gaze to the bold woman in front of him. "You, Miss Parker, will come with me."

He pulled his jacket off a wooden peg and tossed it to her. "Put this on. It's cold out." To Clod he said, "Don't let those men out of here till you hear from me." He walked to the door and waited for Miss Parker to follow. When it was obvious she had no intention of going anywhere without a fight, he lifted a finger in warning. "Don't make me resort to force."

Leveling him with a look of loathing, she shrugged herself into his jacket and followed him outside. "You law officers are all the same," she hissed angrily. "It doesn't matter if it's Thieves Corner or where it is."

He was taken aback by her vengeful voice. And what could she possibly know about a place called Thieves Corner? "I'm taking you home with me," he said patiently.

She stopped dead in her tracks. "I'm not going home with the likes of you."

He turned and faced her. "I'm the sheriff, for chrissakes. I'm taking you to my house where I can watch out for your welfare."

"Is that what you call it, Sheriff? Watching out for my welfare?" She gave him a hateful look. "We have another name for it where I come from."

"Oh? And what might that be?" he asked curiously.

"We call it rape!"

Gunnar drew back, incredulous. "I have no intention . . ." He was so shocked by the idea, he literally sputtered.

She studied him a moment. "Just to be on the safe side, I'll find my own accommodations."

"And where do you propose to spend the night? You've turned down the only two choices you have."

"I would sooner sleep in the streets." She turned and headed for the hotel.

"You're still in my custody, Miss Parker," he called after her.

She slowed her steps, but kept walking.

"After all the trouble you caused, I can hardly let you off scot-free. Besides, someone's got to drill you on the laws of the town."

She kept walking. "Good day, Sheriff Kincaid."

Gunnar watched her, a slow grin curving his mouth. In about two minutes she was going to be damned grateful for the offer he made. He hastened across the street after her, catching up with her inside the newly built lobby of the hotel.

She was furiously pressing on the bell.

"I'll show you to your room," Gunnar said.

Her eyes flared. "You needn't bother."

"It's no bother," he insisted, taking her by the arm and leading her to the stairs.

"That's my trunk," she said.

"You can have the desk clerk bring it to you later."

"But—"

"Come along." The stairs creaked beneath their weight.

"If you don't mind, Sheriff." She pulled her arm away and bounded up the stairs ahead of him.

"Wait!" He raced after her. "Don't open that door."

Paying no heed to his warning, she yanked at the forbidden door. He barely had time to grab her around the waist and keep her from stepping into midair.

Gasping, she held on to him and stared onto the gaping hole at her feet. "Holy blazes! What happened?"

"A fire," he explained, his arms around her. Her slight body trembled next to his and guilt surged through him. He should have explained from the start that the hotel was nothing more than a facade.

"We only had time to restore the lobby. . . ."

She stiffened in his arms. "Restore the lobby? Of all the stupid, asinine things. What good is a lobby without guest rooms?"

He was growing more amused than shocked at her

somewhat colorful choice of words. "It's a long story, but since we'll be spending the night together, I'll save it for later." Her mouth dropped open, but she was too incensed to speak.

Using the silence to his full advantage, he moved a strand of silken hair from her cheek. "There, there, Miss Parker, try to control your exuberance. I've only agreed to give you one night, not marry you."

He regretted his lame attempt at humor, but it was too late. She pushed against him so hard, he lost his balance. He managed to grab hold of the brass-plated handrail just in time to keep from falling backward down the stairs. In the mere seconds it took him to regain his footing, she'd already raced past him and was flying out the door.

Cursing beneath his breath, he ran after her. She was fast, faster than any woman he'd ever seen, but he was faster. He tackled her at the end of the street, in front of the livery stables. Fortunately, they both ended up in a pile of hay.

"Dammit, Miss Parker. Hold still." He was practically on top of her. He held her arms pinned over her head. "Let's get something straight!" he said angrily. "I've never raped a woman in my life. I've never even stolen a kiss from a woman." His gaze dropped down to her lips—but only for an instant, and, he told himself, for no other reason than to emphasize his point. Lifting his eyes to hers, he continued, "You are in my custody until I tell you otherwise. That means you will conduct yourself as a model prisoner. Is that clear?"

It was a long time in coming, but she finally gave a reluctant nod of her head. Not that he had given her any choice.

He pulled away and stood, but kept himself fully alert to any possible attempt on her part to flee.

Miss Parker stood and brushed the hay off her clothes. "You, you . . ." She called him every uncomplimentary name that had ever been thought up to denigrate a lawman—and a few he suspected were made up on the spot. "No wonder this town is so loony . . . a hotel with only a lobby, a church that doesn't exist . . . Why didn't you tell me? I could have killed myself."

"I should have told you," he admitted. "I apologize."

His apology seemed to catch her off guard. The anger and suspicion left her face and she looked as if she wanted to believe his apology was sincere. As if threatened by the thought, she quickly turned and walked away.

He chased after her. "Where do you think you're going?"

"To the jail. I have no intention of spending the night at your house."

"I'm afraid the jail is no longer an option. You're in my custody and that means I'll decide where you'll go and how you'll spend the night."

She turned and gave him a challenging look. "How much is it going to take, Sheriff? Name your price."

Confused, he scratched his head. "My price?" He narrowed his eyes. "You wouldn't be trying to bribe me, now, would you, Miss Parker?"

"Don't look so shocked, Sheriff. I've never met a lawman that couldn't be bribed. So what is it? Will a ten-spot do?"

Curious as to how much higher she was prepared to go, he shook his head.

She shrugged and without a word reached into the bosom of her dress, pulled out four ten-spots, and tossed them on the ground between them. Obviously thinking their business was complete, she turned and casually strode away.

Half in amusement and half in fascination, Gunnar scooped up the bills and fell in step beside her.

"I'm afraid it's not going to be quite so simple, Miss Parker. You will spend the night in my cabin, make no mistake about it."

She stopped dead in her tracks and turned to face him. Without a word, he shoved the money into her torn bodice. Her mouth dropped open, but she made a quick recovery. "I think you will find it a whole lot easier to take the money," she said.

He pulled out his gun and pointed it at her. "I think you'll find it a whole lot easier to do as I say." He reached in his back pocket, pulled out his metal handcuffs, and dangled them in her face.

The gun didn't seem to faze her, but the handcuffs definitely gave her pause. Obviously, the woman valued her freedom. A shadow of indecision crossed her face. "I would prefer not to have to use force," he said, shoving the cuffs back into his pocket. He kept his voice gentle. He had the upper hand with her for once; he could afford to be congenial.

It amused him that she measured him visually before nodding in consent. As if she thought she had a chance of fighting him. Still, he had made the mistake of underestimating her once; he wasn't about to make that mistake twice. Especially now that he knew she was armed.

He held out his hand. "Your weapons, Miss Parker."

She didn't move.

"Don't make me have to search you."

She turned to follow the path up the hill leading to his cabin, obviously thinking if she did what she was told, he would not disarm her.

"Your weapons, Miss Parker."

Her back stiffened for a moment before she bent over. She turned and threw her knife toward him. She was so quick, he had no time to move. The knife landed point down, less than a half an inch from the toe of his boot.

Unable, momentarily, to move, he glanced down at his feet. Damn, the woman was a menace. "Was that skill or luck?"

She laughed aloud, surprising him. "I'd say it was a bit of both, Sheriff."

He bent over and drew the knife out of the ground. "Have you any more weapons, Miss Parker?"

"Indeed," she admitted. "But that's the only one I have any intention of parting with."

He hesitated, not sure what to make of the challenging look she gave him. He could search her, of course, but decided against it. He couldn't say why, but he sensed this was her one and only weapon. He holstered his gun and, holding the lethal-looking knife gingerly, regarded her with new respect. "I had no idea the cosmetics business was so dangerous."

"Nor did I, Sheriff." It was obvious by her tone of voice that she still didn't trust him. Well, the feeling was mutual.

"See that cabin up ahead, beneath those trees? That's mine."

She followed his finger. "How long do you intend to keep me in your *custody*?"

"Pull another knife trick like that, lady, and you'll be mine for the rest of your days." Scowling, he started up the hill. Now that he'd disarmed her, he was fairly confident she would follow without further trouble.

Much to his relief, she did.

# Chapter 8

Abby stood in the cabin's main room. The tall, gently swaying pines blocked out the last of the afternoon sunlight, and the room was too dim to make out much in the way of detail.

Gunnar lit a kerosene lantern, wiping the smoky haze away from the clear glass globe before replacing it. He then knelt on the wide stone hearth and arranged dry leaves and sticks in the stone-faced fireplace. He lit the kindling with a match and waited for the fire to take hold before tossing in a log.

Watching him warily, Abby pulled his coat tight around her shoulders. The room was cold and dank, the corners thick with shadows. On instinct she moved closer to the fireplace, seeking reassurance from the man as much as warmth from the fire. *Please don't let him be like all the other lawmen I've encountered in my past.*

She was suddenly conscious of the condition of her clothes. Feeling anxious and vulnerable without her trusted knife, she glanced around, as she was prone to do upon entering an unfamiliar room, and plotted escape routes. Unfortunately, only one of the two doors led outside. The room had a single window, not very wide and difficult to get to. Her best chance of survival, should the sheriff try anything, was to fight him. She took note of every possible object that could be used as a weapon.

The room was sparsely furnished. A pine table and three mismatched chairs stood between the kitchen and the sitting area. A sofa had been chiseled from a log and was piled high with animal furs. Upended tree trunks served as side tables. One of the tables held a pewter candlestick, another a thick leather-bound book. Dismissing the book as a possible weapon, except in the most dire emergencies, she mentally added the candlestick to her sparse list and studied the wooden-handled shovel standing in a corner.

The room grew less dank as bright flames consumed the log and Abby momentarily abandoned her weapons check to absorb the welcome warmth. Gunnar lifted another of the pitch-pine logs from the wood stack and tossed it into the fire.

"You can have the bedroom," he said. "I'll sleep out here." He looked back over his shoulder. Nervously, she measured the distance to the shovel. He followed her gaze. "There's a lock on the bedroom door."

She glanced at the open door he indicated. It was quite possible she'd misjudged him. Holy blazes, wouldn't that be something? An honorable lawman. The idea was so foreign to her, she immediately dismissed it and increased her guard.

"You needn't give up your bed," she replied, not wanting to explain that she still hadn't learned to trust the night enough to sleep on a bed in unfamiliar surroundings. She much preferred the security of sitting in a chair, ready to defend herself should danger threaten. "I can sleep on the . . . sofa." She eyed an upholstered chair and wished she could cuddle up in its inviting depths.

"Don't think I'm not tempted to keep the comforts of the bed to myself. That sofa is as hard as rock."

Abby pressed down on the seat of the sofa. "I've slept on worse."

Gunnar's eyes locked with hers. "I bet you have, Miss Parker. But if it's not too much to ask, allow me this one gentlemanly sacrifice."

"As you wish."

He lit a candle, stood it in the dull pewter holder,

and handed it to her. "You'll find a lantern by the bed and fresh linens in the bottom bureau drawer."

"Thank you." The candle flickered as she carried it to the doorway of the bedroom. She glanced back at him and for the first time concentrated on the man behind the badge. His handsome rugged face was lit by the fire. He had a strong jawline, a full soft-curving mouth, and a slight indentation on his chin. His thick black hair waved back from a sun-bronzed forehead and curled around his neck. There was nothing in his appearance or manner that felt threatening. If anything, she detected an integrity about him that reminded her of her uncle.

"I'll take the wagon to the hotel and pick up your trunk," he said.

Surprised to feel a twinge of guilt for the trouble she'd caused him, she bit her lower lip. She was no longer angry or even afraid, but she had no intention of lowering her guard. The sheriff might not take bribes, but he was all man, and the only one, other than her uncle, who'd persuaded her to do something against her wishes. He might not be threatening, but the man was clearly dangerous. "I'm most obliged."

He stooped in front of the fireplace to add another log. Flames leaped up the chimney. The log crackled, bringing a welcome glow to the otherwise gloomy room. "I have an old washtub that serves double-duty as a bathtub. It's not much. . . ."

She glanced at the wood slatted barrel. "I've bathed in worse," she said.

He studied her with open curiosity and she wondered what he would think if she told him how much worse.

"You can set your bath up in the bedroom and lock the door." He nodded to the kettle that hung from a black metal hook. "The water should be heated soon. Help yourself."

He grabbed a coat from a wooden peg and picked up her knife from the mantel where he'd set it earlier.

"I'll be back soon." Touching the brim of his hat with a finger, he left the cabin.

No sooner had the rumbling sound of the wagon faded away than she flew to the kitchen area. A wooden box contained a wide assortment of kitchen utensils. The only knife she could find was a poorly made kitchen knife with a celluloid handle. She ran her thumb across the dull blade and searched around for a grinding stone. Unable to find one, she slipped the knife into the leather sheath strapped to her leg. The knife was practically worthless, but its weight offered a small measure of comfort.

Thus armed, she walked into the bedroom, holding the candle in front of her until she located the kerosene lantern.

A four-poster bed commanded most of the room. A simple chest of drawers held a dry sink. A pair of the sheriff's trousers were flung carelessly across the only chair in the room. She set the candle on the bureau. It was freezing cold in the room. She'd much rather set her bath in front of the fire, but she had no way of knowing how soon the sheriff would return. Reminding herself she'd taken a bath in worse conditions, she hurried to the other room to fetch the tub.

By the time she heard the sheriff's wagon outside, she was sitting waist deep in hot water, her body lathered with lye soap. Hating the coarse feel of the homemade bar, she longed for one of the ready-made soaps in her trunk.

Her heart pounding, she studied the two-inch gap at the top of the warped door. A flimsy piece of wire held the door shut. Despite the sheriff's reassurance, the wire could hardly be called a lock.

Arms crossed in front of her bare breasts, she watched the shadow of the sheriff dim the light filtering through the cracks as he paused outside her door.

"Your trunk's outside here," he called. A thud sounded as he set the trunk on the floor.

"Thank you," she answered back, dropping her soap

into the water. He lingered a moment longer before moving away.

Letting out her breath, she lay the back of her head against the rim of the tub, but her body felt charged, like the air during an electrical storm. It was hard to forget the man on the other side of the wall. She could still feel the heat of his fingers where he'd stuffed the ten-spots down her torn bodice, recall the unsettling weight of his lean hard body as it had pressed against her in the hay.

Shivering suddenly, she sank deeper into the water until she was submerged to her neck. The sound of pots and pans offered a measure of security, for it allowed her to keep track of his whereabouts.

So far he'd done nothing that suggested he planned to take advantage of her. Still, she couldn't bring herself to relax, not completely, and even the lulling effect of the soothing hot bathwater failed to calm her tightly wrought nerves.

The spicy fragrance of freshly brewed coffee filtered through her senses and reminded her of her uncle. He'd always insist upon making the coffee whenever he was home. With the memories came the tears.

She'd had the strangest feeling since arriving in Dangling Rope that her uncle was close by, and had even felt his presence in Madam Rosie's sitting room. What did it mean? she wondered. More important, where was he and why hadn't he written to her in all this time?

Following her bath, she wrapped herself in a thick Turkish towel and cracked open the door. Reaching her hand through the opening, she felt for the handle on her trunk, hoping she could pull it into her room sight unseen. Her hand froze at the sound of the sheriff's deep-timbred voice.

"Let me." Not waiting for her consent, he'd scooped the trunk up and pushed his way into the room. He paused for a moment before setting the trunk on the floor next to the bed. It was then she noticed the touch of lace showing beneath the lid.

"Is this all right?" he asked.

She clutched the suddenly inadequate towel with both hands. "Yes, thank you." She hoped he hadn't noticed the lace.

Gunnar set the trunk down and looked up. He was completely taken aback by the sight of soft pink flesh. The towel was wrapped beneath her arms, exposing her shoulders, and the soft fullness of her breasts, before falling smoothly down her waist and molding against the flare of her hips and he wondered what part of her wore the lacy garment that was caught in the lid of her trunk. Her legs proved to be just as shapely without the hosiery and garters, just as womanly. He watched her pull and tug at the towel and decided to give her a little bit of her own medicine. "Don't fret yourself, Miss Parker. I've seen more." And indeed he had seen more, though not in recent memory and certainly not better.

"I'm sure you have, Sheriff."

"Let me know if there's anything else you need."

"Do you treat all your prisoners so well?"

He regarded her thoughtfully. Her wet hair framed her flushed face. Long wet lashes formed a dark ring around her clear blue eyes. It irritated him on some level that he was so easily affected by her. The tip of her tongue glided across her soft-curving lips, and what does he do? He imagines himself kissing her, that's what!

"Just the dangerous ones," he said, not bothering to hide his annoyance. He knew nothing about her. Who she was, where she came from. He would venture to guess, based on her peculiar ways, she was no stranger to trouble, and it was this thought that kept him on edge.

He had enough trouble with his brother. He sure as hell didn't need some damned bribing, loudmouthed, knife-throwing drummer to add to his woes!

# Chapter 9

No sooner had the sheriff left the room than Abby rushed to the door and worked the wire around the wooden peg. Kneeling next to her trunk, she undid the lock and opened the lid. After removing the wooden tray, her hands fell quickly upon the soft lacy shirtwaist her uncle had brought her from San Francisco for her birthday. "Oh, dear, dear Uncle Randall. Where are you?"

She replaced the shirtwaist, pulled out a prim calico frock, and gave it a good shake. No sense giving that sheriff any fancy ideas.

She dressed in front of the small looking glass that hung on the wall above the bureau, and brushed her still-damp hair until it was dry. She then worked the shiny strands into a tight smooth bun. Her face was still flushed from her bath, but dark shadows skirted her eyes, giving her a haunted look.

The weeks spent on the road were beginning to catch up with her. That explained the earlier tears. Perhaps it also explained the strange sense of her uncle's presence that had plagued her since her arrival.

She leaned over her trunk and pulled out a small opaque white jar. This cream was one of the more popular products her uncle sold. She thought about the young woman named Ruby and the horrible disfiguring scar. Was it true? Did her uncle really think he could help the poor woman?

Abby opened the jar and sniffed the faint floral fragrance of the cream. She'd never given much thought to contents. Cosmetics seemed to her a frivolous waste of time, and she had once tried talking her uncle into pursuing a more meaningful trade. But he'd insisted that he provided a much-needed service and had told her about his sister, who had died from arsenic poisoning years earlier.

Arsenic killed off the red blood cells, he'd explained, therefore giving women that prized white porcelain skin. It was a dangerous practice and after his sister's death, Randall Parker went into the cosmetics business. He wanted to spread the word that it was possible to enhance beauty without risking one's health. Unfortunately, most women denied doing anything to enhance their looks, and Uncle Randall was forced to take his products on the road.

Abby wondered how many lives her uncle had saved, and how many he could have saved if only people had listened. She had never personally experimented with the endless array of gels and creams that came to the house. To her way of thinking, women who constantly fretted over their complexions and worried about the effects of the sun were unbearably vain. But today, something clicked inside. People with facial scars like Ruby and like so many of the street people she'd known in the past could be helped by the right creams or powders. She felt a sense of excitement as she considered the possibilities.

Moving the lantern closer to the looking glass, she dabbed a bit of powder beneath her eyes. She stepped back. The talc-based powder erased the dark circles, but she doubted it would cover any major flaws. She dipped her finger in the powder and held it to the light. She suspected the only thing that would cover scars as deep and widespread as Ruby's would be a thick flesh-tone gel.

Deciding to experiment, she impulsively rubbed some lip rouge across her lips. Thinking it a shade too dark, she rubbed her lips until only the faintest touch of red tint remained. Stepping back, she studied herself. The color enhanced her mouth without looking unnatural. She liked what she saw.

An idea began to form. Her uncle's business had dropped considerably in the last few years. With the advent of mail-order catalogues, few women were so isolated as to have to depend solely on peddlers for their goods. What would happen, she wondered, if she and her uncle provided something that could not be purchased through a catalogue or even in those fancy big department stores that were sprouting up in all the major cities? Suppose they offered tips on the proper use of cosmetics?

The sheriff knocked on the door. "Miss Parker, I brought you something to eat."

She hastily glanced in the mirror. Giving her lips a final rubbing and sticking one last hairpin into her smooth shiny bun, she hastened to the door. For the first time since meeting the sheriff, she didn't have to worry about the state of her attire. She was fully dressed, with not a single rip to compromise her modesty.

Feeling confident and in control, she opened the door, only to discover that beneath her carefully nurtured facade she was anything but. Her heart was beating too fast and her body quivering too much to allow for control.

The problem was, with only Gunnar Kincaid to concentrate on, she found herself noticing things she'd not previously noticed. Like his height, which required him to duck beneath the doorway, and the impressive width of his shoulders. Like the way the light danced upon his glossy black hair, and how straight and white his teeth appeared next to his sun-bronzed skin.

His eyes locked with hers. "I'll put this on the end table." Steam curled invitingly from a tin coffee cup.

Putting a stop to the heated glance that stretched between them, she stepped aside. His expression suddenly bland, he brushed past her, placing the tray next to the bed. "It's only cheese and bread," he said, his tone apologetic.

"It's perfect. Thank you." It wasn't all that long ago that such fare would have seemed like a banquet. "I've had—" She caught herself.

"Worse?" He straightened. "Have you, now?" His eyes flickered with curiosity, but much to her relief, he let the matter drop. "Have you made arrangements for the stage to return to Dangling Rope?"

"Arrangements?"

"The stage no longer makes scheduled stops. Before your arrival today, we hadn't seen it for three months."

"Oh." That explained why the stage driver tried to talk her out of coming to Dangling Rope. "Are you saying I'm free to go whenever I choose?"

His gaze settled on her mouth. Feeling self-conscious and wishing she'd not bothered with the rouge, she moistened her lower lip. As if to question the action, he arched a dark eyebrow. "I'm keeping you in protective custody. That's all."

"I don't need your protection, Sheriff."

"I'm well aware of that, Miss Parker. I'm keeping you here to protect the town."

She looked away, blushing. Considering her earlier conduct, he had every reason to think the town might be in jeopardy. Well, let him think what he pleased. She leveled a steady gaze at him. "I won't be leaving for a while."

He tilted his head back in surprise, but said nothing.

"I'm looking for my uncle," she explained. "He was last seen here in Dangling Rope. His name is Randall Parker. Perhaps you've heard of him?"

The sheriff shook his head. "I've only been here three months myself."

"Really? And already you're the sheriff?"

He grinned. "The nice thing about settling in a town like Dangling Rope is you can be anything you want to be and there's no one to stop you."

"Is that why you're here? So no one can stop you?"

"Maybe."

"And the others?"

"The others? Let's see. Mom Bull has always wanted her own restaurant. The only problem is she can't cook worth a pot of fleas. Here she has no competition. Then there's Clod, perhaps you remember him? He's my deputy. His dream is to be a great fiddle player."

"And the other," she asked, "the blond-haired man?"

"You must mean my brother, Nathan."

It surprised her that the two men were related. They looked nothing alike.

"I don't know what his dream is. I doubt if even he knows."

She sensed the sheriff's reluctance to talk about his brother. "I thought every man's dream was to find gold," she said. After traveling across country and meeting so many men who were traveling to the Colorado gold mines, she'd begun to wonder if a dream existed anymore that didn't have to do with gold.

"No amount of gold in the world is going to make Mom Bull a better cook or Clod a better musician." He paused as if he thought she would disagree. "What is your dream, Miss Parker?"

"I told you. To find my uncle."

He studied her thoughtfully. "If you like, I'll make some inquiries for you."

"That won't be necessary," she said, not wanting to feel obligated to him. "I . . . I prefer to talk to people myself."

A frown touched his forehead. "There are some rough characters in the area. You best not take chances."

"If you're so worried about my safety, perhaps you'd be kind enough to return my knife."

"Your safety is of primary concern to me, but so is my own. I wouldn't want you to get any fancy ideas in the middle of the night."

"I almost never get fancy ideas in the middle of the night, Sheriff."

His mouth softened with amusement. "Is that right,

Miss Parker? Well, for the time being, let's keep it that
way. This room's not much, but it's yours as long as
you wish. Meanwhile, I'd appreciate knowing your
whereabouts at all times." He held out his hand. "I'd
also appreciate having my kitchen knife back."

Glowering at him, she reached into her boot. The
knife was so dull, she didn't have to worry about the
blade doing damage to her skirt. She slapped the knife
into his outstretched hand.

"Much obliged, Miss Parker. Now we'll both get a
good night's sleep." He left the room before she had a
chance to respond, closing the door with a firm bang.

"I'll go anywhere I damned well please," she called
after him. "And I don't have to tell you or anyone else!"

Gunnar froze outside her door. For two bits, he'd go
inside and show her who was boss. The only thing
holding him back was the disturbing knowledge that
she was the most intriguing woman he'd ever met. The
urge to kiss those dewy soft lips of hers was so strong,
it was a wonder he'd managed to resist the temptation.

What in the world could he be thinking of? He was
the sheriff. Despite her low regard for lawmen, he took
his responsibilities seriously. He would never take advantage of a woman in his custody.

Besides, she was everything he hated in a woman.
Stridently independent. Brash. It made him shudder
the way she carried on in the jailhouse. Nor would he
forget how she attacked Mr. Mulpepper. Or how she
hauled that knife earlier, barely missing his boot!

God Almighty, it would be safer to kiss a rattlesnake.

She awoke that night with a start. Heart pounding,
she instinctively reached for her knife and was momentarily startled to discover her knife sheath empty. Fully
awake now, she recalled the events of the preceding
day and clutched the blanket to her chin. It was dark
in the room, with only a thin sliver of light showing
around the warped door.

At first she didn't know what had awakened her. Then she heard the angry voices. Holding her breath, she sat forward. She'd felt too anxious to sleep in the bed, choosing instead to sit in the upholstered chair. Now the chair squeaked beneath her weight.

She recognized one of the voices as the sheriff's. "Dammit! Don't blame me for the mess you're in. You're just like . . ."

"Say it, why don't you. I'm just like him."

Abby remembered hearing the second voice at the sheriff's office. She was almost positive it was the sheriff's brother, Nathan.

"That's not what I was going to say," the sheriff said.

"It's written all over your face, big brother, just as it was written all over hers! That's why she chose you over me. You were always so righteous."

"She didn't choose me over you, dammit!"

"What would you call it? She ran off with you, for God's sake! She never gave me a second thought."

"She never cared about anyone, Nathan. That was the way she was."

"But you're the one she held in her arms. I've heard enough of your bullshit to last a lifetime."

"Nathan, dammit, come back here!"

The door to the cabin slammed shut with such force, the flimsy walls shook and the single window in her room rattled.

Shocked by the hatred and anger between the two brothers, Abby lay her head against the back of the chair.

The sheriff was a fine one to talk. Calling her a troublemaker and trying to make her feel guilty for not meeting the high standards of the town. Well, *she* never stole anyone who belonged to someone else. Would never do such a thing.

She adjusted the blanket around her feet, her mind racing with curiosity. It must be some kind of woman, for two men to fight over her. No doubt she was a perfect lady, who always had a roof over her head and who never knew what it meant to miss a meal. Such a woman probably never uttered an improper word in her life and most likely, never had to support herself. Certainly such a woman would never set foot in a brothel.

Abby wondered what had become of her. Nothing remained in the cabin to suggest a woman had lived here. She supposed it must have happened before the two brothers came to Dangling Rope.

She heard the sheriff moving around in the other room. At one point, she sensed him outside her door. She held her breath until he moved away. Trembling with relief, she tried to still her racing pulse. She was safe for the moment, but that was no reason to let down her guard. If the sheriff would steal a woman from his very own brother, who knew what else he was capable of?

During most of the restless night that followed, she couldn't stop thinking of the two brothers—one blond as sunshine, the other dark as a moonless night.

That woman had to be crazy to run off with the sheriff. Even if he was the most handsome and intriguing man Abby had seen in all her born days.

# Chapter 10

She awoke the following morning to the smell of fresh-perked coffee and bacon.

She dressed quickly in the cool morning air, then applied the softest touch of blush to her cheeks. She stood back and regarded herself in the mirror. The additional color made her eyes sparkle and her lips glow. It surprised her how little color was needed to make a noticeable difference.

A knock on the door made her pulse jump. "Breakfast is ready," Sheriff Kincaid called.

"I'll be there in a minute." She glanced in the mirror one last time before hurrying to the door.

The sheriff stood in front of the wood cookstove, his back toward her. He glanced at her over his shoulder, his expression unreadable. "Take a seat and help yourself."

The rough wooden table was set with chipped crockery and metal cutlery. She reached for the platter of flapjacks. "It smells good," she said, feeling awkward. No matter how hard she tried, she couldn't stop thinking about the argument she'd overheard. *What happened to her, Sheriff?* she wondered. *What happened to the woman you stole from your brother?*

Gunnar watched the bacon sizzling in the skillet. He was in no mood for socializing. He'd had a bad night. Actually, he hadn't slept a wink. That senseless fight with his brother hadn't helped. But it wasn't the only thing that had kept him tossing and turning. Not by any means.

His unexpected guest was just as much to blame for his sleepless night as Nathan. It had been a long time since he'd given a woman as much as a passing glance, let alone a thought. He'd been too busy bailing his brother out of trouble.

He lifted the sizzling bacon out of the skillet with a metal spatula and placed the crisp strips onto a plate.

"I like a man who knows his way around a kitchen."

His thoughts fled at the sound of her voice. He turned and locked her in his gaze. "Sometimes a man doesn't have a whole lot of choice what he learns."

"The same is true for a woman," she countered with a look of censure.

She looked pretty as a picture. And delicate as a lily. He always knew looks could be deceiving, but she proved it without a doubt. What kind of life would make a woman learn to fight like a wildcat? Or learn how to use a knife? *I've slept on worse,* she'd said, and somehow he believed her.

Against his better judgment, he reached up to a high wooden shelf where he'd put her knife for safekeeping. He ran a finger along the smooth metal blade before sliding the weapon across the table.

The look of relief and gratitude on her face made him regret having taken it away from her. This weapon, apparently, was more than just a way to protect herself. It represented something deeper and far more profound.

She eyed him speculatively, as if she expected him to change his mind. Finally she picked it up and slid it into her boot.

He reached for the coffeepot and started to pour. Knowing his guest was armed did nothing for his peace of mind, but it sure as hell did plenty for hers. She afforded him a rare smile, causing him to miss her coffee cup.

"I'll get it," she said, jumping to her feet. She grabbed a square of sackcloth and mopped up the puddle of coffee before it had traveled the length of the table.

After filling his own cup, he set the coffeepot on the stove. "Whereabouts are you from?"

"Boston."

"Boston, Massachusetts?" He would have been less surprised had she said Dodge City or one of the other notorious cow towns. He studied her dress. It was plain and practical, similar to the one she'd worn yesterday, but without the torn sleeve. It wasn't exactly the kind of dress one would expect to see in Boston.

He sat opposite her. "Do you have family there?" he asked at length, more curious about her than ever.

"No." She blinked her eyes as if to ward back tears. "Not since my uncle . . ."

Regretting the question, he covered her delicate pale hand with his own and felt something stir inside. It had been a long time since he'd felt skin as soft and smooth as hers. Feeling her fingers tremble, he squeezed her hand tight. "I'm sure your uncle's all right. Probably staked himself a claim like everyone else."

She shook her head. "He would have written and told me." No sign of tears now, only determination and a strong belief that made him ache inside. It wasn't often someone was able to instill that kind of faith in another. Gunnar envied the man.

He was tempted to offer his help, but decided against it. Now that they'd lost their last chance to make something of Dangling Rope, he had no reason to stay. Besides, the woman was trouble. He was as certain of that as she was certain of her uncle's family loyalty.

Following breakfast, Abby made a beeline for the garish pink building marked OPERA HOUSE. The sheriff had given her strict orders to stay away from the brothel, and said it was unseemly for a respectable woman to visit such a place. *Ha!* she thought as she trudged down the hill. *Unseemly, indeed! How dare the man tell me what I can and cannot do!* If he thought her visiting a brothel unseemly, what did he call stealing a woman away from his brother?

She had unfinished business with Madam Rosie and her girls, and she had no intention of leaving town until she had done what she'd come to do.

Madam Rosie greeted her warmly, though she did take the added precaution of propping a chair in front of the door. "Come," she said, leading Abby to the parlor where a Chinese houseboy was cleaning up shards of broken glass. "Girls!" she called at the top of her lungs. "Miss Parker is here. Do hurry!"

Shocked by the condition of the once-beautiful room, Abby stood and stared, not knowing what to say. "I'm so sorry. I don't have much money, but I want to pay for some of these damages."

"Charley's doing that," Madam Rosie said smugly. She held up the bag of gold he'd left behind. "There should be enough here to redecorate the whole place." She sighed and waved a lace handkerchief. "I don't know what the world is coming to. Why, when I was in New Orleans, working on Basin Street, the men were gentlemen. They brought us gifts and treated us like ladies. But these miners . . ." She shook her head. "They come in here, making demands you wouldn't believe."

"You shouldn't have to put up with it," Abby said.

"You're absolutely right. But it's my own fault. I've been far too lenient. From now on everyone coming through that door will have to meet certain standards."

"It seems only right," Abby agreed.

Madam Rosie smiled slowly. "Then you don't think it a bit presumptuous to expect more from our clients."

"Not at all," Abby said. "But that's only my opinion. I'm really not the one to give advice."

"You're a businesswoman," Rosie declared.

"Well, yes, I am," Abby said.

"Then who better to give advice to a fellow businesswoman?" She leaned forward and spoke in a confidential tone. "Business had been rather slow since everyone took off for Cripple Creek. Don't get me wrong. I'm doing all **right**. Some of my loyal customers think it's worth the trip to come here, rather than have to make appointments in advance at some of those la-di-da places. But I'm going to have to eventually do—what do you call it?—advertise. Do you suppose you could help me write up the ads?"

Abby couldn't imagine a respectable newspaper running such an ad. "Well . . . I . . ."

Rosie's girls came bouncing into the room wearing dressing gowns over their corseted bodies. They gathered around Abby like moths around a light and chattered gaily about the events of the night before.

Ginger looked unbearably smug. "I've been in jail more times than I can remember, but never for knocking out a politician."

Meg giggled and Ruby rolled her eyes as if she couldn't bear any more of Ginger's boasting.

"I can't tell you how happy we are that you've come back," Ruby said. "After last night, I thought for sure we'd seen the last of you."

Abby sat on the divan and the women sat around her, with Meg on the floor. "It'll take a lot more than a few drunken miners to chase me out of town."

"W-w-we certainly t-took care of those miners," Meg said quietly.

"We certainly did," Ruby agreed. "It'll be a long time before they cause trouble around here again."

Ginger flicked her hair behind her shoulder. "The sheriff wasn't too happy about how we attacked those politicians."

"How could we have known who they were?" Abby asked. "What were they doing here, anyway?"

Rosie explained. "The sheriff and his brother had some ridiculous plan to make this a county seat. The day this town becomes a county seat, I'll become a schoolmarm."

Ginger studied her hands. "I think we'd make a great county seat."

"It's the only w-w-way the town is going to p-prosper."

Rosie shook her head stubbornly. "I've been through this before. As soon as you let those politicians have their way, the next thing you know, businesswomen like me are out." She drew up a chair and, pointing to Abby's knapsack, sat down. "We put all your cosmetics back. There doesn't appear to be too much damage."

"Thank you," Abby said. She opened up her pack and spread her wares on the table. A quick check told her everything was intact. Meg picked up a jar and sniffed the contents.

"You'll find these facial creams are made from only the purest ingredients," Abby explained. "My uncle refuses to carry anything containing arsenic, mercury, or lead."

Ginger drew a blue bottle from the pocket of her dressing gown. "There's only one product that works for me." The hobnobbed sides of the bottle marked the contents as lethal. "Nothing makes the skin look whiter."

"I'll bet my drawers that's arsenic!" Abby declared, alarmed. "Women have died from using such products."

Shrugging her shoulders carelessly, Ginger replaced the bottle in her pocket.

"W-w-what's this?" Meg asked, picking up a small package.

"That's a very special soap made by a man named Jergens. It's a new product. My uncle's only carried it since last year."

"What does a man know about making soap?" Ginger scoffed.

"Mr. Jergens is a former lumberjack. He learned the importance of using certain lotions to soften his calluses. This bar of soap will keep your skin as soft as a baby's."

"I don't have c-calluses," Meg said. "But the air up here isn't very kind to one's c-complexion. I'll take three b-bars of that lumberjack's soap."

Abby wrote down her order. Next to her Ruby sat holding a bar of soap. "Shall I order you some?" Abby asked.

Ruby gave a mocking little laugh, the scar on her face an ugly red patch. "What good are soft hands when you look like this?"

Not wanting to embarrass her, Abby had avoided looking directly at the scar. But something in the young woman's voice, a plaintive tone beneath a desperate edge, drew Abby's gaze to the reddened skin.

Aware she was being scrutinized, Ruby gave Abby a sneering smile. "Satisfied?" She stood and started to leave.

Abby jumped to her feet. "Wait! Please." Ruby remained standing and Abby continued, "If you let me, I'd like to try something. You said my uncle had talked about a product—"

Ruby started for the door again.

"Oh, come on, Ruby," Ginger coaxed. "What have you got to lose?"

Ruby hesitated. "What do you want with me?"

"I would like to try something. I think I can cover your scar."

Ruby looked skeptical, but she sat down on a chair, holding herself rigid.

Abby reached for a bottle of complexion cream. Ruby was pale-skinned, but even so, the cream was too white. Abby never could understand why society as a whole thought a woman's beauty was based on how closely she resembled a marble statue. It was morbid, to say the least, and so unnatural-looking.

She poured a generous portion into the palm of her hand and added just a touch of red color. Mixing the mixture with her fingertip, she dabbed the light peach-colored mixture with the corner of a fine Mediterranean sponge.

When she lifted the sponge to Ruby's face, the woman drew back.

"It won't hurt," Abby said. "And if you don't like the results, we'll wash it off."

Madam Rosie frowned with impatience. "For goodness' sakes, Ruby. Let Miss Parker try."

"It won't do any good," Ruby said, but she didn't move when Abby touched the sponge to her cheek.

The lotion went on smoothly, but it took three applications before the bright red scar faded, and two more before it disappeared significantly.

Meg's eyes widened in surprise. "W-why Ruby, you c-can hardly see the scar."

"Meg's right," Rosie said. "If you can hardly see it during the day, imagine how you'll look at night when our guests start arriving."

Even Ginger looked impressed. "Well, I'll be a dancing cow."

Ruby stared at the four of them. "You aren't pulling my leg, are you?"

"See for yourself," Abby said, handing her a mirror.

Ruby took a deep breath to brace herself before holding the mirror up to her face. No one spoke, or even moved.

"What do you think?" Abby probed gently.

Ruby suddenly burst into tears. Thrusting the mirror into Abby's hand, she dashed out of the room.

Abby started after her, but Madam Rosie held her back. "Give her time."

"I never meant to . . ."

"I . . . I'll g-go to her," Meg stammered.

Madam Rosie shook her head. "I'll go." She stood and tugged at her corset before leaving the room.

Ginger gave her shoulders a careless shrug. "Ruby tends to be emotional." She applied rouge to her lips and smacked them together. "What do you think?"

"Don't you look s-s-omething?" Meg said.

Ginger looked pleased. "Don't I, though?"

Abby hated to disagree. Anything was better than the arsenic Ginger had admitted taking. But in all honesty, the red rouge clashed with Ginger's hair, highlighting

the brash orange tones. "You have such lovely coloring," she began tactfully. "I think you need a softer
color. Something less red."

"A softer color." Ginger pursed her lips. "Do you
have such a color?"

"Not at the moment." Abby drummed her fingers
impatiently. As far as she knew, most commercial cosmetics came in only one color. No thought had been
given to the unfortunate woman who should never
wear red.

"Perhaps I could find a way to tone down the color,"
Abby said, thinking aloud. "It shouldn't be that
difficult."

"Red looks p-p-erfect on me," Meg said. She spun
around. "W-what do you think?"

Abby agreed. Meg was dark-haired and needed the
bright color. "The color's right. But you're wearing too
much. You look like a hooker," she said, using one of
the many deriding terms so prevalent on the streets of
Boston. Horrified at the slip of her tongue, she immediately tried to make amends, but Ginger brushed her
apologies away with a wave of a hand.

"Mercy me, Miss Parker," Ginger drawled. "Meg *is*
a hooker."

Never one to mince words herself, Abby was nonetheless taken aback by Ginger's candor. "Regardless of
one's profession, the purpose of cosmetics is to enhance the face, not hide it. What do you think about
my face?"

"You're as p-pretty as a p-p-icture," Meg said. "But
unfortunately we don't have your l-looks or your c-
coloring."

"That's nonsense," Abby said. "Each of you has your
own beauty. The coloring on my face was applied this
morning in the privacy of my room."

Both women gasped out loud. "No!"

"You're wearing cosmetics?" Ginger leaned closer
and squinted her face. "It doesn't look like it."

"It's not how much you apply," Abby explained. "It's

how you apply it that makes the difference." Abby dabbed at Ginger's lips with a sponge. "There, that's better."

Ginger looked unconvinced as she stared at herself in the mirror. "I don't want to give the impression I'm one of those church ladies who sit around all day at sewing bees."

Abby laughed. "I doubt anyone would think that!" She turned to Meg. "Let me tone down yours."

"No," Meg said quietly. "C-c-cosmetics hide a lot of things."

"But you're beautiful," Abby said. "You don't have anything to hide."

"Yes, I do. My c-clients see me as a p-professional and that's how I like it. C-cosmetics allow me to keep something of myself p-private. I doubt most of those men would recognize me in p-public with my face b-bare."

Abby drew back. It seemed she still had a lot to learn about cosmetics—and even more to learn about the women who used them.

Abby finished taking their orders, then put the samples back into her pack. She was impatient to steer the conversation around to her uncle. "Yesterday, you said my uncle failed to keep an appointment with you."

Meg nodded. "It w-was so unlike Mr. P-Parker." She gave a wistful sigh. "I hope he's all r-right. He was a t-true gentleman."

"That he was," Ginger agreed. "Always smiling and whistling. He never failed to tip his hat and tell us how much he appreciated our business."

Abby felt a pang in her heart. How she missed him. "That's my uncle, all right." What a handful she was when he first rescued her from the streets.

"He talked about you all the time," Ginger said, putting yet another coat of lip rouge on her mouth.

"He did?"

"Said his life wouldn't have been the same had you not come into it. Said you were the stars and the sun and all that was good about life."

Abby's eyes grew blurry with tears.

Meg gave Ginger a scolding look. "Now l-look what you've g-gone and d-done."

Ginger's eyes rounded in alarmed. "I'm sorry . . . I never meant . . ."

"It's all right," Abby said, dabbing away her tears with the corner of a linen handkerchief. "It helps to talk about him. Do you know of anyone who might have known my uncle?"

Ginger thought for a moment. "As I'm sure you've noticed, there aren't too many people left in Dangling Rope."

Abby bit back her disappointment. She hated the thought of traveling back to Boston with no more knowledge than when she started.

"W-what about M-m-mole?" Meg suggested.

"He's a hermit," Ginger explained. "You probably don't remember him, but he was the man in jail last night who was doing all the complaining. He generally lives on a mountain ledge. Says he can watch the world on his ledge. He might know something. But he probably won't talk to you. He only talks when he wants to talk."

"Where can I find this Mr. Mole?"

"There's an Indian trail that takes you up the mountain. Just as you reach the cutoff, you'll find him."

It wasn't much, but she couldn't afford to leave a single stone unturned. Anxious to track down Mole, she prepared to leave, but Madam Rosie and the girls insisted she stay for the noonday meal.

"P-Please say you'll s-stay," Meg whispered. "It's so seldom M-madam R-rosie allows anyone to stay for dinner."

Since her presence seemed important to Meg, Abby didn't have the heart to disappoint her. "Very well. But I can't stay long."

Dinner was served in the dining room. At first glance, the polished silver and sparkling crystal commanded the eye, giving a look of opulence to the room.

A closer look revealed the skillful darns on the table-cloth and the frayed edges of the linen napkins.

Presiding over the small gathering, Madam Rosie was like the matriarch of a once-wealthy family who refused to lower her standard of living despite hard times. Noticing Abby stare at a French tapestry that hung over the maplewood, she looked pleased. "I'm sure this must remind you of Boston."

Abby smiled, but said nothing. Madam Rosie would be surprised, no doubt, to learn that despite the less than perfect linen, faded carpeting, and stained wallpaper, she'd never sat at a more elegant table.

"The midday meal was always a grand occasion in New Orleans," Madam Rosie explained. Her eyes grew dreamy as she recalled her past.

The Chinese houseboy appeared, carrying plates of sliced roast beef and vegetables. The food was delicious and plentiful. The conversation was lively. Even Ruby had joined them, though it took much persuasion from the others. When she finally arrived at the table during the second course, her face had been scrubbed clean of any cosmetics and the scar stood out, more prominent than ever.

Abby gazed at the woman in puzzlement but said nothing. Cowhide once said that a scar could be a badge of courage or a badge of cowardice, it was up to the person to decide. At the moment, Ruby acted more defiant than anything else and seemed to have purposely brushed her hair away from her face so as not to hide her scar.

Ginger helped herself to the mashed potatoes. "Abby, you must tell us all about your life in Boston."

"I'm afraid you'd find it rather dull," Abby replied. "Not everyone lives in grand manors or attends fancy balls."

The conversation drifted to everyday matters of a brothel.

Ginger rolled her eyes. "I just remembered today is

Thursday." She turned to Abby. "I hate Thursdays. That's Heckman's night."

Madam Rosie paused, her fork between her plate and her mouth. "Heckman pays well."

"But he's so slow," Ginger argued. "I could service three customers for the time it takes the man to—"

Madam Rosie gave Ginger a meaningful look. "Perhaps we could discuss our business affairs later. We have a guest. Besides, it's time you girls went upstairs to prepare for a viewing."

"A-already?" Meg made a face, but she followed the others upstairs, leaving Abby alone with Madam Rosie.

"What's a viewing?"

"Come along and I'll show you." Rosie stood and led the way upstairs to a glass window in front of a tiny cubicle. "A gentleman caller stands right where you are standing now and views each of the girls individually until he finds the one he wants."

Abby was puzzled by the glass. "But wouldn't he want to talk to her?"

"Talk?" Madam Rosie looked incredulous. "Good heavens. I would never allow my girls to go through the indignity of talking while in a state of undress."

Abby stared at Madam Rosie, horrified. "Sin to Moses! You mean they stand there stark-fricking-naked?"

Madam Rosie's eyes grew as wide as saucers and she looked as if her corset had just shrunk two sizes. "My word, Miss Parker, what a way to put it. I prefer to think of it as an unveiling, like an artist unveils a painting. Come to think of it, maybe that's what our advertisement should say." Looking pleased with herself, she led Abby back downstairs. "Now if you'll excuse me, I must prepare to greet our gentleman visitor."

Thanking her for the meal and hospitality, Abby gathered up her cosmetics. She opened the door of the brothel just as a man approached. Dressed in dark gray trousers and a matching sack coat, he lifted his hat in greeting. His black hair had been slicked back with pomade and combed from a center part. It sickened Abby to think of her newfound friends having to go through such a degrading experience on his behalf.

"Good afternoon, miss," he said politely, though his gaze was far too familiar as far as she was concerned. Obviously he thought she worked at the brothel.

"You . . . you . . ." Despite the rather colorful language she'd learned from her years on the street, she couldn't think of a word to adequately describe the man and his kind. "How would you like it if they insisted upon seeing your knocker in advance?" She dropped her gaze contemptuously. "No doubt you'd be rejected on the spot."

The man's mouth fell open, but he was clearly too stunned to speak.

Carrying her knapsack on her back, she marched past him in haughty disgust, leaving him to stare after her.

# Chapter 11

Abby was anxious to question Mr. Mole and was tempted to seek him out at once, but her first priority was, out of necessity, to find more suitable accommodations. She refused to put the sheriff out another night and the hotel was obviously out of the question. While she stood in the middle of Main Street pondering the problem, the man she recognized as the sheriff's brother, Nathan, rode up on his horse.

"Afternoon, Miss Parker." He lifted his hat and smiled. She wondered if his red eyes were from lack of sleep or the whiskey she could smell. "You're looking mighty pretty today."

She smiled back. Although Nathan lacked the rugged good looks of his brother, there was something quite appealing about him. His crooked smile, along with the careless way his hair fell across his forehead, gave him a boyish look.

He dismounted his horse, a piebald gelding he called Blazer, and ran his hand gently along the animal's sleek neck. "Is there any way I can be of assistance?"

Warmed by the man's obvious desire to be kind, she patted Blazer's firm rounded rump. Having overheard the argument he'd had with his brother, she felt strangely uncomfortable in his presence, almost guilty, as if she'd read his private papers or diary.

"I'm looking for a place to stay," she explained. "As you must know, the hotel is out of the question and I have no intention of spending another night at the sheriff's house."

He looked surprised. "You spent the night with Gunnar?"

*So that was his given name.* Gunnar. Not that it mattered, of course. Aware, suddenly, that Nathan could possibly jump to the wrong conclusion, she quickly explained. "Not *with* him. At his house."

"I didn't mean to imply . . . I would never think . . ." He blushed suddenly, and she felt sorry for him. "Anyone can see you're a lady."

She laughed aloud, relieved that after practically confessing she'd overheard the brothers argue, he showed no ill will toward her. "You can still say that? After what you saw at the Opera House?"

"The Opera . . ." He chuckled, proving he had a sense of humor. "Where is it written that a lady can't enjoy a good brawl on occasion?"

"I like your way of thinking," she said. What woman in her right mind would reject Nathan's attentions for those of his arrogant brother's? It made no sense.

"And I like yours. As far as accommodations go, take your pick." He waved his hand to indicate the various wood structures on Main Street. "Every one of these buildings has living quarters upstairs. Some are still furnished. If you'd rather stay outside of town, there're a few empty cabins."

"Don't these buildings belong to someone?"

"Not anymore. Not since gold was discovered in Cripple Creek. No sense letting good buildings go to waste. If I may make a suggestion, Miss Parker, I would say Sleazy's Saloon is your best bet. Sleazy had a few rooms upstairs he'd fixed up for the woman he'd hoped would become his bride."

"What happened to her?" Abby asked.

"She traveled out to Dangling Rope, all right, but she sure didn't stay long. Said it was no place to raise mules, let alone a family. When she left, it liked to break Sleazy's heart. He didn't want no part of the town after that."

"Poor man," Abby said.

"I think he'd feel a whole lot better if he knew the place was being put to good use."

"In that case, I will most certainly put it to good use."

"That's Sleazy's place next to the hotel."

"I'm much obliged, Mr. Kincaid."

"I would be honored if you'd call me Nathan, ma'am."

"Very well, Nathan. As long as you call me Abby."

"Abby." He pushed back his hat and regarded her with yet another of his crooked smiles. "If you require any assistance, please don't hesitate to ask. I live in the cabin up on the hill, three doors away from Gunnar."

She started across the street, before thinking of something. "Oh, dear." She glanced back at Nathan. "My trunk is at the sheriff's cabin . . ."

"No problem! I'll fetch it for you."

"Are you sure you don't mind?"

"Mind? Why would I mind?"

"No reason," she said. If he insisted upon acting as if nothing out of the ordinary had happened between him and his brother, then who was she to argue?

"You go on ahead," he urged. "I'll be by as soon as I fetch your trunk."

She thanked him and continued across the street to the saloon. The batwing doors creaked as she pushed her way inside.

Downstairs was a mess. Overturned chairs and up-ended tables were scattered about the room. Dirty glasses and half-emptied bottles staggered across the bar. A poker hand with four aces was spread fanlike across a green baize gaming table. Cigar butts mingled with the straw and faro cards on the floor. It was as if everyone had gotten up after a brawl and walked away.

She climbed the rickety stairs, fearing the second floor would be in much the same condition. She walked the length of the balcony and flung open the door at the end. She was pleasantly surprised to discover an attractive room furnished with a four-poster

bed stacked high with plush feather pillows and colorful quilts.

The walls were covered with a delicate floral print
that matched the draperies and the upholstered chairs
that flanked either side of the window. A wood-burning
heater filled one corner, a dry sink another.

A daguerreotype of a woman stood on the dresser,
next to a tarnished silver hand mirror. Abby lifted the
frame and blew away the layer of dust. The woman
was young and beautiful. No wonder Sleazy was heart-
broken when she'd refused to stay.

She set the frame down. The air in the room smelled
stale and dusty. She walked over to the window and
felt a welcome rush of pine-scented air as she released
the latch. She leaned over the windowsill and absorbed
the warmth of the sunshine. Below her, Main Street
stood deserted, but it was the sheriff's office that commanded her interest.

The sheriff's black gelding was tethered in front,
along with Nathan's and one other, but there was no
sign of the man.

She turned and surveyed the room. It needed a good
cleaning, but was otherwise more than she could have
ever wished for. She didn't expect to stay in town for
long. What she needed was a horse, though it was
probably too much to expect the rather strange and
surprising town had something as necessary as a working livery stable. Perhaps Nathan could help her with
that problem, too.

Of course, she could always walk across the street
and ask Sheriff Kincaid. No sooner had the thought
occurred to her than she decided against it. He would
most likely give her another lecture as to what she
could or could not do. As if he had the right to tell
anyone how to behave after what he had done to his
very own brother.

After she'd checked out the rest of the second floor,
she heard Nathan call to her from downstairs. She

walked out to the balcony and leaned over the railing. "That was fast. Do you need help?"

"I think I can manage it," he said. He lifted the trunk by the handles and started up the stairs.

"Just set it on the floor by the bed." He swept past her and she followed at his heels. "Where can I get a horse?"

He set the trunk down and straightened. "That's a bit tricky." He walked over to the window and moved a lace curtain aside. "See those three horses in front of the sheriff's office? Those are the only three horses we have in the town proper. One is mine, one is Gunnar's, and that old swayed-back mare is community property. Her name's Logger. You can ride her anytime you like."

Abby studied the sorrowful-looking horse with dismay. Dare she force the poor animal up a mountain? While she watched out the window and mulled over this unappealing prospect, Sheriff Kincaid walked out of his office and mounted his horse.

Handsome and commanding astride his shiny black gelding, Gunnar rode past her window. His head was shaded by the brim of his hat, and his back was rigid and straight. Though she felt nothing but contempt for what he'd done to Nathan, Abby couldn't take her eyes off him.

Behind her Nathan was describing the town's sole eating facility. "Mom Bull's always telling everyone about her hours, but the truth is she can be persuaded to whip you up some chow just about any old time, providing you don't bother her before six A.M. or after midnight."

Gunnar disappeared from sight and she pulled away from the window.

"What do you think?" Nathan asked.

She looked at him blankly. "Think?"

"About Logger. The horse."

"Oh." She smiled to cover her confusion. "I guess he'll have to do."

"If you'd rather, you can use my horse. Just let me know."

"That's very kind of you."

"I guess I better go," he said, though he made no move toward the door. "Let you unpack."

When it appeared he was in no hurry to leave, she casually walked him out of the room and the length of the balcony. "Thank you again, Nathan."

He hesitated at the top of the stairs. "You won't be afraid, will you?" he asked. "Living in this empty building by yourself?"

She glanced down at the deserted saloon below. "I've slept in worse places," she said.

He pressed his hat on his head and descended the stairs. "I'll be at Mom Bull's around seven. I'd be honored if you'd join me."

"Mom Bull's?"

"Remember I told you? The only restaurant in town. I guarantee you've never tasted worse food. Perhaps you'll find the company more appealing?"

She couldn't help but smile at his boyish charm. "I think I might find the company most appealing, but . . . I do have a lot to do."

"Fair enough." He touched his hat with a finger. "I hope to see you later."

She spent the afternoon dusting and sweeping, and was delighted to find a bathtub in a small room that had previously escaped her notice. The bathtub came complete with a waste plug. It seemed that Sleazy spared no expense in trying to please his reluctant bride-to-be.

She aired the bedding and decided that should she feel anxious during the night, either one of the upholstered chairs was comfortable enough to sleep in. Downstairs, she found a bucket and a water pump that worked after much priming.

After she'd finished the chores she'd set for herself, she occupied her time by organizing her dwindling supply of cosmetics. She was determined to create a more

suitable shade of rouge for Ginger. She wandered
about the saloon, gathering glasses from behind the
bar, spoons to stir with. She found a stash of alcohol
hidden in the back room and selected a bottle of
sherry. Alcohol was used as a solvent in complexion
creams.

She tried to think of what other supplies or utensils
she might need. Although many women devised their
own beauty products from ingredients found in the
kitchen, Abby had never done such experimentation.
During the time she lived on the streets, survival commanded her every waking moment. Later, after settling
in with her aunt and uncle, she'd used only those products sold by her uncle. The first night she'd stayed at
her uncle's house, her aunt had filled her bath and
handed her a bar of Ivory soap that actually floated.
But it was the luxury of washing her hair with the
amazing shampoo her uncle had imported from Ger-
many that delighted her the most. Never had her hair
felt so luxuriously soft and fragrant. It had never occurred to her there was such a thing as soap solely for
the hair.

It wasn't until she took over her uncle's business,
had actually met his customers and knew of their special needs, that it occurred to her that most ready-
made complexion creams and cosmetics were of such
poor quality as to be practically useless. Some of the
cold creams had the consistency of library paste. Others were lumpy or watery, and nearly all of them dried
the skin.

Lip rouges and eye paint were often uneven in color
and tended to dry out rather quickly. Abby thought it
no small wonder that a woman using such cosmetics
tended to look like a thick frosted cake.

If she had half a mind, she'd mix her own products.
No sooner had the idea occurred to her than she
grabbed her reticule out of her trunk and headed for
Otis's General Store.

Much to her relief, the store was open, though there

wasn't all that much inside. Most of the shelves were bare and the various bins less than half full.

Otis hurried over to greet her, giving her a toothy smile. "What can I do for you today, Miss Parker?"

"I need mineral oil, beeswax, and borax." She thought for a moment. "Do you have any lanolin? Oh, yes, I'll also need some gum of benzoin, some bay rum, and maybe even some nutmeg oil."

He scratched his head, mumbling beneath his breath. "Lanolin? Nutmeg oil? Let me see." He busied himself behind the counter. "That's a mighty strange order, Miss Parker."

He laid a slab of beeswax on the counter. "I'm afraid I don't have the rest of your order, but I'm heading for Cripple Creek tomorrow. Be glad to pick up what you need."

Abby gave the man a grateful smile. "That would be most generous of you."

He licked the end of his pencil and wrote down her order. "Anything else?"

She thought for a moment. "I think that's all. I have all the sherry I need. By the time I mix this up, I should have enough to last me for a while."

His stared down at the wax. "You're going to mix this with sherry?"

"Absolutely," Abby assured him. "It's the only way."

He leaned over the counter. "Aren't you afraid of destroying the natural properties?"

"The natural properties of alcohol are very drying to the complexion," she explained.

"Is that so?" he asked. He ran his fingers over his pockmarked skin. "That'll be fifty-four cents."

She pulled out her coin purse and counted out the money. "Good day, sir."

# Chapter 12

For the remainder of the day, she worked in her room. She put the wax into a tin can and melted it upon the wood stove. She then mixed in the mineral oil and sherry. With each step, she carefully checked the consistency.

She was so absorbed in her work, she hardly noticed the lateness of the hour until it was almost too dark to see. She lit the wick in the kerosene lamp and replaced the glass globe.

Shadows played along the walls of her room. It was a lonely room; a lonely town. She wished she'd not been so stubborn and had accepted the sheriff's offer to spend another night at his cabin.

No sooner had the thoughts of the sheriff intruded than she found herself glancing outside. Despite the late hour, his horse was in front of his office and a light shone behind the wavy glass windows. The light was strangely comforting and made her feel less lonely.

The sheriff had made no improper advances to her. But knowing what he'd done to that dear sweet brother of his, she'd been right to be wary of him. She should have known to trust her instincts. No wonder she felt so jittery and unlike herself in his presence.

Perhaps that would explain why even now she could recall even his most subtle mannerisms. The way he raked his hair with his fingers before putting on his hat. The way he walked.

During her youth, she'd learned to hide her desperate plight by walking the streets of Thieves Corner with a sense of purpose, hoping to give the impression she had somewhere to go, some important meeting to keep. That's how Gunnar walked. With purpose and meaning.

His smile, now, that was a different story. His smile came and went so quickly, sometimes she wondered if she'd not imagined it. It was the kind of smile seen on people who were afraid to smile, like the homeless. Seldom did you meet someone with a purposeful walk and a homeless smile.

Surprised to discover herself staring into space, she shook herself, and wondered why she was so fascinated with Gunnar Kincaid. Perhaps it was this town that made one's senses so overly aware. With so little else going on, it only made sense people would focus more on each other. As if to prove her theory, she forced herself to think about Nathan. But all she could remember with any real clarity was his blond hair and boyish charm.

When thoughts of Gunnar Kincaid threatened to intrude once again, she decided to finish what she was doing before heading over to Mom Bull's.

She'd planned to work for only another hour, but lost all track of time. A kink in her neck was the first clue as to how much time had passed. She pulled the gold chain from around her neck and checked the time on the chatelaine watch that once belonged to her aunt, and was inscribed with her uncle's name. She was stunned to discover it was almost ten o'clock. Recalling Nathan's invitation, she raced to the window. Mom Bull's Restaurant was dark. The only light burning in the town was the one in the sheriff's office and for some reason, it gave her a sense of comfort to know that Sheriff Kincaid was still close by.

Resigning herself to another supper of hard-boiled eggs, she gazed at the sheriff's window and wondered what he could possibly be doing at this late hour.

Gunnar pushed the pile of survey maps and topography charts aside and stretched his arms over his head.

It was late and he'd been poring over these maps for hours. He'd traced every conceivable route to Dangling Rope from the surrounding towns. Two railroad companies were in a race to reach Cripple Creek and had kept the miners in suspense for months. Hundreds of dollars had been gambled as to which of the iron horses would reach Cripple Creek first.

The Midland Terminal Line would eventually allow passengers to travel between Cripple Creek and Divide. This line was too far north to do much good for Dangling Rope, and the fact that it was behind schedule made it unlikely the company would be receptive to the idea of adding a circular spur.

For this reason, Gunnar concentrated on the Gold Belt Line that would pass within ten miles of Dangling Rope. Upon completion the railway would thread its way north from Florence, wind through a series of spectacular loops through the treacherous and rugged wilds of Phantom Canyon, and climb nearly five thousand feet high. The first train was expected to reach the mining town sometime in July.

His muscles stiff from sitting, he wandered over to the window. It surprised him to see a light on the second floor of Sleazy's Saloon. Usually at this time of night the town was pitch-black. He had seen Nathan carrying Miss Parker's trunk in the saloon earlier, but he never though she'd actually spend the night there.

Suddenly wide awake, he pressed his face closer to the windowpane. What was she doing at this time of night? he wondered. And what in blazes made her so damned stubborn as to refuse his offer to stay at his cabin? It made no sense that she would prefer such lodgings over his.

What a brash woman she was. Never had anyone stood up to him so. Never had he seen a woman with such flashing blue eyes. What would make a woman so bold, so earthy, so lustfully vibrant? Even more of a puzzle was how a woman with such vitality could be so utterly feminine.

Surprised by the sudden direction of his thoughts, he forced himself to concentrate on the problem of saving the town. He'd been working on the problem for the entire day, but every idea so far proved impractical or impossible. After yesterday, the chances of getting the town on the ballot were nil.

He considered giving up and going back to Chicago. He had an offer to join a law firm and he was seriously considering it. The only thing holding him back was Nathan. During these last three months, the two had battled fiercely. They had argued about the past, the future, Nathan's drinking and lack of direction. But despite the hurtful words, the frustration and despair, Gunnar refused to give up. There had to be a way to put a stop to Nathan's destructive behavior.

Saving the town might give Nathan the confidence he lacked. If nothing else, it would give him a home, but whether it would really make that much difference in Nathan's life was anyone's guess.

Chances were Gunnar would never know. Unless a miracle happened, like the train coming to town, Dangling Rope was about to hit the dust like hundreds of towns before it.

The town—damn the town. With its false-front buildings and deserted streets, it seemed as hopeless and empty as Nathan's life. It was a long shot to think that to save one was to save the other.

Gunnar narrowed his eyes upon seeing a movement at Miss Parker's window. A closer look confirmed that it was only the lace curtains moving. Evidently, a breeze was beginning to stir. He glanced at the tall pines behind the saloon to confirm his suspicions. The boughs swept the moonlit sky as if to brush away the stars. His gaze instinctively returned to her window.

He had no desire to go home to his lonely cabin. Hadn't even considered how lonely it was until last night. It amazed him to find her presence had made such a difference to an otherwise dreary cabin. It was as if someone had lit thousands of candles inside—and when she gave one of her rare smiles, it seemed to him the walls had turned to sunshine.

Something—a shadow, a movement of some sort on the street—drew his attention from her window. His forehead pressed against the cool smooth pane of glass, he narrowed his eyes.

After a moment or two, he could pick out the dark form of a man. Hand on his gun, his senses alert, he watched, ready to dash outside if the man made one move toward Sleazy's. Finally the shadowy form moved into the narrow ribbon of waning moonlight that trailed across Main Street, and the silvery glimmer of light danced upon a head of golden hair. His brother was the only man in town with hair that color.

Gunnar had not seen Nathan since the senseless argument the night before. He grimaced at the memory. Fearful that Nathan was following in the footsteps of their scoundrel of a father, and filled with guilt for having been the one his mother had taken with her when the couple had separated, Gunnar had spent the better part of his adult years bailing his younger brother out of trouble.

He'd only been fifteen when he left his mother in some honky-tonk town and traveled back to Philadelphia to find Nathan. After he'd rescued his then-thirteen-year-old brother from the squalor of their father's home, the two traveled to Albany, where Gunnar worked as a clerk for a law firm and put himself through school. One of the lawyers let Gunnar and his brother live in an empty carriage house on his property in exchange for long hours of work and a small salary that barely covered the cost of food and clothing. During all those years they'd lived together, Gunnar had never given up trying to make up to his brother for all the injustices of the past.

It was a losing battle. He knew it was a losing battle and still he kept up the fight. He would probably keep fighting to save his younger brother until his dying days. Nathan had a wild streak in him that, combined with his love of money and alcohol, continued to get him into hot water.

If Gunnar had a sensible bone in his body, he'd leave Dangling Rope and let Nathan solve his own problems. But he couldn't. The pain was too deep, the guilt too strong. The love for his brother unrelenting.

The question on Gunnar's mind at the moment was, why was Nathan watching Miss Parker's window? What dastardly deed was he plotting this time?

# Chapter 13

Early the next morning, Abby left Sleazy's Saloon and walked the short distance to Mom Bull's Restaurant. Dark clouds spilled over the surrounding mountains, but directly overhead the sky was blue. The air felt cold and brisk, and a playful breeze blew off the high peaks, nipping at her cheeks. It was a good day for riding.

Mom Bull greeted her as warmly as a puppy with two tails. She was a big woman with broad movements to match. The frilly lace apron she wore over her bib overalls looked incongruous.

"You just sit right down and I'll fix you somethin' that'll put meat on them bones of yours." She wrapped one enormous hand around the handle of the enameled steel coffeepot and filled Abby's cup. "Nathan was expecting you to join him for dinner and when you didn't show, he sure did look down on the jaw."

Abby felt a surge of guilt. "Oh, dear. I must apologize to him. I completely forgot about the time."

"You don't have to explain none to me. It's his own fault. If he wanted you to dine with him, he should have escorted you over here himself. Men today have no idea how to treat a lady. That's cuz they don't have no proper upbringin'."

Abby thought it was an odd statement coming from the mother of a gunslinger. "Nathan said I could use the horse named Logger. Do I need to ask the sheriff's permission?"

Mom Bull adjusted the waist of her skirts. "Help

yourself. The horse belongs to the town. Gunnar ain't got no say in who uses it."

"Do you know him well? The sheriff, I mean?"

"Never set eyes on him till he rode into town three months ago. Knew his brother, Nathan, though, for over a year. He talked me into comin' here. Said this was gonna be the Boston of the West." She laughed aloud. "You know what? I believed him. Rest my soul, that man could talk a mouse into a hawk's nest, if he had a mind."

"It is a nice town," Abby said. "If only it wasn't so deserted."

"The Kincaid brothers think they're gonna change all that." Mom Bull carried the coffeepot into the kitchen and emerged seconds later with a platter stacked high with flapjacks and strips of charred bacon. The flapjacks were so heavy and tough, Abby was tempted to pull out her own knife, but not wanting to be rude or to hurt the woman's feelings, she resisted the urge.

"How's the food?" Mom Bull asked.

Abby gulped down an unchewable portion. She would like to think she'd had worse, but there couldn't be any worse than this. "It's rather . . . hardy."

Obviously taking this as a compliment, Mom Bull grinned and scooped another helping of burned bacon onto Abby's plate.

"Maybe you can help me. I want this restaurant to be the finest in the West. How can I make it more like those fancy eatin' establ'shments in Boston?"

Abby stared at the woman, thinking she was joking. But it was obvious by Mom Bull's sober expression she was dead serious. Abby glanced at the grim dark surroundings, dirt floor, crudely built tables, and chipped crockery and tried for all the world to think of something charitable to say. "Maybe some flowers on the table would help."

Mom Bull brightened. "Flowers, eh? I never thought of that. What about the food? Is there a way to improve the food? You know, to make it more Boston-like."

Abby stared down at her plate. "Boston is famous for its fish."

"No problem there," Mom Bull said. "Caught me some trout the other day. Thought I'd serve it tonight."

"I suppose that would do," Abby said. "Boston's fish, of course, is ocean fish."

"Ocean fish, eh? I could soak the trout in brine. No one would ever know the difference."

Otis walked in, saving Abby from the temptation of telling Mom Bull what she thought of her brine idea.

Mom Bull greeted him with a hot cup of coffee. "You better double my order of salt."

Otis whipped a writing tablet from the pocket of his shirt and made a note to himself. He gave Abby an odd look as he took a seat at one of the empty tables. "Anything else you need, ma'am, while I'm in Cripple Creek?"

"Maybe a crate of sherry. I don't have as much as I thought. A crate should last me for a while, don't you think?"

Otis sat back in his chair. "Oh, yes, ma'am. A while."

Abby tucked the bacon discreetly into the pocket of her skirt to discard later. She paid Mom Bull and left.

Logger was already saddled. A gentle mare, she nuzzled against Abby's neck. "You think you can take me up the mountain, girl?"

The mare lacked spunk, unlike Gunnar's gelding, which gave a restless whicker and pranced in place. Abby cast a wistful eye on the spirited animal. What she'd give to ride his horse.

It was a perfect day for riding. The clouds had drifted over the valley and only a small patch of blue sky remained. But the air was clear and sparkling. How different it was from Boston, whose skies were gray with factory soot.

As the trail led her higher into the mountains, however, she could see funnels of gray smoke rise from the distant mining towns and it surprised her to feel a sense of outrage at man's intrusive presence in this otherwise spectacular country.

She reached the crossroads before noon and took the less traveled road, away from the mining towns. She searched for a cabin or other signs of habitation. She wondered if she should keep going. Perhaps there was another crossroads farther ahead.

She dismounted and, alarmed by Logger's heavy breathing, led the horse to a little spring that bubbled out of the ground. The horse drank thirstily from the pool of water. Abby dropped down on her knees, cupped her hands, and lifted the water to her parched lips. The water was icy cold and as sweet as the smell of newly sprouted meadow grass. Fields of bluebells spread like fluttering wings from either side of the trickling water. Blue and white columbines nodded star-shaped heads in the cooling breeze.

She sat back on a rock and tucked the stray strands of hair into the brim of her sunbonnet. It suddenly occurred to her that if Mole was truly a hermit, he would hardly be living so close to the main road leading to the mines.

She glanced around, narrowing her eyes to check out the intricate red rock formation overhead. It was entirely possible he could be living in a cave. "Mr. Mole," she called aloud, then listened, hearing only the raucous sound of a magpie in response.

She framed her mouth with her hands. "Yahoo, Mr. Mole." Her voice echoed down the sides of the canyon. This time, she did solicit a response.

"What daya want?"

She jumped to her feet and glanced around. "Where are you?"

"Down here, dammit. Where do ya think I'd be?"

"Down . . . ?" She walked across the dirt road and stared down at a narrow shelf that jutted out of the otherwise sheer red rock.

She vaguely recalled seeing the man in jail. She had no idea what crime he'd been guilty of, but he looked harmless enough. "What da ya want?" he asked again, in a voice that clearly insinuated she better not want anything, because he was of no mind to give it.

Straining her neck so she could better see him, she peered over the edge in hopes she could find a path leading downward. No such access was visible, but a rope was tied to a tree and dangled down the canyon wall. "I need to talk to you, Mr. Mole."

"I ain't talkin' to nobody, especially the woman responsible for gittin' me booted out of jail."

Puzzled by this accusation, she stared down at him. If, indeed, she was responsible for his release, you'd think he'd show a bit of gratitude. "I need to talk to you about my uncle—"

"I said I ain't talkin' and I mean it. Now git outta here and leave me in peace."

"But this will only take a minute."

The man dismissed her with a wave of his hand and disappeared into a lean-to covered with branches.

"Well, I never." Fists at her waist, she tried to decide what to do. She had no intention of leaving until the man had answered her questions.

Mole didn't give her any choice but to trespass on his property. She eyed the rope. Surely that couldn't be the only way down. Biting her lower lip, she squinted her eyes against the sun and stared at the canyon floor. The town of Dangling Rope was but a tiny speck below.

Closing her eyes, she held her hand to her chest and waited for her heart to stop racing. All right, she told herself when at last she could breathe. She'd give the man one more chance. "Please, Mr. Mole, it's terribly important you talk to me. I wouldn't want to climb down there and invade your privacy."

She gave him what she considered a fair amount of time to respond. When he made no reply, she decided the man deserved a third and maybe even a fourth chance. When he continued to ignore her pleas, she changed from one tactic to another; she complimented and humored him to no avail. Patience spent, she paced back and forth restlessly, eyeing the rope and telling herself that however anxious she was to find her dear uncle, hanging from the side of a mountain was *not* an option.

She supposed Mr. Mole knew this. No doubt, he thought himself perfectly safe from her. Suddenly she got an idea. What would happen if she made him *think* she intended to climb down the rope? Surely he wouldn't let her risk her neck.

Swallowing her fear of heights, she rubbed her hands together and tied the end of the rope around her waist. "Yahoo, Mr. Mole. I'm coming down. I've got the rope around my waist. Here I come." She waited. Obviously, the man was no fool; he knew she was bluffing. Maybe if she dangled one leg over the side, he would think she meant business.

Grabbing hold of the rope with both hands, she sat down on the ground and, eyes closed tight, inched one leg slowly, very slowly, over the edge. "Yahoo, Mr. Mole. Get ready."

Adjusting her hold on the rope, she decided to abandon the idea altogether. Obviously, the man was not going to fall for her ploy.

Eyes opened wide, she pulled back from the ledge and stood. A strange rumbling sound seemed to generate up from the canyon, and the ground shook beneath her feet. She tried jumping back, but the edge of the cliff broke away, taking her with it.

An ear-piercing scream filled the air, sending birds into frantic flight. Abby didn't realize at first that the scream came from her until she began choking from the dust. Eyes watery, lungs bursting, she stared down at her dangling feet.

Paralyzed with cold hard terror she clung to the rope and fought to put her frantic thoughts in order. She was hanging from the side of the mountain, swinging back and forth like a pendulum. Sweat rivered down her face as she gasped for air. She was going to die

and nobody—dear God, not a single blazing soul—
would ever know what happened to her.

Dizzy with fear, she reached for a twisted bush that
jutted from the side. This allowed her to pull herself
close enough to the walls of the cliff to get a foothold.

Her body damp with sweat, she held on to the bush
with one hand and the rope with another. She didn't
want to let go; wasn't even sure she could let go if she
wanted to. For all she knew, she was going to spend
the rest of her life dangling from the side of a mountain. "Yahoo, Mr. Mole," she cried when at last she
could find her voice. She was trembling so hard, she
managed little more than a whisper. "Please help me."

She chanced looking downward and was horrified to
discover that Mr. Mole's lean-to was buried under a
pile of rubble. Dear God, the poor man was probably
dead! And all because of her.

Fighting the panic that threatened anew, she forced
herself to calm down. The possibility that Mole might
be injured took precedence over any fear for her own
safety. Somehow, she must reach the top and go for
help.

She wedged the toe of her boot into a slight indentation and forced her weight onto her right foot. Slowly
she inched her hands up the rope. The braided rough
hemp cut into her palms. Taking a deep breath, she
repeated the action with her left foot.

Inch by inch she crawled her way up. She didn't
look up or down or sideways. She concentrated on the
rope in front of her nose and searched for the next
toehold.

She froze at the sound of rumbling. Her heart beat
so fast, she could barely catch her breath. Another part
of the cliff broke loose over her head. She screamed
as rocks slid past her and tumbled to the canyon below.
Once again she fell.

# Chapter 14

Standing in front of the window of his office, Gunnar caught sight of Nathan heading for Sleazy's Saloon. Recalling Nathan outside the saloon on the previous night, Gunnar realized, suddenly, his brother had been trying to restock his alcohol supply.

Now that Miss Parker had moved into the saloon, Nathan was obviously reluctant to walk in anytime he damned well pleased to help himself to whatever whiskey was still stored there. Irritated that his brother's dependency on alcohol controlled both their lives, Gunnar tore open the door and stepped outside.

"Nathan, we need to talk."

Nathan stopped in his tracks. For a moment the two brothers glared at each other.

Finally Nathan walked toward him. Gunnar was stunned by Nathan's appearance. Without any prodding, Nathan had actually shaved and combed his hair, and was dressed in a freshly boiled shirt. Even his boots had been polished to a high shine. Gunnar couldn't believe his eyes.

"I said everything I wanted to say to you the other night."

Gunnar brushed his fingers through his hair. Great Scott, what would possess Nathan to suddenly polish his boots? A closer look revealed Nathan's eyes were less red than usual. Feeling a sense of relief, Gunnar relaxed. Miss Parker's presence had—for the time being, at least—prevented Nathan from replenishing his stock of alcohol. Knowing the reprieve was only temporary, Gunnar decided to make the most of Nathan's sobriety.

"The other night was personal. What I have to say today is about Dangling Rope. I have an idea for saving the town. It's a long shot, but it's worth a try. If you're interested, fine. If not, that's fine, too. It's your neck on the line, not mine."

A silence stretched between them before Nathan finally nodded. He followed Gunnar inside the sheriff's office. "So what's your idea?"

Gunnar tossed a handful of maps on the desk and sat down. "What do you think about bringing the railroad here?"

Nathan looked as if he thought he hadn't heard right. "The railroad? Are you crazy? What makes you think we can talk the railroad into coming here?"

Nathan had every reason to be skeptical. Before last night, Gunnar had thought the idea too far-fetched to be taken seriously.

Placing a tip of his finger on a map, Gunnar pointed to a series of X's. "The Midland train is coming from this direction. It's too far from us to do any good. However, the route of the Florence and Cripple Creek railroad is another story. It wouldn't be all that difficult to put a spur at this point and lay tracks to Dangling Rope." Gunnar drew a line across the map, circling their town.

Nathan studied the markings. "I don't know. I can't imagine why they'd put tracks that go basically nowhere."

"They do it all the time. I can cite at least a dozen places in Kansas and Missouri where the railroad shot off spurs to nowhere because of the promise of some land boom."

Nathan looked incredulous. "Land boom? That isn't going to work. Not now. Everyone knows there's nothing here. Not silver, not gold. Nothing."

Gunnar tossed his pencil onto the desk and sat back in his chair. "There you have it."

"What?"

"Have you been up to Cripple Creek?"

"Of course I've been there. Why?"

"It's a mess. The land is stripped, the air is foul, and you can hardly think for all the noise. There's also talk of a major labor dispute. I'm telling you, Nathan, no man wants to raise a family in such a godawful town. But here . . . ah, now, that's a different matter. And with the train connecting this paradise with the mining camps . . . The railroad would be foolish to pass up this opportunity."

The skepticism left Nathan's face. "You might have something, Gunnar."

Gunnar leaned forward. "I know I have something. But we'll have to act fast. We need to get land grants from the government. We have to make a decision before the tracks reach Tucker's Pass. The sooner we get those grants, the better."

His interest waning, Nathan's face began to cloud with doubt. "I don't know, Gunnar. Even if we get the land grants, what makes you think the railroad will change its route?"

"The train has promised to make it to Cripple Creek by Independence Day. The construction crew is nearly three weeks behind. They'll be lucky if they make it there by the first of August. But by bringing the train through Dangling Rope, they can cut out this entire mountain." He circled a portion of the map. "And half this canyon. Trust me, Nathan. Once we show them a way to make their deadline, they'll beg us to let the train run through town."

Nathan stared at the map. "This could work." He slapped his palm down on the desk. "Hey, this could work!" He paced about the office, thinking aloud. "If I leave for Divide now, I should be able to catch the late-night train to Denver. Tomorrow at this time, I could have those land grants in hand." He leaped up and practically reached the ceiling with his fingertips. "Yippee!"

Surprised by Nathan's unexpected exuberance, Gunnar felt a glimmer of hope. It had been a long time since he'd felt anything but frustration where Nathan was concerned. Wanting to prolong the rapport between them, he walked over to Nathan and gave him a fond slap on the shoulder. "It's up to you, little brother, to use some of that charm of yours on those politicians."

Nathan grinned, then surprised Gunnar by throwing his arms around him. Nathan was not demonstrative by nature, and Gunnar couldn't recall the last time Nathan had showed any outward affection toward him. "Leave it to me." He started for the door, then hesitated. "Gunnar, about the other night. I—"

Gunnar waved his apology away. "Forget it, Nathan. I'd really like to put the past behind us."

Nathan thought for a moment before extending a hand. "I'd like that, big brother."

Grinning, Gunnar shook Nathan's hand, then threw his arms around him for a second time. Nathan hugged him back and suddenly Gunnar's eyes blurred. Damn! His brother hugs him and he becomes a sniveling fool!

Wanting this moment to go on forever, Gunnar tried not to show his irritation when old Mole walked into the office, filling the air with a smell as potent as a distillery filled with skunks.

"Instead of standin' around, jawin' away, you might keep your citizens under better control," he stormed, slurring his words from a toothless mouth.

Gunnar let his arms drop to his side. "What are you talking about, Mole?"

"I'm talkin' about that crazy woman who just destroyed me lodgin's and pretty near sent me to kingdom come."

Gunnar rubbed his forehead. "Crazy woman? What crazy woman?"

"The same woman who started that fight at Rosie's."

"Abby?" Nathan gasped.

Gunnar glanced at his brother, surprised that Nathan was already on personal terms with her.

Old Mole grunted. "I don't know whadda hell her name is, but that's the one. Thanks to her, the whole side of the damned mountain fell on me roof. I barely escaped with me life. You'd think she'd have the common decency to apol'gize. But no, she pract'cally accused me of bein' a murderer and demanded to know where I'd buried the body. You should hear the mouth on that one. Never heard anythin' like it in me life."

Gunnar and Nathan exchanged glances. "Where's she now?" Gunnar asked, almost afraid to ask.

"I told ya. Hangin' from the side of the mountain."

"What?" Both brothers stared at Mole in horror.

Gunnar was the first to recover. "Why the hell did you leave her?" Gunnar grabbed his hat and raced Nathan to the door.

"What the hell did ya expect me to do? She called me a murderer!"

Outside, Gunnar bolted onto his saddle and took off like lightning. Head bent low, he flew out of town and up the trail leading to Minter's Pass with Nathan close behind.

The sun had already dropped behind the high peaks when the two men arrived at their destination. Gunnar quickly tethered his horse to a tree and pulled the length of rope from his saddle. "Where is she?" he shouted. He knew the hermit lived at this pass, but had no idea exactly where.

Nathan pointed down the side of the mountain.

Cursing beneath his breath, Gunnar joined him and, showing more daring than care, peered over the ragged edge of the cliff. "Miss Parker?" he called. "Are you all right?"

Blue eyes flashed up at him from her stark-white face. Never had he seen anyone look so terrified. Fortunately, she was only about fifteen feet down.

"It's about time you got here!" she cried, her voice thick with fear.

"Don't move!" he cautioned. The rope was around her waist and had become entangled in a mass of tree roots.

Next to him, Nathan looked shaken. "Abby, don't worry. We'll save you."

"Hurry!" she gasped in a hoarse whisper.

Gunnar tied his own rope around his waist and motioned to Nathan to tie the other end to his horse. "I'm going down." He glanced at Nathan. Gunnar couldn't recall when he'd last seen his brother look so concerned for someone other than himself. It was another encouraging sign. "When I tell you to, pull her up."

Nathan lay his hand on Gunnar's shoulder. "It's too dangerous. The whole side of the mountain could go. There's got to be another way."

Gunnar shook his head. "She's stuck. She's not going to be able to free herself. Besides . . . she's too frightened to think straight. I'm going down. It's going to be up to you to haul us up."

Nathan gave a nod, his face grim. Working quickly, he tied the one end of Gunnar's rope to Gunnar's horse. Then he tossed a spare rope to Gunnar, who slipped it onto his shoulder.

"It won't be long now, Miss Parker," Gunnar shouted to her. He jumped back when the ground started to give way beneath his feet. Rocks tumbled down the mountainside, leaving a cloud of dust behind.

The two men exchanged worried glances before Gunnar lowered himself over the side.

The landslide that had buried Mole's lean-to had left much of the face of the mountain rough and jagged. Even with his long legs, it was a stretch to get a foothold in the dent that once held an anchoring boulder.

"Holy blazes, be careful!" Abby called up to him, and he could hear the terror in her voice.

He glanced downward. She looked so vulnerable hanging from the side of the cliff, it was hard to equate her with the bold brash woman who had toppled those miners and politicians with seeming ease two days earlier.

He worked his way down until he was directly by her side. She grabbed his outstretched hand and he pulled her toward him. With a tight cry, she wrapped her arms and legs around him and shuddered convulsively. "I've never been so glad to see anyone in my whole life," she sobbed on his shoulder.

"I would have to say the same thing," he said, his own voice hoarse with fear. He tried to loosen her hold around his neck. She was strangling him. "I never thought the day would come I'd tell a pretty woman to take her hands off me, but the truth is, I can't breathe."

"What?" Her face was only inches away from his.

"You're choking me." He made a gasping sound to illustrate.

"Oh," she said limply. "I'm sorry." She loosened her hold, but just barely.

"Hold still." He tied a spare rope around her slender waist. Abby was the luckiest person in the world. The rope was still tied to the tree, but the end that was knotted around her waist was caught on tree roots. It was a miracle she was still alive. "I have to untangle the rope."

Her lips trembled. Her horrified gaze clung to his. "Oh," was all she could manage. *Poor woman,* he thought, feeling sorry for her. *This is probably the first time she's been at a loss for words.*

Hanging in midair, he tried to free the snagged rope. "I need a knife."

"There's one in my boot," she whispered. "Can . . . can you reach it?"

He'd forgotten she carried a knife. He gave her a quick grin. "I'm beginning to understand why you find it necessary to arm yourself. Can you lift your leg?"

"I think so." She pressed her fingers into his back and, pressing her knee against her leg, pulled her foot up.

Reaching beneath her skirt, he ran his fingers up her boot until he felt the handle of her knife. Gripping it tightly, he withdrew it and immediately set to work cutting the rope away from the roots. He slipped the knife into his belt and wrapped his arms tight around her waist.

He glanced up. He could barely see the top of Nathan's blond head, but it shone as bright as a beacon in a dark sea. "Pull us up!" It would have been easier to let Nathan pull her up first, but though they were tied to two different ropes, she wasn't about to let go of him.

Abby tightened her hold on him, her eyes squeezed tight. Her heart was pounding so hard she could hardly breathe. It seemed like an eternity before they finally began to inch upward. She could feel the muscles ripple in the sheriff's back as he pushed his feet against the side of the cliff.

"Give me some slack!" he yelled. "Abby's rope is caught."

Nathan fed them some rope, causing them to drop. Abby screamed and dug her nails into his shoulders.

"Hold on," Gunnar said, his voice hoarse in her ear. She could smell his fear and it was every bit as potent as her own.

He checked the rope around her waist. "Pull us in."

One could have lived out a full life in the time it took them to reach the top—or so it seemed to her.

"I've got you!" Nathan shouted out.

Nathan grabbed her beneath the arms and pulled her away from Gunnar and up over the edge. Her feet at last on solid ground, she trembled with vertigo and fell to her knees in relief as Nathan undid the rope around her waist.

"You're all right," Nathan said soothingly. He wrapped his arms around her, and drew her head to his chest.

She glanced up at him. "Gunnar . . ."

Nathan peered over her shoulder. "He's fine."

She turned her head to see for herself. Gunnar stood a few feet away, undoing the knot at his waist. Saying a silent prayer of thanksgiving, she slumped against Nathan's sturdy body. She would never have forgiven herself had anything happened to either brother because of her.

Nathan lifted a canteen to her lips. "Here, take a drink." Sitting upright, she drank thirstily of the sweet, cool water.

Still breathing hard, she leaned against the trunk of a twisted scrub pine while Nathan offered water to Gunnar, then returned to her side.

"God, Abby, you could have been killed." He looked so worried, she tried to muster a smile for his benefit.

Gunnar watched the timorous though no less dazzling smile and his already quickened pulse took another pounding leap. The color had returned to her face and she was beginning to sound like herself as she proceeded to call Mole the most colorful names Gunnar had ever heard.

"The man is a poppy-cocking, mutton-mongering . . ."

Gunnar smiled to himself as he brushed the dirt off his pants. Still shaken himself, he was amazed at how quickly she'd recovered.

Gunnar slapped his hat against his thigh and, raking his fingers through his hair, dropped his hat in place. He strolled over to Abby's side, handed back her knife, and took her by the arm.

Nathan frowned. "What are you doing?"

"I'm taking her back to town."

"I'll take her."

"I'm the sheriff and Miss Parker has some explaining to do." He leveled a meaningful gaze at Nathan. "You have a train to catch, remember?"

Nathan turned back to Abby. "Will you be all right?"

"She'll be fine," Gunnar assured him. "You go on along and leave Miss Parker to me." With his fingers wrapped firmly around Miss Parker's upper arm, he led her to his horse.

"Do you mind?" she said, pulling away from him. She glared up at him. "You have no right pushing me around!"

"And you have no right trespassing on other people's property."

"Trespassing?" Her eyes widened.

"Thanks to you, old Mole lost his house and he could have been killed."

"If the fool man would build his house in a more suitable location—"

"Get on the horse."

Abby glanced at Nathan who was astride his own animal and was watching from the distance.

"Where's Logger?" she asked.

"Mole rode the horse back into town to get help for you. Lucky for you, he knew more than one way up that mountain. If it wasn't for him, you'd still be dangling from the side."

Her eyes positively sparked with indignation. "If it wasn't for him, I wouldn't have been anywhere near that mountain!"

Feeling the effects of his ordeal, Gunnar had no intention of continuing the argument. He drew himself to his full height and pointed to his horse. "Get on!"

Abby opened her mouth to say something, then obviously changed her mind. Lips pressed tight together, she held on to the horn of the saddle and placed her foot into the stirrups. Gunnar boosted her upward, then mounted behind her. He reached around her slight body to tug on the reins.

Nathan galloped past, tipping his hat. "I'll see you when I get back." In a flash he disappeared on the winding road ahead. The sound of his horse's hooves faded away in the distance.

Abby was sorry to see him go. The sheriff was making her nervous; or rather, it was the way his body seemed to fold around her that threatened her still fragile control. It was hard to think, harder still to keep from trembling.

His head was mere inches from her neck. The heady scent of him combined with the fragrance of leather and woods to produce an overall effect that was as tantalizing to the senses as the smell of freshly baked bread. "What the hell were you doing?" he growled in her ear, his breath hot on her skin. "You could have been killed."

Lord, yes, she could have been. She hardly needed him to state the obvious. "I only wanted to talk to him. To ask him about my uncle."

"So that's who you accused him of murdering." Wisps of her soft silky hair blew in his face. How could a woman who was so soft and tiny be such a nuisance? "You've been in town for three days. Three days, dammit! And you've caused more trouble than a backside full of buckshot."

She stiffened at the accusations, but her sense of dignity failed to protect her from the masculine feel of him, the strength, the power and hardness of him. "How was I supposed to know the mountain was going to fall down? All I wanted to do was talk to him—"

"Hush." He reined his horse and stopped abruptly. His body rigid and alert, his thighs pressed against her hips in a way that seemed both protective and possessive.

"What is it?" she whispered.

"I thought I saw those bushes ahead move. Probably a deer." He dismounted. "Stay here."

She watched him disappear in the brush. The sky was silvery gray. In less than an hour, it would be dark. The air had grown noticeably colder in the last half hour.

Feeling both tired and hungry, Abby remained in the saddle and waited. Suddenly the stillness was shattered by the sound of a gun. Heart pounding, she glanced around. Fearing the sheriff had been shot, she debated about whether to go for help. She decided against it. If he was injured, he would need immediate care.

She slipped from the saddle and grabbed her knife

out of her boot. Crouching low, she followed the same path the sheriff had taken moments earlier. She stilled and listened, but the only sound breaking the silence was babbling water in a nearby creek.

Suddenly a viselike grip closed around her left wrist. Screaming, she whirled about, her knife raised high over her head. Upon seeing the startled face of the sheriff, she almost collapsed with relief. "You nearly scared me to death."

His dark brows knitted together in a furious frown. "Dammit!" He took the knife out of her hand. "I have a feeling I was closer to death than you. Put this thing away and don't let me see it again."

She took the knife from him and slid it into its sheath. "I heard the gunshot and thought you might be hurt," she said peevishly.

Her dirt-streaked face looked so genuinely concerned for his welfare, he didn't have the heart to further take out his irritation on her. "It was just a roving band of Utes. I shot a warning to scare them away."

"Utes!" Her eyes widened.

"Poachers." He walked toward his horse. She followed close behind, but kept looking over her shoulder.

"I thought the Indians had been relocated."

"For the most part they have been. But there're still some small bands roaming about the area. I think even you might find yourself challenged by a warring party of Utes. That's another reason why I don't want you traipsing around by yourself." For once she didn't argue with him and in fact remained stoically silent for the remainder of the return trip.

Main Street was deserted as usual when they reached town. A strange odor drifted from Mom Bull's Restaurant and Gunnar suddenly lost his appetite. The darkness settled over the town like a heavy black blanket. Overhead, the stars gleamed like diamonds.

"Why don't you go and freshen up, then have something to eat? I'll meet you back at the office in, say, an hour." He slid off his horse and lifted her down.

She was standing in the square of light coming from Mom Bull's Restaurant.

"Why?" she asked. "Are you going to arrest me?"

"Not this time." Suddenly aware that his hand lingered at her waist, he quickly pulled away from her. "Though heaven knows I have every right to arrest you. What I'm going to do is help you find your uncle."

Her face softened and for a moment he feared she was going to get all teary-eyed on him. He was grateful when she made an obvious attempt to fight back the tears, but he knew then and there he would do anything to help her. Anything.

Feeling disoriented and suddenly hotter than blazes, he spun around and headed for the safety of his office before he succumbed to the temptation of taking her in his arms and kissing those pretty pink lips of hers.

# Chapter 15

A little less than an hour and a half later, Abby entered his office. Gunnar rose to his feet and suddenly couldn't seem to breathe properly. Even his heartbeats seemed erratic, stopping and starting like an old stubborn mule.

She wore a blue dress the same color as her eyes, with a matching cape. Her hair tumbled down her back in soft damp curls. Despite her feminine attire, she carried herself with bold countenance, revealing none of her earlier fear or vulnerability. It was a shock to his senses to realize that he found her boldness every bit as appealing as her softness.

"You said you'd help me find my uncle." Her eyes challenged him as if she expected him to change his mind.

"That's what I said and that's what I mean to do." It gave him satisfaction to watch the doubt leave her face. "What makes you think he's in these parts?"

Apparently convinced he meant what he said, she sat and waited for him to do likewise. She then told him about her conversation with the inhabitants of the Opera House. "He made an appointment with Ruby to discuss some new product he wanted her to try. He never showed up. That's not like him."

"Your uncle means a lot to you."

She studied him as if trying to decide how little or how much to say. "I was eight when my parents died in a fire. I spent the next two years living in orphanages and various private homes. I ran away from the last orphanage and lived on the streets of Boston."

Gunnar stared at her in astonishment. "By yourself?"

She laughed at his expression. "I wanted stability. I got it. I lived on the same six-block area for seven years." The laughter left her face and was replaced by a dark shadow. "Along with every thief and homeless waif in the city."

"But you were only a child. Good Lord!" He shook his head in disbelief. "I can't believe it. Ten!" He stared at her in amazement. "Is that why you . . . ?"

She glanced at him sideways, her eyes as clear as mountain lakes. "Learned to take care of myself? Believe me, I didn't have much choice. As I told you, I lived on the streets for a total of seven years. I was nearly seventeen by the time my uncle found me."

"Why didn't you live with your uncle from the start?"

"I didn't know I had an uncle. He and his brother— my father—were separated at birth. It took my uncle years to track my father down and when he found out my parents were dead, he continued the search for his brother's child. He never forgave himself for taking so long to find me. I think it's a miracle he found me at all."

She fell silent for a moment before continuing. "He was a father, a mentor, and a guardian angel, all rolled into one. He taught me how to read, write, and add. I kept his books for him. Basically I kept his affairs in order. He tried to teach me how to act like a lady with less success, I'm afraid." there was a trace of laughter in her voice. "He eventually gave up on that one."

Recalling the way she took on the miners at the Opera House, he chuckled. "And now it's your turn to repay the favor by finding him."

She shook her head sadly. "I could never repay him for everything he's done for me." She leaned forward. "Sheriff, my uncle's in trouble. I feel it in my bones."

Gunnar thought for a moment. He was the self-proclaimed sheriff of Dangling Rope, but in reality, his experience in law had been confined to the legal aspects. He could argue a man's case in court, but he had no experience in crime prevention or tracking down missing persons. Family loyalty, however—now, that he could understand.

"I'll talk to Mole," he said. "Ask around at the mines."

"I'll come with you."

"No." He clasped his hands together. "It's rough up at the mines. It's no place for a lady."

She stood and looked as determined as a schoolmarm with a reluctant student. "A *lady* isn't going there. I am."

He locked eyes with her, aware of the visual battle in progress. Weighing his chances of winning this particular war—and not liking the odds—he stood. He placed his hands on the desk and leaned toward her. "If you go with me, you'll do as I say."

Following his lead, she rested her hands on the desk and stretched herself to the fullest extent of her five-foot-three height. "I'm very good at following orders when I see the need," she said. They were almost nose to nose. *Mouth to mouth.*

His lungs suddenly screaming for air, he backed away from the desk. "Meet me here tomorrow before sunup."

"I'll be here. But I want another horse and I want a good one."

"I'm afraid Logger's the only horse available. Anything else, Miss Parker? A gun, perhaps?"

"No need. I have my own weapons." She turned to the door. "See you tomorrow, Sheriff."

The sky was still dark that next morning when Gunnar left his cabin. It was early May, but it was cold enough to snow. Gunnar had never seen such changeable weather in his life. One day the weather was so warm it almost felt like summer, and the next day a blizzard was likely to whip across the mountains and canyons, dumping several feet of snow in its path.

Holding a lantern in one hand and shoving the other hand into the fur-lined pocket of his coat, he headed toward Main Street. It was still two hours before dawn. By the time Miss Parker rose and crossed the street to meet him, he would be halfway to Cripple Creek.

He grinned to himself. He wished he could see her face when she discovered him gone. It was for her own good. Those miners could be rough and who could predict the problems they might encounter should they meet up with those damned poaching Utes?

In any case, trouble seemed to follow her wherever she went. First she was nearly raped at the Opera House, then she practically got herself killed on the mountain, and could just as easily have taken him with her. He was right to be concerned.

Upon reaching Main Street, he glanced at the dark upper floor of Sleazy's Saloon. He had made a show of checking the shoes on Logger the previous night and otherwise grooming both horses before leading them to the livery stable and locking them into their stalls. He also made certain she heard him ask Mom Bull to pack two lunches. He knew full well she had watched his every move from her window.

He walked into the livery stable and stopped in his tracks. Both stalls were empty. "What the devil!" He spun on his heel and walked with long strides toward town.

She was waiting for him in front of the sheriff's office, sitting astride Logger and looking a bit too smug for his peace of mind. "Good morning, Sheriff."

Gritting his teeth, he stood staring at her. He didn't like the idea of someone beating him at his own game. Especially a woman. And most especially this particular woman. "Good morning, Miss Parker," he said, calmly and benignly. He would not give her the satisfaction of hearing the slightest hint of defeat in his voice. "What brings you here so early?"

"It's a little trick I learned on the streets of Boston. Never let the other person get a head start."

Despite the blow to his ego, he grinned. All right, he'd give the woman her due. This time. But it better be the last time. "It would seem I underestimated the streets of Boston."

"Don't feel bad, Sheriff. You're not the first one to make that mistake."

Finding little comfort in the knowledge, he rubbed his chin with his hand and started for his office.

"Your horse is saddled and ready to go," she said. "There's bread and cheese in your saddlebags."

He turned to stare at his horse. No one else in town dared handle his spirited mount. "Don't tell me you learned to handle horses on the streets of Boston."

"No," she said. "Before his death, my father ran a stable. I used to help him out."

"Is there anything else about your earlier life I should know?"

"Not that I can think of."

"Well, if you happen to think of anything, Miss Parker, let me know. I'm not particularly fond of surprises." Gunnar set his lantern on the porch and mounted his steed. He led the way out of town. The sky was still dark overhead, but a silvery thread of light appeared in the east.

They followed the winding trail up the mountain and picked up the stagecoach road leading to the mining towns.

They reached the deserted Cambridge Silver Mines by nine. Old Mole swaggered from one of the abandoned shacks to greet them.

"Not you agin!" he snarled at Abby. He glared at her through squinty red eyes. "Ain't you caused me enough trouble?"

"I'm not going to cause you any more trouble," Abby began. "I just want to ask you about my uncle."

Mole looked far from appeased. He folded his arms

in front of him. "Is that the same uncle you accused me of murd'rin'?"

"I know I went overboard," Abby admitted. "I tend to overreact in times of crisis. I can't tell you how sorry I am."

"Save your apol'gies. I don't know nothin'." Mole turned and started back to the shack.

"Wait!" Gunnar called after him. "This is an official visit."

Mole spit out a stream of yellow tobacco juice. "Would you like to know what ya kin do with ya o'fficial business?"

"Mr. Mole, please listen to what we have to say." Abby dismounted and looked at the small man beseechingly. "Please."

"Please?" The man let out a cackling laugh. "Such a lady, you are." He turned to an old prospector who was wandering past, his belongings tied to the side of a mule. "Ya shodda heard this one danglin' from that rope. Called me a prick, she did." He cited a few more choice names Abby reputedly called him. The prospector hurried away as if not wanting to hear more, and Gunnar arched a dark brow at her. Abby shrugged and looked anything but repentant.

Mole seemed to take offense at the prospector's lack of interest. "She called me an oyster-faced, murderin' prick," he shouted, waving his hand at the prospector. "Now she's all ladylike . . ." He lifted himself on his toes and imitated the walk of a proper lady.

"Oh, all right," Abby said. "I apologize. I tend to say things when I get upset that I don't mean."

"You were spittin' fire," old Mole said, looking aggrieved. "And you meant everythin' you said!"

"I was dangling in midair and you were standing around doing nothing."

"What was I s'pposed to do? You're the one who got yourself in such a almighty fix."

"I wouldn't have been in that fix had you lived in a proper place."

"I can live where I damn well please!"

Gunnar had heard enough. "Quiet!" he ordered. "Both of you." Abby and old Mole glanced at him as if he were the one causing the trouble. "I'll do the talking," he said, fixing his steady gaze on Abby.

"If you have something to say, say it," old Mole said irritably. "I ain't got all day."

"Thank you." The sheriff pushed back his hat and hung his thumbs from his belt. "Now, Miss Parker here is looking for her uncle. We thought perhaps you might have seen him hereabouts somewhere. Name's Randall Parker."

"Parker . . ." Mole wagged a crooked finger in Abby's face. "Don't you go puttin' yurself off as his r'lative."

Abby's heart skipped a beat. "You know him?"

"I know him well enuff."

"When did you last see him?" Gunnar asked.

Old Mole scratched his whiskered chin.

"It's terribly important," Abby urged.

"You ain't really Parker's kin, are you?" He leveled his watery eyes on her as if searching for a family resemblance.

"I truly am."

Old Mole looked dubious, but he shrugged his bone-thin shoulders, spat another stream of yellow tobacco juice into the ground, and scratched his head. "The man did me a favor. I guess I owe him."

Abby caught her breath. "My uncle did you a favor?"

"That he did. I was soakin' my achin' feet in Cripple Creek and mindin' me own business, when along came this peddler and sat down beside me. Said I wouldn't have problems with me feet if I washed my socks out at night. Hell, I said, I don't have no socks. You know what he did? Gave me a pair of woolen socks. Took them right out of his pack." He lifted the legs of his stained canvas trousers to show her. She had no trouble recognizing the gray-ribbed socks as a pair her aunt had knitted shortly before her death.

Abby clasped her hands together and held them next

to her chest. She tried to speak, but her voice was blocked by the choking sensation in her throat. Socks were a peddler's most important piece of clothing. To part with a pair was no small sacrifice. How like her uncle to do such a thing.

She jumped at the sound of an explosion. Dust rose from the valley below them, spiraling upward like a cloud of smoke. The horses whinnied and stirred and scuffed the ground with their hooves. Overhead, a flock of noisy magpies took to the sky.

Gunnar grabbed hold of the reins and held the horses steady. "Dynamite," he said. "The railroad crew is blasting through that mountain back yonder."

"Oh." Abby turned back to Mole, impatient to find out what else he knew.

"Do you remember when you last saw Parker?" Gunnar asked.

"Seems to me it was 'round September. I remember we had an early snowstorm and that creek was icy cold. Pretty near froze me toes off."

Abby turned to Gunnar. "That's when he was here last."

Gunnar continued questioning Mole. "Do you know where he was going?"

"Said he was headin' on up to Cripple Creek. He was on the way to deliver his order to the ladies on Myers Street. That's all I kin tell ya."

Abby had hoped for more, of course, but she felt encouraged. Every little bit of information, no matter how small, might help them put the puzzle together. "Thank you," she said.

"I don't need your thanks. Just you stay away from me. Ya hear?" Old Mole shuffled off, disappearing in the tall pines.

Gunnar made no effort to stop the man. "Looks like we better head for Cripple Creek. It's just beyond those hills over there. If we hurry, we could make it by early afternoon. See what we can find out."

Gunnar took the reins of both horses and led the

animals downhill to the little creek. While the horse drank liberally from the cool sweet waters, Abby studied the lovely wildflowers growing about her feet.

She leaned down and picked one of the soft pink blooms. It was the exact shade of pink she had tried so hard to create in her room. Thinking she would try to make a dye out of the blossoms, she gathered a handful of flowers and tucked them into her knapsack.

*Oh, Uncle Randall, where are you?* she wondered, watching a magpie hopping along the edge of the creek. *And why do I have this feeling you're trying to tell me something?*

Lost in her thoughts, she was unaware that Gunnar had walked back with the horses until he spoke. "I'm going to find your uncle, Miss Parker. That's a promise."

The warm sincerity on his face filled her with new hope. Suddenly she felt less alone in the world. She smiled and dropped the last of the wildflowers into the pocket of her pack. "You can call me Abby."

"Abby." He rolled the name in his mouth as if not wanting to part with it. "How like you to have a name that sounds like a monastery."

"Perhaps you'd prefer to call me Abigail."

"Abby will do," he said. "If you'll agree to call me Gunnar."

"Gunnar, eh?" she said. "The name suits you—" Her mouth dropped open and suddenly she couldn't find her voice.

Glancing at her wild hand gestures, Gunnar spun around. "What in blazes?" Too late, he realized they were surrounded by a Ute war party.

# Chapter 16

Acting out of pure instinct, Abby reached for her knife.

Gunnar grabbed her by the arm, preventing her from pulling her weapon from her boot. "Don't move."

Reluctantly, she straightened. She watched the small band of Utes creep toward them with a combination of fear and fascination.

There were eight in all, dressed in a strange blend of traditional Ute attire and white man's accessories. Rawhide hats such as many miners wore and canvas pants were mixed with fringed V-necked shirts and matching buckskin breechcloths. Only one Ute wore the traditional regalia, including fringed leggings.

"I'll do the talking," Gunnar said beneath his breath.

For once Abby didn't argue with him. Mainly because she was having a hard time finding her tongue.

Gunnar's horse pawed the ground and moved its head up and down. Moving slow so as not to alarm the Utes, Gunnar stroked the horse's neck. "It's all right, boy."

A striped-faced warrior stepped forward, a quiver and bow case strapped to his back. The tall eagle-feathered bonnet marked him as a leader. His eyes were fixed on Gunnar's black gelding. "Owns Six Horses."

Encouraged by the Indian's ability to speak English, Abby caught her breath. Why, the man was just trying to be friendly, and if he owned that many horses, maybe he'd be willing to sell one. "That's impressive," she said, smiling. She took a step forward and pointed to herself. "Owns no horses."

Gunnar pulled her back. Had the woman no fear? "I think he's telling us his name," he said in a low voice.

"Oh."

Owns Six Horses nodded to the other warriors, who began closing in. Soon they formed a tight circle around Abby and Gunnar. More dynamite exploded in the distance and the leader turned in the direction of the blast. "No like iron horse."

Gunnar narrowed his eyes. "The railroad is a good thing. It can make this area prosper—"

"Not good thing!" Owns Six Horses shouted, his voice hard. He shook his fist over his head. "It take away our land."

"This land is not yours," Gunnar said quietly.

"This land belongs to the Great Spirit." He nodded and a fierce-looking warrior stepped into the middle of the circle. Another nod from the leader, and the warrior raised his spear and pointed it at Gunnar's chest.

Abby choked back a cry. She had never seen such a lethal weapon in all her born days.

While the warrior held Gunnar at bay with the spear, another Ute bound Gunnar's hands. The bear-teeth necklace around the man's neck rattled as he wrapped a length of rawhide around Gunnar's wrists.

Eyes wide with fear, Abby pressed her fingers against her mouth. She had heard horror stories of white men and women captured by Indians. Somehow this confrontation seemed so much worse than any she'd experienced on the streets of Boston, mainly because it was so unexpected. In the city, she would never have let her guard down. Here, she'd been lulled by the serene beauty of the area into thinking her surroundings safe. If she survived this ambush, she'd not make the same mistake twice.

Owns Six Horses said something to the others in the Ute language, then moved toward her. He stood just under six feet tall. Beneath his feathered headgear, his black hair fell to his shoulders in two straight plaits.

But it was his weathered face that caught her attention, more accurately his war paint.

"Oh!" she cried out as he grabbed her hands and prepared to bind them.

He gave a scowling look. "White squaw keep still!"

"I was just noticing your face," she explained, not wanting to risk making him angry, but unable to contain her curiosity.

He surprised her by releasing her. He stepped back and touched his face with his hand.

"I like the war paint on your forehead," she explained.

When he seemed not to understand, she pointed to her own forehead and traced an invisible design that matched his own. "I like."

Understanding flickered in the depths of his glittering black eyes. "White squaw like?"

She nodded with uncertainty, hoping he understood what it was she liked. "White squaw like war paint," she said with firm emphasis. Once again she pointed to his forehead.

He turned and spoke to the other Indians. Soon the lot of them were laughing and repeating the words. "White squaw like."

"War paint," Abby added, so there'd be no misunderstanding.

"War paint," the Utes said in unison.

"I would like war paint." For good measure, she pointed to herself. "Me want war paint."

One of the Indians began chanting, "Me want war paint."

The others followed his lead. Soon the woods echoed with their delighted voices.

Finally the leader held up his hand and the others fell silent. "Owns Six Horses," he said a word in his native language, which she could not understand. He moved his hand in a circle to indicate his meaning.

"Mix," Abby said. "Owns Six Horses mixes . . . the war paint. You mix the paint yourself. I understand."

She nodded her head vigorously. She was so delighted at the thought of communicating with the leader, she clapped her hands and laughed aloud. She called over to Gunnar, who was tied to a tree and appeared to be the only one not enjoying this rather amazing exchange of information. "He mixes his own war paint."

"Well, now, isn't that just fine and dandy?" Gunnar grumbled. "I would have sworn he'd ordered it through the mail-order catalogue."

Making a face at him, Abby turned back to Owns Six Horses. "Could you show me how to mix war paint?"

The Indian looked puzzled. "White squaw want war paint?"

Abby nodded. "I'll show you." She led him to her horse and reached into her peddler's knapsack she carried with her at all times for a small jar of rouge.

Owns Six Horses took the jar from her and stuck his forefinger into the bright red cream. He lifted his finger and held it up.

"Not good color," she said.

"Not good," he repeated after her. He handed the container back and spoke rapidly to the others. "You ride," he told her.

She started for her own horse, but he stopped her. "You ride that one." He pointed to Gunnar's horse. Obviously, he didn't think much of Logger and motioned to the others to leave the swaybacked horse behind.

Not wanting to chance upsetting him, she grabbed her knapsack and did as she was told. Astride Gunnar's horse, she watched two Indians force Gunnar to his feet and breathed a sigh of relief when it appeared they were not going to harm him.

"We go find berry!" the leader yelled over his shoulder. He grinned at Abby as he grabbed the reins of her horse. "Make war paint!"

The horses moved forward, with Gunnar bringing up the rear on foot.

Gunnar stumbled as he was pulled along. The horse

picked up speed, forcing him to run to keep up. He glowered at the line of horses in front of him. "If this isn't a fine kettle of fish!" he muttered. *She* was allowed to ride on *his* horse, while he was forced to stumble on foot through wild, snake-infested terrain. And for what? To search out some bloody berry to make war paint!

It wouldn't have been so bad had Abby not been enjoying herself so much. He could hear her laughter from the front of the line, where she rode by Owns Six Horses's side. What the hell was so damned funny? And what was this fascination of hers with war paint, for God's sake? If he lived through this day, he planned to wage his own private war on one irksome blue-eyed nuisance—and he wouldn't need any war paint.

It was late afternoon by the time they reached their destination, and still fairly warm. Later, when the wind picked up, it would likely turn cold. Owns Six Horses slid off the bare back of his painted horse and motioned Abby to a cluster of berry bushes.

The bushes were covered with pink berries. "War paint," Owns Six Horses said, grinning.

"It's perfect," Abby said, reaching for a berry.

"No do!" The Ute said gruffly. "Pick berries here only." He indicated with his hands the middle part of the bush.

"Why only in the middle of the bush?" she asked, thinking it had something to do with the ripeness of the berries or the color.

Owns Six Horses explained. "Top bush for birds. Lower bush for wildlife. Middle bush for man."

Abby regarded the leader thoughtfully. While living on the streets of Boston, she'd learned to take what she needed, with no thought of others. It was every man for himself. Any woman or child who didn't adhere to that one unbreakable rule of survival quickly starved or froze to death. Life for these Utes had to be equally hard, and yet their own survival, apparently, never took precedence over nature as a whole.

Shamed by the selfishness of some of her earlier survival tactics, she felt both humbled and reverent as she reached for a berry, this time taking care to keep within the acceptable range. She placed the berry into her pack, and apparently satisfied she showed adequate respect for nature, Owns Six Horses nodded with approval. "What squaw called?"

"Oh, you mean my name. My name is Abby."

Owns Six Horses frowned. "What squaw called?" he repeated.

"Abby," she repeated. Thinking, perhaps, he was looking for a more descriptive name, she added, "Some people call me Traveling Lady but—"

"Traveling Lady," he repeated slowly.

She nodded and added inanely, "It means . . . to travel." She indicated her meaning by imitating a train with her hand.

The Indian's face grew red with rage as he yelled in her face. "No like iron horse!"

Practically jumping out of her skin, she fell back. Her mouth dropping open, she watched Owns Six Horses mount his painted pony and lead the others back down the trail, taking Gunnar's horse with them.

Almost as quickly as the Utes had made their appearance, they had disappeared, riding over the ridge and leaving a cloud of dust in their wake.

Abandoning the berry bush, Abby hurried over to Gunnar. "Are you all right?" She fell to her knees and ran her hand down his arm to check for herself.

He glared at her, his eyes as black as midnight. "You had to see the berry bushes, didn't you? I hope you're satisfied." He groaned. "My feet will never be the same."

"It's probably because you're wearing the wrong socks."

"What?"

"Your socks. My uncle insists that only fine worsted wool will do. Lamb's wool is the best."

"I don't believe this," he muttered to himself. "I'm in agony and she blames my socks."

Abby checked the rawhide wrapped around his wrists. She lifted up the hem of her skirt and drew her knife out of her boot. The blade glinted in the low-riding sunlight as she sliced through the rawhide at his wrists. After freeing his hands, she quickly slashed the rawhide at his ankles.

"Dammit, be careful with that thing," he growled, though he admired her skill.

His hands and legs free, he rubbed the circulation back into his wrists. His ankles were sore from the rawhide, his feet ached, and they were miles from nowhere. Without so much as a horse, it could take hours before they reached help. He doubted his aching feet could hold out that long.

In any case, they didn't have hours, or at least not as many hours as they needed. It would soon be dark. And there was no way in hell he was going to traipse through the mountains at night.

While he pondered the problem of getting back to town, Abby had returned to the berry bushes and was busily humming to herself as she filled her pack with berries.

Gunnar shook his head. Damn woman! What did she think this was? A picnic?

The sun suddenly disappeared behind a mountain peak. The air was still fairly warm, but the temperature would drop quickly during the night. He glanced around, looking for landmarks. He'd been too busy try-ing to stay on his feet during the ordeal to pay attention to where they were going. He had no idea where they were. As near as he could tell, they were in a remote wilderness miles away from the nearest town or min-ing camp.

It seemed they had no choice but to make them-selves as comfortable as possible and start off in the morning.

Having filled a pocket of her pack with berries, Abby walked over to his side. "What are you doing?"

"Making a fire. What does it look like I'm doing?"

She lifted her chin and looked miffed. "You don't have to be so ornery."

"I have every right to be as ornery as I want to be. You gave me that right when you cooked up that little scheme to go into the war paint business."

Her eyes flashed with indignation. "So now I'm to blame. You're the one who wants to bring the railroad to town."

"There's nothing wrong with that."

"That's not what Owns Six Horses said."

"Thanks to you, that's now *seven* horses he owns." he glared at her. "Not that it matters, but what did he say?"

"He said the iron horse will bring more white men to the area who will strip the land and dirty the waters. Who can blame him for opposing the railroad?"

"No one can stop the railroad from going to the mines." Gunnar arranged the rocks he'd gathered into a circle. They had less than an hour of daylight left and he meant to make the most of it. "All I'm doing is bringing the train a little farther west."

"But he's right about the railroad scarring the land."

"It's man's greed that's responsible," Gunnar said. "The land is scarred from mining. No railroad could do the damage that has already been done to the region by the mining companies."

Abby studied his profile, surprised by the plaintive tone in his voice.

He turned toward her and for a moment their gazes locked in mutual understanding, but rather than derive any satisfaction from their sudden rapport, she was shaken by it.

"I'm afraid the railroad is here to stay," he said, turning away.

So were they, she thought, if the amount of firewood he was gathering was any indication.

Following his lead, she searched for pine cones and kindling wood. It had been a long time since she'd slept outside. Indeed, after her uncle had rescued her, she swore she'd never sleep outside again.

An unfamiliar rattling sound snapped her out of her thoughts. Sensing some innate danger, she instinctively spun around. That's when she saw the coiled rattlesnake inches away from Gunnar's hand, ready to strike.

# Chapter 17

A flash of lightning whizzed by Gunnar and hit the ground directly in front of the snake. It wasn't until Gunnar saw the hilt of the knife standing on end that he realized what had happened. Abby had done her knife trick, and not a moment too soon. Much to his relief, the reptile slid away, barely seeming to skim the ground as it slid through the underbrush. The sound of its rattles faded in the distance.

"You can move now, Sheriff," Abby said. She casually walked over to the spot where the snake had been seconds earlier and pulled her knife out of the ground. She twirled the weapon once, then yanked up her skirt to tuck it into place. "Didn't want to hurt the poor thing," she said. "Just wanted to scare it off."

*Poor thing.* Gunnar straightened and wiped the sweat off his forehead. "Don't tell me they have rattlesnakes in Boston."

Abby grinned. "They have them, all right. The only difference is they walk around on two legs." She tugged on the side of his vest that held his sheriff's star. "Some of them even wear police badges."

He studied her a moment, wondering if corrupt policemen had made her suspicious of all lawmen. It would certainly explain why she thought he could be bribed.

He scooped up another handful of pine needles, making certain, this time, that nothing lurked amid the dry brown foliage. "It'll be dark soon. I'm not about to go traipsing through that brush in the dark. You better start making yourself a bed."

"I don't need a bed," she said. "I never sleep when I'm on the street." It was her way of dealing with danger. Sitting up with one eye open and one hand on a weapon.

Gunnar glanced in one direction, then the other. "Don't see a single street anywhere, but suit yourself."

She sat on a log and watched Gunnar try to start a fire by rubbing two sticks together. It was an interesting concept and she was curious if such a thing actually worked. After about twenty minutes of nothing but an occasional spark, she decided it was a waste of time. "I have some matches in my knapsack."

His hands stilled and he lifted his eyes in surprise. "You have matches? Why the hell didn't you say so?"

"You didn't ask." She drew the box of lucifers from her peddler's pack and tossed the box to him.

He struck a match and touched the flame to the pine needles and twigs. Smoke rose as the fire slowly took hold. "What else have you got in that damned pack of yours?"

"Just the usual things," she replied. "Things no peddler would be without. Socks." She drew out a small kettle for boiling water and a little tin of tea leaves.

Lord, he thought watching her in astonishment. She *did* think she was at a tea party.

She ran the short distance to the creek and dipped her kettle into the water. "Want some tea?" she called gaily.

"No," he said, his ill humor escalating.

She placed the kettle on a log next to the fire. "The berries don't taste very good. They're rather bitter. I guess they're not for eating."

"Guess not," he said, though he was hungry enough to welcome even Mom Bull's fare. He wished now he'd eaten the remainder of the bread and cheese still in his saddlebags.

"Would you care for a boiled egg?"

"A what?"

"An egg. I always carry hard-boiled eggs in my pack. Never know when they might come in handy." She handed him an egg. "I have some salt if you like. It brings out the taste."

"The egg's fine the way it is," he grumbled.

"Save the eggshells," she said. "We can use them to make coffee."

"You have coffee in there, too?"

She nodded.

"Well, now . . . if I have to be stuck in the middle of nowhere, I guess you're the one to be stuck with."

The temperature was dropping rapidly. Gunnar huddled closer to the warmth of the fire. He rolled the collar up on his shirt, cursing himself for having left his jacket with his horse, and tucked his hands beneath his arms. While he struggled to keep warm, Abby seemed perfectly at home.

She sipped her tea and ate her egg as if being stranded on a mountain were a normal everyday occurrence. She then washed out her tin cup, refilled her little kettle with water, and put it back by the fire. He watched incredulously. Damned if she wasn't carrying on like some little homemaker on the old homestead!

She disappeared into the dark shadows and he could hear the rustle of her skirts. Half expecting her to come out dressed in her night attire, he was surprised—and more than a little relieved—when she appeared again, still fully clothed.

Instead of settling down as he'd hoped, she poured hot water over some dark object in her hand. "Now what are you doing?" he asked, his teeth chattering.

"I'm washing out my stockings," she said.

"Your what?"

"My stockings," she repeated. "Peddlers never fail to wash out their socks every night. Saves a lot of foot problems. You ought to try it."

"There's nothing wrong with my feet that some rest won't cure," he grumbled.

Without another word, she squeezed out her stockings and spread them to dry on a large rounded rock next to the fire.

When she finally settled down on a log opposite him and planted her bare feet next to the fire, it was all he could do to keep his gaze from traveling to her pretty toes.

She reached into her pack, pulled out a dark wool blanket, and wrapped it around her shoulders. "Night, Sheriff," she called.

He grunted in response. *Isn't that dandy? She thought to bring a blanket.* He was freezing his behind off and she was wrapped snugly in a blanket.

"Are you going to sit up all night?" he asked, irritated.

She nodded. "I don't sleep at night on the streets or"—she glanced around—"on a mountain. Do you realize how vulnerable you are when you sleep?"

Looking at her in disbelief, he stretched himself out on the bed of pine needles he'd made for himself earlier. He couldn't be any more vulnerable lying down than sitting up—nor more uncomfortable. His face was hot and his back was icy cold. He rolled to his back. Overhead, the jagged tops of the tall pines framed a star-studded sky. His right arm was burning up.

He flopped over to his side. Now his front side was cold and his behind hot. He peered over his shoulder at Abby. She looked as snug as a bug cocooned in her blanket.

The burning log cast a rosy glow across her face. Her eyes were fixed upon the fire, her lashes forming a dark fringe. She looked quiet and reserved, almost angelic. Anyone stumbling upon such a woman would probably never suspect she was armed and potentially dangerous.

Oh, but she was dangerous, all right. He felt it in his bones. She had an acid tongue and a lethal throw and a way about her that touched a man to the quick.

Gunnar rolled over to face the fire. It was a mistake. For it allowed him to focus his attention fully on her.

She was a beauty, all right, with all her odd ways. But, oh, how her smile could light up the darkest of nights, and those eyes, those big blue beautiful eyes . . . Why, a man could drown in them if he had half a mind to.

The sound of moving bushes behind him brought him to his feet in a flash. He reached for his gun out of habit, cursing beneath his breath to find it not there. The Utes had taken it, along with his coat and his horse.

Abby crouched next to him, feral style, her knife drawn. "What do you think it is?"

"Shhhh." He cocked his head and strained his ears. The babbling rush of the creek drowned out all but the loudest sounds. An owl hooted overhead, filling the night with questions before taking to the air in silent flight.

"Must have been a deer," he said at last. "Maybe a rabbit."

"Oh." She glanced at the darkness around them, then slipped her knife back into its sheath.

Gunnar lowered himself to the ground and tossed another log into the fire pit.

"Do . . . do you mind if I sit next to you?" she asked.

His hand stilled for a moment. He met her eyes and sucked in his breath. "If you like." He became very busy poking at the fire with a stick he'd found nearby.

"It's cold," she said, not wanting to admit it was fear that had driven her to his side.

"I guess we should be happy it's not winter." He sat on the bed of needles next to her.

"Would . . . would you like to share my blanket?" she asked.

His eyes seemed to sparkle with amusement. "Are you sure you want to share your blanket with a lawman?"

"If you had a blanket, I'm sure you'd share it with

me. It makes no sense for you to freeze your knocker off!"

He stared at her, shocked. "Did ... did you say ... knocker?"

He looked so utterly horrified, she hardly knew what to say. For goodness' sakes she could have said a whole lot worse. "If there's a more polite way of talking about a man's anatomy, I should be most happy to oblige."

She waited as if she actually thought there was a polite way for a man and woman who were relatively strangers to talk about such things.

"Give me the damn blanket," he said. He took the blanket from her.

She drew her legs beneath her skirt and snuggled up to his side. He pulled the blanket around his back and wrapped her in his arms.

She nestled closer and rested her head on his shoulder. He felt a jolt to his senses. Dear God, it was only her head on his shoulder, but it felt like so much more. On the outside he was as rigid as a poker. On the inside, he was as soft as warm ashes.

He tried to concentrate on the fire, the dark shadows shifting in the background, the stars overhead. Anything but the faint floral scent of her hair.

"Do you really believe the railroad is a good thing for the area?" She spoke in a voice as soft as a baby's sigh.

"I wouldn't be trying to bring it here if I thought it would hurt."

She moved her head and looked up at him. "Not even to save your brother's skin?"

The warm glow of the fire flickered softly across her face. Her eyes danced with orange flames. "So you know about that, do you?"

"Nathan told me."

"What else did Nathan tell you?"

"Not much. But I know there's a terrible strain between you two."

"There has been in the past."

"I suppose you can't blame him, really, can you? For feeling the way he does."

He stared at her, trying to comprehend her meaning. Had Nathan discussed their personal problems with her? To his knowledge, Nathan had never discussed such things with anyone. Was this sudden sharing of his past yet another sign that Nathan was finally growing up? Gunnar wanted to believe it was true; he was desperate enough to believe anything was possible. "Blame him?"

"Oh, dear. There I go again. Saying what I have no right saying."

Certainly nothing she could say would shock him more than what she'd already said. What had she called it? A knocker? Fighting a sudden bolt of energy that coursed through him, he adjusted his position. The damned ground was hard as rock. The cursed woman soft as feathers. He buried his nose into her hair and all but forgot any discomforts.

"Say what you want," he drawled. "When a man and woman share the same bed, they should be completely open with one another."

"The same . . ." She giggled softly. "I guess we are sharing the same bed." After a pause, she shrugged her shoulders lightly. "Very well, then. I think you should know I overheard you and your brother arguing the night I stayed at your cabin."

"I thought you might have."

"It was hard not to," she said, feeling defensive, though there was nothing reproachful in his manner.

"You needn't apologize. The problems between my brother and me aren't exactly secret."

"I would have thought . . . I mean, since you did steal a woman away from him . . . I wouldn't think you'd want anyone to know."

"A woman?" He pulled back slightly, astonished. "You think I stole a woman?"

"Well . . . I . . ." Words escaping her, she could only stare up at him.

He laughed aloud. "That woman he accused me of stealing was our mother and I was seven years old at the time."

"S-seven?" she stammered. Never had she felt so foolish in her life. "I'm so sorry. I mean . . . I . . ."

Their gazes locked. She looked so distressed, he felt sorry for her. "Don't fret yourself over it. Anyone would have made the same mistake." Now he understood the cold looks she'd given him the morning following the argument. "Is that why you've been so unfriendly-like to me?"

"I wasn't unfriendly-like," she said.

He thought for a moment. "You were unfriendly-like."

A shadow touched her forehead. "He blames you unfairly, yet you're still trying to save his neck."

"It's a long story," he said, in a voice he hoped would discourage her questions. He had no interest in talking about the past with her. There were too many other things he'd rather talk about. Like how did she get her hair to smell so fragrant? Like where did she get those big blue eyes of hers? Like the beautiful night sky.

"We have a long night ahead of us." She dropped her voice low to match his. "And I don't think either one of us is going to get much rest."

He gazed helplessly at her tempting soft lips and despite his initial resistance, found himself talking about the past. He told her about his mother and how she'd taken him with her—how she'd left Nathan and their father—to follow some misguided dream of singing onstage.

Abby heard the pain in his voice, saw the same pain reflected tenfold in his face. "Why did she take you and not Nathan?"

Gunnar rested his head on hers and stared into the fire. "I was part of her act. I could sing, I could dance. The audience loved the mother and son routine." He laughed a bitter laugh. "After the curtain came down, that was the end of my mother's interest in me until the following night when it was time to go onstage again."

Abby tried to imagine Gunnar at seven, dancing his heart out for his mother, only to face her rejection. "It must have been a very difficult life for you."

"It was difficult. Every day, it seemed, we were in a different city. Every night I sang and danced, trying to make my mother look good. I guess I knew she had no talent and I felt it was my job to hide it. The audience loved it. When you're a child, you don't have to be good. We traveled like this for four and half years until . . ."

"Until?"

Gunnar took a deep breath. "When I turned eleven and shot up six feet tall, the audience was no longer interested in our act."

"Where is your mother now?" Abby asked.

"She drank herself to death."

"Oh, Gunnar . . ." She lifted her hand to his face and caressed his cheek before reaching up to touch his shadowed brow. "How awful. It's sad to think a woman would desert a husband and two children just to perform onstage."

His eyes smoldered as he gazed at her and she felt a delicious tremor shoot down her heated body.

"Two? She didn't desert me. She took me with her. Nathan's the one she deserted. Nathan and my father."

Abby studied him quietly, aware of the heat that emanated from his powerful body. There was strength in his face, and integrity. The last thing she expected to see as she searched the depths of his eyes, studied the fine lines at the corners of his eyes and the gentle curve of his mouth, was vulnerability. More prevalent was the hungry desire that had flared suddenly in his eyes, and though she didn't understand it fully, she felt an almost unbearable urge to answer his silent call. "There are all kinds of ways to desert a person," she said softly.

"Nothing she did to me can compare to what she did to Nathan."

"Even so, it seems strange he would still blame you."

"Strange? I can't blame him for that."

"You were a child."

"Nathan never saw me as a child. To him I was always the older brother. Mother's favorite."

"And yet, she deserted you, too."

He shook his head. "Why do you keep saying that? She didn't desert me, Abby. She took me everywhere with her. I was with her to the very end."

"Why do you find it so difficult to see the truth?" she asked, feeling his body tense in denial.

"Dammit, Abby! She deserted Nathan. He was five years old and she walked out on him, taking me with her. I'll never forget that day as long as I live. The look on his face . . . my father's face. Never!"

He pulled away from her, leaving the blanket draped around her shoulders as he knelt in front of the fire. For the longest while, a tense silence hung between them.

# Chapter 18

Abby held the blanket tight and chastised herself for probing into his past. It was none of her business. "Gunnar," she began tentatively. "I had no right to say what I said."

He tossed more wood into the fire, along with some pine cones, but made no effort to rejoin her.

Cursing herself for interfering and unable to stand the strain between them, she dropped to her knees by his side and rested her head between his shoulder blades. "Gunnar . . . I . . ."

He turned toward her, his face bathed with flickering light. Desire smoldered in the depths of his eyes and a shiver of anticipation rippled through her. She lay a hand on his cheek, knowing full well what he wanted of her, and what she wanted of him.

His mouth softened as he gazed at her. His hands slid down her arms in a sensuous journey to her waist. She absorbed his very essence as a plant absorbs the warming sun after a long winter. She imagined she could hear the special music of the stars and could feel the presence of every living creature within miles. But mostly, she was centered on him; on the look, the scent, and the feel of him.

Gunnar slid his hands along her slender hips and gazed into her beautiful luminous eyes. God, he wanted this woman. Wanted her more than he thought it possible to want anyone. Sensing the awakening flames in her, his own desire no longer simmered, it erupted with such force he could hardly breathe.

In a moment of unbearable need and passion, he crushed her in his arms and pressed his lips hard against hers. He moaned her name between kisses, tracing her lips with his tongue and searing a fiery path of kisses down her neck, before finding her mouth again and starting the process all over.

Caught in a golden web of wonderful sensations, Abby melted against him. Her lips burned with heavenly fire. Warmth spread like golden honey down her body.

He whispered her name and practically devoured her with his fiery lips and tongue. His kisses sparked far deeper needs than any kiss could satisfy. Her passionate responses promised more than any kiss could deliver. At last, he lay on his back, pulling her with him.

Abby eagerly pressed her body along his, her breasts crushed against the hardness of his chest. Never had she lain with a man so intimately. Never had she felt so alive or floated at such dizzying heights.

He unbuttoned her waistshirt and slipped his hand inside, covering the soft mound of her breast with the most wonderful warm sensations. She impatiently tugged at his shirt, wanting to give to him as he was giving to her.

"Abby . . ." Her name seemed to melt into a passionate sigh. "If you don't want this, you better get the hell away from me."

She lifted her head and looked him square in the face. "You don't have any half-arsed ideas that a woman should be a lady in bed, do you?"

His eyes flared and he groaned aloud. "You sure as hell haven't been a lady any other place." He rolled her on her back and suddenly his hands, his lips, his body were all over her until every inch of her body prickled with the heat of his touch. His hand reached beneath her skirt, skimming her bare leg lightly all the way to her thigh. She arched toward him, wanting him desperately to touch the one place his hands had yet to reach.

They both froze upon hearing a male voice call from the distance. "Gunnar! Abby? Can you hear me?"

Gunnar dragged his mouth away from hers. "Nathan!" It was a gasp of protest, more than surprise. He drew back and jumped to his feet.

Her senses reeling in confusion, Abby fought for some semblance of control. She quickly checked her hair and tried desperately to make the pearl buttons on her shirtwaist go through the tiny holes, but there didn't seem to be much she could do to cool down her hot flesh. If her cheeks were as red as they felt, Nathan would surely know something was afoot.

Gunnar picked up the blanket that had fallen by the wayside and wrapped it tenderly around her shoulders. His face was lined in regret. But it was the look in his eyes that made the interruption bearable, for the look held a promise of things to come.

Shuddering with anticipation, she smiled back, signaling back a few promises of her own. His eyes flared with warm approval as he lifted her hand to his mouth and pressed his fevered lips against her skin. Finally he stood and called out in a husky voice, "Nathan! Over here."

Nathan emerged from the shadows, holding a lantern. He glanced at Gunnar, but his eyes quickly searched for and found Abby. "Are you two all right?"

"We're fine," Gunnar said. "How did you know . . ."

"Ole Mole saw the Utes take you captive. He rode Logger back to town to fetch help." Nathan grinned. "You should have heard the man complaining. Said it was the last time he was going to rescue you, Abby."

Gunnar grinned. "Well, if I have anything to say about it, this will be the last time she'll need rescuing."

Nathan continued to gaze at Abby. "I've been searching since I got home and heard what happened. I spotted your campfire from below. The others are waiting."

"Others?" Gunnar asked.

"Otis and Clod came with me. We brought extra horses."

Gunnar covered the fire with dirt while Abby repacked her knapsack.

"Let me," Nathan said, taking her pack from her and flinging it over his shoulders. "Are you all right?"

Her face still flushed and lips still swollen from Gunnar's kisses, she sat on a log, her back to Nathan, and pulled on her boots. "Of course I'm all right."

"The Indians didn't harm you?"

She kept her face hidden. "Not at all."

"That's a relief. You must live under a lucky star." Nathan waited for her to finish tying her boots, then searched her face, his eyes probing. "Are you sure you haven't caught a chill?"

She stared at him. "What?"

"You look feverish."

"Oh. Perhaps—"

"Since when have you become such an old mother hen?" Gunnar teased, cuffing his brother playfully on the arm.

Nathan gave a sheepish grin. "I hope you're not coming down with something." He pulled off his jacket and wrapped it around her shoulders. "The wind has changed. I think a storm might be brewing."

"This blanket's quite warm," she protested.

Ignoring her protests, Nathan placed an arm around her shoulders and led her through the brush. She felt Gunnar's eyes on her back as he took up the rear.

Otis and Clod were waiting on the trail below them. Otis spotted them first. "Well, if you two ain't a sight for sore eyes. I thought Nathan was half-arse crazy traipsin' around the mountains at night. Tried to talk him into waitin' till mornin', but he'd hear none of it."

Nathan took the reins of his horse from Otis. "You can ride with me, Abby."

"Thank you, Nathan. But that won't be necessary, I'll ride Logger."

"Mole said the Utes took your horse," Clod added. "We picked up this horse in Victor. His name's Lucky."

Gunnar patted the horse's black sleek neck. "Lucky, eh?"

Otis spit. "Don't know if he's better than your last horse, but he's sure an improvement over Logger."

Abby placed her foot in the stirrups and swung herself into the saddle. "Hush, now, or you'll hurt Logger's feelings."

Nathan stood by her side, measuring her physical condition. "We have quite a ride ahead of us, I'm afraid. If you need to stop and rest, let me know."

"I'm perfectly fine," she assured him.

He gazed at her for a moment, then, apparently satisfied by what he saw, mounted his horse and took the lead.

Abby glanced back, but it was too dark to see much. As far as she could tell, Gunnar took up the rear, behind Otis. She took her place in line behind Nathan.

It seemed the journey down the mountainside would never end. She wanted it to end so she and Gunnar could finish what they had begun. By rights she should be miserably cold and tired and hungry. Instead, she felt like the happiest woman alive.

Warmed by the memory of his arms, she must have dozed off, for the next thing she knew, Gunnar was by her side, shaking her.

"Are you all right?" he asked, his voice low.

She nodded and he brushed his hand against the side of her face. Her skin tingled at his touch, her pulse quickened. Heat rippled through her, reawakening the aching need inside. She wished with all her heart that Nathan hadn't found them so soon. Longing to be back in his arms, she squeezed his hand. She felt a sense of loss when the narrowing trail forced him to drop back and fall in line behind her.

At last they found the stagecoach road and followed it back to the looping trail that led to Dangling Rope.

They reached town just as the sun began to rise. Abby was so exhausted, it was all she could do to stay upright in her saddle.

Nathan dismounted and quickly hurried to her side to help her off her horse. She didn't really need his help, but she was too tired to argue. Still, she was surprised when he lifted her in his arms and carried her to the saloon.

She glanced over Nathan's shoulder to search for Gunnar. He smiled and winked at her before he turned away and headed toward his own cabin.

# Chapter 19

It rained for the next three days. Mud was ankle-deep in the streets of Dangling Rope. The rain drummed the roof of Sleazy's Saloon and beat relentlessly against Abby's bedroom window.

Abby had awakened at the end of that first day with a sore throat and fever. Nathan had stopped by to see how she was doing and, against her wishes, had insisted upon summoning Mom Bull.

For three days and three nights, Mom Bull had guarded her door against visitors. Despite her rough ways, Mom Bull had a surprisingly gentle bedside manner. She sponged Abby's forehead, fed her soup, and straightened her bed.

Abby faded in and out of a fevered sleep. She dreamed wonderful warm dreams of being in Gunnar's loving arms. But she was also plagued with nightmares. Dreams of her uncle followed much the same theme. He beckoned to her from a distant mountain, but try as she might to reach him, she could never catch up to him.

After one such dream, she sat straight up in her bed. Her chest heaved with each gasping breath. She was soaking wet and her nightgown clung to her body.

Mom Bull stood next to her bed, shaking her head. "You ain't gonna get any sleep if you keep gettin' yourself all worked up over some nightmare."

Hands pressed against her chest, Abby lay back against her pillow. Not even Mom Bull's comforting presence could take away the horror of losing her uncle again, if only in her sleep. She thought of Gunnar and the horror of the nightmare began to fade away. "Is . . . is Gunnar all right? He doesn't have a fever or anything, does he?"

"Gunnar's as fit as a fiddle. They both are, but if Gunnar and Nathan don't stop acting like a coupla expectant fathers, I'm gonna be at the end of my rope."

"Expectant fathers?" Abby asked, confused.

"You should see them. They've been camped downstairs off and on since hearin' you weren't up to snuff."

Abby lifted the blanket up to her nose to cover a smile. It wasn't a dream, then. Gunnar really did care for her.

Mom Bull straightened the bed. "It does my heart good to see the two brothers gettin' along, though. Even if it is drivin' me up the wall. You shoulda seen the two of them goin' at it when Gunnar first came to town. They liked to kill each other."

Abby thought about the fight they'd had her first night in town. "I think they genuinely care for each other."

"That they do. And as long as Nathan stays away from the juice . . ." She shrugged. "He's got a wild streak. Just like my boy. You can try to tame it, but in the end there ain't much anyone can do but pray. Gunnar ain't learned that yet, but he will."

A wild streak? Nathan? Why, he'd struck her as being one of the most gentle and kindest men she ever met. If anyone had a wild streak it was Gunnar. Just thinking of how he'd unleashed some of his wildness on her the night they were stranded in the mountains was enough to make her feel all tingly inside. She sank lower into the bed, feeling hot and weak in a way that had nothing to do with her illness and everything to do with Gunnar.

Gunnar sat at one of Sleazy's tables opposite Nathan and kept his voice low so as not to disturb Abby. They were discussing Nathan's trip to Denver, but the conversation was plagued with long pauses. Neither man seemed able to keep his mind on the tedious details of bringing a railroad to town. Gunnar's mind kept wandering back to the night he and Abby had been stranded on the mountaintop. He, at least, had an excuse for being distracted, but he sure in blazes didn't know what Nathan's problem was.

"You're not holding back anything, are you?" Gunnar asked.

Nathan's forehead wrinkled in annoyance. "Dammit, Gunnar. I'm telling you everything I know."

"All right, all right, I'm sorry." He glanced to the top of the stairs, where Mom Bull had parked herself like a bloody fool sergeant-at-arms. "Must be the weather."

"We should have heard from the railroad by now," Nathan said. Otis had agreed to wait at the telegraph office in Colorado Springs for messages.

"This rain has probably closed the road again." Gunnar's gaze darted back to the stairs. Enough was enough. He intended to see Abby today, if he had to climb in her window!

"That's another good reason to bring the train here. We're pretty near trapped every time it rains or snows." The corner of Nathan's mouth suddenly lifted in a half-smile. "I tell you, big brother, I was brilliant. The railroad would be foolish to turn us down."

"What did I tell you?" It did Gunnar's heart good to see Nathan looking clear-eyed and confident.

Nathan had taken the trouble to shave, which was more than Gunnar had done. His hair, still wet from the rain, had obviously been combed. As far as Gunnar knew, Nathan hadn't touched a drop of alcohol in several days. Nathan's hand shook earlier, but after he'd had himself a cup of Mom Bull's coffee, the shaking had stopped. Nathan's behavior of late gave Gunnar a lot of reasons to feel encouraged. Instead, he felt a sense of uneasiness.

It was too soon to hope Nathan had changed. Change took time, months, maybe even years; it didn't occur overnight. Cutting down on alcohol had helped, of course, but was that the only explanation?

"I've been meaning to talk to you about something," Nathan began.

Gunnar held his breath, thinking his brother was about to confess to some dastardly deed. It wouldn't be the first time and it would explain why Nathan appeared to be sitting on a keg of explosives timed to go off at any moment.

"What do you say, big brother, about staying on?"

Gunnar blinked, thinking he'd heard wrong. "You mean you want me to stay here, in Dangling Rope?"

"Don't look so shocked. Once the railroad comes to town, we're going to need a sheriff more than ever."

Gunnar leaned back, balancing his chair on two legs. He was deeply moved. His brother asking him to stay? He never thought he'd see the day. "I don't know. A law firm in Chicago made an offer."

"You hate Chicago."

What Nathan said was true, but still Gunnar hesitated. Not because he didn't like the idea of making a home in Dangling Rope, but because he was still caught off guard by his newly discovered feelings for Abby. How could one glorious night spent in her company make such a difference? Lord, it only took one kiss to know he loved her; two kisses to know he wanted to spend the rest of his life with her.

"I'll think about it," he said. Before he committed to the town, he had to know Abby's true feelings for him. *You don't have any half-arsed ideas that a woman should be a lady in bed, do you?* Trying to control a shiver that suddenly ran through him, he reached for his coffee cup.

"I hope you think about it," Nathan urged. "When you get right down to it, you and me, we're the only family we've got."

"I know," Gunnar said. He was tempted to tell Nathan about his feelings for Abby. The problem was nothing had been settled. If the intensity of their passion was as unexpected and surprising to her as it had been to him, they both could use some time to sort things out. It was too early to make assumptions.

Nathan stood and stretched. It had been a long day. "I think I'll go and get some coffee. Coming?"

Gunnar raised a brow but said nothing. Nathan had drunk a half dozen cups or so since noon. "I'll be there in a bit." Maybe with Nathan gone, Mom Bull would let him see for himself how Abby was doing.

No sooner had Nathan left than he dashed upstairs and pleaded his case. "Come on, Mom Bull. That's a girl. I won't stay but a minute."

"It won't do you any good. She's asleep."

Not do any good? To stand in the same room as the woman he loved? To touch her? To breathe the same air? To gaze at her. How could that not do him good? "She won't even know I'm there." When reason failed to win her over, he threw himself on his knees, hands together, like a love-struck suitor.

Mom Bull laughed at his antics. "Don't you say a word to anyone that I let you in. Otis and Nathan and all the rest will have my head."

He made a show of locking his lips by turning a key in pantomime. "Not a word."

"All right, then. You have one minute."

He kissed Mom Bull on the cheek and tiptoed his way into Abby's room. Her soft, even breathing told him she was still asleep.

Holding his breath, he tiptoed to the bed, then stood transfixed next to her side. His heart swelled with the most unbelievable feelings of warmth and love as he gazed down at her. Even in sleep, she was beautiful. Her dark full lashes fanned out like the points of a star across her softly flushed cheeks. Her mouth was curved upward, as if she were dreaming lovely sweet dreams. He dared hope she was smiling because of him, would always smile because of him.

Longing to take her in his arms, he consoled himself by brushing his lips tenderly against her forehead. "I love you, Miss Abigail Parker, lady or no lady," he whispered, and it seemed to him the little dimple on her cheek deepened.

Mom Bull motioned to him from the door and, carrying the vision of Abby in his heart, he tiptoed out of the room, feeling once again restored.

Nathan rushed into the sheriff's office later that day, waving a paper over his head. "The railroad is coming to town!"

Gunnar jumped to his feet and gave a whooping sound. "They agreed to everything. No conditions. Nothing?"

Nathan hedged. "More or less."

The smile died on Gunnar's face. He sat down slowly. "What do you mean by more or less?"

"The railroad gets half the stock in the Dangling Rope Town Company and asked that we allow them to locate their maintenance shop and roundtable here. I tried to get them to take less stock, but they wouldn't hear of it."

"Do they know that less than a dozen people call this town home?"

"Not exactly. Actually the matter never came up. I mentioned the town had a sheriff and a mayor and a librarian and they just naturally jumped to all the wrong conclusions."

"Naturally." Gunnar chuckled. "I wonder what conclusions they might have jumped to had they known we also have a lady drummer."

Nathan laughed. "I can just imagine. Actually, there is another condition written into the contract."

Gunnar let his chair fall forward. He should have known it was too good to be true.

"If they don't reach us by June fifteenth the deal's off. They'll just leave us out of the loop and go straight across the canyon to Cripple Creek."

"June fifteenth." Gunnar stared at the calendar on his desk. "That's only four weeks away."

"Twenty-seven days to be exact."

Gunnar rubbed a hand over his stubbly beard. "Can it be done?"

"I talked to the railroad supervisor and he told me it could be done, but only if there're no setbacks. A setback of a single day would make all the difference. They've already lost valuable time due to this latest storm."

Gunnar's thoughts whirled. "There's not much we can do about the weather."

"No, but the railroad crew is more concerned about Indian trouble than the weather. The railroad crew has been plagued by those damned poaching Utes. They've already set fire to a boxcar filled with railroad ties. I talked to the railroad commissioner. They've got armed guards stationed in the area, but nowhere near enough."

"What about the army?"

"They've been notified. But so far the army's downplayed the problems. They don't want to admit the reservation idea isn't working."

Gunnar stood and paced about the office. "The Ute leader made it perfectly clear that he was none too happy about the railroad. They don't even know we're bringing it this far east to Dangling Rope."

Nathan looked worried. "Do you think they'll cause any real trouble?"

"Hard to know." The Utes hadn't done any real harm to Abby or himself. And the way Abby and Owns Six—make that Seven—Horses had carried on, talking and laughing like they were on a picnic, it was hard to imagine the leader resorting to violence. Still, it hadn't been all that many years ago that the Utes had killed that Indian Agent Meeker. All Meeker tried to do was to turn a meadow the Indians used for a racetrack into farmland.

"I think it would be wise to exercise caution." Gunnar rubbed his hands together. "Anything else I need to know?"

"No, but I asked the railroad for regular reports on their progress. If they're not going to make their deadlines, I think we should know in advance."

"I agree."

"The railroad construction engineer has some questions as to where we want to put the depot. I told him you'd ride out in the morning to talk to him."

"I'll go first thing," Gunnar said.

Nathan's chair scraped against the wooden floor. "I guess I better tell the others." Grinning wide as a sickle moon, he reached for his hat and pressed it on his head. "Dangling Rope is gonna have itself a railroad!"

# Chapter 20

Abby awoke the following day fully recovered from her illness and anxious to make up for lost time. The rain had stopped and the sun was making a gallant attempt to burn through the clouds.

She was disappointed to learn from Mom Bull that Gunnar had left before dawn to meet with the railroad crew, and wasn't expected back much before nightfall. She was anxious to see him, talk to him, tell him all the things she'd not had a chance to tell him the night they'd been stranded.

Feeling restless, she decided to experiment with the berries she'd gathered. After breakfast, she washed and crushed the berries, then beat them until the mixture was as creamy as pudding.

She smoothed a dollop of cream across her cheek with a sponge, staring at herself in the mirror as she worked. A beige-pink, the color was as delicate as the first blush of a rose. It would be perfect for Ginger.

She glanced outside on the off chance Gunnar had returned early. Disappointed that his horse was nowhere in sight, she drew away from the window. Her body ached, but not from any lingering illness. No, this time it was the memories of the night spent with Gunnar that kept her feeling as if she would explode into a million pieces if she didn't see him soon.

Never had she known that being with a man could be so wonderful. She'd been accosted on several occasions while on the streets. Fortunately, she'd always managed to escape before anything much had happened, but she had secretly feared the memory of rough hands and foul mouths might make it difficult to trust a man enough to have any sort of normal life.

She never thought she could so willingly let a man kiss or touch her the way Gunnar had kissed and touched her—would touch her again if she had anything to say about it. Quelling the eagerness that made her feel raw-edged with anticipation, she moved away from the window and wiped the cream off her face.

The berry base left an unsightly stain. She washed her face with Jergens' soap to no avail. Finally she scrubbed her face with lye soap. The soap removed the last traces of berry juice but left her skin feeling taut and dry. She experimented with the various products in her pack in search of a less damaging complexion wash.

After much trial and error, she mixed melted wax and olive oil together, added a bit more benzoin gum powder than usual, tossed in a few other ingredients for good measure, and finished with a dash of wine. After rubbing more berry cream on her face, she poured this latest lotion onto a piece of cotton and rubbed it gently over the rosy spot. She glanced in the mirror. This time, not a trace of berry stain remained. She smiled to herself. She was ready to try her new rouge on Ginger.

Less than twenty minutes later, Abby was greeted by Madam Rosie, who quickly ushered her into the front sitting room. "We heard about your dreadful ordeal in the mountains with those terrible savages."

"Terrible savages?" Abby sat down on the velvet divan. "I don't know where you heard such a thing. The truth is, we didn't see a single miner."

Madam Rosie looked blank. "Miners? I was referring to Indians."

"Oh."

Ginger and Meg joined them, dressed in multilayered petticoats. They pranced around the room in their bare feet, bombarding Abby with questions about her encounter with the Utes. Laughing at the absurdity of their questions, she tried to ease their fears. "Actually, if it weren't for my encounter with the Utes, I wouldn't have developed this new rouge just for you, Ginger." She reached into her pack and unscrewed the top off a jar.

Curious, Ginger settled herself on a chair and flicked her long orange-red hair away from her face.

"Hold still." Abby wiped Ginger's face until every last speck of red rouge had been removed.

Abby dabbed the color across Ginger's high cheekbones. She then blended the cream with a wet sponge until her face looked as smooth as satin.

Abby stood back, amazed at the difference.

"It's p-perfect," Meg exclaimed.

Even Ruby, who had just joined them, agreed. "Perfect!"

"Now let's add some lip coloring." Abby applied a thicker rouge in the same soft color to Ginger's mouth. "What do you think?" she asked the others.

Meg was so overwhelmed by Ginger's amazing transformation, she looked about to burst into tears. "Oh, Ginger. I'm s-so h-happy for you."

Only Rosie seemed to have reservations. "Her lips seem a bit too pale, don't you think? I don't want the girls to fade into the woodwork."

"I don't think there's any danger of that," Abby said. She handed Ginger a hand mirror.

Looking skeptical, Ginger took the mirror and lifted it to her face. Her mouth formed a perfect o and her eyebrows curved upward in two high arches. For several moments, she didn't say a word. She only stared at her image as if watching an apparition.

"Say something!" Ruby said impatiently. "Do you like it or don't you?"

"I love it," Ginger said. "I . . . I don't know what to say."

Abby knew exactly what she wanted Ginger to say. "Just promise me you'll stop using that poison."

"I'll think about it."

Meg tried out Abby's new rouge, though it was no-where near as effective on her. "I really think you sh-should s-stay in D-dangling Rope and open up one of those f-fancy salons like they have in Paris."

"How's she going to make a living?" Ruby scoffed. "There's hardly enough of us to support a gnat."

"The g-girls would come down from C-cripple Creek and Victor," Meg persisted. "B-besides, Nathan said the t-train is coming this way. Why, that w-will b-bring people from f-far and wide."

"Meg's right," Ruby said. "Especially when word reaches them how you've turned dear Ginger here into a raving beauty. I bet there isn't anyone in the world who can customize colors like you do."

"Oh, I'm sure there is," Abby said modestly. "In Paris." Despite her protests, her head swam with possi-bilities. She had not previously considered extending her stay in Colorado. She fully intended to return to Boston just as soon as she'd found her uncle.

The possibility of her uncle being lost to her forever was too painful to contemplate. The problem was, she would soon have to replenish her supplies, and she was almost out of money. Of course, if Gunnar asked her to stay, she wouldn't hesitate a moment. *Please hurry back, Gunnar. I so need to talk to you!*

"It's a g-great idea," Meg was saying. "P-please say you'll give it s-some thought."

"I'll think about it," Abby promised.

The girls insisted she stay for the noontime meal, but she politely declined, not wanting to run into an-other one of their guests.

After leaving the Opera House, she ran into Nathan. "Abby!" He gave her a delighted smile. "I can't tell you how good it is to see you up and about."

"It's good to be up and about," she said.

"Have you heard the news?"

"Are you talking about the train?"

He looked as disappointed as a child who was told

Santa Claus didn't exist. "Who told you? Not my brother?"

"I haven't seen Gunnar. Actually, I heard it from Meg. Oh, Nathan. It's wonderful! I . . . I think."

"What do you mean you think?"

"You know how the Utes feel. Owns Six Horses will probably be furious to learn the train is going to cover more ground than before."

"To hell with the Utes." Seeing the disapproval on her face, he quickly tried to make amends. "I'm sorry, Abby, but we can't let the Utes dictate to us. They have no business being here in the first place. They belong on the reservation. If we could get the army to do its job . . ."

Abby was ashamed to think that before her meeting with the Utes, she would have agreed with Nathan's views. Owns Six Horses had told her horror stories about Utah's Uintah-Ouray and Colorado's Southern Ute reservations. He'd said his people were hunters, not farmers, and had grown fat and lazy on the reservations, away from their beloved mountains. "Would you stay on one of those reservations?" she asked.

Nathan blinked in surprise. "Me? I'm not an Indian."

"The point I'm trying to make is that you're free to come and go as you please. To live the life you want to live. Why shouldn't Indians know that same freedom?"

"I understand your point. But I don't try to tell people what they can and cannot do with the land."

"The Indians have special regard for this land."

"So do I," Nathan said, his face earnest. "Do you know how many towns I've tried to build in the past? Dozens! But every time I think things are going well, something happens and the town goes bust. This time . . ." He gazed around like a loving parent gazing at his young. "Granted, the town's not much yet, but when the railroad comes, it'll be great, Abby. You just wait and see!"

Abby found herself caught up in his enthusiasm. She was reminded how she felt the day her uncle first took her home with him. She stood in the small room he said was hers and stared about in wonder, not wanting to move for fear the vision would disappear before her eyes. "Most men are satisfied with building a house," she said softly, knowing there was much about him— about both brothers—she didn't understand. "You want to build a town."

Nathan's gold-colored hair waved in the cool afternoon breeze that was blowing down from the high peaks. "I always wanted to live in a place like this. You have Boston to call home. Me? My pa kept to himself and we lived miles away from our closest neighbor. I never really felt as if I belonged." He gave her a quick smile that was more somber than bright. "I didn't mean to bore you with all this."

She laid her hand on his arm. "You're not boring me."

"I'm not?"

"Not at all. But I don't think you realize that to Meg and Ginger and even Mom Bull, this is already home."

Nathan's gaze grew intense. "What about you, Abby? Would . . . you ever consider calling Dangling Rope home?"

"I don't know," she said honestly. "It would depend on my uncle's plans. That is, if I ever find him."

"You will, Abby. Why, Gunnar is as determined to find him as you are. Every day you were sick, he wrote letters to innkeepers and saloon owners. He even arranged to put a notice in each of Cripple Creek's numerous newspapers."

Abby didn't think it possible, but the love she felt for Gunnar grew even deeper, more intense. "Gunnar did that?"

"Yes, he did. He would have told you himself, but Mom Bull guarded you like the national treasury."

Abby smiled. "The national treasury, eh?" It gave her a warm glow to know that Gunnar had continued the search in her absence. It helped to relieve her own guilt for having lost so much time. "Meg had an interesting idea. She wants me to stay in Dangling Rope and open up a complexion salon, like the ones in Paris."

Nathan's face lit up. "Why, Abby, that's wonderful!"

"Do you really think so?"

"Of course I think so. Don't you? Just think of all the business you'll do. There're enough brothels in the mining towns to make you a very rich woman."

Abby laughed at the idea of being rich, and together they continued walking, trying their best to avoid the mud holes remaining from the rain. "Do you suppose it's only women in brothels who are interested in their appearance?"

Nathan shrugged his shoulders. "I guess so. Why would an ordinary woman want to paint herself up? Especially if she's already married or as beautiful as you?"

She blushed. She'd never thought of herself as beautiful. Her eyes were too far apart, her lips too full. But since she'd taken over her uncle's business, she'd learned to search out the beauty that she'd recently come to believe was inherent in everyone. Even Mom Bull with all her peculiar ways and unwomanly traits radiated an inner glow that seemed to Abby beautiful in itself. "Businesswomen in Boston use color enhancement on their faces."

"We don't have any businesswomen in Dangling Rope," Nathan said. "Not unless you count Rosie and her girls."

"Of course I count them," Abby said. "For your information, I consider myself a businesswoman, and don't forget Mom Bull."

Nathan chuckled. "You think Mom Bull's going to want to get all painted up?"

"Stranger things have happened."

Nathan laughed louder. "I can't argue with you there."

They had reached Sleazy's Saloon. Abby pointed to the sign over the batwing doors. "What do you think of my changing the sign to read Abby's Complexion

Salon?" She wrinkled her nose. "That's not right. It should be Miss Parker's Complexion Salon. That's better."

Nathan gazed down at her. "You're serious about this, aren't you?"

"I don't know. Maybe." She thought of Ruby and what she could do for her if given the chance. She thought of Meg and how she hid herself behind her painted face, how Ginger had stared at herself in the mirror that morning as if seeing herself for the first time. Her goal wouldn't be to make a woman more beautiful. What she wanted to do was help women gain a better sense of themselves. She glanced up at Nathan, her excitement growing. "Come to think of it, I'm very serious."

Nathan couldn't have looked happier had he struck gold. "Really, Abby? You plan to stay?"

"For a while," she said.

"Ya-hooo!" He grabbed her by the shoulders. "Let's celebrate tonight. You and me!"

"What?"

"Let's celebrate the coming of the train and your complexion salon. I'll ask Mom Bull to fix chicken and dumplings and we'll get Clod to play his fiddle. What do you say?"

"Shouldn't we invite Gunnar to celebrate with us?"

"Of course we'll invite Gunnar. If he gets back in time. We'll invite anyone you want. So what do you say?"

"I say let's celebrate!"

Nathan let out another whooping sound, picked her up, and twirled her around. "Nathan . . . for goodness' sakes . . ." But his laughter was contagious and she was soon laughing with him.

# Chapter 21

Gunnar didn't make it back to town until well after midnight. The sound of Clod's fiddle floated up from Mom Bull's Restaurant, but otherwise there was no other sign of life. The window over Sleazy's Saloon was dark. Apparently, Abby was asleep. It was all he could do to keep from going to her. She needed her rest, he told himself. They had tomorrow, the day after—the rest of their lives to be together. Tonight, he would let her sleep. But if he had his way, it would be the last full night of sleep she'd ever have.

Frustrated by the chain of events that had kept them apart for the last four days, he left his horse at the livery stables and ran the short distance up the hill to his cabin.

Tomorrow, come hell or high water, nothing was going to keep him away from her.

It was barely dawn when Gunnar left his cabin. The air was cool and clear. The ground was still soaked and a large pool of water spanned the distance between his cabin and the woods, forcing him to abandon the trail and cut through Main Street.

It was much too early to pay Abby a call. But since he couldn't sleep, he decided a brisk walk would be just the thing to clear his head. Perhaps he would pick some wildflowers for her. That is, if any survived the rain. Yes, indeed, columbines or mountain wood lilies for her hair. He smiled at the thought and the love in his heart was so great, he didn't know how he would get through the next hour until he once again held her in his arms.

He only wished he had something substantial to tell Abby about her uncle. While at the railroad construction site, he'd questioned members of the crew. Not one knew Parker, but he did happen to run across a miner who placed the peddler around the Butterfly mines around the middle of September.

His thoughts were interrupted by the sound of Nathan's voice. "Hey, big brother, wait for me!"

Turning, Gunnar waited for Nathan to catch up.

"Where are you off to so early?" Nathan asked.

"Thought I'd take a walk." Gunnar eyed Nathan in surprise. He couldn't recall ever seeing Nathan willingly dressed at this ungodly hour of the day. Not only was he dressed, he was freshly shaved and his hair was neatly combed. "Where are *you* off to?"

"Nowhere," Nathan said, a strange intensity in his voice. "I couldn't sleep. I was anxious to hear how your meeting went with the construction crew."

"Everything went like clockwork." He placed his arm around Nathan's shoulder and the two walked side by side. "They expect to lay a mile of track a day. At that rate, they should reach us in plenty of time."

Nathan glanced sideways at Gunnar, a grin on his face. "Hey, big brother, we can do this, can't we? Just you and me."

*Just you and me.* Gunnar hugged the words to his already overflowing heart. Could it be true? Had the brother he loved more than life itself finally given up his wild, destructive ways? God, it was a miracle. "You bet we can."

Gunnar took the lead as they followed a narrow deer trail through the woods.

"I've got more news." Nathan called from behind, and because he sounded out of breath, Gunnar stopped to rest.

Nathan leaned against a tree. "Abby's decided to stay in Dangling Rope for a while."

Gunnar's heart leaped with joy. *Here? She's staying here for me?* "Are you sure?"

Nathan's grin broadened until his entire face seemed to shine. "Said she was going to open up a complexion salon."

"What?"

"Hard to believe, isn't it? We're gonna be the first town in Colorado to have such a shop. I tell you, that Abby Parker is some lady! If anyone can make a success out of such a business, it's her. I'd bet my life on it."

Gunnar felt a sense of uneasiness as Nathan raved on about her. Abby this and Abby that . . . it seemed to Gunnar that Nathan was obsessed with her. Gunnar rubbed his jaw and shifted nervously. What was going on here?

"Abby decided to use Sleazy's Saloon for her business," Nathan continued. "She's already talked Mom Bull into painting a sign. Said she could use the bar for a counter and the liquor shelves for her jars and vials."

Gunnar grimaced and started to walk faster, this time forcing Nathan to scramble to keep up. He recalled his own mother with her harsh-painted face. She'd used her painted face as an excuse to keep him away. "Mustn't mess up Mama's face," she'd say, whenever he'd attempted to show her the least affection.

"Does she expect to make a living at this sort of thing?" Gunnar asked, telling himself he was imagining things. Nathan was only two years younger, but he was still only a kid at heart. What could he possibly know about love? "Other than Madam Rosie and her girls, who else is going to purchase her cosmetics?"

"I asked Abby the very same thing. She said once the train comes to town, businesswomen will travel to Dangling Rope all the way from Denver."

"Businesswomen? You mean like Rosie's girls?"

"No, *business*women. You know, like Mom Bull. Dammit, Gunnar, do you have to walk so fast?"

Gunnar stopped and turned. "Mom Bull, eh?" He

watched Nathan closely, measuring every smile, every frown, every nuance in a desperate attempt to disprove his growing suspicions.

Nathan's hands hardly trembled this morning and his normally red unfocused eyes looked clear and as bright as a winter star. Little of the troubled boy and even less of the troubled man was visible. It was a miracle, that's what it was, seeing Nathan happy and actually looking forward to the future. Nathan had given up alcohol. That's why he looked so confident— why he acted, sounded, even walked differently. It had nothing to do with Abby. Nothing!

"How do you expect us to attract families if we kow-tow to a bunch of painted ladies?"

"You know what your problem is, Gunnar? You take life too seriously."

"Maybe you're right." They walked in silence through the woods, following a deer trail clear up to the ridge that overlooked the valley. The sky grew lighter and birds darted in and out of dripping bushes, twittering noisily. Overhead, patches of blue sky broke through the clouds.

Most of the wildflowers had been damaged in the rain. Abby would not be wearing flowers in her hair today, Gunnar thought ruefully, but one day soon, he would shower her with blossoms.

They circled back to town. Gunnar glanced at his clock, noting it was only seven. No matter, he couldn't stay away from her a moment longer. In five minutes, he would be in her arms. Make that four . . .

Nathan's step grew hesitant upon reaching Main Street. "Gunnar. I need to talk to you about something."

He sounded so serious, Gunnar swallowed his impatience and turned in alarm. "What is it?"

Nathan walked in a circle, his hands in his pockets, his head lifted toward the sky. "Promise you won't laugh."

"What is it with you, Nathan? One minute you accuse me of being too serious. Now you're worried about me laughing."

Nathan faced Gunnar. "You must think I'm crazy. Maybe I am."

"Quit beating around the bush, Nathan. Just spit it out."

"All right." Nathan took a breath and braced himself. "I think I'm in love."

Gunnar stared at him. "What?"

"Don't look so shocked, big brother. I hear it can happen to the best of us." He glanced around to make certain no one else was listening, then lowered his voice. "I think I'm in love with Abby."

Gunnar felt as if every last drop of blood had been drained from his body. Dear God, how could this be true? He sucked in his breath. "You don't even know her that well."

"I think I know her very well. We've spent a lot of time together and last night . . ." Suddenly, he seemed overcome with emotion.

Gunnar felt sick. *Last night? When he thought it more important to let her have her rest than take her in his arms?* "What . . . what happened last night?"

"We celebrated the railroad and her decision to stay here. We ate at Mom Bull's and danced to Clod's music and do you know something? It seemed to me the best food I ever ate and the best music I ever heard. Now, if that isn't love, I don't know what is."

Gunnar didn't want to hear this. He didn't want to hear that Nathan held Abby in his arms. Or danced with her. Or even ate with her.

"Do you think she'll have me?" Nathan asked.

"How the hell would I know?" Gunnar snapped. Nathan looked surprised, then hurt. Gunnar swallowed hard. His prayers had finally been answered. Nathan had found someone to love. But why in heaven's name did it have to be Abby?

Gunnar saw her, suddenly. Dressed in a pretty floral

frock, she stood in front of Sleazy's Saloon looking like an angel as she gazed at him.

Nathan spotted her and waved, but Gunnar stood frozen in shock and disbelief. Helplessly, he watched his brother go to her, and at that moment knew everything Nathan had told him was true.

Nathan loved her. Lord, it was written all over his face as he greeted her, emanated from every pore of his body. Gunnar cursed himself. How could he have been so utterly blind?

Unable to watch a moment longer, Gunnar spun on his heel and half ran, half walked up the muddied hill to his cabin.

Why hadn't he seen this coming? All those days and nights he'd sat with Nathan in Sleazy's Saloon during Abby's illness, it had never once occurred to him that his brother was there for any reason other than to talk over business and out of friendly concern for Abby.

He shuddered to think what would happen if Nathan learned the truth about him and Abby. If Nathan had so much as a clue, it would send him over the edge again. Maybe this time for good.

Gunnar's mind reeled in confusion, clouds of despair muddling his thinking. Memories of Abby, memories of Nathan all combined to create a living hell. He recalled seeing Nathan's young face the day his mother had deserted him. He could almost feel the heated passion of Abby's lips on his. Abby, Nathan. Nathan, Abby. Choking with despair, he stumbled up the steps of his cabin.

Inside, he paced around the tiny room trying to shake off the anguish. Abby, Nathan. Their names kept running through his mind. Dammit, they were the two people in all the world he loved more than life itself. Now one of them—Abby, his dear sweet Abby—was lost to him forever.

For he'd already stolen one woman from his brother. Dear God, how could he steal another?

# Chapter 22

Gunnar found her in Sleazy's Saloon sorting through bottles of sherry and bay rum. He owed her something, some explanation for avoiding her these past few days. He'd waited until he was certain he could face her without making a fool of himself. He'd rehearsed his speech, written and rewritten it in his mind, practiced saying it aloud. His success depended on how well he kept a clamp on his heart and a lock on his emotions.

His heart nearly stopped at the sight of her and for a frightening moment he could hardly breathe. This wasn't going to work. How could he pretend he had no feelings for her when he couldn't even seem to think in her presence? He was just about to leave when she looked up and caught him red-handed, staring at her in a way that belied everything he came to say.

"Gunnar?"

He tried to read her face and couldn't. She had every right to be angry with him. She had tried to talk to him on several occasions, but each time he'd brushed her away, making up some excuse for having to leave his office and ride like a damned coward out of town. Regretting the way he'd treated her, he cleared his throat and hoped to God she couldn't hear the way his heart was thumping. "I need to have a word with you." His voice sounded gruff, almost insolent in tone. So much for trying to sound impassive.

She searched his face with a probing gaze, then frowned.

Hoping to break the tension between them, he

glanced around. Sleazy's Saloon never looked so good. "You've been working hard."

It was obvious by the impatient look on her face that she had no intention of discussing her remodeling plans. "Why have you been avoiding me?" So there it was, the question he didn't want to answer, stretching between them like a life-threatening wound in need of immediate attention.

"I needed time to think about what happened between us last week."

The look on her face was one of confusion. "Do . . . do you regret what happened?"

"I could never . . ." He sucked in his breath. "Of course not. I could never regret it."

"Then why are you acting this way?"

"I'm not acting any particular way." He pressed his fingers into the brim of his hat and tried to recall the words he'd spent half the night rehearsing. "I'm afraid you might have misunderstood my intentions."

She looked him square in the face. "I understood your every intention, Gunnar Kincaid. Just as I'm sure you understood mine."

"Yours?" He stared at her.

"My intention was to . . ." She stopped as if to search for the right word. "Shake the blanket with you."

"My God, Abby!" It pained him to think she would use such a flippant expression to describe what had almost happened between them.

Seeing his stricken face, she touched her fingers to her lips. "That's the most polite way I know to describe what we—"

"Polite?" If this was her idea of being polite, then he would just as soon she go back to speaking street language. "What you and I . . . we weren't going to . . . *shake the blanket!*"

"We weren't?"

"No, Abby! Dammit, no! We were going to make love." He shook his head in dismay. Now she'd done it. Made him think things he had no intention of thinking; say things he never meant to say.

"Oh." Her eyes softened as she considered what was obviously a new idea. Suddenly he ached for her. Ached with the knowledge that her years on the streets had taught her so much about survival, but so little about life and love and all that was beautiful in the world.

Abby was deeply moved. Lord, she'd heard so many crude ways of saying it, but never had she heard the act between a man and woman described in such a simple, beautiful way. "Can you call it that?" she asked, truly intrigued. "Making love?"

He feared the restraints on his emotions were about to snap. "The other night I wanted to make love to you." He stared down at the hat in his hands. He couldn't bear to look at her for fear of what he might see in her eyes—what she might see in his. "I don't regret anything that happened. But it's over, do you understand?"

Abby stared at him in shock and disbelief. Feelings of anger and hurt exploded inside. Wanting to hurt him in return, she lashed out, "Is that why you came here today? To tell me it's over?" She laughed an ugly, hateful laugh. "Is there really any difference between shaking the blanket and making love? I think not. You can take your pretty words and go!"

Her words were like bullets to his soul. He longed to carry her upstairs to prove there was a difference. In a moment of madness, he cleared the distance between them. Grabbing her by the waist, he dragged her to him and pressed his mouth hungrily on hers.

She pushed him away angrily. "Don't you ever do that again!"

Shocked by the contempt on her face—shocked even more by his own inexcusable actions—he backed away. "I'm sorry, Abby . . . I better go, before I . . . before we . . ."

"Make love?" she retorted with a mocking look.

"Go any further." He turned to leave, desperate to put as much distance between them as possible. "I want you to know I'll continue to look for your uncle and I won't stop until he's found."

"Go to hell, Sheriff!"

Long after Gunnar had left, Abby stared at the bat-wing doors that had swung back and forth in his wake and which now stood as still and silent as her heart. *Oh, Gunnar.* She squeezed her eyes tight to hold back the tears. None of this made sense. None of it!

Immobilized by grief, she went through the motions of her day, hardly knowing what she was doing. Nathan stopped by and, thinking she was on the verge of a relapse, made her promise to get some extra rest.

Though Nathan meant to be kind, she was relieved when he left. She was in no mood for company.

Thoughts of Gunnar's kisses haunted her; the tender, loving kisses on the mountain, the desperate but no less passionate kiss only hours before. He *did* love her. It was the only thing that made sense. Her hopes rose as she listened to her heart. If only she could drown out the more sensible voice inside her head that kept telling her over and over she was a fool to ever have trusted a lawman.

It was after dark by the time her anger had flared into outrage. How dare the man take advantage of her, then toss her aside like a bag of potatoes! Who did he think he was?

Around midnight, it became increasingly clear that all the denials and anger in the world weren't going to erase the pain.

*Oh, Gunnar,* she thought, her anguish so deep, so intense, it felt like a lump inside. *How could you do this to me? How could you turn my heart inside out and then walk away?*

Hurt and confused, angry and humiliated, she worked herself into a cleaning frenzy that spanned the next few days. She scrubbed and oiled the wood floors, walls, and stairs of Sleazy's Saloon until every tobacco and alcohol stain was gone. Every square inch of brass, from the foot railings below the bar to the lantern hooks on the walls, was polished until it gleamed, every window buffed to a sparkling shine.

As she worked, her mood swings went from deep despair to a nonchalant "who cares what the sheriff thinks" attitude that did nothing to chase away the heartache, but did wonders for the saloon.

Mom Bull said she never saw the likes of it. "Why, the fool woman would scrub the marks off a rattler if you gave her half a chance!"

Nathan tried to talk Gunnar into helping him move out the gaming tables and crates of unneeded liquor.

"What's the matter with you, big brother?" Nathan asked. "You act like Abby has the plague or something. How come you keep trying to avoid her?"

"I'm not trying to avoid anybody," Gunnar argued. "I've been busy. Someone's got to make certain the railroad stays on schedule."

"Why don't you just admit it? You don't want Abby to open up a complexion salon."

"All we need is a bunch of women with painted faces running about," he grumbled, though in reality this had nothing to do with his ill temper. Still, the thought made him shudder. His mother hadn't started painting her face until she'd started her stage career. He remembered clearly the shock of seeing her for the first time with her lips painted scarlet and her cheeks redder than two tree-ripe apples. She looked so unattainable, lost to him. *Lost to him like Abby was lost to him.*

"I think you're being mule-headed," Nathan said. "Just because Mother . . ." His face darkened. "Gunnar, you've been trying to make me put the past behind me. Maybe it's time for you to follow your own advice."

Gunnar raked both hands through his hair. "The past has nothing to do with this." *It had everything to do with it.*

"Abby needs our support—"

Gunnar jumped to his feet. "All right! You want me to move furniture? I'll move furniture!" He stormed out of his office and marched across the street to Sleazy's Saloon, with Nathan close behind.

"Dammit, Gunnar, what's eating you?"

"How many times do I have to tell you, nothing's eating me?" He pushed his way through the batwing doors and froze.

Abby stood behind the counter. She looked up in speechless surprise. A spark seemed to snap between them before a mask of indifference settled on her face.

Aware of Nathan stacking chairs behind him, he fought to keep his voice normal. "I came to help Nathan move furniture."

"Oh." She sounded vague, removed somehow, so different than her usual self. "I thought . . ."

His heart skipped a beat. He swallowed hard. He moved closer to the counter and picked up a chair. Keeping his voice low, he asked, "You thought what, Abby?" *That I've decided to act on my love for you, even though it would kill my brother?*

She looked at him oddly, but when she spoke, her voice was almost as cold as her eyes. "I thought you had news about my uncle."

It was a reasonable assumption on her part, thinking he'd come to talk about her uncle. Still, he felt like she'd taken that confounded knife of hers and thrust it into his heart. He felt as if he'd failed her on so many levels. The least he could have done was to have found her uncle. "I'm afraid I know nothing more than before," he said.

Their gazes met, locked for a moment, before they both glanced away, she to stare at the bottle of bay rum in her hand, he to study a knot in one of the floor planks.

Nathan moved a table aside, the legs scraping across the floor. "Shall we get started, big brother? We're going to store these gaming tables in the building next door."

Gunnar followed Nathan across the room and lifted the end of a green baize table. It took several trips back and forth to empty the room of unnecessary tables. Gunnar fought every urge to steal a glance at Abby. But invariably, he couldn't seem to help himself. It was as if his eyes, his very senses, even, took on a life of their own. He wondered if she was having as much trouble ignoring him.

Probably not, judging from the way she was mixing her paints as if nothing else existed or even mattered. As much as it hurt to know she could so easily forget him, he was happy for her. It would be best for all concerned if she never thought about their kisses. Never thought about that night on the mountain. Never recalled the unspoken promises they'd made seconds before their rescue. It would kill him to know she was hurting. God only knew he was tortured enough for both of them.

Still, there was a less than noble, all too human part of him that didn't want her to forget.

Abby stared in dismay at her own handwriting. She had inadvertently written the word *kiss* for *cup*. *One kiss of baby rum*. She was even more surprised to discover Gunnar's name amid her notes. Since it was obvious her mind wasn't on her work, she laid her notebook aside and decided to arrange her supplies on the shelf behind the bar. The only problem was, the full mirror offered too much temptation. Instead of paying full attention to her tasks, she invariably found herself watching Gunnar.

At one point, when his gaze met hers in the mirror, an empty sherry bottle slipped through her fingers and shattered into a million tiny pieces at her feet. Heaven help her! She couldn't seem to concentrate when Gunnar was nearby. He made her nerves stand on edge; worse than that, made her heart jump like melted lard on a hot griddle.

Not that he paid her any heed. The man acted like

she was a stranger. He didn't look at her, he glared. Nor did he talk as much as growl. For two cents, she'd be tempted to tell him exactly what she thought of him and his kiss. *His wonderful, sensuous kiss that had kept her walking on eggshells ever since.*

"Would you like me to sweep that up for you?" Gunnar spoke from the other side of the bar.

She whirled around to face him. "What?"

"The glass. Would you like me to sweep it up?"

"I'm quite capable of cleaning up my own glass," she said, her voice tight.

"Very well." Gunnar glanced back as Nathan returned from carrying a stack of chairs next door. "If there's nothing else you need me for . . ."

"Thank you, big brother, you've been a big help." An eager looked flashed in Nathan's eyes. "Without all that furniture in here, there's enough room to hold a dance."

Abby glanced around the room. "I do believe you're right."

Nathan gave Gunnar a brotherly pat on the back. "I'm heading out to check on the railroad. Want to go for a ride?"

"Why not?" Gunnar's eyes locked with Abby's for the briefest of moments before he followed Nathan out the door.

# Chapter 23

A week later, Meg arrived at the complexion salon, bringing a bottle of lemon juice Abby had requested. "Don't tell the c-cook I r-raided his p-pantry or he'll be on the warpath."

"I won't say a word," Abby promised. She placed the bottle on the shelf with her other supplies.

With her back and her elbows resting against the counter, Meg glanced around. "Y-you've done wonders."

"I couldn't have done it without help," Abby said. "Nathan has been a dear." She had no idea what she would have done without him. "And Gunnar has taken over the search for my uncle, which has freed my time considerably. Of course, I'll always be grateful for your help."

"W-what's going on between you and the sh-sheriff?"

Abby felt her cheeks flare. "Going on? Why . . . why, nothing's going on. Why do you ask?"

"It's just a feeling I g-get whenever the two of you are in the s-same room. And just a m-moment ago . . . when you m-mentioned him . . . you had this f-funny look on your f-face."

"The sheriff and I don't always see eye-to-eye. That's probably why I had that look on my face."

Meg looked unconvinced. "Then why does he k-keep c-coming here?"

"He's not here any more often than Nathan."

"B-but Nathan has a g-good reason to be here. He's h-helping you set up your b-business."

"The sheriff keeps me informed on his investigation

into my uncle's disappearance. He keeps me fully informed of any leads."

"Has he had any l-leads?" Meg asked curiously.

"Not yet. He was here yesterday to help Nathan change the doors." The oak doors were a vast improvement over the batwings. "Nothing wrong with that, is there?"

"I s-suppose not," Meg said. "But if you and he don't see eye-to-eye, why would he k-knock himself out to help you?"

"He's not knocking himself out. He's only doing what he thinks is best for the town. A facial salon is infinitely better than an empty building and might encourage other businesses to locate here."

"I s-suppose you're right," Meg said.

Eager to change the subject, Abby pointed to her new doors. "So what do you think?"

"They m-make a b-big difference," Meg said.

Abby nodded, but in reality she thought the place still lacked the proper ambience. She'd come to the conclusion that no matter how much she cleaned and polished, Sleazy's Saloon would never remotely resemble anything found in Paris.

"Some c-curtains would help," Meg offered. "And maybe a p-painting or two. I'm sure you could find what you need in D-denver."

"I'm afraid any decorating touches will have to wait until after my shop starts making a profit," Abby said.

Meg pursed her lips. "If it's m-money you need, I'll be h-happy t-to help."

Abby reached for Meg's hand and squeezed it warmly. "That's very kind of you, Meg. But I couldn't take money from you."

"It would give me great p-pleasure to h-help you. I've been s-saving my money. I keep hoping that one day I'll have the c-courage to leave the brothel."

"Oh, Meg, that's wonderful!"

Meg smiled at Abby's enthusiastic response, but the smile was fleeting, at best, and held more sadness than joy. "I don't know if th-that day will ever c-come. I've lived in a brothel nearly all my life. I don't know how to live any other way."

Abby recalled being in much the same predicament. "Between the age of ten and seventeen, I lived on the streets of Boston in a part of town known as Thieves Corner."

Meg looked horrified. "B-by yourself?"

Abby nodded. "When my uncle found me, I was afraid to go with him."

Meg stared at Abby in total disbelief. "Afraid to leave the s-streets?"

"I know it sounds crazy. But it's true. I couldn't imagine living any other way."

"But you did go with your uncle."

"Yes, I did, and I could never go back to that old life. That's how you'll feel one day, Meg, once you've tried other options."

"It's not the s-same for me," Meg said, her voice hoarse. "You c-can read and write. I never learned to do th-those things. The truth is there's nothing else I can do to s-support myself. N-nothing."

"That's nonsense," Abby said. "Look at Mom Bull. She can't cook worth a copper penny, but that didn't keep her from opening up her own restaurant."

Meg looked more depressed than ever. "If M-mom B-bull's wasn't the only restaurant in town, she'd have failed from the m-moment she opened her d-doors."

"I'm not so sure. She makes everyone feel so welcome, the food takes on less importance than you would expect." Abby thought for a moment. "I've got an idea. Why don't you work for me?"

"You?"

"Why not? I'll teach you how to mix cosmetics and take orders. Eventually, I'll teach you how to add and subtract." She released Meg's hand. "You can be my assistant."

Meg looked flustered. "I d-don't think th . . . th . . . that's a good idea."

Despite the skepticism on Meg's face, Abby persisted. "It wouldn't be that hard. I can't afford to pay you at first. But as soon as the railway reaches town, I'm positive we'll have enough customers to support us both. Think about it, Meg. Please."

"I'll th-think about it. B-but don't be d-disappointed if I don't take you up on the offer. I really don't think I'm ready to g-give up the only l-life I've ever really known. Not yet." Meg jumped as a loud boom rattled the windows, her eyes wide with fright. "Wh-what was that?"

"Dynamite," Nathan called from the doorway. At the sound of his voice both women turned to greet him. He closed the door behind him and joined them at the bar. "Me and Gunnar rode out to Beaver Canyon yesterday. The railroad is right on schedule."

"Then we better get this place ready," Abby said. Another boom sounded, this one rattling the bottles on the wall behind her. "When that train rolls into town, I want to be open for business."

Mom Bull walked into the salon, carrying a sign. "What do you think?" she asked. She propped it up next to a wall for everyone to see. The sign read MISS PARKER'S COMPLEXION SALOON.

"It's *salon*, not *saloon*, with only one O," Abby said. "It's a French word."

Mom Bull scowled at Abby. She didn't take kindly to people messing around with the English language. "French! How do you expect to attract customers with foreign words? I say we keep the word *saloon*."

"But that will mislead people," Abby said. "*Saloon* is a barroom. As you can plainly see, this is not a barroom."

"Then what's all that sherry doing there?"

"Alcohol is good for the skin," Abby explained.

Mom Bull shook her head. "I've been drinkin' whiskey for years, and it ain't done nothin' for my skin."

"She has a point there," Nathan whispered for

Abby's benefit. Aloud he said, "Let's get that sign up where it belongs."

"The one O has to go," Abby insisted.

Mom Bull conceded. "Oh, all right."

The four of them trooped outside. Nathan stood the sign against the building and Mom Bull crossed out an O with blue paint.

Nathan jammed a hammer into the deep pocket of his canvas overalls and climbed the wooden ladder while Meg and Abby held on.

"Where do you want it?" Nathan called down.

"Over the door."

"Need some help?" Gunnar spoke from behind her. Abby's heart started to beat as fast as a galloping horse, and her knees threatened to buckle. *What a fine kettle of fish*, she thought irritated. *The sheriff opens his mouth and I start acting like a schoolgirl.*

Nathan called down from the top of the ladder. "You can hand me the sign, big brother."

Gunnar lifted the sign. His arm brushed against Abby's shoulder as he handed the sign up to Nathan.

Jolted, Abby raised her eyes to his for an instant before they both turned away—she to get a better grip of the ladder, he to follow the progress of the sign. Meg was looking at her with an odd expression and Abby could guess what she was thinking. Blushing, she said the first thing that popped into her head. "I think this calls for a celebration."

"I think that's a g-great idea," Meg said, looking up at Nathan. "I'll have our c-cook make something special for the occasion."

"That'll be wonderful." Abby squeezed Nathan's arm when he descended the ladder, and wondered about the dark look on Meg's face.

The celebration was held during the afternoon at Madam Rosie's request, so as not to interfere with working hours.

Clod didn't need any persuasion to play his fiddle, and Mom Bull, after spending half the afternoon pouting because she'd not been asked to cater the food, finally agreed to accompany him on her mouth organ, but only after much persuasion on Otis's part.

"D-did you notice how Otis c-can talk M-mom B-bull into just about anything?" Meg whispered in Abby's ear.

"Really?" Abby glanced over at Otis, who was clapping his hands in tune to the music. Mom Bull and Otis? She giggled at the thought.

Nathan grabbed Abby by the hand. "I'm not much of a dancer," he said. "But if you'll do me the honor, I promise not to complain should you crush my toes."

Abby laughed. "That's mighty generous of you. But be forewarned I fully expect to complain should you crush mine."

He slid his arm around her waist. Soon they were two-stepping up and down Main Street to the occasional boom of dynamite blasting in the distance.

"Pretty soon we're going to have something really exciting to celebrate." Abby shouted to be heard over the music.

"We are?" He twirled her around, then drew her by his side and gazed into her face with quiet intensity. "What's that?"

"Why, the railroad, of course."

As if he had overheard their conversation, Clod started making quick raspy jerks on his fiddle and Abby could have sworn a train was coming through town. Mom Bull mimicked the high notes of a fast passenger train on her mouth organ, then imitated the sound of a train clacking along the tracks. Finally, Clod pulled his bow across the top string and mimicked the long lonely sound of a train whistle, then bowed to the applause.

Standing on the boardwalk, Meg and Ginger clapped their hands and stomped their feet. As soon as Clod and Mom Bull started playing a medley of folk songs, Meg cut in. "You can't h-hog the only d-dancer in town."

Meg flung her arms around Nathan's neck. Smiling at the startled look on his face, Abby wandered over to Gunnar, who was helping himself to a glass of sarsaparilla.

"We need to talk," she said.

He regarded her with dark hooded eyes. "You don't have to worry, Abby. What happened between you and me . . . Our secret's safe. Nathan need never know."

Her cheeks grew hot. What in the world did Nathan have to do with anything? "That's not what I wanted to talk about," she said uncertainly. It hadn't occurred to her that he would reveal their secret, or even that he might think she meant to discuss something he'd made clear was of no consequence to him. "I—"

Nathan surprised her by coming up from behind and slipping a possessive arm around her waist. "What are you two looking so serious about?"

Abby gently pushed his arm away. "Gunnar and I were about to discuss the search for my uncle."

Nathan looked from one to the other. "I apologize," he said, sounding petulant. "I thought this was a party."

"It *is* a p-party," Meg said, tugging at his arm. Nathan laughed and shrugged his shoulders good-naturedly before allowing Meg to pull him away.

Gunnar's jaw tightened as he finished filling the glass in his hand. "I haven't forgotten about your uncle, Abby. Or my promise to help you find him."

Abby took a deep breath to steady her nerves. Trying to act normal in Gunnar's presence was the hardest thing she ever had to do. If it wasn't for her uncle, she'd leave town and put as much distance as possible between Gunnar and herself. It was the only way she could think to make the pain go away. "I thought perhaps you'd rather not continue the search."

"Why would you think that?"

She could think of a lot of reasons, all of them personal, and not one of them was she willing to discuss.

When she didn't reply, he set his glass down. "You

can't give up, Abby. Not yet. Now that the roads aren't so muddy, I plan to go to Cripple Creek tomorrow to ask around. No one's responded to the notices I placed in the newspapers, but you never know. Not everyone reads the paper."

"I want to go with you." When he made no reply, she pressed. "Please, Gunnar. I need to be actively involved in the search."

"I won't be taking you away from your new shop, will I?"

She was angered and confused by the note of concern in his voice. *Don't do this to me,* she cried silently. *Don't ignore me one minute and act like you care the next.* "It's not as if I have any customers."

"It would probably be better if I went alone. You know what happened last time." His voice sounded strangely wistful, but his eyes remained dark and hooded, letting nothing in and even less out. She had the strangest feeling he was both pulling her toward him and pushing her away. No wonder her emotions were tied up in a knot.

"Last time?" she squeaked out. *When you took me in your arms and kissed me?* Was that the time he referred to? She didn't know and she wasn't about to ask.

"With the Indians."

She swallowed hard. "Oh." Feeling utterly foolish, and on the verge of tears, she gazed at Meg and Nathan as they danced up and down the street. "There hasn't been any more trouble with the Utes since, has there?"

"No," he admitted. "But that doesn't mean there won't be in the future. Especially as the railroad advances closer."

"I'll take my chances," she said.

She saw the disapproval in his eyes, but he didn't try to talk her out of going.

"I'll have two horses ready in the morning." His voice sounded so normal, so matter-of-fact, she felt a squeezing hurt inside.

"At the usual time?" she asked, referring to the way he tried to trick her the last time.

He stared at her unflinching. "Let's make it seven, this time. No tricks." To prove his intention, he handed her a glass of sarsaparilla.

She tried, really tried, to keep her emotions in check. But when his fingers brushed against her hand, her heart took to beating like a drum, and her pulse took to leaping around until it was almost impossible to keep her feet planted on the ground. "Thank you," she murmured, taking a quick sip.

Her cheeks burning with unwelcome warmth, she glanced across the way to find Nathan looking in their direction, his face almost as glum as his brother's.

She forced a smile. "How about another dance?" she called, setting her glass down. Clod was fiddling as fast as his bow would fly. Besides, it was time for Meg to head back to the Opera House.

Nathan's brooding look disappeared as she fought off her depression, lifted the hem of her skirt, and danced toward him.

She hoped no one else would notice how hollow her laughter was, or guess that her gaiety was a sham, designed to hide a broken heart.

Wondering if Gunnar could see through her facade, she glanced back, only to find him gone.

# Chapter 24

Abby awoke abruptly, her heart beating so fast she could hardly breathe. It was the dream again, that same terrible dream in which she saw her uncle beckoning from the distance. In her dreams, she ran toward him, but try as she might, she never could catch him, and eventually he was gone for good.

Shaken by the lingering effects of the nightmare, she walked barefooted to the window. Although it was too dark to see the face of her watch, she could pick out two horses in front of the sheriff's office. Evidently, Gunnar meant to keep his word. She quickly dressed and hurried to Mom Bull's for breakfast. Already, Gunnar was sitting at a corner table, drinking coffee and reading a week-old Denver newspaper.

Mom Bull poured Abby a cup of Arbuckle's coffee. "Another early bird." She set the cup on an empty table and hurried back to her cookstove.

Abby picked up the cup and walked over to Gunnar. "May I join you?"

He shrugged as if it didn't matter and nodded his head at the empty chair. He then buried his head behind the newspaper.

She sat down and stared at the bold headlines. That fool politician Wrightwood had made the front page. It seems he resigned from office to become a monk, all because of some religious experience. Abby wondered if he'd had his experience before or after the brawl at the Opera House.

She drank her cup of coffee and ate every last bite

of the flapjacks and bacon Mom Bull set in front of her. Not once during the time it took her to swallow the unpalatable food did he bother to look up at her.

Finally she could stand it no more. "Are we going to spend the entire day ignoring each other?"

The newspaper lowered, revealing his eyes. "I'm not ignoring you."

She sighed. "Gunnar, whatever happened before . . . I'm willing to forget everything, if you are. It would make it so much easier for us to work together."

His eyes brimmed with unreadable emotions and for a moment she feared she'd made matters worse. Finally he folded the paper in two and tossed it aside. "It makes sense." He stood. "Shall we get started?"

Nodding mutely, she watched him walk to the door, and fought against the burning tears that threatened to give away her emotions.

They left Mom Bull's just as the hot rays of golden sunlight spilled over the tops of the tall gently swaying pine trees. It was going to be a blazer.

"Do you think we'll have any trouble with the Utes?" she called from atop her horse.

The huskiness in her voice caused Gunnar to look up sharply. His haste cost him dearly, for he'd not braced himself. Without having taken the time to harden his heart, his soul, his very being, he was struck anew by the depth of his feelings for her. He was a man with no weapons in the middle of a battlefield. His only choice was to surrender.

"I hope not," he said, thinking how beautiful she looked, framed against the mountains and the sky. Her golden hair tumbled carelessly down her back, with the slightest wisps framing her face. Her lovely blue eyes held a haunting sadness that made him resolve anew to find her uncle. Her soft curving mouth tightened as he watched her.

He mounted Lucky. The spirited horse circled about and nodded its head. "If we do happen to meet up with the Utes, I'd be eternally grateful if you'd refrain from commenting on their war paint." With a loud "Gid-up," he galloped away.

Abby made a face behind his back and gave chase. It promised to be a long and difficult day.

The journey to Victor was uneventful. The sun was directly overhead by the time they followed a well-traveled dirt road. They stopped at the various mining camps that clung to the side of the mountain like fragile weeds, and made inquiries.

They reached the bustling little town of Victor just after midday. At the foot of Battle Mountain, the town was hot and dusty and was comprised of a few hastily built false-fronted pine buildings. Long lines of miners snaked from the numerous eating houses and horse-drawn water tanks. The men, some covered with dust and grime, cast appreciative glances at Abby.

"Any of you know a Randall Parker?" Gunnar called out.

The men shuffled and bantered her uncle's name among themselves. "Parker? Anyone know a Randall Parker?" The miners shrugged in turn and shook their heads. Abby and Gunnar continued on through town, passing through Squaw's Gulch on the way to Cripple Creek.

Blinding rays of sunlight danced upon the many galvanized roofs of the mining companies strewn along the way. Closer to town, canvas homes dotted the bald hills. A mule-driven wagon rumbled past them, followed by the Hundley stagecoach pulled by a team of six lively horses.

Abby was surprised to see small children playing among the canvas houses. On the outskirts of town, clapboard structures came into view, some with fine trimmed porches and bay windows.

Abby had no idea Cripple Creek was such a large town. Her amazement grew as they rode past the newly constructed train station to Bennett Street, which took them to the very center of town. Two- and three-story false-faced buildings lined the eighty-foot-wide street.

Traffic was nearly at a standstill. Horse-drawn vehicles of every description vied for a place to park. Horses, mules, and pushcarts were forced onto the boardwalk. Scampering out of harm's way, pedestrians raised their fists and shouted obscenities.

Gunnar tethered their horses to the wooden railing in front of the hotel. "Let's talk to the desk clerk."

"My uncle wouldn't stay at a hotel," she said. "Not unless the weather was bad or he was unable to find a suitable place to camp."

"It won't hurt to try," Gunnar said.

Abby followed him into the lobby of the Palace Hotel. The sleepy-eyed clerk listened politely to the description of Abby's uncle, then yawned and shrugged his bony shoulder. "Sounds like a hundred other men who've come through those doors."

"Let's go," Gunnar said, clearly disgusted with the man's lack of interest. "Maybe the ladies on Myers Street will have some answers." He glanced at her. "The Old Homestead, as they call it, caters only to rich prospectors."

"You mean millionaires?" she asked, intrigued.

"Exactly. Madam Hazel Vernon has high standards about who she lets onto her premises. She refuses to let an armed man enter her establishment. I suggest you keep that knife of yours out of sight."

They rode their horses past the numerous houses of ill repute that lined the "row." On the north side of the street stood one-woman shacks made of weathered pine. Women of all nationalities filled the doorways, some making overt gestures.

"How disgusting," Abby said, shocked. "At least Madam Rosie's girls never make a public display of themselves."

"Rosie takes care of her girls. These women are more or less on their own. If they don't do business, they don't eat."

Embarrassed for having judged the women without regard for their desperate and needy circumstances,

Abby flushed. She knew what it was like to be hungry. Soul-searing hungry. The kind of hunger that could drive an otherwise honest person to thievery. She wasn't proud of the times she'd pinched a loaf of bread or snared an apple from a grocer or fruit cart to abate the gnawing hunger pains. But this selling of one's body puzzled her. Could a person really be *that* hungry?

She stared into the disfigured face of one woman and was reminded of the look in Ruby's eyes upon seeing her own scarless face in the mirror.

She halted her horse in front of the dark-skinned woman, meaning to offer her some fragrant soap as a gift. But the woman disappeared inside her shack before Abby had a chance to make her intentions known.

Abby trotted her horse next to Gunnar's. "I wish I could do something to help these women. There has to be something else they can do besides sell their bodies."

"This is the only life these women know," Gunnar said. "Some, given the choice, would probably hesitate to leave."

She thought of Meg and knew he spoke the truth. She remembered the days she'd stood on Thieves Corner staring at the fine carriages in the distance and hating herself for not having the courage to leave the place she'd called home. How strange that the unknown held a far greater fear than the familiar, no matter how horrifying the present circumstances might be.

Gunnar tied both their horses to the wooden railing in front of the building known as the Homestead, and rang the bell.

A Chinese houseboy showed them into the elegantly furnished parlor, replete with rich velvet upholstery and gilded picture frames. Unlike Madam Rosie's, this house was furnished with only the finest of European silk wallpapers, tapestries, and carpets, and there wasn't a faded or worn piece of fabric in the place.

No sooner had they sat upon the elegant velvet sofa

than Madam Vernon came sweeping into the room, dressed in a surprisingly modest and tailored silk skirt and shirtwaist. If it weren't for her bright red lip rouge and elaborately upswept coiffure, Abby would have mistaken her for one of the many office workers employed in the Boston business district.

Gunnar stood and introduced them. Madam Vernon regarded Abby with surprise. It wasn't often that a woman visited the premises. "Have you an appointment?" she asked, taking note of the sheriff's badge on Gunnar's vest.

"I'm here on official business," he explained.

She regarded him coolly. "You don't have official business here. I pay my sixteen dollars and make sure the girls pay their four."

Gunnar looked taken aback by the woman's hostility. "I've no doubt you're a law-abiding citizen, Miss Vernon."

"You bet I'm a law-abiding citizen, Sheriff. Now you can take your official business elsewhere. I don't answer questions and I don't name names."

Abby rose to her feet. "It's about my uncle," she said beseechingly. "His name is Randall Parker. He's a—"

"I know who he is!" Madam Vernon snapped, startling Abby into silence. "I paid the scoundrel good money to send me a case of French perfume and I never heard from him again."

Abby's heart skipped a beat. Her uncle had made it to Cripple Creek, then. "I'm sorry about your money. I'll make certain every penny you paid is returned. My uncle would never do anything dishonest. That's why I know something awful has happened to him." Abby's voice broke and she quickly pulled a handkerchief out of her reticule.

Gunnar moved to her side and slipped an arm around her shoulders. He meant to comfort her, but his closeness only made matters worse, for it only reminded her that her uncle wasn't the only one lost to her. "Miss Parker has not heard from her uncle in many months. If you could tell us when you last saw him, it would be most helpful."

Madam Vernon gave Abby a sympathetic look. "I'm sorry about your uncle. I just naturally assumed he'd taken my money under false pretenses. Oh, dear." Her gaze traveled from Abby to Gunnar. "My policy's not to divulge information."

"Please. It would mean so much to me."

The woman hesitated, but after a moment she shrugged in resignation and rose to her feet. "Very well." She walked over to her desk and flipped through the pages of her ledger. "Here it is." Abby and Gunnar leaned over the desk to better see the entry she indicated. "I paid your uncle for our order on September nineteenth of last year. He said he would have it to me no later than March."

Abby inhaled. "That means he was here the day after his appointment with Madam Rosie."

"Is that significant?" Madam Vernon asked.

"I don't know." Abby stared up at Gunnar, who was jotting something down on his writing tablet. "We know my uncle saw Madam Rosie on Tuesday and promised to return on Thursday. He never kept his second appointment."

Madam Vernon closed her ledger. "Since he was in Cripple Creek on Wednesday, do you think something might have happened to him here?"

"That's what we're going to find out," Gunnar said.

They thanked Madam Vernon and left, stopping at several cribs along the way to inquire about Abby's uncle. No one else seemed to know him and, as one woman pointed out, most couldn't afford the luxury of special-ordering cosmetics from "no overpriced peddler."

The sheriff of Cripple Creek offered even less help. A stout cigar-smoking man who walked with a limp, he made it clear that he wasn't responsible for anyone who did business on the row. "As long as those women pay their taxes and don't set foot in town except during designated times, I don't have much call to visit the row. As for keeping track of the patrons—"

"My uncle was not a patron!" Abby said angrily. The sheriff reminded her of the corrupt lawmen in and around Thieves Corner. "He was an honest business-man."

The sheriff sneered. "It's been my experience that honest businessmen don't disappear in thin air."

"I wonder that you've had experience with honest people," she retorted.

"I think we better go." Gunnar pushed her toward the door. "Thank you for your help, Sheriff," he added, his voice thick with irony. "I hope one day to return the courtesy."

Abby's depression increased as they left Cripple Creek. Halfway to Dangling Rope, they veered off to the Butterfly mines to talk to the owner. Buzz Camp-bell was a portly man with a broad red face and an unkempt mustache, who stood legs apart, hands across his chest, glaring at them as they approached. Abby shuddered. The man would look menacing even in Thieves Corner.

"We're looking for a man by the name of Randall Parker," Gunnar explained. "Have you heard of him?"

The man's face grew darker as if he resented the intrusion. "Can't say that I have." He walked away without so much as a backward glance.

"He was a peddler," Gunnar called after him to no avail, but he did attract the attention of a small gather-ing of miners gathered around a well. "Sold women's cosmetics."

A burly man with frizzy red hair and a beard to match stepped forward. "Funny you should mention women's cosmetics. I found a canvas knapsack a time back hanging on the side of a tree south of here. I remember it looked like someone's camp. Thought I'd found myself a treasure trove, but all that was inside was a bunch of ladies' face paint."

"That had to be my uncle's!" Abby said excitedly.

"What did you do with the pack?" Gunnar asked.

"Tossed it aside," the man replied. "Didn't have no use for it personally." This brought a round of laughter from his co-workers.

"Could you tell me where you tossed it?" Gunnar persisted.

The man scratched his head. "All's I remember, it was somewhere along the creek." He pointed. "No more than a mile or so away."

Abby's heart fluttered anxiously. "I can't tell you how much this means to me."

The man's face grew as red as his beard. "I'm always happy to help a lady. If you ever need more help, just ask for Hoss."

She gave him a brilliant smile. "Thank you, Hoss." The man's face grew redder, and the other men took to needling him.

"Much obliged," Gunnar said, nudging his horse forward. Gunnar took off in a hurry and, thinking his behavior a bit abrupt, she waved her thanks to the men and galloped after him.

"You could have been a bit friendlier back there," she called as she reached his side.

"You were friendly enough for both of us," he replied, his profile hard and rigid.

"Gunnar?"

He turned his head. A probing query lit his eyes, but the look on his face was forbidding. "We're going to have to start back soon. If we're going to check out that campsite, we'd better hurry."

It took less than fifteen minutes to find the area described by the miner. They dismounted where the road split and walked along the bank of the fast-running creek.

The area was dotted with fire rings. The hot smoking ashes of a recent fire still glowed from the center of a lava rock pit. Obviously the area was a popular one and anything left behind by Abby's uncle was probably long gone.

Gunnar covered the hot ashes with dirt and checked around the base of each tree, looking for the remains of a canvas knapsack. Nothing. He walked the length of the campsite, while Abby crisscrossed it. Between the two of them, they probably covered every square inch. Frustrated, he kicked a rock aside and saw something half buried in the dirt. He bent over and picked up a piece of gray fabric. It was a man's sock.

He recalled Abby washing out her stockings around the campfire. The vision brought an involuntary smile to his face. Prettiest toes he ever did see.

He shook off the dirt. The sock had been neatly darned. Chances were the man had a wife—or maybe even a niece.

"Did you find something?" Abby asked.

"I'm not sure." He handed her the sock. She stared at it as if looking at a ghost. She swayed slightly and he grabbed her by the elbow to steady her.

"Are you sure, Abby? Are you sure it's his?"

She lifted her lashes, her eyes glistening with tears. "My Aunt Ida knitted this sock. After she died, he refused to part with any of the socks she made him, no matter how worn. I darned it for him. Right here, see?" She held her hand to her mouth, muffling her sobs.

He folded her in his arms. "Don't cry, Abby." He pressed his lips to her forehead, absorbing the sweet fragrance of her hair and skin. "We'll find him. I swear to you."

She sobbed quietly, her head on his shoulder, her body trembling next to his until her pain and grief were as much his as they were hers. He had no idea how long he held her. Time, suddenly, had no meaning, and he would have held her indefinitely had she not pulled away, leaving him feeling lost and his arms empty.

She brushed away the tears and looked up at him. He honestly thought he was going to drown in the softness of her liquid blue eyes. Wanted to.

"I'm sorry," she whispered. "I don't know what came

over me. . . . The socks . . ." Her voice trailed off and she strode quickly to her horse. "We better head back." This time her voice sounded nearly normal, with only the slightest tremor.

Not wanting her to act brave for his benefit, he cleared the distance between them. He hesitated a moment before reaching out and swinging her around to face him. "Abby, don't pretend with me."

The look on her face at that moment nearly tore him apart. "Pretend?" she whispered. "Like you pretend with me?"

A curse escaped him as he crushed her to him and hungrily covered her mouth.

The powerful force he unleashed on her brought an equally powerful response. Their warm, sweet lips and hot tongues worked in a harmonic, though no less frantic pace.

He fumbled with the top button of her waistshirt. Realizing he was going to have to give more attention to the tiny buttons, he pulled his mouth away and looked deep into her eyes. He wanted her to feel what he felt, want what he wanted, know what he knew.

"I . . . I don't think we should . . . not here," she said.

Reality hit him like a fist. He realized how close they were to the main road. Anyone passing by would spot them. Miners. Railroad crew. *Nathan.*

That last thought startled him. It was as if someone had suddenly stabbed him in the back with a knife. Nathan had no reason to be on that road. He was nowhere near the Butterfly mines. He wouldn't ever know, dammit! Never!

Gunnar turned to his horse and hung over the saddle. He couldn't look at her, for if he did, he wouldn't be responsible for his actions. To surrender to the burning desire that pulsed through his body would be the same as firing a loaded gun into his brother's heart.

"Gunnar?"

He closed his eyes tight. Lord, this was killing him! "It'll soon be dark," he said by way of explanation.

"We'd better start back." He dragged himself into his saddle and waited for her to do likewise.

When he finally got the nerve to look back at her, she looked dazed and confused, her lips red and moist from his kiss. He focused his attention straight ahead and wondered in the name of God how he was going to keep away from her after today.

# Chapter 25

The next day Gunnar sat in his office staring down at Parker's woolen sock. He fingered the tiny neat stitches, the result of Abby's handiwork. He'd been tempted—was now tempted—to go to her and finish what they had begun twice before.

Only one thing kept him from following the dictates of his heart. Only one thing could.

Nathan! Just thinking about his brother filled him with unspeakable guilt that was far stronger than any guilt he'd felt in the past. *How can I tell you about my own feelings for Abby? How can I not?*

He dropped the sock in a desk drawer and reached for his hat just as the door swung open.

"Going somewhere, big brother?" Nathan walked into the office dressed in a pin-striped suit and a derby hat. He looked like one of the big city politicians he detested.

"Well, now, if you don't look all spiffed up." It looked like Nathan had purchased some new clothes while he was in Denver. "Why are you all dressed up?"

Nathan grinned. "I thought since I was the mayor, I'd best dress the part."

Nathan sat down on the ladder-back chair in front of Gunnar's desk, taking care not to disturb the creases in his pants. "You're looking at the new Nathan Kincaid. I decided it's high time I settled down and lived a respectable life."

"Settle down? You?" Gunnar set his hat on the desk.

It wasn't so long ago he would have given his right arm to hear Nathan say this very thing.

"I told you my feelings for Abby."

Gunnar felt himself sink into a dark deep abyss. "I believe you said something to that effect."

"Something?" Nathan looked surprised. "I guess I wasn't as clear as I thought. Maybe I didn't want to admit the extent of my feelings until I knew what my chances were. You know, of her loving me back."

Gunnar lowered himself into his chair. "Have you talked to her? Told her how you feel?"

"Not in so many words. But I have this feeling. I can't explain it. You know when you're with someone and things seem to feel right? She's got to feel it, too, don't you think?"

"It's hard to tell. Abby . . ." Her name seemed to stick in his throat. It was as if he wanted to hold on to whatever part of her he could, if only the sound of her name. He cleared his throat and pressed his fingers together. "She's not like most women."

"I know. Maybe that's why I love her so." Nathan fingered his hat, his eyes shining bright as tinfoil. "I never thought I could feel about a woman like I feel about her. She makes me feel wanted and important. She brings out the best in me. She's shown me life can be beautiful. I'm a changed man because of her."

Gunnar sat perfectly still, afraid to move for fear of giving away his own feelings. Everything Nathan said applied equally to him. Conflicting emotions nearly ripped him apart. His love for his brother ran deep—so deep that he couldn't really resent or begrudge Nathan whatever happiness or joy came his way. But it hurt, dammit, to hear another man talk about her this way. Hurt to high heaven. "Nathan, you know I've always wanted what was best for you."

"I know, big brother. Even though I didn't want it for myself. But things are different now. I'm going to make you proud of me. Just wait and see."

"I *am* proud of you."

Nathan grew misty-eyed. "I can't tell you how good that makes me feel. Especially after everything we've been through."

Gunnar stared at his brother, ashamed of the emotions that seethed like hot lava below the surface. Jealousy and rage filled him. Heartache and despair depleted him. But the most cruel irony of all was the look of joy and pleasure on Nathan's face. Dear God, how could he deny his brother this chance at happiness?

"Nathan . . ." He weighed his words carefully. "It's possible she might not return your feelings."

The hopeless, shattered look that crossed Nathan's face was almost identical to the bleak expression on his face the day their mother had deserted him. The look linked the man to the child of long ago. All the grief, all the guilt that had haunted Gunnar these many years came back to haunt him anew.

"She loves me," Nathan said simply. "I'm convinced of it." Nathan moved restlessly, as if he had something pressing to do. "The least you can do is look happy for me."

"I *am* happy for you. Of course I'm happy for you . . . but . . ."

"But?" Nathan regarded his brother with fond tolerance. "You think I'm going to get hurt again."

Hurt. Gunnar pounced on the word like a cat on an injured bird. He'd once thought he knew everything there was to know about hurting. He'd thought wrong.

Gunnar stared unseeing at the pencil that had somehow found its way into his hand and snapped it in two. "It's a possibility."

"Not this time." Nathan sounded so sure, so confident, his voice resonated with vibrancy.

Gunnar tossed the pencil pieces into the wastepaper basket. "Abby's had a tough life. She needs someone who will give her a stable home."

"And you don't think I can do that?"

"You've never stayed in one place long enough to call it home."

"Dangling Rope is my home," Nathan said.

"For now."

"This is different, big brother." His left foot resting on his knee, Nathan played with the cuff of his pants. "When gold was discovered at Cripple Creek and everyone left the town I'd built from the ground up, I felt as if I'd been deserted again. I was angry, and all that crap from the past—I don't know. It drove me crazy."

"So you started drinking again."

"Yeah. I drank myself into a stupor." Nathan gave a bitter laugh. "Strange, isn't it? The very things I hated about our parents are the very same things I hate most about myself. I could have left like the others. I could have left, just like our dear mother left."

"Why didn't you?"

"It occurred to me one night when I was feeling sorry for myself that everyone who remained in this town had been deserted, one way or another. Otis's wife had left him. Ruby was abandoned by her mother after the fire. Ginger came from an abusive home and was once beaten so severely by a stepfather, she was left to die."

"I didn't know. You'd think she'd have nothing to do with men after a background like that."

"I guess we all have different ways of dealing with pain," Nathan said.

"Maybe so." Gunnar said, thinking of Ginger. Who would have guessed that behind the red-painted lips and bold dresses was a woman in pain? He thought of his mother; had she, too, been in pain? Was that why she wore those flamboyant clothes and those dreadful cosmetics? To hide the pain?

"It's people like Ginger and Otis and even Mom Bull who made me decide to stay and fight for them, like Mother never fought for me."

"And Abby? Where does she fit in?"

The anger and bitterness on Nathan's face faded and

was replaced by a glow that made Gunnar die yet another death. "She's not like any other woman I've ever known. But we're so much alike, I swear to God. She calls herself a Traveling Lady, but I think this is her way of protecting herself from rejection. Think about it, Gunnar. Abby and me, we both like people to think we're roamers at heart. And do you know why? Because we have some cockamamie idea that it'll give us an escape should we have to face rejection again."

Gunnar hated knowing that Nathan understood something about Abby that had escaped his own understanding.

"I'm going to ask her to be my wife. I hope when that day comes, you'll be my best man."

Gunnar pressed his fingers together hard. Things were moving too fast. He had a responsibility here, to Nathan. "What if she doesn't love you?"

"Is it so hard for you to believe a woman could love me?"

"That's not what I'm saying. I think you should slow down. You haven't known her all that long. Besides, she's trying to find her uncle and start a new business. She might not be ready to rush into marriage."

Nathan's frown faded. "You're right, big brother." Nathan stood and placed his hat on his head. "I'll give her some time, but not much." He gave Gunnar a crooked smile. "So what do you say? You gonna be my best man?"

Gunnar forced the words out. "What do you think?"

Nathan's smile broadened. "One day, I hope I can return the favor." He left, closing the door after him.

Gunnar waited until he was certain his brother was out of sight before leaving the office. Abby called to him from across the street, but he couldn't face her, not now, not after agreeing to be the best man at her wedding.

He swung into his saddle and raced out of town, refusing to look in her direction.

The hooves of his horse thundered against a ground

packed hard by the last rains. Somehow his muddled mind conjured up some crazy mixed-up idea that if he rode fast enough, far enough, long enough he could quiet his raging dark thoughts.

He lowered his head as his horse raced beneath a series of low-hanging branches. Maybe he'd put too much stock in those kisses of hers. *Just because she acted as if she wanted me to do a whole lot more than just kiss her doesn't necessarily mean much.* They'd been stranded on the mountaintop the first time, and the second time she wasn't herself. Who could blame her? He'd just found her uncle's sock. She needed comforting and he was more than happy to provide it. He would have provided a lot more had she let him.

The thing he had to think about was Nathan's happiness. He should be happy for the boy. *Was* happy for him. This was the very thing Gunnar had hoped for all these years. Someone for Nathan to love. It was an answer to a prayer.

But why did it have to be Abby he loved? Abby with her bright smile and dancing blue eyes? Why did it have to be the one woman in all the world whom Gunnar himself could love? Did love. Would always love.

# Chapter 26

Abby paced in front of her salon waiting for Gunnar. It worried her the way he raced out of town earlier.

Holy blazes, where could he have been going in such a fired-up hurry? He didn't even look at her when she'd called to him. He must have heard her. How could he not?

Upon returning from Cripple Creek the previous night, they had agreed to ride today to the Loser's Gulch mines area. It was crazy the way they'd made plans, standing a few feet apart with only the dark between them, and acting as if nothing untoward had happened.

She berated herself for playing such games. What was the matter with him? One minute he made her feel like the most beautiful and cherished woman in the world, the next minute he ignored her. Enough was enough. If Gunnar Kincaid couldn't make up his mind, then she would make it up for him. They were finished. From now on it would be business between them—nothing else! It would break her heart even more to pretend she had no feelings for him. Oh, Lord, it would kill her. But she couldn't continue to let herself be turned inside out, upside down. Not anymore.

She lifted her neck chain and checked her watch. It was a half hour past the time they'd agreed to meet. It wasn't like Gunnar to be late.

She spun around at the sound of a horse. Despite her vow to try to control her feelings, her heart thudded and her pulse raced as she narrowed her eyes on the advancing rider, trying to make out Gunnar. Only it was Nathan who rode toward her, not Gunnar, and there was no denying the disappointment she felt. She waved, but her heart wasn't in it. "Have you seen your brother?"

Nathan tugged on the reins, and his horse reared back on its hind legs before coming to a standstill. Grinning at her like a mischievous schoolboy, Nathan leaned on the horn of his saddle. "Not since this morning. Why?"

"He rode out of town in a hurry. Do you suppose there's a problem with the railroad?"

"Not that I know of."

"We planned to ride out to the Loser's Gulch mine to make inquiries about my uncle. It's not like Gunnar to take off without telling anyone where he's going."

Nathan narrowed his eyes in the direction of the railroad. "If you like, I'll ride out to the railroad camp and see if he's there."

"I'll go with you." Abby rushed across the street and quickly mounted Logger. Soon she and Nathan were racing out of town, the sun at their backs.

It took nearly two hours to reach the summit of Tucker's Pass. The echoing sound of pounding steel rose from the canyon below as the crew of the narrow-gauge Florence and Cripple Creek Railroad worked at a furious pace in a race to meet their deadlines.

The loud clangs echoed along the hard granite walls and deep canyons surrounding the rugged terrain. The low drone of the railroad workers floated upward in song. Abby couldn't make out the words from this distance, but she caught the energy and excitement as the men worked their way ever closer to Dangling Rope.

Abby was amazed at the size of the railroad camp.

"That's a work train," Nathan explained, pointing to the dozen or so cars that were attached to the narrow-gauge engine. "Each car serves a different purpose. One is a blacksmith shop. Another stores tools. The railroad workers bunk in that middle car. The one right behind it is the commissary."

"It's like a small city," Abby said, truly impressed. Behind the work engine were two flatcars loaded with spikes and rails, bolts and fishplates.

She watched four men carry a long shiny rail to the front of the line. The track boss shouted "Down!" and the men dropped it in place. The first workers were followed by a crew of gaugers who measured the distance between the rails. Close behind were the spikers swinging sledgehammers, the sun glistening on their bronzed bare backs.

"Are they going to reach Dangling Rope in time?" she asked. It didn't seem as if it were possible, considering the ground yet to be covered.

"As long as they continue to lay a mile of track a day, they should reach us in time. It'll be cutting it close," Nathan admitted. "Let's hope we don't have any more trouble with the Utes."

Abby searched the basin of the canyon, hoping to catch sight of Gunnar or his horse. "I don't see him. Is it possible we missed him?"

"This is the only road leading into town. I can't imagine us missing him, unless he didn't follow the trail."

"Well, I can!" Abby said. "He probably went to the mine without me. Of all the low-down . . ."

Nathan's eyes warmed with amusement. "Now, calm yourself down, Abby. First of all we don't know that's where he's at. Second, if he did go to the mine, then he probably had a good reason for wanting to go alone."

Abby wasn't eager to concede Nathan might have a point. "He better have a good reason."

"He's an honorable man, my brother," Nathan said quietly. "It's taken me a long time to realize that."

Surprised by the emotion in his voice, Abby studied his face. "The first night I was in town, I stayed at Gunnar's cabin. I overheard the two of you argue."

The brim of Nathan's hat shaded his eyes, but the

pain reflected in their depths was very much in evidence. "Then you know about our mother."

Feeling foolish for having originally jumped to the wrong conclusion, she nodded. "Do you still blame Gunnar for taking her away?"

Nathan took a long time to answer. "I don't know who I blame."

The tortured look on his face made her regret her probing question. "We don't have to talk about this, Nathan."

"I want you to understand. . . . It's important to me." He fell silent for a moment before continuing. "Maybe I was just plain unlovable. Maybe that's why she left."

Abby inhaled. The two brothers were alike in one regard; neither one was willing to blame his mother for what she'd done. Abby reached out and stroked Nathan's arm. "You know that's not true, Nathan. You've got many fine qualities that make you very lovable."

He leaned toward her. "Do you mean that, Abby? Do you really mean it?"

His earnestness made her smile. Sometimes he seemed so endearingly young, almost boyish, like a colt just discovering the world. "Of course I mean it. Come on. I'll race you back to town!"

Gunnar had just left Abby's salon looking for her when he heard the horses. Standing in the middle of the street, he waited until the riders came into view.

Abby's horse was ahead, with Nathan close behind.

Gunnar's heart lurched at the sight of her, astride her horse, laughing as carefree as a child at Christmas. Her sunbonnet had fallen to her back, its shiny blue ribbons still tied beneath her chin. Her long golden hair blew carelessly in the wind, her cheeks flushed a pretty pink.

For a moment he watched her unnoticed. He stood absorbing the sight and sound of her like a hungry man denied food for far too long, recalling every time she'd smiled at him. Maybe that's why it hurt so much when she looked at him from atop her horse and the smile died on her lips.

Hurt? Damn, that was the least of it. He felt as if someone had suddenly stepped on him and crushed him to the ground.

Behind her, Nathan lifted his hand in greeting, then dismounted. Nathan gazed up at Abby, as if sharing some delicious secret with her, before turning to Gunnar. "We looked for you at the railroad camp." When Gunnar made no reply, Nathan glanced up at Abby, said something about a cup of coffee, then quickly walked into Mom Bull's.

After Nathan had left, Abby turned to Gunnar. Her eyes flashed angrily. "Why didn't you tell me you had no intention of taking me up to Loser's Gulch? I don't like being treated like a child!"

"I'm sorry, Abby. I told you I have every intention of helping you find your uncle and I mean it."

She studied his face, puzzled by the look he gave her. It was as if they were strangers. "Is that why you failed to keep our appointment?"

"I said I was sorry, Abby."

"I don't want your apologies, Gunnar. I thought . . . when you raced out of town, I thought something was wrong."

Gunnar gazed at the mountains in the distance. "Nothing's wrong," he said, wishing she'd stop looking at him with those soft blue questioning eyes. He could handle her anger; in fact, welcomed it. It made what he had to do so much easier. But seeing the look in her eyes, hearing the huskiness in her voice—it was killing him.

"I wanted to talk to the miners before they went home for the day. It was a waste of time. No one knows anything about your uncle." With that brisk, almost curt explanation, he walked away as quickly as he could without breaking into a full run.

# Chapter 27

Early the following afternoon, a woman entered Abby's complexion salon. Despite the heat, the woman was wrapped in a blue cloak, her face covered with a veil. "Are you Miss Parker?" she asked, her voice low.

Abby set her mixing spoon down and wiped her hands on a towel. "I am," she replied. "How may I help you?"

The woman cast an anxious glance over her shoulder before moving away from the door. "I'm Mrs. Campbell." This time she spoke louder, the soft drawl of her southern accent seeming to contradict the urgency in her voice. "I heard you can perform miracles with your cosmetics."

"I'm not sure about the miracle part. Campbell?" Abby recognized the name. "Your husband owns the Butterfly gold mines, doesn't he?"

For a fleeting moment, Mrs. Campbell had the look of a frightened deer. Thinking she was about to flee, Abby walked around the counter and beckoned the woman to sit.

Mrs. Campbell remained standing. "I'd rather you didn't mention my being here." Her voice held a hysterical edge. After a pause, she gave a nervous little laugh. "You know how men are."

"You needn't worry, Mrs. Campbell. My customers' names are my business and no one else's. Please take a seat at the counter."

Mrs. Campbell hesitated so long, Abby thought she'd

changed her mind. "Would you rather come back another time?"

The woman shook her head and sat upon one of the stools in front of the bar.

Abby moved the hood of the cloak away from Mrs. Campbell's cheek. Shocked and horrified at the sight that greeted her, she drew her hand away. The whole left side of the woman's face was swollen and bruised. "Your face . . ."

"I was thrown from my horse," Mrs. Campbell explained quickly. "So stupid of me, really. I've been around horses pretty near all my life. You'd think I'd know better than to get myself thrown."

"Anyone can get thrown from a horse," Abby said. "Have you seen a doctor?"

"A doctor?" The woman looked startled. "Why, there's no sense in bothering the doctor. Poor Dr. Ashbrooke has his hands filled with sick people. Besides, what could the doctor possibly do? It'll heal soon enough. Meanwhile, I thought . . ." She glanced down at her hands.

"I think we should wait until the swelling goes down before we try cosmetics," Abby said. "Perhaps in a day or two—"

"No, I can't wait that long!" Abby was surprised by the adamant tone in her voice. Upon seeing the alarm on Abby's face, the woman quickly apologized. "Please forgive me. You see, if my husband sees me like this, he'll forbid me to ride my horse."

"I really think we should wait. You could get an infection."

"Please." The woman's fingers pressed into Abby's arm, her eyes beseeching. "It looks worse than it is." The young woman looked almost desperate, and close to tears. "I bruise very easily. Sometimes I'm covered all over in bruises. My friend Emma-Lou says I need a good tonic to purify the blood. Please, you can't imagine how much it would mean to me."

Abby reluctantly agreed. "Very well." Much to Abby's

relief, the woman seemed to relax slightly, though her gaze kept darting toward the door. "Please tell me if I hurt you."

Mrs. Campbell looked visibly relieved when Abby began setting out her supplies. "I'm really much obliged to you, Miss Parker."

Though the afternoon sun slanted through the windows, Abby lit a lantern for more light and studied the texture of Mrs. Campbell's skin. At first glance the woman appeared tired, almost haggard in appearance. In reality, she was younger than Abby had first supposed, probably not past her early twenties.

Like most of the women who lived in mining towns, her complexion was dull, her brown hair hung limp and lifeless. But these were minor problems that could be easily remedied. The swollen bruised cheek offered far more of a challenge.

Abby reached for a clean sponge. "You have a very pretty face."

The woman glanced away and blushed. "You don't have to say nice things to me, Miss Parker. I know I'm not much to look at."

Abby's hand stilled. "Who told you that?"

"Ain't no one has to tell me. All's I have to do is look in the mirror."

"Well, there's looking and there's looking. I guess we have to make you look a little harder."

Mrs. Campbell glanced at the door as if she were tempted to leave. Obviously the woman wasn't used to compliments.

Abby stood squarely in front of her, hoping to discourage any thought of escape. "Let me know if this hurts." Abby gently cleansed Mrs. Campbell's face with complexion wash, leaving the bruised skin until last. The woman winced when the sponge reached her cheek, but said nothing.

Abby stilled her hand. "Are you sure you want me to do this?"

Mrs. Campbell lifted her chin. "Quite sure."

Abby finished the cleansing and drying process, then reached for a jar of Burnett's face powder. It took several light coats to cover the bruise. By the time she applied the final coat, the bruise was hardly noticeable, though her cheek was still slightly swollen, giving her face a lopsided look.

Abby reached for the pale pink cheek blush and lip rouge she had prepared herself and proceeded to paint the full-rounded lips and well-defined cheekbones. This helped to fool the eye by drawing attention away from the bruise. She purposely used a light touch and the end results looked amazingly natural.

She stepped back and gave Mrs. Campbell's face a thorough visual check. She was right about the woman's looks. She really was pretty. And if she did something with her hair . . .

"How . . . how does it look?" Mrs. Campbell asked.

"Why don't you see for yourself?" Abby gave her a hand mirror.

Mrs. Campbell slowly drew the mirror up to her face. Her eyes widened as she turned her head from side to side, her fingertips flying to her cheek. "I . . . I can't believe that's me. I look . . ."

"Beautiful," Abby finished for her when it became clear the woman couldn't state the obvious aloud. Abby reached for a bottle and set it on the counter. "If you wash your hair with this shampoo, it will bring out the gold highlights."

"I don't know how to thank you." The poor woman sounded close to tears.

"Don't cry," Abby said gently. "You'll mess up your face."

This brought a shadow of a smile to Mrs. Campbell's lips. "I don't want to do that." She lifted the mirror to her face again. Aware of Abby watching her, she dropped the mirror to her lap and tittered in embarrassment. "Why, Miss Parker, you must think I'm the most conceited woman in the world. Looking at myself like that."

"My uncle used to say that it's our duty to look at ourselves in the mirror before we inflict ourselves on others."

"Your uncle . . . said that?"

"Yes," Abby said quietly. Then, to keep her own eyes from tearing with fond memories of her uncle, she quickly busied herself and replaced the lids on each of the jars. "Make certain your face is clean and dry before you apply the powder, Mrs. Campbell."

"I'd really like for you to call me Lucy."

"Lucy it is, then. My friends call me Abby."

"I . . . I better go. I want to get home before it's dark. How much do I owe you?"

Abby added the prices together and wrote them out neatly on a receipt. "These cosmetics should last you for a while."

Lucy paid Abby from her coin purse and gathered up the various bottles Abby had set out for her. "Miss Parker . . ."

"Abby."

"Abby. I can't tell you how grateful I am."

"I'm glad I could be of service," Abby said.

"If there's anything I could do for you . . ."

Abby thought for a moment. "Maybe there is. I'd appreciate it if you'd encourage your friends to stop by."

"I don't know if I can help you. I wouldn't be getting myself all painted up if it weren't for my . . . my accident. If the other women knew what I was doing to my face, they'd think I was one of those dreadful women on Myers Street."

"I can assure you that in Boston and New York, cosmetics are used by respectable and well-educated businesswomen to enhance their appearances."

Lucy sniffed. "You call them what you want, but that doesn't change the facts."

"I'm not talking about the women who work in brothels. I'm talking about women who work in office buildings. I even know a woman doctor who wouldn't think of being seen in public without her lip rouge."

Lucy looked amazed. "Is that really true?"

"Absolutely," Abby assured her. "And I do believe the time will come when all women will make use of cosmetics."

"Oh, I don't know about that," Lucy said.

"You don't think most women make use of facial creams and other concoctions now, in private? Let me tell you they do, and some of the products they use are extremely dangerous."

"All right, I'll talk to the others. But I can't promise anything." Lucy lifted her hood over her head and reached for the package of cosmetics. "I really must go. It'll take me some time to get back." She started for the door.

"Be careful on your horse," Abby called after her.

Lucy paused, her hand on the doorknob. "My horse?"

"I wouldn't want you to be thrown again."

"Oh, yes, of course, my horse. Good day." Lucy hurried outside.

Abby watched her through the window, her every instinct telling her that the woman was lying. Abby was willing to bet that Mrs. Lucy Campbell hadn't been thrown by any old horse.

# Chapter 28

Lucy Campbell remained very much on Abby's mind during the week that followed. She couldn't seem to shake the feeling the woman desperately needed help.

Even Gunnar noticed her preoccupation. He had come to the salon to tell her he'd reached another dead end in the search for her uncle.

"Abby?" Sitting at one of the tables next to her, he leaned forward, his rugged square face only inches away. "Did you hear what I said? No one seems to know anything. I've gone to every mining camp and town in and around Cripple Creek. It's as if your uncle vanished in midair."

The last of her hopes plummeted. It appeared she would never know what happened to her dear, sweet uncle.

"I don't know where to go from here," Gunnar said honestly. "I'm sorry, Abby." He searched her face. She could feel the heat of his gaze as his eyes lingered longer than necessary on her lips. It was only after he looked away that she could breathe. "I wish I knew what to do."

"Someone has to know something," she said stubbornly.

Gunnar lifted his eyes to hers. He looked so frustrated and dejected, her heart melted and it was all she could do to keep from reaching up and brushing away the anguished shadow at his brow. Despite the abrupt and puzzling way he'd pushed her away following that kiss on the mountain and again after their trip to Cripple Creek, he had worked diligently to track down her uncle. Regardless of how he'd hurt and humiliated her, she would always be grateful to him.

"Gunnar, I appreciate everything you've done." She kept herself rigid, contained, for fear of letting down her guard. As long as she kept a clamp on her emotions, she'd be all right, and he need never know how much she was hurting. "I can't tell you how much." She started to rise from her chair, but he stopped her, his hand on her arm. Unable to help herself, she covered his hand with her own and squeezed tight. For several moments they sat side by side, letting that one squeezing touch be the link connecting them.

At last he released her and she was left to wage yet another battle for control.

"I'm not giving up, Abby. I want you to know that." For a moment, she thought he was going to kiss her. Indeed, his lips were so close to hers, she could almost smell the warm sweetness of his breath. Then he stood abruptly, almost knocking over the chair in his haste.

Feeling shunned, she rose and crossed to the counter, pretending to straighten her supplies. Thinking herself safe from his scrutiny, she forgot about the mirror on the back wall until she looked up and realized he could see her tears.

"Abby?" He touched her shoulder and she felt as if he'd set her afire. "What's wrong?"

"What's wrong?" she repeated. *What's wrong?* One moment he would kiss her, the next he would push her away. He was driving her crazy. She took a deep breath before facing him, but her feelings were so tangled with anger and hurt and confusion, nothing seemed to make sense. Unable to say what was really on her mind, she stammered out her concern for Lucy Campbell.

"I'm sure it's her husband who hit her," she finished, her voice barely audible. If only he weren't standing so close, looking at her so intently.

"You could be right," he said, the dislike for Lucy's

husband written all over his face. "But there's not much I can do. Not unless she approaches me directly."

"I didn't like that man from the moment I set eyes on him."

"Calm down," he said gently, touching her arm.

Their gazes locked for a quick instant before they both turned away, he to glance out the window and she to straighten the already orderly bottles on the counter.

"She will never come to you," Abby said.

"Not even if you ask her to?"

"I don't think she'd ever do anything she considers disloyal to her husband."

"I'll talk to her if you like," he offered.

"No . . . if she found out I broke her confidence, she'll never trust me again."

Gunnar raked his fingers through his hair and donned his hat. He looked as frustrated as Abby felt. "Let me know if you change your mind."

After Gunnar left, Abby sat in her empty salon and wondered if she should return to Boston. It was obvious she wasn't going to find her uncle. She wasn't even all that certain she could make a success of her complexion salon. At least not here, in Colorado. Maybe she'd have a better chance of success in one of the big cities. If that was the case, she had no reason to stay in Dangling Rope. She thought of Gunnar and felt more depressed than ever.

She was almost tempted to close up her shop and leave town immediately when two women walked into the salon.

One of the women introduced herself. "I'm Hannah Walsh." She stood tall and straight, and had red shiny cheeks and fuzzy gray hair. "This is my friend Louise Baker. Mrs. Campbell told us you're the one responsible for giving her a new face. We got to thinking, maybe a new face isn't such a bad idea. This mountain air plays havoc with the complexion, doesn't it, Louise?"

"Absolutely," Louise agreed. She was a small, thin, mousy woman with dull splotchy skin and brown hair. "Even though I never go outside without a hat, my skin still feels as rough as the bark on a tree."

"Take a seat at the counter," Abby said, "and we'll see what we can do."

Hannah and Louise were the first of a long succession of women to ride into Dangling Rope during the following days to visit the "miracle worker." The women, mostly miners' wives, arrived in carriages and on horseback. One woman arrived in town on a burro. They came from Cripple Creek, Florence, Divide, and Manitou Springs. One determined schoolteacher traveled clear from Denver.

Mom Bull cooked up a storm to accommodate all her new customers, and the smell of burned teacakes and biscuits permeated the air. Not wanting to miss out, Otis established regular business hours for his general store and Clod took to fiddling for the ladies as they waited their turn.

Madam Rosie took a more dismal view of the sudden increase in visitors. One hot morning in mid-June, less than two weeks before the train was scheduled to arrive in town, she stormed out of the Opera House and marched in a beeline straight to the sheriff's office, feathers flying everywhere.

"Sheriff Kincaid! This has got to stop!" she complained.

Gunnar frowned up at her. "A good morning to you, too, Rosie."

Rosie impaled him with a glare. "I suppose you think this is funny. I'll have you know, I pay good money to do business in this town and I expect something in return."

"What are you talking about, Rosie?"

"I'm talking about Abby and that . . . that French salon of hers. Since she's been fancying up those miners' wives, business has been down. The men are afraid to leave their fancy wives alone!"

"What do you expect me to do about it?" Gunnar asked. "I can't make a man leave his wife if he doesn't want to."

"Well, you better, Sheriff, or I'm not paying any business taxes at the end of the month!" She gave her corset a tug and slammed out of his office.

Smiling to himself, Gunnar reached for his hat. Things sure hadn't been the same since Abby opened up that salon of hers. Hell, they hadn't been the same since she hit town. *He* hadn't been the same.

Outside, Gunnar stared in disbelief at the number of horse-drawn vehicles parked along Main Street. Equally amazing was the size of the crowd that was gathered in front of the salon. The high-pitched chatter of the women almost drowned out the loud blasts of dynamite that sounded from the distance.

The carriages were parked every which way, with no regard for order. Gunnar dodged around a buggy and was forced to climb over the wheels of a springboard wagon in order to cross the street.

Abby stood on a chair in front of the counter and lifted her voice to be heard in the back of the room. "A woman can look pretty just about anytime she puts her mind to it. If the professional women of Boston and New York think it important enough to enhance their appearances, why shouldn't housewives?"

The women applauded and begged for more, and Abby happily complied. "Who wants to be first?" she asked, and over a dozen hands shot into the air.

Otis and Nathan joined Gunnar as he stood just inside the doorway, behind the crowd.

"Is it true?" Otis whispered. "Is Dangling Rope really gonna have a millinery?"

"That's what I hear," Gunnar said. A Miss Tucker had stopped by his office to inquire about renting out one of the buildings.

"And what's this about a dressmaker?" Otis continued. "Parisian Fashions is going to open next door to

Abby's place as soon as the train arrives," Gunnar replied.

Otis shoved his hands in his pockets and grumbled, "Who ever thought Dangling Rope would turn into a damned ladies' parlor?"

Later that same afternoon, after Abby's customers had left for the day, and while she was busy replenishing her supply of facial creams, a black man walked into her salon and stood anxiously at the doorway, clutching an old felt hat to his chest. He wore old canvas pants and an old leather vest.

"Hate to disturb you, ma'am," he said. "I'd be much obliged if you could help me with a problem I've been havin'."

Abby wiped her hands on her apron. "I'll try," she said, curious. Other than Gunnar, Nathan, and sometimes Otis, who stopped by to deliver supplies, men generally refused to step foot inside her shop.

"My name's Abraham Lincoln Smith, but everyone calls me Abe. My wife, Beulah, has this scar. . . ." He ran his hand alongside his cheek and jaw. "It don't bother me none. I think she's beautiful just the way she is. But it bothers her and I thought . . . One of Beulah's lady friends told me about you. Said maybe you could help."

"I might be able to," Abby said. She'd never worked on dark skin. She'd have to experiment. "When can she come to see me?"

Abe flashed a smile. "I can bring her anytime you say, ma'am."

"Shall we say tomorrow, then? Sometime in the afternoon?"

"No problem with the time." He stood by the door and continued to finger the brim of his hat. "But there is a problem you best know about. I haven't had any luck with my claim. Been working away at it for months and so far, nothing. I wouldn't be botherin' you with my problems normally, but I don't have any

way of payin' for them there cosm'tics. I'm real handy
with my hands, though. If you need any shelves or
cabinets built, I'd be mighty happy to work off what
it'll cost."

"That's very generous of you," Abby said. "But I believe I have all the shelves and cabinets I need."

"I see." He looked so disappointed, Abby felt sorry
for him. "I'm sorry to have troubled you." He turned
to leave.

"Wait, don't go." Abby quickly closed the distance
between them. "Just because I don't need shelves
doesn't mean you and I can't do business."

"I don't cotton to charity, ma'am, if that's what you
have in mind."

"I don't cotton much to charity, myself," she said.
"What I had in mind is called credit. It means—"

"I know what it means," Abe said. "As far as I know,
the only folks who can buy on credit is rich white
folks."

"That might be true in other places, but in my shop
the only requirement for buying on credit is honesty.
You are an honest man, are you not, Mr. Smith?"

He grinned, his teeth white next to his dark skin.
"Oh, yes, ma'am. I'm not smart enough to be anything
but honest."

"I think it takes a smart man to be honest," she said.
"So do we have a deal?"

"Oh, yes, ma'am, and I'll do everythin' in my power
to pay you back."

He turned to leave and almost plowed straight into
Mom Bull. Stammering his apologies to Mom Bull and
his gratitude to Abby, he rushed outside, let out a yelp,
and threw his hat into the air.

Mom Bull scowled after him, her fists on her hips.
"One day, someone's going to look that happy when
they leave my restaurant."

Gunnar stepped up behind her. "Why, Mom Bull,"
he drawled, "everyone's that happy when they leave

your restaurant." He winked at Abby, who stifled a laugh.

"Yeah, well, they don't show it none." Mom Bull stomped off, leaving Abby and Gunnar to stand staring at each other, neither able to speak, suddenly.

Finally Gunnar pulled off his hat. "Do you have a moment, Abby?"

Feeling giddy with warmth, Abby nodded. "Come on in."

He followed her to the counter and slid onto a stool. "Madam Rosie stopped in the office this morning. She's not too happy about how things are going."

"Things?" Abby sat on a stool next to him. "What kind of things, Gunnar?"

"It seems that since business has picked up at your salon, the miners haven't been showing up at the Opera House."

She wrinkled her forehead. "What could one possibly have to do with the other?"

"It seems that the miners want to stay home with their own wives."

Abby drew back in astonishment. "Really?" A smile as bright as the sun spread across her face. She threw back her head and laughed. "Now, isn't that a fine kettle of fish?"

He laughed with her, enjoying the sound of their voices as they blended together. Suddenly he reached for her hand. "Abby . . . I . . ."

The laughter died on her face and in its place was a look of wariness. "What is it, Gunnar?"

He hated the distrust he saw in her eyes, but who could blame her? He wished to God he'd been honest with her from the start. How shortsighted of him to think he could suddenly withdraw, with no explanation, nothing. She had the right to know why there could never be anything more between them. God only knew he owed her that much. "I think you should know—"

"So what's so funny?" Nathan said, walking into the

salon. "I heard you two laughing from clear across the street."

Gunnar snatched his hand away and both he and Abby swung around to stare at Nathan.

Nathan looked from one to another. "Well?"

Gunnar stood and reached for his hat. "You tell him, Abby." Without another word, he walked with long strides to the door and was gone.

Abe returned the following afternoon with his wife, Beulah, a pleasant woman with gentle soulful eyes.

"I'm pleased to meet you, Mrs. Smith," Abby said. "Sit over here and we'll get to work."

Beulah was dressed in a bright calico wrapper frock. A large bosomy woman with kinky black hair, she had a high forehead, a wide nose, and thick lips. The bright pink scar ran from her left eyebrow all the way to her chin. Abe explained that Beulah had fallen against a hot poker as a child.

The woman glanced at her husband, who nodded in encouragement. "I'm not sure this is a good idea."

"Now, Beulah, you promised to hear what Miss Parker had to say."

Beulah eyed Abby warily before taking a seat. She fidgeted nervously with her skirt while Abby studied her skin texture. Abby had mixed some face powders in anticipation of Beulah's arrival. But she'd overestimated the skin tone. Beulah's skin color was much lighter than her husband's, almost a golden tan.

Abby toned down the mixture with white face powder and stirred. When she was satisfied with the color, she cleansed Beulah's face. She carefully applied lotion, explaining each stage as she worked.

"Well, I'll be!" Abe exclaimed at length. "The scar's plain gone out of sight."

Beulah gave her husband a look of skepticism. "You ain't pulling my leg, are you, Abe?"

Abe looked the soul of innocence. "Now, would I do that?"

"In a minute you can see for yourself," Abby said. She worked a third layer of lotion across the scar and blended it until the skin was a uniform color.

"Now just a touch of lip color," Abby said.

"Oh, dear," Beulah said, glancing at her husband. "I don't know about having my lips painted."

Her husband shrugged. "What can it hurt to see what it looks like?"

"Your lips are your best features," Abby said. "A little color on your lips will make them stand out better and will add sparkle to your pretty brown eyes."

After she had applied the color, she stood back to view the results. A quick look at the woman's husband told her she had achieved her goal.

"My, don't you look like an angel," Abe said with a broad smile.

Beulah still looked skeptical. "You're not just sayin' that to be nice, are you?"

Abby handed Beulah a hand mirror. "See for yourself."

Beulah held the mirror in front of her face. For several moments, she spoke not a word. She only stared.

"What did I tell you?" Abe asked at length.

"You told me right," Beulah said, her usually strong voice sounding husky.

Abby set the jar of newly blended facial cream on the counter. "Take this with you. It should last you for a month or two."

"Why, bless my soul, Miss Parker, that's mighty nice of you. But we can't afford to spend money on this old face of mine. We can't hardly afford to feed our-selves—"

"Now, baby, don't you go frettin' yourself about money. Miss Parker, here, she's agreed to let me buy on credit."

Beulah's eyes grew wide as saucers. "Are you crazy, girl? The only ones who can buy on credit are—"

"All my trustworthy clients can buy on credit," Abby

said firmly. She pushed her ledger toward Abe. "If you would be kind enough to sign right here."

Abe beamed. "It would make me proud to sign." He took the black enamel fountain pen from her and scratched out the letter A, which was all he knew how to write. He took a stepped backward so Beulah could see his signature. "Isn't that a wondrous sight?" he asked.

"A wondrous sight," Beulah agreed, tears in her eyes. "Never thought I'd see the day we would have the honor of owing someone money." She picked up her jar of facial cream and held it close to her ample bosom.

Abe took Abby's hand in his. "Thank you, Miss Parker. And don't you worry none. I intend to make good on every penny I owe you."

"I have no doubt," Abby said.

She followed the couple outside and waved as they drove off in their mud wagon.

Nathan passed them as they left town. He rode up to the salon on his horse and tipped his hat with his usual boyish charm. "Good afternoon, Abby. I was wondering if you'd like to join me at Mom Bull's for a bite to eat."

She shaded her eyes against the slanting sun. "I'd love to," she said. "I just need a minute to close up."

"I'll meet you in, let's say, fifteen minutes."

Abby watched him ride off, wishing with all her heart that Gunnar was as open and warm as his brother.

# Chapter 29

During the week that followed, Abby's complexion salon enjoyed a steady flow of customers. Hannah had recommended Abby to Pauline Brooks, who recommended her to Jennifer Crandall, who told everyone she knew. Word of mouth spread from one mining town to the next and the flow of wagons streaming into Dangling Rope increased to the point that Gunnar couldn't even ride his horse through town during daytime hours.

It was the damnedest thing Gunnar had ever witnessed. Who would have thought that a complexion salon, of all things, would be so popular?

Along with Abby's popularity, Gunnar found his services as a law enforcer in more demand than ever before. Husbands stormed into his office as regular as clockwork to complain about their wives' sudden obsession with their appearances. Sometimes the men were lined up in front waiting for him when he arrived in the morning.

"Can't get a decent meal around my place!" one shouted in Gunnar's ear.

"A decent meal?" another sneered. "I'd be happy for a boiled shirt."

The miners were usually gone by noon, and that's when the prostitutes descended on him, filing into his office in a cloud of perfume and feathers. Not only was the Opera House affected by Abby's business, even Cripple Creek's illustrious Madam Vernon felt threatened.

Madam Rosie had fallen into the habit of storming into his office almost daily and, on that particular day, was more incensed than usual. "She's putting us out of business."

"It's true," said a well-known madam from Victor. "Business is down by half."

The eight women who crowded into his office all began talking at once. Women who were normally staunch enemies stood together like allies.

"Quiet!" Gunnar said. He swiped at the feathers in his face. "One at a time. Now what about single miners? Surely there's enough of them to keep you in business."

One of the women gave a disgusted harumph. "Most of them can't afford the services offered by my girls. I cater to the men who've struck it big and, unfortunately, as soon as a man has a little money in his pocket, he goes and gets himself a wife."

It was with the greatest relief that Gunnar saw the last of the protesters leave for the day, but he knew the reprieve was only temporary. First thing in the morning, they'd be back.

He settled down at his desk and labored on the new town ordinance. Something had to be done about the traffic problems. The railroad crew would be arriving soon and if Abby's customers were allowed to continue with their lawless ways, there'd be no room for men to work.

When the last of the carriages pulled away from the complexion salon, Gunnar hurried across the street just as Abby changed the sign in the window to read CLOSED.

He stepped inside. "Is that sign for me?"

She sank into a chair, exhausted. "It depends on what brings you here."

He straddled a chair opposite her. "I noticed that some of your customers have been a bit careless when driving through town."

"Careless? How?"

"A couple of the ladies were seen racing up Main Street."

Amusement flickered in her eyes. "That's because they were in a hurry to prepare supper for their husbands."

"It's no excuse," Gunnar said. "Besides, it's not just speed that's the problem. I caught a few of your customers parking haphazardly."

She pursed her lips prettily and he was suddenly forced to remind himself that her lips were no longer his concern. "Is that against the law?"

He grimaced. What should be against the law was how the memories of their kisses kept pushing their way into his thoughts. "As a matter of fact, it is."

She looked doubtful. "Are you sure?"

"Of course I'm sure. I'm afraid we're going to have to put a time limit as to how long a wagon will be allowed to park on Main Street."

Abby's eyes widened. "A time limit? But why?"

"Once the train comes into town, we're going to attract a lot more businesses. Main Street isn't going to be large enough to hold everyone."

"That seems like an awful lot of laws for a little town like Dangling Rope," she said.

"It's going to be a large town soon." He stood and hung a copy of his ordinance on a nail by the front door. "If we don't begin setting down the laws now, we'll have everyone running wild."

"Well, we certainly can't have people running wild," she said heartily. It wasn't people she was thinking about; it was passionate feelings like the ones that ran rampant on the ridge when he kissed her and that were running rampant now, at least on her part. "Does everything have to be so controlled?"

His eyes met hers for a fleeting second, before he turned away. "Not everything," he said. "Just most things."

A crowd waited in front of Abby's salon early that Friday morning as she unlocked the front door and turned the CLOSED sign to OPEN. "What the . . ." She stepped outside, surprised to find close to a hundred men out front.

A grizzly man with long unkempt hair stepped forward. Recognizing the man as Lucy's husband, it was all she could do to hide her distaste.

"Are you Miss Parker?"

"I am," Abby said. She cast an anxious glance at the sheriff's office. His horse was tethered in front, but there was no sign of Gunnar. Holy blazes, where was he? "What can I do for you?"

"You the owner of this here compl'xion s'loon?"

"That's *salon*. Yes, I am."

"In that case, the boys and me have something to say to you. We don't cotton to the idea of our women-folks having their faces all gussied up with paint."

"Yeah!" several men shouted in unison.

"I don't want to come home nights and not find supper on the table," someone hollered from atop his horse.

This brought a murmur of agreement from the angry crowd.

One man pointed a finger at Abby from the driver's seat of his buckboard. "Daya know what my old lady said to me last night? She told me to fix my own supper."

"That's nothin'," another miner added. "My wife kept looking at herself in a mirror and said she was going back home to Iowa where her beauty would be 'ppreciated."

Campbell thrust his face into Abby's. "It ain't decent the way you turned our womenfolks aginst us."

Abby stepped back, but held her ground. "I've not turned anyone against you."

"Oh, no!" Campbell grabbed her roughly by the arm.

Her anger flared. "Get your hands off me."

"And who's gonna make me?"

"I am." silence reigned as Gunnar pushed his way through the crowd to Abby's side. "You'll take your hands off her this minute or you'll spend the night in jail."

Campbell released Abby and turned to face Gunnar. "I'm warnin' you, Sheriff, you better keep Miss Parker the hell away from my wife." The man cast a contemptuous glance at Abby before mounting his horse and riding away. Almost as soon as Campbell had left, the crowd quickly dispersed.

Watching the various rigs pull away, Abby rubbed her arm. "I can't stand that man!"

Gunnar cupped her elbow. "Did he hurt you?"

Confused by what she saw in his face and heard in his voice, she could only stare at him. When she failed to reply, he wordlessly restated his question with an arched eyebrow.

"I've been hurt worse," she stammered, dropping her arms to her side. Being roughed up was almost an everyday occurrence on Thieves Corner.

He looked at her sharply. "Let me see." He lifted her arm and ever so gently rolled up her sleeve. Two red spots showed on her arm where Campbell had pressed his fingers into her skin. Gunnar's jaw tightened as he released her arm. "If he ever touches you again, I'll . . ."

This time the depth of feeling in his voice frightened her. She'd feel terrible if Gunnar resorted to violence on her behalf. "It's nothing compared to what he did to his wife."

"You don't know that for a fact—"

"I know," she said quietly.

"Abby, there's nothing I can do. Not unless Mrs. Campbell makes a complaint."

"She's too frightened to make a complaint."

"I'll talk to her."

"No, Gunnar, you mustn't. If she knows I talked to you, she'll stay away. Then we'll never be able to help her."

He raked his fingers through his hair and sighed in frustration. "All right, see if you can earn her trust.

Maybe when she knows we're on her side, she'll make a complaint."

Abby knew what he suggested made sense. But earning Lucy's trust could take time. Too much time. Every day Lucy spent with her violent husband, her life was in danger. Abby felt it in her bones.

That night, a loud boom shook the town. Abby jumped out of bed and raced to the window. The speed of the moving light on the hill below Gunnar's cabin confirmed her suspicions. Something was definitely wrong.

She waited until Gunnar reached town, then hung out the open window. "The explosion, Gunnar. What was it?"

He looked up at her. "That's what I aim to find out. Go back to bed, Abby, before you catch cold."

Nathan came running, his open shirt hanging out of his pants and his red suspenders flopping at his sides. "Are you all right, Abby?"

"I'm fine."

Gunnar greeted his brother with a nod. "I think the sound came from Tucker's Pass. Is the railroad crew working at night?"

"Not that I know of." Nathan rubbed his temple. "The engineer said he didn't have enough men to work a triple shift."

Both men turned toward the sound of running feet. Otis emerged from the darkness, buttoning his shirt. From across the street, Mom Bull opened the window on the second story of her building and stuck out her head. "Keep your voices down. I'm tryin' to get my beauty sleep."

After a short discussion, the three men decided to ride out to the pass.

Abby was unable to sleep for the remainder of the night. She sat in the chair in front of the window, her ears straining to pick up the slightest sound.

The men still hadn't returned by morning. At the

first sign of daybreak, Abby quickly dressed. She was on her way to Mom Bull's for coffee when she heard the sound of horses in the distance. She stopped in her tracks and waited.

Gunnar led the way. He looked tired.

She met him in front of the sheriff's office. "Is everything all right?"

He held her gaze as he dismounted. "It looks like the train won't be making its deadline."

"Oh, no," she whispered. Without the train, the town had no chance of surviving.

Nathan rode up behind him and slid out of the saddle. Abby had never seen him look so defeated.

"It was those damned Injuns!" Otis spit out, riding up from the rear. "Owns Six Horses and his men blew up the bloody pass."

Abby searched Gunnar's face. "Was anyone hurt?"

"Fortunately not," Gunnar said quietly.

Otis wiped his forehead with his arm. "I'm gonna get me some shut-eye."

"I think all three of you need sleep," Abby said.

Nathan managed a crooked smile for her benefit. "I'll see you later."

She nodded and waited until Nathan and Otis had left. "Can't something be done about the railroad?"

Gunnar shook his head. "We don't have enough manpower."

"But what about the miners? Couldn't we ask them to help?"

He sighed wearily. "Do you think Campbell is going to let us use his men for the purpose of laying track to Dangling Rope?"

"There are other mines," she said.

"None as close as Campbell's or that have as many men." He stroked the neck of his horse. "I'm sorry, Abby. I know you were counting on the train for your business."

"It's not my business I'm worried about. It's Nathan. This meant a lot to him."

A strange look crossed his face. "You . . . you really care for my brother, don't you?"

"Of course I care for him," she replied. "Nathan is warm and friendly and, as Mom Bull says, can charm a mouse into a hawk's nest."

His eyes glittered with some unnamed emotion. "Help him through this, Abby. You're the only one who can." He walked away, not giving her a chance to respond.

Sensing things were not as they seemed, she puzzled over the exchange as she headed for the salon. What he asked of her was no more than what any concerned brother would ask of a friend. So why did she find Gunnar's request so disturbing?

Maybe she was imagining things, she thought. Or maybe it was simply disappointment that made her feel suddenly weepy and at odds with herself. She tried to shrug off her depression. She wasn't going to be much help in cheering Nathan in this present state of mind. Besides, what did it matter that the train didn't come to town? Nathan, Mom Bull, and all the rest would have to find some other town to call home.

As for herself, well, she would travel back to Boston and close out her uncle's affairs. She didn't need roots; didn't need a permanent place to call home. That's why they called her Traveling Lady. Her trunk was always packed. Ready. She would simply move on to the next place—and the next. As she'd done so many times in the past and would probably do countless times in the future.

The only difference was, this time she didn't want to go.

# Chapter 30

Later that same day Lucy showed up at the salon. She looked as wild-eyed and jittery as a cornered deer. Her eyes were red as if she'd been crying. Abby stared in horror at the ugly new bruise on her cheek.

"Lucy, your face—"

"I don't want to talk about it," Lucy said. "I . . . I can't stay long." She shrank away from the window of the salon to stand in the shadows. "I came to get another jar of face cream."

"Another . . ." Abby stared at her incredulous. "I gave you a three-month supply."

Lucy's lower lip trembled. "I shared it with a friend and . . ."

Abby decided there was no point in making the woman feel any more embarrassed or uncomfortable than she obviously was. Without further comment, she set a jar of face cream on the counter. "Is one enough?"

"Enough?"

"Do you want an extra jar for your friend?"

"I'll just take the one." Lucy pulled a gold coin from her coin purse.

Trying to make the woman relax, Abby searched for a topic of conversation. "I don't know if you've heard. The Utes blew up Tucker's Pass. That means the railroad won't make it here on time."

Lucy looked horrified. "That's terrible. Have you reported the Utes to the Indian Agency?"

"I'm sure the railroad will make a full report. But that

isn't going to help us get the train through. Unless . . ."
Abby hesitated, not sure how much she should say.

"Unless what?" Lucy prodded.

"We need men to lay track. Your husband has a large
workforce. Do you suppose there's any chance at all
he might consider letting us use his men, just for a
few days?"

Lucy grew as pale as new-fallen snow. If Abby had
the slightest doubt her suspicions were true, they were
forever wiped away by the look on Lucy's face. "No,
no, that's not possible."

"But it wouldn't hurt to ask," Abby said gently, wishing she'd not said anything. "Would it be . . . a problem
if one of us talks to him?"

"I don't think that would be a good idea. He would
never agree to loan his men out." She grabbed her
package and half ran to the door. "Don't tell anyone I
was here. Please."

"Lucy, I think you should know I told—"

Lucy bumped into Gunnar as she ran from the shop,
and almost dropped her package. Stammering apologies and looking about to burst into tears, she dashed
past him.

"Mrs. Campbell!" Gunnar called after her. "Is something wrong?" But already she was racing away, the
wheels of her wagon kicking up dust in its wake. He
turned to Abby, looking more tired than he had earlier.
"Is she all right?"

"No, she's not all right. How can she be? Living with
that terrible man. Did you see her face?"

"I'm afraid I couldn't see much of anything. She was
going too fast."

"I'm telling you, Gunnar. If we don't do something,
he's going to do serious harm to her."

"Abby, I told you. I can't do anything without Lucy's
cooperation. I'll talk to her, like I said, but that's about
all I can do."

Abby shook her head. "She's not going to talk to you.
She won't even be honest with me." She studied the

rugged lines of his face. There was a permanence about him that was as irresistible as it was dangerous. If she ever truly allowed herself to believe that something or someone could be a permanent presence in her life, she would be in serious trouble.

"You look like you're about ready to be laid in the locker," she said.

He shook his head, but he did manage a heart-stopping grin. "That bad, eh?" He pulled out a chair and sat, tossing his hat on the table. "I went to see Campbell."

"You saw Campbell?" Abby sat next to him. "Holy blazes, Gunnar, you didn't say anything about Lucy, did you?" She shuddered to think what the man would do if he knew his dirty little secret was out.

"Her name never came up. I asked him to loan us some men."

"What did he say?" Seeing his reluctance to answer, she squared her shoulders. "You can tell me. I daresay I've heard worse."

His mouth lifted in amusement. "Knowing you, you've probably even said worse."

"That bad, eh?" She met the smile he gave her with one of her own. It seemed silly for two grown people to sit smiling at each other for no apparent reason, but that's what they were doing—and might have kept doing—had Abe and Beulah Smith not walked into the salon.

As if caught doing something outside the law, Gunnar grabbed his hat and Abby jumped to her feet, practically knocking over her chair.

Beulah and Abe glanced at each other. Beulah's scar was barely visible beneath the careful application of facial cream. "Hope we're not troubling you none, ma'am," Abe said politely.

"Not at all," Abby managed to say, and for no reason felt her cheeks grow hot.

"I don't mean to run off like this," Gunnar said, heading for the door, "but I'm going to hit the sack."

After Gunnar had left, Abe stole a glance at his wife,

who gave a slight nod. "The missus and me, we would like to take a look at your books." His voice sounded apologetic. "That is, if you don't mind."

It was a simple request, but no less puzzling. "I'm not sure I understand what you mean."

Beulah spoke up. "What Abe is trying to say is that we've never had the honor of having credit. That's why we'd like to see our name on your ledger." She looked embarrassed. "I know it sounds foolish. But it kinda gives us the feelin' of being important."

"I don't think it sounds foolish at all," Abby said. She fetched her ledger from behind the counter and opened it up for them to see. Abe and Beulah stood staring at the large bold *A* marking their name, like first-time parents gazing down at a newborn.

Not content to simply look, Beulah traced the letter with a thick blunt-nailed finger. "That's mighty nice," she said proudly. "Never thought we'd have the privilege of owin' money to no one."

"And I'm gonna pay back every cent," Abe said. "Just like I said I would."

Abby smiled. Until her uncle had come into her life, she'd not put much faith in other people's promises. But she believed Mr. Abe Lincoln Smith.

Abe pushed the ledger toward her. "I surely do appr'ciate you lettin' us look at your ledger. If there's anything we can do for you . . ."

"Thank you, I—" Suddenly she had an idea. "Maybe there is. You know we're trying to bring the railroad to Dangling Rope."

Abe nodded. "I heard what those injuns did. It's a mighty shame."

"We need workers. Do you think you could get some miners to lay track for a few days?"

Abe shook his head. "Oh, no, ma'am. Those miners ain't gonna do nothin' that interferes with their quest for gold."

Beulah placed her hands at her waist. "It's a crying

shame those men can't do a little for the community."
She thought for a moment. "If you like, I'll lay track."

Abe shook his head as if he didn't think he was
hearing right. "Now, Beulah, what do you know about
layin' rails?"

"Not a thing," Beulah admitted. "But I bet it's no
harder than having a baby. And I've had a whole half
dozen of those."

Beulah had given Abby an idea. "How many women
do you think would help us?"

Abe scratched his temple. "I don't like the sound
of this."

Ignoring her husband, Beulah did a mental count.
"I can round up a goodly number. Maybe twenty or
more."

"I think I can get Meg and Ginger to help," Abby
said. "Maybe even Mom Bull." She was thinking aloud.
"Beulah, would you have your friends meet me here
first thing tomorrow morning?"

"I don't like the sound of this," Abe repeated.

"Tomorrow it is," Beulah said, looking self-
important.

The following morning, Beulah and Abe rode into
town, followed by a long line of wagons. The women
parked illegally in front of the complexion salon and
charged inside, anxious to volunteer their services—
anything—for the miracle worker.

Abby stood on a chair behind the counter so everyone could hear her. She faced the crowd. "Ladies, as
you might have heard, we have problems with the railroad. We haven't been able to convince any of the
miners to help out. That's why I'm asking for your
help."

A dark-haired woman known as Emma Lou Watkins
raised her hand. "I resent being asked to attend a meeting with the likes of these women." She glared at Ginger, who was dressed in a shocking red gown.

"If you don't want my help, say so," Ginger said,
glaring back.

"We need everyone who is willing to work," Abby said, pointedly.

Beulah raised her hand. "I say if the men refuse to help, it's up to us womenfolk to do the job. We've got strong backs and hard muscles. You can't pick up no child without them. I say it's time we showed our menfolk what we're made of."

"Count me in," called Mom Bull, chomping on her cigar, and others echoed her cry.

The women pushed and shoved their way to the counter to add their names to the list of volunteers. "All right, ladies," Abby said after everyone had signed up, "let's go."

Dust stirred and birds took to the air as wagons and horses raced out of town and headed toward Tucker's Pass. It took them a little over an hour to reach the railroad camp.

Gunnar was talking to the chief railroad engineer when he heard the racket. His first thought was that the Utes had returned. "Take cover!" he yelled, diving beneath a railroad car and pulling out his gun. Following his lead, the railroad workers scattered about, looking for a place to hide.

His gun aimed, Gunnar laid on his stomach and waited. He heard Abby's voice before seeing her. "Yoohoo," she called gaily. "We're here."

"What the . . ." He crawled out from under the boxcar and slammed his gun into its holster. "What the hell are you doing here?"

She looked startled by his anger. "You said you needed people to lay track, so here we are."

Gunnar glanced at the mob of women behind her. "Are you crazy? Laying track is backbreaking work. It's a man's job."

Eyes flashing, Abby dismounted and faced him. Shoulders held rigid and head held high, she looked as determined as a charging bull. "It seems to me there aren't a whole lot of men willing to do their job!"

His voice rose as he towered over her, but only to

hide the drumming sound of his heart as he gazed at her. "What about the Utes? Do you think Owns Six Horses is going to give up and let the train come into town unchallenged? You could be putting these ladies' lives in jeopardy!"

It was a chilling thought and one she'd not considered. "We're staying," she insisted. She wasn't about to give up easily.

Gunnar turned and strode away angrily.

Abby stared after him. "Meg, go and talk to the foreman. Tell him to get everyone started."

"Where are you g-going?" Meg asked.

"I'm going to make sure that no one gets hurt." Abby swung onto her horse. She had no idea where the Utes were camped, but her instincts told her to follow the creek. She only hoped she'd find them before there was any more trouble.

# Chapter 31

Gunnar set his jaw angrily as he searched for the railroad foreman. Of all the harebrained ideas Abby had thought up since her arrival in Dangling Rope, this latest was the worst. Women laying railroad track! It was ridiculous. Unheard-of. Preposterous! The women could be hurt. *Abby could be hurt!*

Burt Stonewall, the railroad foreman, took the prospect of working with a bunch of women in stride. When Gunnar had informed him of the sorry state of affairs, Burt simply shrugged his hefty shoulders, scratched the balding spot at the back of his head, and said, "They got two arms, two hands like everyone else."

Gunnar couldn't believe his ears. "Have you seen the size of these women? Why, a strong wind would blow the lot of them downhill."

Burt eyed Mom Bull, who towered over at least half of his men. "They ain't no smaller than some I've worked with in the past."

"What about the Utes? What happens if they come back?"

"If I were a Ute, I'd sure want to avoid that one," Burt said, pointing to Mom Bull.

As if she had heard her name, Mom Bull turned and glared at him. "What're you staring at?"

Burt touched his hat with a finger. "Not a thing, ma'am." He walked off.

Nathan rode to Gunnar's side. "What's going on? I heard Abby's here."

"She is and if you really care for her—"

"Of course I care for her," Nathan said defensively, "You know I care for her!"

Gunnar pressed a fist into his palm. "We need a guard up there. Make sure no Utes come anywhere near here."

"But—"

"Go, dammit!"

Without another word, Nathan rode off. Gunnar glanced around, looking for Abby. Where the hell was she? She was here a minute ago.

He mounted his horse and rode over to where Meg was waiting to be assigned a job. "Have you seen Abby?"

"S-she took off. S-said s-something about making sure no one causes t-trouble."

Gunnar followed Meg's finger. Damn! She wouldn't be tracking after the Utes, would she?

He kneed his horse and raced after her.

An hour after Abby had left the railroad camp, she sat upon her horse and gazed down an embankment. A cluster of bleached buckskin tepees were staggered along the side of the fast-running mountain stream.

Farther on, two women giggled as they spread their wash across a sunny meadow. The scene was so peaceful, it was hard to believe these same Indians had blown up the pass the night before.

Coaxing her horse across the rocky stream, she moved closer to the Indian camp. A golden-limbed youth spotted her, then ran quickly into one of the tepees. Owns Six Horses emerged a moment later and waited for her.

He lifted his hand in greeting as she neared. "How, Traveling Lady."

She returned the greeting.

"Like war paint," he said, pointing to her lips. "It look better on head." He touched his forehead. "But hard to take off."

"I found a way to remove it," she said. She reached into her knapsack and pulled out a small glass jar. When he showed no understanding of what she had said, she hopped to the ground. "I'll show you." He watched as she poured a small amount of the lotion on a sponge and carefully dabbed at her lips. "See?"

Owns Six Horses moved closer. Squinting, he leaned over and studied her mouth. "That good stuff," he announced. He spun around on his moccasined feet and walked away. "Come," he said over his shoulder. He beckoned with his arm.

Abby hurried to catch up to him and fell in step by his side. "I need to talk to you about the railroad."

"No talk iron horse," Owns Six Horses said. "Talk berry cream."

He led her past several tepees until they reached the one at the far end of camp. Streamers fluttered from the top of the three-pole tepee.

Owns Six Horses introduced her to an older Indian. "White squaw make face cream." He turned to Abby. "Show." He stooped over so she could reach his face. Startled at first, she soon understood his meaning. She quickly applied her cleansing cream and wiped away the red stripe from his forehead and cheeks.

The older man coughed and nodded, but apparently spoke no English. Owns Six Horses and the man spoke rapidly in their native tongue.

Finally Owns Six Horses interpreted for her. "He like Traveling Lady magic. He want."

Abby handed the older man the jar and received a toothy grin in return.

"He like," Owns Six Horses repeated. "Me like."

"I have more in my pack," Abby said, anxious to earn the Utes' trust. She started toward her horse with the Indian close at her heels, and pulled a jar from her pack.

"What's wrong with him?" she asked, pointing to an older Indian lying next to a campfire. The poor man was coughing so hard, Abby feared he would never catch his breath. It was similar to the cough that plagued many of the residents of Thieves Corner.

"Crooked Neck sick," Owns Six Horses explained. "He wait for Great Spirit to take him."

"What's wrong with him?"

"He have gold sickness."

His answer surprised her. "For white man, gold sickness is greed," she explained. "Not a disease."

"White man's greed fills the water with poison and makes the skies gray. I bring my family back to this land where my ancestors roamed, and now many of my people have this sickness, including my son." Owns Six Horses pointed to a tepee where a woman sat holding a small child.

"I'm so sorry," she said, her mind racing. What could be causing this illness? "Perhaps you'd let me fetch the white man's doctor from Cripple Creek?"

"No want white man's doctor!" Owns Six Horses said angrily. "Want white man to go. White man change everything. Elk gone. Deer gone. Bear gone. Water smell strange. Now iron horse come." He turned and walked away.

"Wait!" She rushed after him, but he had already heaved his sturdy body onto the bare back of his painted horse and had streaked away as quick as the wind.

Abby glanced around anxiously. With Owns Six Horses gone, she felt vulnerable. Several Utes, mostly women and children, stared back at her.

She paused next to the dying man. His skin was pale, almost pasty; the whites of his eyes had a yellow cast.

What was it, really? Poison? *Water smell strange,* Owns Six Horses had complained. She picked up a clay water jug and sniffed, but she smelled nothing out of the ordinary.

Crooked Neck looked up at her beseechingly, as if he thought she could put him out of his misery. On impulse, she handed him a jar of cleansing cream and wished with all her heart there was something she could do for him.

He clutched the jar in his hands and said something she didn't understand. Thinking he was thanking her, she nodded and hurried to her horse.

Fifteen minutes later, she met Gunnar on the trail.

He reined his horse in front of her. "Where the hell have you been? I thought . . ." A fleeting look of concern flashed across his face, but like a playful sun darting behind the clouds, it was gone, dark anger taking its place.

"I went to see Owns Six Horses," she said quietly.

"Good God, Abby. If something had happened to you, I'd . . ." He glanced away, but not soon enough to hide the look of torture on his face.

"You'd what?" she asked, needing to know.

"I'd have a hard time explaining it to Nathan."

The breath left her lungs as if she'd been kicked in the stomach. Did the man not have a thought that didn't involve his brother? "If Nathan is so damned concerned, why didn't he come?"

"He didn't know you were missing. He's guarding the pass. Did you talk to Owns Six Horses?"

"He refused to discuss the railroad." Her voice was cold and exact, allowing nothing of her aching heart to escape. "So as you can see, we both wasted our time." She galloped past him and headed back to construction headquarters.

She could feel Gunnar's eyes bore into her back as he followed, but for the most part she ignored him, determined to do whatever was necessary to forget she'd ever been in his arms. Besides, she couldn't get the vision of the old man out of her mind. Were the miners putting something into the water? Or was it a change in diet that was the culprit, caused by the shortage of game?

It was nearly noon by the time they reached headquarters. Somehow, the chief engineer had managed to put everyone to work.

Several of the women were filling a horse-drawn wagon with railroad ties. Ruby was carrying buckets of water to a railroad car that was the kitchen. The regular cooks, dishwashers, and kitchen helpers had been put to work laying track, and their ranks had been replaced with women volunteers. Mom Bull's voice could be heard over the others, giving orders. "Come on, you lubbers!" she yelled. "We got a meal to prepare!"

Abby's only hope was that the railroad workers didn't go on strike after tasting one of Mom Bull's meals.

Abby walked over to where the foreman was standing. "Do you think we have a chance? Can we reach Dangling Rope by Friday?"

"Not at this rate. My men are digging through the pass and the women . . ." He glanced over at Ginger, who kept checking her face in her hand mirror. "There's only so much they can do."

A cloud of dust rose in the distance. It was Nathan riding full speed, waving his hand. "Utes!" he called, pointing to the cliffs that towered over them.

Abby shaded her eyes against the midday sun. She could barely make out the outline of three men on horseback atop the cliff. She was unable to determine if Owns Six Horses was among the three men. She dropped her hand worriedly. The Indians weren't against the railroad for mere philosophical reasons as she had once thought. Members of the small band were dying; Owns Six Horses's son was dying. It was quite possible the Indians weren't just trying to stop a train; they might very well be seeking revenge.

The foreman spit onto the ground. "I've notified the railroad and told them to send a wire to the Indian Agency."

"What will happen to them?" she asked.

"They'll be sent to the reservation where they belong."

"No one deserves to be confined to a reservation!" she said hotly.

Gunnar put a steadying hand on her shoulder. He shook his head at the foreman, discouraging the man from continuing the discussion. The man grabbed his maps and stomped away. His hand still on Abby's shoulder, Gunnar glanced at his brother. "Better warn the crew at the pass."

"Gee-up!" Nathan shouted at his horse, riding off.

Abby's anger turned to fear. She would never forgive herself if any of the women were hurt. She whirled about to face Gunnar. "Do you think there'll be trouble?"

"Not if I can help it. But I think you'd better tell the women to leave. Just to be on the safe side."

He took off at a run, giving orders to a group of bolters. She scurried down the hill to where Ruby and Beulah were loading ties onto the back of a wagon.

Ruby's face was covered in dirt, her gingham dress wet with sweat. She grinned at Abby and nodded enviously at one of the railroad employees who worked shirtless. "This is the first time I've ever had a job where I couldn't take my clothes off."

Not wanting to overly alarm them, Abby lifted an armload of ties and followed the other two women to the wagon. "It's time to head back to town."

Ruby emptied her arms and wiped the sweat off her brow. "So soon?"

"Don't ask questions. Just go."

Ruby's eyes grew round. "Oh, my God. Look up there!"

Beulah rolled her eyes. "Mercy me."

"Keep calm," Abby cautioned. "Just stay together and act natural. Go."

After making certain that Beulah and Ruby had safely left the area, Abby followed the shiny rails of the newly laid track around a curve. In the distance, Abe and Otis stood opposite each other, taking turns pounding in spikes. She waited until she was certain the Indians could no longer see her before she lifted the hem of her skirt and ran. "Abe, Otis!" she called. "Go back to town. Hurry!"

One by one, the volunteers returned to their wagons and left. The Utes remained at their post, but they made no threatening moves, and for that Abby was grateful.

Astride her horse, she waited until the last of the women had left. Seeing Gunnar in the distance, she galloped toward him. "Are you coming, Gunnar?"

"I'm staying with Nathan. Someone's got to keep watch."

"Forget the railroad," she begged. "Please, Gunnar, it's not worth it."

He looked up at her, his hand on the neck of her horse. "Go," he whispered. Before she had a chance to argue, he slapped the rump of her horse and the animal took off in a run.

For the remainder of the day, Abby paced the floor of her room hoping and praying that Nathan and Gunnar would hurry home.

They rode into town just before sunset and at the first sound of horses, she rushed outside to greet them. The two brothers looked so exhausted, she ached for them.

"Any trouble?" she asked.

"None," Nathan said. "After you and the others left, the Indians disappeared and we never saw them again."

Gunnar loosened his saddle. "I have a feeling as long as no work is being done on the railroad, they'll leave us alone."

Abby wasn't convinced. Should something happen to Owns Six Horses's son, anything was likely to occur.

Nathan squeezed her arm, his gaze warm. "I'm going to clean up and have me an early night."

"Don't you want something to eat? Mom Bull said she'll keep something hot."

Nathan whispered in her ear, his hand on her shoulder. "Don't tell her, but after she left, the railroad cook fixed up some venison stew." He rubbed his stomach. "Best stuff I've ever tasted."

Aware of Gunnar's watchful eyes, she was relieved when Nathan broke the intimate circle and mounted his horse. "See you both later." He mounted his horse and galloped away.

Gunnar's gaze locked with Abby's before he lifted his saddle off his horse. He stomped his feet onto the wooden porch as he carried the saddle into the sheriff's office and set it in a corner.

Abby followed him inside. "I guess I owe you an apology."

He looked surprised. "For what?"

"For being so foolhardy stubborn. You were right. I put a lot of people's lives in jeopardy."

"No harm was done," he said.

"But it could have been and I—" She stopped upon hearing the sound of horses.

"What the . . ." Gunnar spun toward the open door. "Damn! It's Utes!"

# Chapter 32

Gunnar squeezed her arm, his face grim. "Stay here!"

"Gunnar, be careful." Her plea was wasted, as he'd already left the office, the door slamming shut between them.

She raced to the window. Her breath caught in her lungs as she watched.

Gunnar walked over to the leader. Abby strained her ears to hear what was being said, to no avail. Otis had emerged from Mom Bull's Restaurant, but stood back.

It was obvious by the expression on Owns Six Horses's face and the hand gestures of the men involved that an argument had erupted. Desperate to know what was going on, Abby cracked open the door and was startled to hear her name.

"Me want Traveling Lady," Owns Six Horses said.

Gunnar's voice was thin-edged with anger. "You talk to me."

Taking a deep breath, Abby walked outside. "It's all right, Gunnar. I'll talk to him."

At the sight of her, Owns Six Horses slid from the back of his horse. "Traveling Lady tell me how make medicine."

Gunnar looked from the Ute leader to Abby, his forehead creased. "What medicine? What's he talking about, Abby?"

"I don't know," Abby said. "All I gave him was some cleansing cream. For the complexion."

Otis swore under his breath. "Are you saying these

savages half-scared the shit out of me for some dang-
arsed face cream?"

"Watch what you say," Abby cautioned beneath her
breath. Things were tense enough without Otis tossing
out insults. To Owns Six Horses, she said, "Are you
talking about the jar of cream I gave you?"

He nodded. "Me want."

"I think I have a jar or two I can give you."

"No!" Owns Six Horses face grew fierce. "Me want
to know how make."

"But why?" Abby asked.

"Medicine make Crooked Neck well. He strong
again."

Abby was puzzled. "I don't understand. How could
face cream cure an illness?"

Owns Six Horses grinned. "Crooked Neck ate cream
and now bad spirits gone. Face cream make good
medicine."

Abby's eyes widened. "He *ate* the face cream?"

Gunnar shook his head in confusion. "I don't understand. How could Abby's face cream cure an illness?"

"Maybe it was all that alcohol she puts in it," Otis
growled. "The woman's gotta be plain loco the way she
wastes good sherry."

Abby's mind raced. It wasn't the alcohol; it had to
be something else. But what? Olive oil? Oil of nutmeg?
A combination of all the ingredients?

"Owns Six Horses make cream for son."

"Give him the bloody recipe," Otis said. "Maybe then
they'll leave us alone."

Abby ignored him. She remembered her lessons well.
Those who survived any length of time on the streets
knew the value of bartering. "I will give you a jar for
your son," she said. "But I will tell you how to make
the magic cream only if the railroad reaches town by
Friday."

Owns Six Horses glared at her. "Iron horse bad
thing."

"A lot of people think it's a good thing," Gunnar replied.

"White men think good thing. My people know truth."

"Sometimes the truth isn't always what it seems," Abby said. She stepped between Gunnar and the Ute leader. "The truth is that something is affecting your people. Maybe it's a chemical in the water or in the game you eat. I can give you the recipe, but the ingredients are not readily available in this area, and my supply is limited. We need the train to keep the supply on hand, but if it doesn't meet its deadline . . ."

Owns Six Horses took a long time to reply. Finally he nodded his head slowly. "My people not stop train."

Relief washed over her. "I'll be right back." She raced to the salon and grabbed a jar of cream off a shelf. In her haste, she knocked over a carton of benzoin. She stood the box upright, her heart racing. Benzoin! Wasn't that what the doctor had given Cowhide to clear the fluid from his lungs the winter he'd had pneumonia? Smiling to herself, she replaced the box on the shelf. Who would guess that a jar of complexion cleanser would serve a medicinal purpose?

The men were still waiting for her when she returned. "This is for your son." She handed Owns Six Horses the jar. "I'll give you the recipe when the train arrives in town."

Owns Six Horses held the jar in his hand. "You save my son," he said. "Owns Six Horses not forget."

He strode to his horse on moccasined feet and rode out of town, followed by his men.

"Yee-haw!" Gunnar hooted. He grabbed her around the waist and whirled her about.

Mom Bull ran out to join the fun and lifted Otis clear off his feet. Meg and Ginger, hearing the commotion, rushed to Main Street to see what all the fuss was about.

Nathan, who from his cabin had seen the Utes leave, raced to town on foot. Puzzled by the sound of laugh-

ter, he stopped in his tracks, his eyes riveted on Abby
and Gunnar. Abby had never looked prettier than she
did at that moment with the setting sun at her back,
laughing up at Gunnar.

Gunnar, standing tall and lean, swung her around
with the grace of a country gentleman. Gunnar's laughter mixed with hers as he gazed down at her.

Stunned by what he saw, what he felt, what he instinctively knew at that moment, Nathan froze. He
watched the exchange with a sense of impending
doom. Gunnar and Abby? Was it possible? Had he
been so wrapped up in his own feelings that he'd not
noticed his own brother trying to steal Abby away?

Nathan clenched his hands tight. He'd been a fool
to trust Gunnar. An utter fool. No more. Gunnar had
deprived him of their mother, but by George, he wasn't
going to cheat him out of Abby.

Meg moved to his side, but it wasn't until she slipped
her arm around his that he was aware of her presence.
"T-they d-dance w-well together, d-don't you think?"

"I suppose so," he said.

"I w-wish I c-c-ould d-dance like that," Meg said
shyly. When he made no reply, she continued, "Do . . .
do you like to dance?"

He shook his head and pushed her arm away. "I
hate to dance." He spun on his heel and half ran, half
stumbled back to his cabin.

# Chapter 33

That night, Abby, Gunnar and Otis sat around a table in Mom Bull's Restaurant, drinking strong-brewed Arbuckle's.

"I can't believe it," Otis complained. "The battle with the Utes was won with facial cream. Abby, you should have been around for the Indian Wars."

Gunnar laughed, but his expression soon grew serious. "Our biggest challenge is still ahead. We have three miles of track left to lay in seventy hours."

Beulah and Abe Smith entered the restaurant and Abby motioned the two over to their table. "We heard the problem with the Utes has been resolved," Beulah said.

Otis was still shaking his head in disbelief. "You heard right."

"We're planning our next move," Abby explained.

Gunnar made a few notations on a writing tablet. "Burt said he'll need to double his present work crew. Some prospectors have agreed to help out for a share or two of the railroad, but we have nowhere near enough to make a difference."

Abby ran a fingertip around the rim of her cup. "We're going to have to put the women to work laying track. We have no other choice."

Otis grunted. "They ain't enuf women on the face of the earth that could lay that track in time." He imitated Ginger checking her appearance in a hand-held mirror, and brought a howl of laughter from the other men.

Beulah scowled at her husband. "That's not true."

Her husband tried to smooth things over. "I'm sure Otis is just blowin' off steam. Why, I bet you could drive a spike as good as any man."

"You're darn-tooting I could!"

"I'm sure the same could be said for Mom Bull, here," Gunnar added. "Anyone who could put this much punch in a cup of coffee should be laying railroad track."

Mom Bull accepted his comments about her coffee as a compliment, and gave him one of her rare smiles. "You'll say anything for another piece of homemade berry pie."

Gunnar winked at Abby and rolled his eyes toward the ceiling. The crust of the pie was as heavy as lead, and the berries sour enough to pucker a wooden bowl, but he good-naturedly accepted a second piece.

Otis lay two table knives side by side, like train rails. "It can't be done," he said finally. "No way, nohow, can a bunch of women lay that much track."

"It's not only women doing the work," Abby argued. "The railroad crew is still intact."

Otis maintained his stubborn stance. "Yeah, but they think it's a good day when they lay a mile of track. That still leaves two miles to the rest of you. I'm tellin' ya, it can't be done."

Abby rose to her feet. She was a woman of action, not talk. "We'll just have to see, won't we? Beulah, would you tell the other women to meet me at construction headquarters at dawn tomorrow?"

Beulah's brown eyes registered approval. "I'd be happy to. Come on, Abe, we've got work to do."

Mom Bull hung up her apron. "I'll go and talk to Rosie's girls." She bit down on a cigar. "And I'm gonna tell them to leave their mirrors at home!"

Abby followed Mom Bull out the door. The two parted company outside. Abby was surprised to find Nathan waiting for her in front of the salon. He was dressed in a suit and vest, his hair slicked back.

"Don't you look dapper?" she said, surprised. She glanced at the shay hitched at the back of his horse. "Are you going somewhere?"

"I was hoping you'd take a ride with me. The night is young and the stars are just waiting to be enjoyed."

"I suppose I could," she said reluctantly. "As long as we're not gone too long. I want to be at the railroad camp at the first light of day."

"The railroad camp?"

"I guess you haven't heard what's happened." She quickly explained about the Utes. "I'm surprised you didn't hear all the commotion."

"I guess I was asleep," he said vaguely.

Abby studied him for a moment. She wondered if he was coming down with something. He looked a bit pale and kept running his finger along his collar as if he felt hot. "We have three miles of track left to go. We're trying to round up as many people as possible to help out." She flashed him a smile. "How are you at laying track?"

"I guess we're going to find out, aren't we?" He nodded toward the shay. "Shall we?" He helped her onto the wagon and took his seat beside her. He mopped his forehead with a handkerchief, then took the reins.

"Are you feeling all right, Nathan?"

He glanced at her in surprise. "Yes, of course. Why do you ask?"

"No reason."

He flicked the reins and the horse moved forward.

Abby sat back, prepared to enjoy the ride. "Otis said we haven't got a chance of getting that track laid in time."

"What does Otis know?"

They followed the wagon trail until it grew dark and only the lights from the Opera House marked the town of Dangling Rope behind them. Nathan slowed the pace of his horse as the rig continued upward. The trees began to thin and only the starlit peaks obstructed their view of the sky.

Nathan pulled the shay onto an area that overlooked the deep valley below. A big silvery moon rode above the tall peaks of the mountains, casting a frosted glow on the landscape below.

Abby inhaled the sweet fragrance of the night. After spending nearly all her life in the city, it had never occurred to her that she could love the wilderness. She sighed a deep sigh. "I love it here."

She felt his eyes on her. "I'm so happy to hear you say that, Abby. I was afraid you'd miss the city. Miss Boston."

She thought over what he said. "It's not the place, you know, as much as the people. Without my uncle . . . well, there's really nobody left in Boston I care about. Not like the people I care about here."

"Am . . . am I one of those people, Abby? The ones you care about?"

"Oh, Nathan, of course you are!" she exclaimed. "You, Meg, Otis, Mom Bull, and all the rest. You're like family."

"I feel the same way, Abby."

She smiled. "This is going to be a wonderful town one day, Nathan. I feel it in my bones. I only wish . . ."

"What, Abby? What do you wish?"

"I wish I knew where my uncle was."

"I'm sorry." He turned on his seat to face her. "I wish I knew what I could do to help."

"I'm afraid there's nothing to be done. Gunnar has done everything possible."

"Still, I wish I could do something to help. I feel so helpless."

"That's very kind of you to offer, but—"

"Kind? Is that what you think I am? Kind?"

She laughed nervously, not sure what to make of the restless energy that seemed to emanate from him, the strange gleam in his eyes. "You make it sound as if I accused you of something illegal. It's no crime to be kind."

"Dammit, Abby, I'm not being kind. I want to help you."

She pulled her shawl around her shoulders. "Gunnar contacted all the newspapers in the area and nothing came of it."

"Gunnar again," he said sulkily. "I should have known."

"For goodness' sakes, Nathan. What's gotten into you tonight?"

He grabbed her by the arms, frightening her. "Don't you know?"

"Know . . . what?" she whispered.

"How much you mean to me. Marry me, Abby, please say you will."

Her mouth dropped open. "What?"

"Don't look so surprised. Surely you must know how I feel about you. I've loved you from the first day I saw you."

"I . . . I . . . don't know what to say."

"Say you have feelings for me. Say you want to spend the rest of your life with me." He dropped his head to her shoulder and she smelled whiskey on his breath. "Oh, dear, sweet Abby. Say you'll marry me."

Abby's mind spun in confusion. Things were going too fast. "Nathan, please . . ." She pushed him away and jumped out of the wagon.

"Abby!" He caught up with her. "Talk to me!"

Her heart was pounding so fast, she could hardly find her voice. There was none of the boyish charm she had always found so appealing. "I . . . thought we were friends," she stammered.

"We are friends. Of course we're friends. But what I feel for you . . . what I thought you felt for me . . . it's more than friendship. Surely you can't deny that!"

"I never meant to give you the wrong idea."

"Wrong idea!" He sounded stricken and hurt, but there was anger on his face and anger in his eyes.

She wanted so much for the anger to go away, for Nathan and her to be friends again and forget everything that had happened tonight. "You've been such a good friend, Nathan. I don't know what I would have done without your help."

"You must know this isn't what I want to hear."

"Nathan, please. I'm saying all the wrong things, I know. . . . You caught me off guard. Had I the least inkling of how you felt, I'm sure I would know better what to say to you. If you don't mind, I think you better take me home."

To his credit, he didn't argue with her. Instead, he spun on his heel and walked with long strides to the wagon. Reluctantly, she followed.

Neither spoke during the return trip. Abby didn't know how to bridge the strained silence between them, or even if she should try. Berating herself for the way she handled things, she tried to think of some way to make things right. She was still shaken and even the beautiful night sky seemed to have lost its earlier luster.

After what seemed to Abby an interminable journey, Nathan finally pulled the shay in front of the salon. The lights were ablaze at Mom Bull's Restaurant. Clod could be heard playing a lively rendition of "Oh, Susanna" on his fiddle, accompanied by the sound of stomping feet and loud whoops.

The sheriff's office was dark.

Nathan jumped to the ground and hurried around the back of the shay to assist her down. She would have preferred he leave immediately, but he insisted upon seeing her safely inside. Unwilling to further reject him or chance making matters worse, she mutely accepted his offer.

Although the salon still retained the heat of the day, she stood shivering in the dark while he lit a lantern and set it on the table. The light revealed lines in his face she'd not previously noticed.

"We better . . ." She took a deep breath. "We have a hard day tomorrow. . . ."

He stood fingering his hat. "How long do I have to wait for your answer?"

She bit down on her lower lip. To her way of thinking, she'd given him her answer. She pulled off her shawl and draped it over a chair. The easy way out would be to ask for time. But it didn't seem fair to feed a man's hopes. "Nathan, I'm really very flattered, but . . ."

"I just want a chance, Abby. That's all I'm asking you to give me. I can make a good life for you. You can have your salon, everything. If you want, I'll search the very ends of the earth for your uncle. I'd do anything for you. Anything!"

His love for her was so clearly written on his face, in his voice, in his eyes, she wondered at not having seen it before. She had no idea what to say, what to do. He looked so earnest, she didn't have the heart to tell him that no amount of time was going to make her change her mind. For some utterly insane reason, she was in love with his brother.

Partly because she felt guilty, but mostly because she couldn't bear to look at the devastation on Nathan's face, she did something she'd never done before; she opted for the easy way out. Anything to put an end to this torturous night. "Perhaps it would be best to talk about this after the train arrives. We'll both be better prepared to think about our future then."

"You're right." The anger had left his voice, but the hope she saw in his eyes worried her. "I should have waited. Gunnar told me not to rush into things."

"Gunnar?" She stared at him. "Gunnar knew how you felt?"

"Don't look so surprised, Abby. He *is* my brother and my feelings for you weren't exactly a secret. He said you had a lot on your mind with your new business and your uncle. I should have listened to him."

Gunnar knew how his brother felt and he never said a word? "I don't want to give you false hope."

"Any hope is better than none. Take your time and

think about it. Please, Abby. I want you to be sure of
your feelings before you give me your answer." He
backed toward the door. "We won't talk about this
again until you're ready. You let me know when that
is."

"Nathan, wait."

She rushed after him, but by the time she reached
the front of the salon, he was already behind the reins.
"I'll see you bright and early in the morning," he called
to her. He swung the shay around and headed in the
direction of the livery stables.

Moments later, she carried the lantern up the stairs
and sat on the edge of the bed, feeling utterly miserable. *Oh, Nathan. What have I done to you?*

Why hadn't she seen it coming? Maybe she could
have nipped it in the bud. Why hadn't Gunnar said
something?

Unable to sleep, she wandered over to the window
and sat huddled in the chair, thinking about Nathan,
about Gunnar. Mostly about Gunnar. About loving
him.

Words he'd spoken in the past kept repeating themselves in her mind. Kisses that should be only memories still burned her lips.

The thing that was so hard—so painfully, devastat-
ingly hard—was that every time they'd grown closer,
he'd pulled away from her. It seemed to her they were
so far apart, she doubted they could ever find their way
back to each other.

Was it because he knew of Nathan's feelings for her?
She couldn't bear to think Gunnar would sacrifice his
own happiness for the sake of his brother. And what
about her happiness? Did it not matter to Gunnar how
she felt?

She drew her legs to her chest and laid her head on
her knees. Oh, yes, it was Gunnar she loved. But it
was painfully clear that the only thing he cared about
was Nathan. Gunnar would never forgive her for hurting his brother.

She knew that as surely as she knew her name.

# Chapter 34

It was foggy that morning as Gunnar hurried down the hill toward town, the thick mist swirling about him like ghostly shadows. He was surprised to find a lantern lit in the stables and Nathan already saddling the horses.

"What are you doing up so early?"

Nathan grinned, as if enjoying some private joke. "I couldn't sleep."

Gunnar studied his brother closely, sensing an underlying excitement. Well, who could blame him? The very air around them seemed to reverberate with excitement. Strangely enough, even the livery seemed to lean less, as if whatever energy was in the air affected it. God almighty, if they managed to bring the train to town, it would be a miracle.

Nathan finished tightening the girth on Logger. "I did it, Gunnar. Last night, I did it."

"Did what?"

"I asked Abby to marry me."

Gunnar felt as if the ground suddenly had given way beneath his feet. "So . . ." He forced himself to breathe. "What . . . what was her answer?"

Nathan laughed. "As if there were any doubt. Abby thought we should wait until after the train arrives in town before making any definite plans."

"That's . . . probably wise." Gunnar managed to keep his voice normal, but he was grateful for the cover of darkness. There was no way in hell he could manage to look happy.

"I wasn't going to ask her so soon. I took her driving

last night and, I don't know, it just popped out. Maybe it was the way the stars were reflected in her eyes."

Gunnar squeezed his hands until his fingers cut into his palms. *Spare me the details,* he begged silently. *I don't want to know about the stars in her eyes.*

"I guess I'm not the only man to lose his head in the presence of a woman."

"I guess you're not," Gunnar mumbled. Losing one's head was the least of it; it was losing the heart that was the real problem.

Harnessing his horse, Gunnar followed Nathan down Main Street. He couldn't think, suddenly, couldn't feel. It was as if he'd become part of the ghostly fog and his fate was to spend the rest of his days floating in a mindless sea.

Nathan tied his and Abby's horses to the post in front of the sheriff's office. "Abby should be here any minute. Her lights have been on for nearly a half hour."

Gunnar glanced at the curtained window above the salon. His heart felt so heavy in his chest, it was a wonder he could still stand. It was all he could do to keep from going to her and demanding to know how she could kiss him and hold him and practically let him make love to her, when all this time it was Nathan she loved. "I think I'll go on ahead," he said.

"That's a good idea. Abby and me will be along shortly."

Gunnar pressed his hat lower and pressed his heels into the side of his horse. He rode to the construction site and saw nothing; not the sun burning through the fog, not the wagons rushing by, not the miners' wives who waved as they galloped past him.

Pulled apart, that's how he felt. Broken. Shattered. Half of him felt numb, the other half hurt like hell. So it was final; Abby had agreed to be Nathan's wife.

Abby hesitated upon seeing Nathan waiting for her. He greeted her with a carefree smile and she relaxed.

"Good morning, Abby."

Relieved that the awkwardness between them had disappeared, she smiled back. Maybe Nathan realized they'd make better friends than marriage partners. Grateful that things were back to normal, she accepted a boost from him as she mounted Logger.

"Gunnar went on ahead," he said, mounting his own horse.

Outside of town they met up with Abe. Perched on the seat of the mud wagon next to him, Beulah waved. "It's a good day to build a railroad!" she called.

Nathan whipped off his hat and waved it over his head. "Ya-hoo!" he yelled, and Abby laughed at his exuberance. He really was a dear man, and he was doing everything in his power to make her feel comfortable in his presence.

Upon reaching the railroad construction headquarters, Abby was gratified to see so many people waiting in line outside the chow train. Mom Bull and Otis. Lucy stood talking to Beulah and Abe. All three waved at Abby and Nathan. Clod was deep in conversation with a new fellow reputed to be opening up a barbershop in Dangling Rope as soon as the railroad arrived.

Ginger and Meg walked over to greet Abby. "You'll never believe who came with us," Ginger said.

Abby followed Ginger's finger to the water car. "Rosie?" she mouthed. She never thought she'd see the day Rosie would join the railroad crew.

"This is the first time she's ever been seen in public without her girdle," Ginger said, keeping her voice low. "Said she has no intention of wearing the darn thing while doing a man's job."

Abby laughed. "Good for her."

The volunteers stood in the food line and carried their tin plates to one of the railroad cars that served as a dining room.

Abby and Nathan sat down at a table toward the center of the car, next to Burt. After eating mainly Mom Bull's food since arriving in Dangling Rope, Abby had forgotten what it was like to eat flapjacks that were light and fluffy.

"Do you think she'd mind if I came courting?" Burt asked.

Abby stared across the table at him. Thinking he must mean Meg or even Ginger, she pursed her lips thoughtfully. Rosie wouldn't take kindly to losing one of her girls. "Which one do you have in mind?"

The question seemed to surprise him. "Which one? Why, Mom Bull, of course."

Abby was so surprised, she almost choked. Holy blazes, there must be something in the air. First Nathan announced his feelings for her; now this. She coughed to clear her voice, and Nathan patted her on the back.

"Are you all right?" Burt asked.

"I'm fine," she said, taking a quick gulp of coffee to clear her throat.

Burt waited until she had recovered. "Well, what do you think? Will Mom Bull have me or won't she?"

Despite his unconventional taste in women, Abby liked the man. He drove his men hard and shouted loud, but beneath his rough exterior, she sensed he was kind and fair. "She'd be a fool not to."

Nathan frowned. "What about Otis?" he asked. "Wouldn't he be a bit put out?"

"Who's Otis?" Burt asked.

"Why, he's the deputy sheriff of Dangling Rope," Nathan explained. "And he won't take kindly to anyone messing around with his woman."

"She's not his woman," Abby said.

"We don't know that for a fact," Nathan argued.

Abby leaned forward and lowered her voice. "I think it's up to Mom Bull to decide who comes courting."

"I agree." Burt stood. "We better get started. We want to get as much done before nightfall as possible."

Outside, the rail boss stood in front of the new recruits, shaking his head in disbelief. Obviously, he didn't share Burt's opinion that women could do an adequate job. He glared at Gunnar. "You said you were going to get me more help. What do you give me? A bunch of women. What do you expect me to do with them? Throw a tea party?"

Abby was irritated by the man. "We came to work, sir. And that's what we intend to do!"

The man stepped in front of her. "Very well. Then listen, because I'm only going to say this once. You'll each man a sledgehammer. It'll be three strokes to the spike, ten spikes to the rail, and four hundred rails to the mile. Any questions?" His expression strictly forbade any discussion, let alone questions. When no one was brave enough to raise a hand, he shouted, "Get to work!"

Glaring at him, Abby reached for one of the sledgehammers, which was heavy enough to require the use of both hands, and fell in line behind the others.

Presently, the rail boss yelled at her. "Hey, you, start over there!"

"My name is Miss Parker!" she yelled back. Scowling at him, she trudged to a portion of shiny rails that ran along the evenly spaced cross ties. Already the gaugers had measured the rails to make certain the distance between them met the requirements of the narrow-gauge train.

From the distance came the sound of blasting as the graders cut through the gorges. Straddling the rail, she lifted the head of the wooden-handled sledgehammer over her shoulder and dropped it forward. The sledgehammer met the heavy steel spike with a loud resonating clang and a shower of blue sparks, but failed to produce any noticeable results.

"That's one!" the rail boss shouted in her ear, before moving down the line.

Abby lifted the sledgehammer a second time and a third. The spike hadn't budged. She glared at the back of the rail boss. Three strikes, indeed! Who did he think he was fooling?

Abby dropped the head of the sledgehammer to the

ground and rubbed her hands together. Bracing herself, she filled her lungs with air, picked up the sledgehammer, and lifted it overhead. This time the head of the spike dropped lower. It took eighteen strikes in all before the head of the spike was level.

Soon, the mountains echoed with the sound of picks and sledgehammers.

Toward midmorning, Gunnar took over the chore for her, freeing her to take on the less backbreaking chore of laying cross ties. Relieved to be free of the sledgehammer, she nonetheless found his presence a distraction. His bare back glistening in the morning sun as he worked, he lifted his sledgehammer over his head and brought it down with thunderous force.

It grew hotter by the hour, and by the time the sun was overhead and the train whistle blew for lunch, she thought she would die from heat. Her hair was wet with perspiration, her damp clothes clinging to her body.

She walked downstream to a quiet spot beneath a grove of aspens, the leaves fluttering in the soft breeze. She sat on the ground and pulled off her boots and stockings.

She stuck her knife in one boot and, holding the hem of her skirt up high, she waded out to the middle of the stream. The palms of her hands were covered in blisters. She dangled her hand in the sparkling clear stream. The icy water stung her hands for a moment, but the pain soon subsided and a soothing numbness took its place.

She looked up to see Gunnar watching her from the bank. Grateful that he'd taken over the spiker's job for her, she beckoned to him. "Why don't you join me?" she called. Fortunately, the rush of water drowned out the tremulous sound of her voice. "The water feels great."

He stared at her for a heart-jolting moment and looked about to turn away. But he surprised her by stooping to roll up the cuffs of his trousers. He tossed his hat on the bank, and his dark hair gleamed in the sun as he waded into the water, and curled softly around his neck.

Her pulse quickened as he neared and, thinking the dark look on his face was due to exhaustion, she gave him a sympathetic smile. "I have nothing but respect for the men who do this work on a daily basis."

"The water feels good," he said, avoiding her eyes. As if on impulse, he abandoned any attempt to stay dry and dived headfirst in the water, disappearing altogether before emerging directly in front of her. Water streamed off his head to his shoulders. His hair was plastered against his head, giving him a playful appearance that belied the haunting dark expression on his face as he gazed at her.

She blew on her palms and he caught her hands in his. He sucked in his breath as he examined each blister in turn. He pulled a wet handkerchief from his trousers pocket and wrapped it tenderly around one reddened palm, avoiding her eyes as he worked.

"I hear congratulations are in order," he said hoarsely.

"Congratulations?"

He lifted his eyes to hers. "Nathan told me the two of you are getting married."

She stared at him in astonishment. "He told you that?"

Gunnar arched a dark brow. His hooded eyes gave no hint as to what he was thinking, the stern set of his jaw and mouth gave even less. "Why wouldn't he tell me? I'm his brother."

"But it's not true!"

His face clouded in confusion. "Not true? What do you mean, it's not true?"

Stung by the censure in his voice, she lashed out at him. "You don't have to sound so . . ."

He grimaced as if in pain. "so what, Abby?"

"So angry!"

"All I want to know is whether or not you're going to marry my brother. He says you are."

"He's mistaken."

"Mistaken?" His voice held a note of disbelief. "How could he make a mistake like that?"

"By hearing only what he wants to hear. I tried to tell him no, but he wouldn't listen. He begged me to think it over. I told him we'd talk about it after the train arrived."

Gunnar looked thunderstruck. "My God, Abby. He actually thinks . . ." He gazed at her with quiet intensity. "You're not going to . . . ?"

She shook her head mutely, not knowing what to say.

His eyes softened as he considered her answer, softened and grew almost misty, softened and turned to gold. Then suddenly, cruelly, his eyes hardened and grew distant. "It'll kill him."

Hot fury rose inside her. "That's all you care about, isn't it? Your brother! You don't care a fig about me or how I feel."

"That's not true, Abby. I . . . care for you. Very deeply."

"Oh, no, you don't!" she stormed. "Otherwise you wouldn't have treated me so coldly after what happened between us."

"Nothing happened," he said firmly as if denying it would erase the memory.

"You kissed me," she shouted at him, not caring who heard. "Not once, but three times. Isn't that something?"

"I had no right to touch you, Abby." He reached for her arm, but she pulled away. If he had no right to touch her before, he had even less right to touch her now.

His face closed, as if guarding a secret. "Abby, please understand, after Nathan told me he loved you, I couldn't—"

"So it's true!" More hurt than angry, she fired accusations like bullets. "You knew and you didn't care!" Desperate to mask her true feelings, she gave an ugly mocking laugh. "How considerate of you! It seems there's nothing you won't do for your brother."

"What's that supposed to mean?" He caught her by the arm and when she fought him off, they both fell into the water.

Kicking frantically, she splashed in a crazy circle before regaining her balance. "Now look at what you've done," she sputtered.

"I'm sorry," he said, feeling totally inadequate and confused. What an appealing sight she made. Her wet clothes clinging to the gentle curves of her body; her thin white waistshirt transparent enough to make a man forget any promises he'd made to himself. He slipped an arm around her waist and crushed her to him. "I didn't mean to get you all wet."

"Let me go." She pressed against his chest with both arms, but he refused to budge.

"Not until you tell me what's going on. Why did you turn Nathan down?"

"It's none of your business."

"He told me you loved him."

"He should have checked with me first."

Gunnar's grip tightened. "If he didn't, I did. You said you cared for him. Don't deny it, Abby. I heard you with my own ears."

"Caring isn't the same as loving someone. Not the way I love you."

He held her so close, her breasts were pressed hard against his chest. He held her so close it was as if the two of them had become one. "What . . . what did you say?" he gasped at last.

"I said I love you."

She felt a shudder travel the length of his body. When he spoke, his voice was hoarse. "Nathan was convinced you loved him."

"I never did anything to make him think that."

"Nothing?"

"Nothing!"

The muscle fluttered at his jawline as his gaze bored into her. His bold embrace and probing eyes told her no lie had a chance, no secret was safe. Satisfied he had the truth, he cursed beneath his breath and let her go.

Fast action on her part to regain her balance was all that kept her from falling into the water a second time. "Why?" she demanded to know. "Why are you so eager to give me up for your brother?"

"It's not a matter of giving you up. I believed Nathan when he told me you had feelings for him." Hands at his waist, he shrugged and sighed, like a man tired of fighting. "I don't know, Abby. Maybe on some level I wanted it to be true. Maybe I thought losing you to Nathan was just punishment for being the one our mother took with her." He paused and a waiting silence stretched between them. "Don't look at me like that," he pleaded. "Try to understand. He's not the same person since you've come into his life. You bring out his best. How could I possibly take away the one woman in all the world that caused such a miraculous change in my brother?"

She stared at him aghast. Something snapped inside. "You leather-headed, jingle-brained, heart-cheating . . ." She called him every name she could think of. It was an old habit learned from the streets, but at the moment she didn't have a lot of resources left. When the name-calling failed to relieve the anger and hurt, she beat on his chest with her fists, ignoring the pain of her sore muscles and hands. He grabbed her by the wrists, but she wiggled free. "What about my feelings?" she cried.

"I told you, Abby. I honestly thought you had feelings for him. Had I known . . . if I thought you really cared for me . . ."

She stared at him in disbelief. "You can honestly deny knowing how I felt after the night we spent together?"

"That was a crazy night, Abby. Things happen when two people are together under such circumstances."

"Is that all it was to you, Gunnar? Just a crazy night?" Not wanting to hear his answer, she pushed against his chest hard, but this only made him clamp down on her shoulders.

Their gazes met, setting off sparks between them. "Don't you know, Abby? That was the most wonderful night in the world for me. That was the night I fell in love with you."

Abby pressed her hand hard against her mouth, not sure she'd heard right. But the moment of confusion only lasted for a fleeting moment. For suddenly she was in his arms, his warm hot lips on hers, and nothing seemed to exist but the love flowing between them.

He kissed her long and hard—and she returned his kiss with equal fervor. But something, some self-protective instinct, perhaps, made her push him away. "Oh, no, you don't," she cried. "You're not doing this again. You're not kissing me, only to ignore me. I won't have it, Gunnar!" They stood staring at each other, heedless of the quick rushing water at their knees.

"I love you, Abby." His voice rang deep with meaning and was filled with passion, but this time she heard what she didn't want to hear the first time; a thin edge of regret. And it was this regret that spoke the loudest. The simple truth was, he would never forgive himself for loving her.

Swallowing hard, she fought for control. "I can't be part of your guilt, Gunnar. What happened in the past between you and Nathan happened. I can't have it play a part in my life."

"Abby . . ." His fingertips touched the hands at her side, and the pain inside her grew to unbearable proportions. A million unspoken words hung between them. He pressed his forehead against hers. "I'll talk to Nathan. I've got to. It's the only thing that makes sense. He never understood about Mother. Dear God, I only hope he understands about us."

She gazed up at him, her heart filled with hope. Could she really expect Gunnar to put their feelings for each other above all else? "And if he doesn't?" she whispered.

Gunnar didn't reply. He didn't have to. She already knew that whatever happened, Gunnar would always put his brother first.

The rest of the day was a blur as far as Abby was concerned. She had been assigned another job, this one placing ties on the ground. It was hard on the back, but easier on the hands. She tried to keep her mind on her work, but it was difficult. She could see Gunnar behind her, pounding spikes. Ahead of her Nathan worked with the blasting crew. Two brothers as different as day and night. She hated knowing that loving one meant hurting the other.

She wandered over to the water tank for a drink. Beulah joined her, looking upset. "Have you seen that poor baby's face?" she said. She was staring at Lucy who worked a distance away. "That man of hers is beating her more and more lately. If you ask me, he's gonna do real damage one day."

At the end of the day, the foreman blew the whistle and the men headed for the stream to clean up for supper. Nathan searched her out, finding her washing her hands. His face was covered with sweat and grime, his hair plastered with mud, but his eyes danced merrily.

"It's hard to get through that mountain," he said. He cupped his hands with water and splashed his face. "We're hoping to blast our way through tonight."

She handed him a bar of soap. "You're working through the night?"

He nodded. He lathered his arms to his elbows. "We don't have a choice. We only have until noon Friday. That's less than forty-two hours away." He dried himself off with a towel and tossed it aside. "I'll see you back in town."

She nodded. "Nathan." He turned. "Be careful." He nodded and strolled away.

Meg ran up to her. "S-s-s-omething's w-wrong with Ginger."

"Oh, no!" Abby followed Meg to where a small crowd was gathered. Ginger lay on the ground, her face pale, her voice weak.

Madam Rosie looked visibly shaken. "She just fainted dead away," she explained. "And she's not even wearing a corset."

Abby knelt on the ground next to the pale woman. "Maybe you've had too much sun, Ginger."

Gunnar joined them. "I'll take her back to Dangling Rope."

Abby nodded. "I think that's best."

Gunnar lifted Ginger in his arms and headed toward the wagons.

Abby started to follow, but a glint of light caught her eye. A closer look revealed a blue hobnobbed bottle, the kind that held arsenic, half hidden in the dirt where Ginger had lain only moments earlier. She picked it up and followed Gunnar.

# Chapter 35

Abby woke the following morning and was hardly able to move. Every bone, every joint, every muscle in her body ached. It took her forever to crawl out of bed and work her way through her morning ablutions. Finally she placed a hand on the small of her back and hobbled down the stairs.

Gunnar was waiting for her outside, the horses already saddled. He lifted his hand when he saw her, and it irked her that he showed not the least bit of stiffness or difficulty in moving.

She took little shuffling steps toward him, her legs resisting every step of the way.

He assessed her from head to toe, his eyes soft with sympathy and so much more. Yesterday, then, hadn't been a dream. "Abby?" He caressed her cheek. "Are you all right?"

She tried to straighten and grimaced. "Perfectly. Why wouldn't I be?" she glanced toward the Opera House. "I wonder how Ginger is today." Ginger had seemed her old self last night, but Rosie had promised to send away for the doctor as a precaution. "I'll wager she's poisoning herself with arsenic."

"Arsenic? Are you sure?"

"What do you think gives her that porcelain look?"

"She takes poison just so she looks a certain way?" His eyes were wide in astonishment. "She could kill herself."

Abby thought of her uncle's sister and nodded sadly.

"She wouldn't be the first one. That's why I'm determined to make my salon a success."

Gunnar tightened the cinch around Logger. "Did the blasting keep you awake?"

"I was too tired."

Mom Bull walked out of her restaurant, wearing her apron. "Have you seen that fool man Otis?"

"Not since last night," Gunnar said. "Why?"

"He never showed up for breakfast. All because Burt asked me if he could come a courtin'."

Gunnar's brows lifted. "Why, Mom Bull. You do have a way with men."

"It's like my mother used to say; the way to a man's heart is through his stomach." She stuck her cigar in her mouth and traipsed back to the restaurant.

Almost as soon as Mom Bull disappeared, a horse and wagon rolled into town. Recognizing the driver as Lucy, Abby limped to the side of the street and waited for her.

Lucy wore a bonnet with a wide floppy brim that all but hid her face. She kept her face lowered as she spoke. "I can't work on the railroad anymore."

"Lucy, did he—"

"I . . . I can't talk right now." Lucy tugged on the reins and the wagon made a wide circle in the middle of Main Street. As quickly as she'd come, she was gone.

Forgetting her sore muscles and aching joints, Abby stared after her, hands at her waist. "He hit her again!"

Gunnar rested his hands on her shoulder. "Calm down, Abby."

She spun around to face him. "If I ever get my hands on the man, I'll . . ." She stopped upon seeing Meg.

Meg looked distressed. "I'm s-sorry to interrupt, b-but I thought you should know that M-Madam Rosie has f-forbidden me and the others to w-w-work on the railroad."

"But why?" Abby asked. "Didn't you make it back in time?"

"It's Ginger," Meg explained. "She's all r-right. But M-madam Rosie said she didn't want to take a chance on the rest of us c-collapsing in the s-sun."

"It wasn't the sun, Meg. I'm convinced it's something she's taken for her complexion. You must talk to her and tell her how dangerous it is. Yesterday was a warning. Next time she might not be so lucky."

Meg paled. "I'll do what I c-can."

"And tell the doctor what I said. Maybe he'll talk some sense into her."

Meg nodded. "I b-best get back."

Abby sympathized as Meg limped back to the Opera House. "What are we going to do, Gunnar? Our workers are backing out."

A loud boom sounded, shaking the ground. The horses whinnied and danced around nervously. His eyes leveled in the direction of the explosion, Gunnar frowned. "It sounds like they're still trying to blast their way through that mountain."

He accidentally brushed against her sore shoulder and she grimaced in pain. "I'm sorry, Abby." His brow knitted in a worried frown. "I think you should stay here and get some rest. I'll ride out to construction headquarters. If they failed to get through that mountain last night, I'm afraid it's over. There's no way we can meet the deadline."

For once in her life, Abby didn't argue. She was more than happy to slip back upstairs to her room and bury her aching body beneath the covers.

She was still asleep when a knock came at the door. "Abby, it's Gunnar."

Surprised to find the shadows of late afternoon outside her window, she reached for her dressing gown. "Just a minute," she called. Recalling she was fully dressed, she abandoned the dressing gown and slumped back against the pillow. "Come in," she called.

The door moaned on its hinges and Gunnar peered through the open crack. "Sorry to waken you." He pushed the door wide and gazed at her with tender concern.

She searched his face. "The railroad?"

He carried a wooden chair to the side of her bed and straddled it, leaning his arms on the back. "The railroad isn't going to make it by tomorrow," he said. "It took longer to blast through that mountain than expected and a couple of men were injured."

"Oh, no," Abby gasped. "Nathan?"

"Nathan's fine. Fortunately no one was seriously injured. But the men have been sent to Denver for medical care. That means we have a severe shortage of trained men. Even if we managed to round up enough volunteers, there simply isn't enough men to train them, and we still have a mile and a half of track to lay by noon tomorrow."

Abby swallowed hard. She wasn't used to defeat, didn't know how to handle it.

"I'm sorry, Abby. We tried."

"I know." She reached up to wipe away a tear from her cheek.

"Let me get you a handkerchief." He opened the top bureau drawer, and looked at her in surprise upon finding it empty.

"In my trunk," she said, pointing to the foot of the bed.

He dropped down on a knee and released the latch, his fingers caressing the lace that had caught in the crack. The handkerchiefs were stacked neatly in the set-up tray, next to the bonnet box. He picked up one lace handkerchief and dropped the lid back in place. "Wouldn't it be easier to use the bureau drawers?"

"I always keep my things in my trunk," she said.

He sat down on the bed next to her and lifted a corner of the handkerchief to her face. Gently, he dabbed away a shimmering tear. "Did you say always? Don't you ever unpack? Even at home?"

She regarded him with liquid eyes before shaking her head ever so slightly.

His hand stilled. "Why not?"

"After my father died, I was sent to an orphanage. From there, I went to live with several different families who had expressed an interest in adopting me. No sooner had I unpacked my things than I would be sent back to the orphanage. Sometimes they'd pack me up so quickly, some of my most precious belongings were left behind, including a letter my father sent me as a child. I decided to keep my things in my trunk so that I would never lose anything again, no matter how quickly I was packed up."

"I don't understand, Abby. Why did the families keep sending you back to the orphanage?"

"Once it was because I grew too fast for one family and they couldn't afford to keep me in clothes. Another family, a doctor and his wife, decided I wasn't bright enough. Then there was the family who deemed me a melancholy child. After a while, I didn't wait for them to think up some excuse to be rid of me. I left at the first sign of trouble. It was easier to leave of my own accord than to wait for the orphanage director to appear on the doorstep."

Gunnar was stunned. "What was the matter with these people? Melancholy? What does that mean? And what is a child to do but grow?" He looked so angry on her behalf, she felt her heart swell with feelings of love. "And what was that nonsense about you not being bright enough? What kind of reasons are those for rejecting a child?"

"Is wanting a stage career a better reason?" she asked.

The question seemed to surprise him and it took him a moment to reply. "No reason is good enough for a mother to abandon her child."

She pushed a lock of hair away from his forehead, caressing his sun-bronzed forehead with her fingertips.

Thrilling to her intoxicating touch, he wrapped her hand in his and pressed it against his lips. "So you never had a permanent home?" he murmured next to her skin.

She laid her free hand on his head. "Not until my uncle found me. Even then, I never unpacked, just in case. A part of me feared he would grow tired of my street ways. I guess I'll always be a traveling lady." The tears started to flow again, this time fast and furious, until a hot liquid path trailed down her cheeks.

"Abby?" He pulled her in his arms.

"Oh, Gunnar." She sobbed next to his strong firm chest. "I wanted so much to make Dangling Rope a home . . . just like Nathan wanted."

"I know." He stroked her head tenderly.

"Poor Nathan," she whispered. She clutched at Gunnar's vest. "Go to him. He needs you."

He gazed down at her, long and hard. Her eyes were luminous. He ran a finger up one tear-stained cheek. "I'm staying here with you, Abby."

"But Nathan . . ."

He touched her lips with his fingers before feathering her mouth with kisses. "I've always put Nathan's needs before anyone else's, even my own." His lips brushed against hers as he spoke. "For weeks now, I've resisted my feelings for you because I didn't want to hurt him. I can't go on doing this, Abby. I was afraid it would kill him to know I love you. The truth is, keeping my love for you inside is killing me."

He covered her mouth hungrily, then eased her back against the pillow, feathering a fiery path of kisses down her neck.

His movements slow and precise so as not to injure her sore muscles, he covered one breast with his hand and gently massaged it. She moaned with pleasure and arched toward him.

Smiling to himself, he wrapped his fingers around the soft-heaving mound, feeling her peak grow taut beneath the thin fabric of her shirtwaist.

He pulled off his boots and stretched himself beside her. Absorbing the sweet essence of her heated body, he dragged a kiss down her neck to the high-collared gingham shirtwaist. He released the tiny pearl buttons on her bodice, then slipped his hand inside to capture the naked firmness of her breast. Her nipple pressed against his palm like a tiny rosebud; her breath bathed his neck with sweet moist warmth.

"Oh, Abby," he whispered. "I've wanted this for so long. Do you know how much I love you?" He gave her a quick smile. "I know, I know. You've heard better."

"Oh, no, Gunnar!" She doubled her arms around his neck. "I've never heard better or felt better than I feel right now. Not ever!"

"I'm glad to hear that. Before this night is over, I hope you'll feel the same about a few other things."

He gently slid her shirtwaist off her shoulder and down her arms. He then pulled her sleeveless camisole off her and tossed it aside. Her breasts were naked beneath his gaze and he couldn't recall seeing anything more exquisitely beautiful.

He flicked his tongue across one ivory mound and then the other before covering one red-tipped bud with his mouth.

She moaned and wiggled beneath him. "Dear God in heaven, don't stop."

Chuckling softly, he unfastened her skirt. "I don't intend to, my love." He felt her impatience as he pulled the skirt down the length of her slender legs and tossed it aside. As quickly as his urgent fingers would allow, he undid the drawstring on her lace-trimmed drawers and drew them downward. He trailed a hot fiery path with his lips and tongue, capturing every square inch of skin he uncovered until she was writhing in pleasure.

At last she lay before him, naked and beautiful and utterly desirable. All except a leather strap at her ankle where she kept her knife. He reached down and felt her tense. A look of fear flashed across her face. He drew his hand away, stunned to recall having seen that look before on the night he'd taken her knife away.

She met his gaze. "I'm sorry, Gunnar."

He pushed a strand of hair away from her forehead. He was the one who should apologize, for not knowing, on that long-ago day when he'd disarmed her, what he knew now. "I'm not going to take your knife away, Abby."

She looked at him with so much love, he felt as if he were floating on a cloud. "It's all right, Gunnar. You can unbuckle the sheath," she whispered. He recognized the gesture for what it was: an act of faith and trust on her part. Gunnar had once envied her uncle because of her belief in him. Now, he felt humbled by the look of trust in her eyes. Never did he think it possible to love anyone as much as he loved her at that moment.

The knife came off, followed by his shirt and pants. "That's some knocker you have," she whispered in his ear.

No longer surprised by anything she said, he gasped in pleasure as her fingers traveled across his thighs and squeezed him. "Good Lord, Abby . . ."

Running her hands the length of his body, she explored the hard lean lines of his chest, his hips, his back, setting his already burning flesh on fire. "You really are a traveling lady," he gasped.

His body vibrating with liquid fire, he caught her by the wrists and pushed her back against the bed. He rolled on top of her, his throbbing manhood perched upon her damp warm nest of curls. "Get ready, Traveling Lady," he whispered. "This is one trip we're taking together."

# Chapter 36

Gunnar awoke the next morning and positioned himself so that every possible part of him was pressed against the sleeping woman in his arms. She stirred next to him. Her lashes fluttered like the wings of a butterfly, but she didn't awaken.

His heart felt as if it would burst with contentment and joy as he gazed down at her. He smiled and buried his nose in her flower-scented hair. What a wondrous night they had shared. After their initial lovemaking, he'd dressed and walked across to Mom Bull's to get them both something to eat. Together they'd sat on the bed eating burned stew and rock-hard dumplings and thinking it the best food they had ever tasted. Afterward, they'd made love again. And again.

Just thinking of the night filled him with new longing. To think he'd almost thrown it all away because of some crazy, mixed-up sense of duty.

Still, the guilt persisted. It was too deeply embedded to stay quiet for long. Now, as he held her in his arms, stroking her, absorbing the warmth and sweet fragrance of her lovely body, he shuddered with the raw ragged edge of guilt.

What kind of man was he? How could he allow himself to feel such pleasure? Knowing as he did how his love for Abby would surely destroy his brother.

Feeling a sudden dread, Gunnar gently pulled his arms from around her. She sighed softly, but her eyes remained closed. Swallowing hard, he pressed his lips into her forehead, then slid out of bed.

Their clothes had been tossed around the room in careless abandon. He smiled upon seeing her camisole puddled onto the floor next to his shirt.

He picked up the lacy garment and smoothed it over a chair, then quickly threw on his clothes.

He tiptoed from Abby's room and hurried downstairs.

The town was swaddled in the usual early morning fog. The hazy mist swirled around him, cutting visibility. Muted sounds drifted out of nowhere, without a clue as to what they were or where they were coming from.

He stood in front of Abby's salon and tried to make out Nathan's cabin. But the fog blotted out the hill behind Main Street. There was no way of knowing if his brother was home. Sickened by what he must do, he started across the street.

"Gunnar!"

Upon hearing his brother's voice behind him, Gunnar spun around. "Nathan?"

Nathan sprang out of the mists like a wild and hungry panther. "You couldn't keep your filthy hands off her, could you?"

Gunnar stared at the dark angry face and wondered when his brother had become such a stranger. "Nathan, I'm sorry—"

"Sorry? You son-of-a . . ." The last word muffled, Nathan attacked him with flying fists.

Taken by surprise, Gunnar flew back against the building, hard. The attack was so quick and furious, Gunnar hardly knew what hit him. Taking a sharp jab to the side, he barely managed to prevent a secondary blow to his jaw. "Dammit, Nathan. What's the matter with you?"

"You!" he shouted in deadly earnest, his face contorted in jealousy and hate. "You knew all along how I felt about Abby. First you steal my mother and now the one woman—"

"I didn't steal her." He started to walk away. There was no talking to Nathan when he was like this.

Nathan grabbed him from behind, spun him around, and let another fist fly. Gunnar hit the ground hard.

"Dammit, Nathan! Will you listen?"

Nathan flew at him. Gunnar pushed him back with the soles of his boots, then struggled to his feet.

Circling around him, Nathan glared menacingly, his voice low and dangerous. "I'll never forget the day Mother walked out, taking you with her. Oh, you were the golden child, the one with perfect manners and charm . . ." On and on he went, spilling all the venom and hatred that had built up through the years.

Nathan's anger was no surprise to Gunnar. He'd let enough of his anger slip out over the years to convince Gunnar that a lot of his problems with the law were a direct result of what had happened that day. No, Nathan's anger was no surprise. What surprised Gunnar was the depth of his own anger.

Eyes ablaze, Nathan came at him, swinging his fist. Gunnar ducked, then grabbed him by the collar. Their contorted faces only inches apart, Gunnar breathed hard in Nathan's face. "You think I had it so great, eh? Traveling from town to town, city to city. Never having a place to call home. Never knowing from one day to the next where my next meal was coming from?" The words began coming so fast, they hardly made sense. "You think I had it so good!" Gunnar let out a hollow laugh. "She used me, Nathan. And when I couldn't do her any good, she left me, too!"

Nathan sneered. "You want me to feel sorry for you. Is that it? You had Mother's love. That's a hell of a lot more than I had."

Gunnar released Nathan with a shove. "I hate to spoil your delusion, little brother. But the woman who was our mother didn't know the meaning of love."

"Damn you, Gunnar. You're not getting out of it that easy." Head low, Nathan rammed straight into him. Gunnar tried to ward him off, but failed to deflate the blow. Something exploded in his head; flashing lights blurred his vision. With a shake of his head, he struck Nathan's jaw with a quick clumsy punch.

"Stop it!"

At the sound of Abby's frantic voice, Gunnar looked up at Abby's window. It was a mistake, for it allowed Nathan to hammer yet another raw-knuckled fist into his face.

Reeling backward, Gunnar fought against the dark fog that was closing in. He pressed his body against a post to keep from falling. He tasted blood as he turned, fists ready. The look on Nathan's face confirmed his own fear. This would be a fight to the finish.

Nathan lurched at Gunnar, his face in a murderous rage. Locked together, the two men struggled and rolled into the middle of the street, kicking up dust.

Abby watched in horror from her window. "Stop it!" she cried out again. "Stop it, both of you!" Otis ran out of Mom Bull's Restaurant, saw the battling brothers, and froze in his tracks.

Abby leaned out of the window, holding the sheet to cover her nakedness. "Otis, do something!"

"It's a family fight, Abby. Can't interfere with family."

"If you won't stop them, then I will!" She quickly donned her dressing gown and grabbed her knife off the bed table where Gunnar had laid it the night before.

By the time she reached ground level, Nathan and Gunnar were pounding on each other without mercy, their angry voices almost savage in intensity as they hurled accusations back and forth.

"Stop it!" Knife poised, she lunged forward. Somehow, she would make them stop. Mom Bull grabbed her by the arm.

"Leave 'em be," she said.

Abby tried to pull herself free, but Mom Bull held on with the power of steel. Abby beseeched her. "They're going to kill each other!"

Her cry was drowned out by a loud whistle that sliced through the air in a shrill squeal. Suddenly the air rang out with the sound of clanging bells. A strange rumbling shook the ground and rattled the windows. Thinking it was an earthquake, Abby froze in terror. Even Mom Bull had the good sense to look frightened as she dropped her hold on Abby.

"The train's coming!" Otis shouted.

"The what?" Abby couldn't believe her ears. Then she saw the tracks running down the middle of the street.

The two brothers rolled away from each other, just as the engine loomed out of the fog and headed straight for them.

Gunnar, poised on hands and knees, shook his head in a daze. Nathan lay on his side, holding his head.

The horn gave a loud blast and Abby screamed for Gunnar and Nathan to get out of the way.

Gunnar glanced up at the advancing train and staggered to his feet, but Nathan's prone body remained motionless.

Abby dashed toward him, but it was Gunnar who reached Nathan first, followed by Otis. Together they lifted Nathan out of the path of the oncoming train.

The twenty-ton iron horse steamed down Main Street, wobbling dangerously like a child's spinning top about to fall over on its side.

"What's wrong with it?" Abby asked Clod, shouting to be heard over the clanging bells and loud hisses. "Why is it shaking like that?"

"There ain't nothin' wrong with it," Clod said. He threw his hat skyward, then jumped on the cowcatcher. A number of railroad workers clung to the shiny black smokestack, waving their hats in the air and yelling at the top of their lungs.

The air brakes hissed and the train slowed. Then suddenly the tracks separated. The slow-moving locomotive derailed but stayed upright, coming to a full stop mere inches away from the front of the hotel.

For a moment, no one moved. The porter, a youth no older than twenty, was the first to jump from the passenger car. He looked shaken, but managed a grin for the small gathering.

Behind him several politicians disembarked, including Mulpepper and Clayton, whom Abby recalled meeting during the fracas at the Opera House. Mulpepper lit into Gunnar.

"What the hell is this, Kincaid? We could have been killed!"

Gunnar, still dazed, wiped the blood away from his lip. Before he had a chance to answer, a group of horsemen galloped into town.

"Utes!" someone shouted from atop the engine.

A moment of panic ensued. Mulpepper dived beneath the still hissing engine, with Clayton close behind.

"It's all right, Mr. Mulpepper," Abby called to him, recognizing the head horseman as Owns Six Horses.

The chief slipped off the saddleless horse in front of Abby. "Iron horse come to town. Now Traveling Lady tell how to make medicine face cream."

Mulpepper crawled out from under the train, fuming angrily. He brushed himself off and glared at Abby. "I almost get killed and this . . . this savage is worried about face cream!"

Abby glowered back at the incensed politician. "This man's name is Owns Six Horses."

Mulpepper scowled. "Yes, well, I want an explanation. Who's responsible for this travesty?"

"I have no idea what you're talking about," Gunnar said, rubbing his bruised chin.

Mulpepper kicked the wayward rail and grimaced. Holding his injured foot in his hand, he jumped about on one foot, sputtering. "Do you see that? Do you see that?" he yelled for all to hear. "The tracks are just lying in the street. Do you hear me? There's nothing holding them in place. You can't have makeshift tracks!"

Mom Bull towered over the legislator. "The train was supposed to git here by June fifteenth, and that's what it did."

Owns Six Horses grinned. "My people worked all night."

Abby spun her head to face him. "You laid the tracks?" She couldn't believe it. Thanks to the Utes, they'd accomplished the impossible. "How can we ever thank you?"

"No need," Owns Six Horses said grimly. "Just need face cream."

"Face cream!" Mulpepper's eyes looked to pop out of his head. "What's wrong with this town? You failed to get the tracks laid properly. Look at this." He lifted his foot as if to kick the rail again, but thought better of it. "There's not a spike anywhere!"

Abby took a closer look at the shiny rails. Mulpepper was right; not a bolt was in sight. It was a miracle the train had traveled as far as it had without derailing.

Mom Bull grabbed the man by his collar and pulled him off his feet. "Is there somethin' wrong with yer hearin'? The train was supposed to reach town by June fifteenth. Ain't nobody said nothin' about the train havin' to stay upright."

"She's right!" Burt said, edging out Otis to stand by Mom Bull's side.

"Course she's right," Otis said, edging out Burt.

Mulpepper straightened his shirt. "Well . . . I . . ."

No one heard what he said for the loud cheering. The folks of Dangling Rope had something to celebrate, and by George, that's what they intended to do.

# Chapter 37

Later that night, Gunnar sat alone in his cabin and nursed his injuries. His hand hurt, his head hurt, his sides hurt. Still, nothing compared to how he felt inside. Never would he forget the look on Nathan's face when Nathan confronted him in front of Abby's place that morning. It was the same devastating gut-wrenching look that had haunted Gunnar since the day he was dragged away by his mother.

Gunnar dropped his head into his hands. Ever since he was seven years old, he'd done his damnedest to forget the look of horror and anguish on Nathan's young face the day he'd been left behind. But after seeing the same look repeated this morning, he knew he never could.

He leaned his head against the back of the chair. His aching jaw forgotten, he squeezed his eyes tight. *Oh, Abby! After the wonderful night we spent together, how can I find the strength, the fortitude, the courage to stay away from you?*

A knock sounded at his door. "Gunnar?"

His eyes flew open at the sound of Abby's voice. The door opened and she stepped into the yellow circle of light cast by the kerosene lantern. Her presence brought a rush of blood through his veins.

She searched his face, her gaze lingering on the redness on his chin. "Are you all right?"

He opened his mouth and grimaced. No, he wasn't all right, dammit. Would never be all right again.

"Yeah," he managed at last. He ached, physically ached, to touch her.

Wanting her more than he thought it possible to want anyone, he watched her draw up a chair and sit by his side. "Have . . . have you seen Nathan?" he asked.

Abby sat and bit down on her lower lip. He could guess by the accusatory look on her face what she was thinking. Even now, after everything they'd shared, after everything that had happened between them, his first thought was for Nathan. If only that were true . . .

"Meg is taking care of him."

"Meg?" He shifted in his chair and rubbed his leg. "Damned stupid kid. I didn't want to fight him." He slammed his hand down hard on the table and winced in pain.

Abby started forward, but he brushed her away. He was having enough trouble keeping his hands away from her. A hurt look crossed her face and he felt a shattering lurch inside as if some vital part of him had broken away. It took every bit of energy he could muster to keep the memories of the previous night from demolishing his resolve. It was not the time to think. Or to feel. Or even remember. "My ribs," he offered by way of explanation.

"I'm so sorry," she whispered. "I never meant to cause trouble between you and Nathan."

Gunnar shook his head. "That fight wasn't about you." When the truth had hit him, exactly, he couldn't say. He supposed it was during the time he and Nathan had tried to kill each other. Didn't someone once say that a man facing death only dealt with the truth? Maybe that's what dying was all about. "What happened this morning . . . that was about me."

"You?"

"All these years, I've felt guilty because of what our mother did to Nathan. I tried to make it up to him. I even tried to deny my love for you."

The pain in her face matched his own. "I know."

The tears that sprang to her eyes nearly tore his heart in two. It made what he had to do that much more difficult, and maybe even impossible.

"I never meant you to suffer because of me." He took her hand in his and held it tight. It was a mistake to touch her. He knew it was a mistake, but he couldn't seem to help himself. He pressed her hand hard against his face. "I didn't know until today how much anger I've buried over the years. You were right, Abby. I didn't want to admit it, but you were right. In her own unique way, our mother deserted us both. I don't think she meant it." Catching himself, he shook his head. Even now, after all this time, he still felt the need to defend her. Nothing, it seemed, was more painful than to admit one's own mother was lacking in basic human qualities. Maybe that's why Nathan had placed the blame on Gunnar's shoulders. Maybe that's why Gunnar had let him.

He dropped Abby's hand and struggled to his feet. "I've got to go to him." He was in no condition to go anywhere.

She reached out to him. "I don't think that's a good idea. Give him some time. Please, Gunnar."

"If anything happens to him, I'll never forgive myself."

"It's not up to you to protect him."

"I owe him that."

"You don't owe him anything, Gunnar." She pressed her hand against his back.

"If I don't save him, who will?" He turned to face her, but the bleak look on his face was as much of a barrier as was his back. "Last night . . . I should never . . . I knew, dammit, what my loving you would do to my brother. I'm going to have to live with that for the rest of my life." He stepped back, putting as much distance between them as possible. He lifted his hat off the wooden peg by the door and pressed it on his aching head.

"Gunnar . . . if you push me away again, it will be the last time."

"Abby . . ."

"I mean it. You talk about what all of this is doing to you, to Nathan. It's killing me, too, Gunnar."

He paused, his hand on the latch. "I hate knowing that. It makes what I have to do . . ." His voice broke as he turned his tortured face toward her. "I love you, Abby. No matter what happens, nothing will ever change that."

"I know that. I also know you love your brother more."

He felt shocked, then angry. "That's not true, Abby. How could you think such a thing after the night we spent together? Nathan's my responsibility. Don't you understand? I can't just walk away from him!"

"Nathan's a man. You have no responsibility to him!"

"He's my brother!" He ran his fingers through his hair. "Abby, I could never live with myself knowing that any happiness of mine is based on my brother's misery. . . . No matter how much I love you, I'd always be weighed down with guilt. Eventually, I'm afraid, the guilt would end up destroying what you and I have together."

She looked at him in disbelief. "It's you who is destroying that!"

"My choice is to destroy him or to destroy us." He sighed a deep and anguished sigh that seemed to rise from the very depths of him. "Last night, I thought I could give myself to you heart and soul and not worry about Nathan. But that was a lie. This morning . . . I can't betray him. No matter how much I want to, dammit! I can't do that to him."

Her eyes flashed angrily. "If you think I'm going to fall in love with your brother just to appease your conscience . . ."

"Abby, don't do this to me."

"What about what you're doing to me?" her voice

held a thin edge of hysteria. "Don't I have any say in this? Doesn't it matter how I feel?"

"Of course it matters. This wouldn't be so damned hard if it didn't matter."

"Last night . . . what we shared . . . I thought it meant something."

"It did mean something. It meant the world to me, Abby. You mean the world to me."

"And still you can walk away as if nothing happened?"

"If you think that's what I'm doing, then you don't know me."

"I think, perhaps, I don't want to!" She whirled around and shot out the door.

"Abby, wait!" By the time he reached the porch, she'd already disappeared. He called her name, over and over, until his voice echoed along the canyon walls and rose to the very treetops in an anguished plaintive wail. When he finally stopped calling her, the world echoed the dead silence of his heart.

Abby ran through the woods, stumbling over fallen logs and fighting off low-growing branches with her hands. She ran until she could run no more. Gasping for air, she bent over trying to breathe. It was the sound of yipping coyotes that finally made her turn back.

The Opera House stood like a shining beacon in the distance. Closer to Main Street, the sound of Clod's fiddle broke the silence. The railroad crew were camped just outside of town and little dots of light shimmered from among the trees. On Main Street, the town was divided down the middle by the derailed train.

Abby considered leaving town. There really was no reason for her to stay. She'd failed to find her uncle. There was nothing more to do but face the fact he was gone—perhaps forever. It was the story of her life. Everyone she ever loved eventually left her.

Moving by memory, she let herself inside the dark salon and groped her way to the counter. Her hands shaking, she searched for the box of matches and lit a candle. A small sound like a sigh told her she was not alone. Startled, she instinctively reached for her knife and spun around. She could see someone huddled in the far shadows. "Nathan?" she whispered.

"It's Lucy."

"Lucy!" She slipped the knife back in place. "Holy blazes, you nearly scared me to death." She lit a lantern and carried it over to where the woman sat. The flickering light revealed an ugly red mark across Lucy's tear-streaked cheek. "Oh, no, your face!"

Abby set the lantern down and squeezed Lucy's small trembling hand. "Stay here. I'm going to fetch some water."

She raced to the back room, where she kept a bucket of freshly drawn water. Fetching a cup of water and a sponge, she hurried back to Lucy's side. She lifted the dampened sponge to Lucy's face. "This might hurt a bit."

Lucy cried out at her touch and cast a worried glance at the doorway.

Abby drew the sponge away. "You're safe here. I won't let him hurt you."

"If he had a mind to come here, you couldn't stop him. No one could."

"Don't be so sure of that," Abby said. "He's a coward, Lucy. Men who would harm a woman are cowards."

"He may be a coward in your eyes, Abby. But that don't make him any less dangerous."

Abby gently dabbed the area beneath Lucy's eyes. The swollen skin was already beginning to turn blue. "Why do you stay with him?"

"He's my husband."

"Don't you have family that you could stay with?"

She nodded. "My family lives in North Carolina." For a moment she fell silent, a faraway look in her eye. "What kind of a woman would I be if I deserted my husband?"

"A husband's job is to love and protect his family. He's the one who's deserted you." Abby pressed the sponge next to Lucy's cheek. "Hold this," she said. It was warm inside the salon, but Lucy was shaking and her skin felt like ice. "Let's go upstairs. You can stay with me tonight."

Lucy cast another worried glance at the door. "I . . . I don't know if I should. If he finds me with you, he could kill me. He could kill us both."

"Lucy, listen to me. A man like that preys on fear. You've got to be strong."

She lifted the lantern and offered Lucy her arm. Lucy clung to Abby's arm like a frightened child as they climbed the stairs. Abby made Lucy lie down on the bed, and covered her with a warm quilt.

"What am I going to do?" Lucy sobbed into the pillow.

Abby sat on the edge of the bed and rubbed Lucy's back. "We'll talk about it in the morning. Right now you need to get some sleep."

"What if he comes looking for me?"

"I'll watch from the window. It'll be all right, Lucy, I promise. I'm going downstairs to move your rig. I'll hide your horse and wagon in the livery. He won't even know you're here. I'll be back as quickly as possible."

Abby left the room, closing the door softly behind her, and ran down the stairs. Outside, she stopped and listened. Mom Bull's lights were out and all was quiet. The full moon bathed the ground in a silvery light, adding to her anxiety. When she lived on the streets, she dreaded the full moon, for it was always at this time of month when crime reached a peak. She much preferred the protection of a moonless night.

Heart pounding, she followed the outline of the engine. Anyone could be hiding behind its bulky shape. She pulled her knife from her boot. Cautiously, she walked around the front of the engine and circled the length of the train. Satisfied that no one was hiding in the shadows, she replaced her knife and drove Lucy's wagon to the livery stable. She unhitched the horse and led it into one of the empty stalls, next to Logger's. She then locked the door and replaced the key in a tin box that was kept hidden in a nearby bush.

She ran back to the salon, staying in the shadow of the buildings. To her greatest relief, all was quiet. She slipped inside the salon and locked the door after her, then dashed upstairs.

She couldn't have been gone for more than ten minutes, fifteen at the most, but already Lucy was asleep.

Abby curled up in the upholstered chair and stared out the window. Never had she felt so utterly miserable. It was hard to believe how much had changed in twenty-four hours. Last night, she'd felt safe and happy in Gunnar's arms. For the first time in her life, she'd known what it meant to love and be loved as a woman. This only made her grief and pain that much harder to bear.

*No, Gunnar. I'll never understand. Never!*

Her bleak thoughts were interrupted around midnight by the sound of a horse's hooves. She leaned closer to the window and strained her ears. Her heart pounded so loud, she feared it could be heard a mile away. It was Lucy's husband. She was sure of it!

# Chapter 38

The horseman rode slowly down Main Street. The precise clip-clop of his horse sounded menacing in the otherwise silent night. Abby shrank back as the man came into view. He stopped directly in front of the salon and Abby stood frozen against the wall, afraid to breathe. A minute passed. Two.

Fearing he would enter the building, she dropped soundlessly to the floor on hands and knees. Although it was too dark to know for certain, Abby was almost positive it was Campbell looking for his wife. Thank God she'd thought to hide Lucy's horse and wagon.

She glanced back at the bed. Lucy had cried out earlier, but at the moment she was perfectly still, her breathing soft.

Abby turned back to the window. She couldn't see the horse, but she could sense the man's presence. She pulled the knife out of her boot. Although her weapon had gotten her out of many dangerous situations in the past, she'd never seriously harmed anyone. She prayed she wouldn't have to tonight.

Seconds passed. Minutes. Rising slowly, she peered over the windowsill. The moon had moved behind a cluster of tall pines, and it was too dark to make out anything more than the man's shadowy form.

Finally he rode away and all was quiet. Gasping for air, Abby leaned against the windowsill and searched the street below.

Out of habit she glanced toward Gunnar's cabin. A

light was burning. It wasn't like Gunnar to be up so late. So he couldn't sleep, either.

Slipping the knife back in her boot, she settled back in her chair, her nerves on edge. *Just don't let Lucy's husband come back,* she prayed.

She was accustomed to staying awake nights. All those years she'd lived on the streets, she'd never once closed an eye except in the full light of day.

Still, the night seemed to stretch on forever as she sat waiting for the first glimmer of dawn. It came at almost the same instant as the windows of Mom Bull's Restaurant lit up. Soon afterward, Otis rode into town and tethered his horse to the railing in front of Mom Bull's. It was another normal morning in Dangling Rope.

Abby tiptoed from the room and hurried downstairs. She unlocked the door and searched the dimly lit street before crossing to Mom Bull's. Already, the railroad crew was hard at work driving spikes into the hastily laid tracks. Abby's nerves were already on edge and the constant pounding made her more jumpy.

Otis sat at a corner table, drinking a cup of coffee. From the kitchen came the sound of pots and pans as Mom Bull prepared his breakfast.

Otis studied Abby over the rim of his cup. "You're up and about early, ain't you?"

She sat on the chair opposite him. "I need your help."

Otis set his cup down. "Every time a woman needs my help, it means I'm in trouble."

"It's Lu . . . Mrs. Campbell. I need you to take her to the Denver train station."

"Denver? What's wrong with Divide?"

"I'm afraid her husband would look for her there. I'm hoping that by the time he realizes she's gone to Denver, her train would have already left."

She was asking a lot of him. With the derailed train, Main Street was a disaster. Wagonloads of railroad ties were parked haphazardly, blocking the road. Getting out of town was going to be a challenge. "I'm afraid her life might be in danger."

Otis rubbed his chin. "I don't know, Abby. I don't want to get into hot water with that husband of hers."

"How can you think of your own neck at a time like this?"

He shrugged. "I make it a habit to think about my neck ever' time the opport'nity presents itself."

"Please, Otis. I'd ask Gunnar or Nathan, but . . ." She fell silent.

Mom Bull gave him a hearty slap on the back. "You ain't got nothin' better to do."

"Oh, awright," he said, grimacing. He gazed up at Mom Bull. "Why is it I can't ever say no to a pretty lady?"

Mom Bull slid a plate filled with eggs and beans in front of him and winked at Abby. "That's one of your best traits, Otis. Recognizin' a beautiful woman when you see one."

A horseman rode by and Abby whirled around to glance outside the window. To her relief, it was Burt. "I'll have Lucy meet you in about twenty minutes."

"Awright."

"Her horse and wagon's in the livery, but you better take yours." She threw her arms around him. "Thank you, Otis."

"Now, don't go gettin' all gushy," he said, blushing.

Abby raced back to the salon and flew up the stairs. "Lucy, wake up."

Lucy's eyes flew open. For a moment she looked disoriented. Finally, a look of raw fear glittered in her eyes and her face paled. "Is he . . ."

"No. Your husband's not here. I didn't mean to alarm you. But we've no time to waste. Otis is going to take you to Denver. From there you can catch the train to North Carolina and your family."

"I don't know if I should leave. . . ."

"Listen to me, Lucy. If you don't leave, something awful is going to happen to you. I feel it in my bones."

"Oh, Abby." Her eyes filled with tears. "I'm afraid you're right, but I don't have any money."

"I have a little. Enough for train fare." Abby reached under her mattress and retrieved some bills. "Take this. It's not much." The black and blue bruises on Lucy's face sickened her and Abby's anger flared. The man should be horsewhipped. "Hurry, Lucy. Please."

Lucy climbed out of bed and stared in the mirror. "Oh, God . . ."

Abby pulled the pins out of Lucy's hair. "He'll never do this again to you, Lucy. I promise."

"If my husband finds out you helped me . . ."

Abby ran a brush through Lucy's hair. It was obvious Lucy was in no frame of mind to groom herself. "He's not going to find out."

Lucy stood motionless, watching her through the mirror. "Abby . . . I don't deserve your kindness."

Abby tossed the hairbrush on the bureau and handed Lucy her sunbonnet. "That's nonsense, Lucy. You're a very special person. You deserve the best in life."

Lucy twisted the ribbons on her bonnet, but made no motion to put it on. "You don't know what you're saying." Her tears began to flow again. "If you knew why he hit me, you'd hate me."

"It doesn't matter why he hit you. Nothing gives anyone the right to abuse another person. Nothing."

Lucy wiped away her tears with the palms of her hands. "That's what your uncle said."

Abby stared at her, not sure she'd heard right. "Did . . . did you say my uncle?"

Lucy nodded her head and lowered herself onto the bed. "I think it's time you knew what happened to your uncle."

# Chapter 39

Abby's mind reeled in confusion and bewilderment. "You know what happened to my uncle? But why didn't you say so before?"

"I couldn't." Lucy bit her lip and glanced away.

"What do you mean, you couldn't?" Abby shook her. "You've got to tell me everything you know!"

"Oh, Abby, I wanted to tell you, but . . ." Fresh tears filled her eyes and her body trembled with her sobs.

Feeling guilty for snapping at her, Abby handed her a clean handkerchief. "Lucy, I didn't mean to—"

"It's all right," Lucy said. She dabbed away the tears. She was shaking so hard, her voice trembled.

Feeling sorry for the woman, Abby swallowed her impatience and hugged her. "Please, you must tell me what you know about my uncle."

Terror glittered in Lucy's eyes, but she lifted her chin and made a determined effort to overcome her fear. "Your uncle's dead."

Abby drew back, her stomach clenched in a knot. Naturally, she'd considered the possibility her uncle might not be alive. How could she not? But to hear the words spoken aloud was still a horrendous shock. She struggled to hold her emotions in check. "How . . . how do you know?"

Lucy balled the handkerchief in her hands. "I saw him die with my own eyes. I'm so sorry, Abby. . . . I would give anything not to have to tell you this."

For a moment, Abby was too stunned to speak. When she finally found her voice, it was high-pitched and shaky. "You *saw* my uncle die? Lucy, why did you wait so long to tell me this?" Lucy flinched as if she thought Abby would strike her and Abby regretted her harsh-spoken words. "I'm sorry, Lucy. I didn't mean to shout at you and I'm not going to hit you." She brushed a wisp of hair away from Lucy's face. "Are . . . are you certain it was my uncle?"

Lucy glanced uneasily at the window. "It had to be your uncle." Her voice was barely a whisper as she continued. "The man who died was a drummer. He came up to the Butterfly mines to show his wares. I saw him in Cripple Creek one day, showing a group of women some ready-made soap. So when he came to the cabin, I recognized him." Lucy's voice broke. "My husband and I were out back by the woodshed. I guess your uncle heard us. He came around the house and that's when he saw . . ." Lucy started to sob uncontrollably.

Abby wrapped her arms around Lucy's trembling body and rocked her until the sobs subsided. Finally she asked the question she was almost sure she knew the answer to. "What did my uncle see, Lucy?"

"My husband . . . he was hitting me. There'd been a terrible cave-in and he lost some of his men. . . . He and the others spent the night in town drinking." She wiped away the tears with her fingers. "He don't mean nothing by it, Abby. If only he didn't drink . . ."

Abby couldn't believe Lucy was still making excuses for the man. "Are you saying my uncle saw your husband beating you?"

Lucy's body shook violently, but this time she kept the tears at bay. "I pleaded with your uncle not to get involved. He wouldn't listen . . ."

Abby clutched the oak bedpost. She felt cold, nauseated. "How . . . how did he die?"

"They got into a terrible fight." Lucy's voice was so soft Abby had to strain to hear. "My husband struck him on the head with a piece of pipe."

The last chilling words were like daggers to her

heart. Abby pressed her fingers to her mouth. All these months she'd searched for him, she'd considered every possible explanation for her uncle's disappearance; but nothing was as horrible as the truth.

"Do you know where my uncle's buried?"

"No. My . . . my husband took his body away in the wagon. I don't know what he did with him after that."

Someone pounded on the door of the salon. Lucy turned deadly white.

Otis's voice filtered through the open bedroom window. "I thought you said we were in a hurry," he complained. "I didn't even get to finish my breakfast."

Abby thrust her head out the window. "We're coming, Otis."

"Abby." Lucy clutched at Abby's arm. "I wanted to tell you weeks ago. Honest I did. I couldn't because, though he might be a brutal man, he's still my husband."

"He's a murderer."

"I know." Lucy covered her mouth with her hand. "He's also the father of my child."

Abby's gaze dropped to Lucy's slender waistline. "You're expecting a baby?"

Lucy nodded. "What you said about something terrible happening if I stay with him . . . I'm afraid you're right. I'm afraid he might make me lose the baby. It wouldn't be the first time. . . ."

"Holy blazes, Lucy . . . is that why he beat you? Because you're carrying his child?"

Lucy shook her head. "He doesn't know about this child. I'm afraid if he knew, it would only make him more possessive of me."

"Beulah told me the beatings have gotten worse lately. If it's not the baby, then what?"

"My husband was furious when he learned you were in town. He forbade me to talk to you. When he saw me leaving your shop, he . . ." She was sobbing hard. "I kept coming and he kept . . . He was furious that I had spent the day at the railroad site. He's afraid I might tell someone what he's done."

It horrified Abby to think she was the cause of Lucy's torment. "Oh, Lucy, I'm so sorry."

"You have nothing to be sorry for. I'm the one who should be apologizing to you. I wanted so much to tell you the truth. That's why I came to your shop that first day . . . to tell you. But I couldn't, so I pretended I came to see you for face cream. I knew he'd kill me if I told you. But after yesterday . . . I'm afraid it doesn't matter much. He's gonna kill me anyway."

"Don't say that, Lucy. You mustn't even think it. You're going back to your family and you're going to have a beautiful baby and a beautiful life."

At the sound of horses, Lucy stiffened.

"Stay here," Abby said. She raced to the window. "It's all right," she called. "It's only the railroad crew." They were lucky this time, but who knew when Campbell would arrive? "We better not keep Otis waiting any longer."

Abby led the way to the stairs. Before they descended, Lucy reached for her arm. "Abby, I'm so sorry about your uncle."

"I'm just grateful you told me, Lucy. I would have spent the rest of my life not knowing the truth." She gave Lucy a hug. "You take care of that baby, you hear?"

Lucy managed a faint smile, her first around Abby. "If it's a boy, I would like to name him Randall, after your uncle."

Abby battled back the tears that stung her eyes. She had to be strong for Lucy's sake. "You said you didn't even know my uncle."

"I know he was a kind and honest man. He lost his life trying to protect me from my husband. I also know that those who knew him loved him very much. What better person to name my child after?"

Swallowing the lump in her throat, Abby threw her

arms around Lucy one last time. "I would be honored to have you name your son after my uncle."

Otis whisked Lucy out of town with no trouble, though he was forced to wait for the road to clear. On the chance they might meet up with Campbell, Otis insisted Lucy hide in the back of the wagon, beneath a blanket. As an added precaution, Abe Lincoln Smith agreed to accompany them as far as Divide, but Abby knew she wouldn't rest until Otis returned and reported Lucy's safe arrival in Denver.

As soon as the wagon was out of sight, Abby crossed to the sheriff's office.

Gunnar was just walking out the door. Surprised to see her, he froze. "I didn't think you'd want to see me after last night." The look on his face said he wouldn't blame her.

Last night? Was it only last night that she'd last seen Gunnar? So much had happened. Grief-stricken upon learning of her uncle's death, all she could think about at the moment was how much she wanted to be held by him. "I—I know what happened to my uncle," she stammered.

His eyes narrowed speculatively as he studied her face. "Abby?" He grabbed her arm and she collapsed against him.

Suddenly she was in his arms, pressed against his chest, desperately clinging to him. The tears came now, fast and furious, blurring her vision and dissolving the last thread of control. She needed Gunnar at that moment and she didn't care who knew it. Nathan included!

He pulled her inside the office and closed the door. Holding her tight, he whispered words of comfort into her hair. Only after her sobs had subsided did he question her. "Do you want to tell me what happened?"

The horrible truth burst out of her like steam escaping from a boiler. "Lucy's husband killed him."

He stiffened in surprise. "Campbell?" He lifted her

chin and searched her face, his expression incredulous. "Are you sure?"

She nodded. "Lucy told me. She said my uncle witnessed her husband hitting her. When my uncle tried to stop him, he and Campbell got into a fight."

Gunnar drew her closer, locking her in his arms as if he would never let her go. "I'm so sorry, Abby."

"He was a good man," she sobbed. "He was more like a father to me than my own." More tears welled up in her eyes, spilling onto his shirt. "I never told him that, about the father part. . . . Now it's too late."

Gunnar caught her face in his hands and wiped away her tears with his thumbs. "I think he knew everything he needed to know," he said, his brown eyes soft as velvet. "He knew how much you loved him and that's all that counts."

It was a comforting thought and one that helped her regain control. "I'm all right now," she said at last. She backed away from him, feeling oddly drained.

He poured her a glass of water and handed it to her.

She accepted the glass and took a long bracing sip before sitting. "I guess deep down a part of me always knew he was dead. It's just not fair that a man as peace-loving as my uncle should come to such a violent end. I only wish . . ."

He knelt by her side and stroked her arm. "What, Abby? What do you wish?"

She met his gaze. "I wish I knew what Campbell did with his body."

The lines deepened at his brow. "Lucy didn't tell you?"

Abby set the empty glass on the desk. "She doesn't know."

Gunnar studied her for a long moment, and she saw her own pain and sorrow carved into every line of his face. Finally he stood and checked his gun. "Will you be all right?"

Her stomach churned in dread. "Yes, but where are you going?"

"To find Campbell." He was out the door before she could respond.

"Wait!" She dashed outside after him and had to shout to be heard above the hammering of the railroad crew. "Gunnar! Wait!" He'd already mounted his horse. "The man is dangerous."

"The man's a murderer and a wife beater. It's time he's brought to justice." He snapped the reins and took off in a gallop.

Fearing for Gunnar's safety, Abby frantically glanced around. Nathan stepped out of Mom Bull's and, meeting her gaze, turned and headed in the opposite direction.

"Nathan, wait!" She lifted the hem of her skirt and chased after him. He refused to slow his pace, forcing her to run to keep up with him. "Gunnar's going after Campbell. You've got to stop him."

Nathan swung around to face her. He looked so unlike himself, she hardly recognized him. His bruised face was filled with contempt, his mouth twisted in cynicism. He held a bottle of whiskey in his hand. He took a sip, wiped his mouth with his arm, and replaced the cap. "Stop him? Why?"

"Campbell killed my uncle. He's capable of anything."

Nathan's mouth tightened into a harsh straight line. He turned and started up the hill. "Gunnar can take care of himself."

"What's the matter with you, Nathan? Campbell's dangerous. Gunnar could be killed."

He stopped and glanced back at her, his face dark and angry. "So what do you expect me to do about it?"

"Go after him. He wouldn't listen to me. But he'll listen to you, I know he will. You're his brother."

"I'm not any brother of his!" He spit out the word as if it held poison.

Her temper flared. How dare he abandon Gunnar in his time of need! After all Gunnar had done for him.

"Don't you think it's about time you stop blaming Gunnar for your mother's behavior?"

"Don't get involved in this, Abby. You don't know what you're talking about."

"I think I do, Nathan. Gunnar was only seven when your mother left you. He was a child. She made his life hell."

"You'll have to forgive me for not feeling sorry for him. But I have my own hell to deal with."

"It wasn't his fault."

"Oh, no?" He backed down the hill and planted himself in front of her. "He was the golden boy. The one who always said the right thing, did the right thing. 'Why can't you be like your brother?' Mama used to say. Well, he got Mama and he got you."

"Not me," Abby whispered. "He won't let himself love me because of what it's done to you." Her voice broke. "There's nothing he wouldn't do for you. Nothing."

"He knew how I felt about you, Abby. I told him how I felt. But that didn't stop him—"

"He tried, Nathan. He kept pulling away from me and I didn't know why. I'm the one you should be angry with. Had I been more honest about my feelings, maybe none of this would have happened." He turned to leave, but she grabbed him by the arm. "I wish to God you hadn't found out about Gunnar and me the way you did. It was inexcusable. Neither Gunnar nor I wanted to hurt you, but in the end, that's exactly what we did, and for that I'm truly sorry."

He gave her a look of contempt and pushed her away. "I don't need your apologies. I don't even need your pity."

"Please, Nathan, I beg of you. Whatever your feelings toward me, your feelings toward the past . . . none of that can matter. Not now. Gunnar needs you."

"He doesn't need me. He doesn't even need you, Abby!"

She swallowed hard, trying to think what she could say to penetrate through the hard mask of his anger and bitterness.

He gave a mocking laugh. "To think I loved you. I must be the greatest fool alive."

"Please don't, Nathan."

"Don't what, Abby?" he grated. The look of unbelievable pain and torture crossed his face. "I was willing to do anything for you." The softness in his eyes was almost as difficult to bear as his anger. She hated this, hated knowing what she'd done to him.

"Nathan . . . I . . ."

Something snapped in him and his eyes grew hard again, hateful. "But you wanted the golden boy. I wasn't good enough."

"I never thought that! You have so much goodness in you. What you've done for this town. For the people . . ."

"Don't, Abby." His voice grew husky. "Don't try to make me something I'm not."

"Everything I said is true. Nathan, don't do this to yourself. Go to your brother. If you don't, I'm afraid we'll both be sorry."

He looked at her long and hard and she dared to hope the strange look in his eyes meant he was about to relent. But her hopes were soon dashed when he took another thirsty gulp of his whiskey and started up the hill.

Frustrated and angry, she called after him. "How could you do this? You're the only family he has left! Dammit, Nathan. What kind of man are you?"

Nathan never looked back.

Not knowing what else to do, who else to turn to, she rushed back to Main Street. Otis and Abe were gone, and Clod was nowhere in sight. Who else was left? Except . . .

She ran to the sheriff's office and mounted Logger.

It was a challenge to ride her horse around the amazing amount of railroad equipment, but once she was out of town, she flew like the wind toward the Utes' camp. She couldn't think of a single reason why Owns Six Horses and his men would help her, but she was desperate enough to try anything.

# Chapter 40

Gunnar spotted Campbell's cabin set in a small clearing amid a grove of tall pines. With his eyes narrowed beneath his furrowed brow, he searched for signs of life. An empty clothesline stretched between the cabin and a shed. No horses occupied the corral. Not even a whisper of smoke rose from the tall stone chimney. The only sign of life was a noisy bluejay.

Gunnar had checked the mines, but Campbell's men claimed they hadn't seen him since yesterday. Lucy Campbell's disappearance could explain Campbell's absence. He could be out looking for her.

Still, it struck Gunnar as strange that Campbell hadn't asked for the sheriff's help in finding her. Wouldn't most husbands, even abusive ones, report a missing person to the authorities?

Gunnar dismounted and tied Lucky to the wooden fence. He kept a leisurely pace as he made his way to the front door. No sense giving Campbell reason to be suspicious.

He knocked, and when no one answered, he tried the door latch. It was locked from inside.

"Campbell!" he called. "It's Sheriff Kincaid. I need to talk to you."

He spun around at the sound of a running horse and charged down the steps. He caught only a glimpse of the rider, but it was enough for him to determine it was Campbell.

With lightning speed, Gunnar raced back to his horse and tugged the reins from the bush. He swung into his saddle and pressed his heels hard against his horse's ribs. "Let's go, boy!" Kicking up a cloud of dust, his horse tore up the trail, slicing through the woods like a cannonball.

The path veered sharply upward and narrowed before coming to a dead end at the base of a granite wall. Gunnar brought his horse to a halt. Shading his eyes against the bright midday sun, he finally spotted Campbell scrambling over huge granite boulders. Gunnar swung down from his saddle and gave chase. Body bent forward for balance, he jumped from rock to rock.

"Give it up, Campbell," he yelled. The man glanced back at him and nearly slipped. Rocks fell from beneath his feet, forcing Gunnar to take a less direct approach. This turned out to be a blessing. Rather than slow him down, the hard granite offered more stability than the loose sandstone beneath Campbell's feet.

He could see the panic on Campbell's face as the distance closed between them. "Don't make it any more difficult on yourself, Campbell!"

"You'll have to git me." Campbell reached a high ledge that jutted out over a steep canyon. He started across. He was almost to the end by the time Gunnar reached the ledge.

"You stay right where you are!" Campbell moved out farther. "Or I'll jump."

Gunnar froze. The louse would probably do it. "I'll make you a deal. You tell me what I want to know and I'll do everything I can to see you get a fair trial."

Campbell gave a mocking laugh. "Now ain't that right nice of you, Sheriff?" His face frowned in curiosity. "Whatya want to know?"

"Abby's uncle. Where'd you bury him?"

Campbell's mouth curled upward. "Now, why would I tell you that?"

"Because if you don't, I'll make your life hell—"

"You ain't doing nothin' to me, Kincaid." He moved closer to the end.

"Don't do it, Campbell!" He held out his hand and

beckoned him. "I swear, I'll do everything in my power to see you get a fair trial."

"You won't be happy until you see me hang. Well, I ain't gonna give you the satisfaction." He spun around and lifted his arms as if to jump. Instead he froze. For several seconds neither man moved. Then Campbell sobbed. "She left me. My Lucy left me."

Gunnar swore beneath his breath. The last thing he wanted to do was walk out on that ledge to save Campbell's skin.

"Steady, now," he called. "Back away. Come on, Campbell, you can do it." His clothes covered in red dust, the man stood as still as one of the red sandstone rock formations that rose from the canyon below. Cursing, Gunnar began to inch his way toward Campbell, his arm outward. "Take hold of my hand," he coaxed gently.

Campbell made no effort to move. Gunnar inched closer, keeping his eyes leveled at Campbell so as not to look down. At last he caught hold of Campbell's arm. "All right, now. I'll lead you back. Slowly."

Sweat beaded Gunnar's forehead as they started back. Campbell's eyes were fixed straight ahead and every step he took was a result of much prodding on Gunnar's part.

Within a few feet of safety, Campbell suddenly snapped out of his stupor. Taking Gunnar by surprise, Campbell thrust out his arm and sent him flying toward the edge. Only fast action on Gunnar's part prevented him from going over.

Gunnar hoisted himself to his feet, but Campbell kicked his legs out from under him. Down on all fours, Gunnar reached for his gun just as Campbell jumped him.

Abby followed Owns Six Horses along the old Indian trail that was almost hidden by the thick underbrush. The trail took so many twists and turns through the woods, Abby began to wonder if they were making any headway.

There were eight of them in the war party, including Abby, who, like her Ute companions, wore feathers and war paint. After finding no sign of Campbell at the Butterfly mines, Abby had persuaded Mole to direct them to Campbell's cabin.

"But I ain't gonna rescue you no more," the hermit yelled after her. "This is the last time. The last time! Ya hear me?"

Campbell's cabin was deserted, but Owns Six Horses pointed to the still-fresh tracks and gave a knowing nod. "Sheriff."

"How can you be sure?" Abby asked.

"I know," he said. "This way." He veered his horse to the left and galloped toward the woods. Abby and the others followed. They found Gunnar's horse and, hidden behind a boulder, a bay belonging to Campbell.

A movement overhead caught Abby's eyes. "I see them!" She steadied her horse and pointed at the high rocky ledge that jutted out over the canyon.

Owns Six Horses studied the ledge and the men on it. "Your friend in big trouble."

"Can't we do something?"

The Ute leader shook his head. "Too far."

Her heart in her throat, Abby watched the battling pair. It was impossible to determine which man, if either, held the advantage.

Suddenly the man she knew was Campbell rose to his feet. Gunnar remained on the ground. She didn't even know if he was alive. Campbell picked up a rock the size of a melon and held it over his head.

"Dear God, no!" Abby opened her mouth to scream, but no sound came out.

A single shot rang out, echoing along the walls of the canyon and sending a flock of protesting ravens to the sky.

For a frozen moment, Campbell stood perfectly still.

Finally, as if in a strange slow dance, the rock fell to the ground and he crumpled backward.

Gunnar made a desperate grab for the man's leg, but there was nothing he could do. Campbell fell over the ledge with an ear-piercing scream and disappeared into the depths of the canyon.

The silence that followed was almost chilling in its intensity. Gasping for air, Gunnar held himself on hands and knees and tried to shake off the fog that tiptoed on the edge of his consciousness. His head ached; his sides were sore. He didn't trust himself to stand. He searched for his gun, but apparently the weapon had fallen below during the struggle.

His heart skipped a beat, suddenly, and he lifted his head. "Abby?" He listened again. Did he only imagine he heard her calling to him? He feared he was losing ground to the darkness that was fast closing in. He forced himself to crawl along the rock, head held low. Upon reaching safe ground, he leaned his back against a boulder.

A fuzzy form swam before his eyes. Blinking hard, he was surprised to find Nathan standing in front of him, gun in hand.

Gunnar wiped the blood away from his chin. He hardly recognized Nathan. He'd always thought of Nathan as the little brother his mother had left behind. The little brother who needed his care. The little brother who must be protected at all costs.

Today, Gunnar saw Nathan for perhaps the first time. He was a grown man and the Colt revolver in his hand made him a formidable one. Abby was right; Nathan didn't need his older brother to watch out for him. It was a startling revelation, bringing with it a strange combination of relief and regret. "You . . . you saved my life."

"Hard to believe, isn't it, big brother?" Nathan blew on the barrel of the gun and pushed it into his belt.

"You were always so strong and in control and I was always the weakling."

"I never thought of you as a weakling."

"Yes, you did. I've lost track of how many times you came to my rescue." Nathan gave a strange, haunting laugh. "How I hated you all those times."

His head clearing, Gunnar stared hard at his brother. "Hated me? Why?"

"I wanted to punish you and the only way I could see to accomplish that was to hurt myself. Only you wouldn't let me. You kept coming to my rescue. I felt like the man who kept trying to commit suicide and always failed." He wiped his chin with the back of his hand. "It's crazy, isn't it?"

"Nothing's crazy," Gunnar said.

"Dammit, Gunnar. Everything's crazy. You. Me. This whole damned world. Do you know what's really crazy? I saw you on the ledge with Campbell and I realized that I didn't resent you taking Mother away as much as I resented her taking *you* away from me."

"You're right. That is crazy."

Nathan narrowed his eyes thoughtfully. "The thing is, she never was much of a mother to me, even before she left. Hell, even when we were kids, it was you and me against the world." He gave a tight-edged laugh and sank to his knees. "All I know is that when I saw you and Campbell out there, I wasn't going to let him take you away from me, too."

Gunnar's heart stopped racing and he felt drained. Reaching for every bit of strength he had left, he lifted his hand toward Nathan. "I'm sure as hell glad you felt that way."

Nathan grabbed his hand. "Me too."

Gunnar grimaced. If his ribs hadn't been broken following his fight with Nathan, they most definitely were now. "I liked taking care of you," Gunnar said. "You were a great kid." All the frustration and anger of those long-ago days returned and he could almost see the hard stubborn set of his mother's profile the countless times he'd pleaded with her to return home. "I begged her to go home."

"Forget it." Nathan released him and stood. "It doesn't matter anymore. None of what happened in the past matters."

"You're right," Gunnar said, making a few resolutions of his own. "You're not that kid anymore and you don't need me bailing you out of trouble." Gunnar shook his head. "God, I hate this. Every time I face death, I come up with all this wisdom." He grimaced against the pain. "Where'd you get the gun?"

Nathan touched the ivory-handled weapon. "It just so happened my old enemy came into town to check on his mother's investment."

Gunnar's eyes widened. "Bull Crankshaw's here?"

"He didn't want to loan me his gun, but old Mom Bull threatened to make him eat brined trout if he didn't."

Gunnar laughed and grabbed for his side.

Nathan frowned. "You better see a doctor."

"Wait. There's something else you should know."

"What's that?"

"I'm going to ask Abby to be my wife. I hope to God she'll have me after what I put her through. Can you handle that, Nathan? Knowing Abby and I are together?"

Nathan's expression darkened. "The question is, big brother, can you handle it? Knowing how I feel about her?"

"I hope so, Nathan. I really hope so."

Both men turned at the sound of Abby's voice. "Gunnar! Where are you? How dare you scare me like that, Gunnar Kincaid! If you don't answer me this minute, I'll . . ."

Nathan's eyes met Gunnar's. "You better go to her." He stood, but Gunnar grabbed him by the arm. "I never meant to fall in love with her. I fought against my feelings. I wanted you to be happy. . . . I swear to

God I would have done anything to keep from loving her."

Nathan surprised Gunnar by dropping to his knees and hugging him. Gunnar's ribs hurt, but he managed to hug his brother back, man to man, and it felt wonderful. He felt wonderful.

Nathan released him. "Go to her, Gunnar."

Gunnar arched an eyebrow. "No more 'big brother'?"

"No more little brother." Nathan glanced up as Abby's voice grew closer. He quickly spun about and disappeared in the thick brush.

He heard the sound of snapping branches behind him. "Gunnar?"

"Abby?"

He tried to catch sight of her in the heavy growth of trees and bushes. "Abby!" No sooner had he called her name for a second time than he was attacked by feathers and beads. "What the . . ."

Arms around his neck, she looked up at him with eyes as big and blue as mountain lakes. She was dressed in full Ute regalia, her face striped in war paint. And she'd never looked as beautiful to him as she looked at that moment.

"Owns Six Horses wouldn't let me ride with his war party unless I was properly attired," she explained.

Never had he known the joy and happiness he knew at that moment as he folded her, feathers and all, in his arms. "Abby, I love you."

She stared up at him with eyes filled with longing and desire. "I know," she whispered, and he caught the sadness in her voice.

"This time it's different, Abby. I *love* you. Do you hear me? And I want to marry you."

She looked stunned. "But you said . . ." She searched his face. "I thought . . . What about Nathan?"

"Nathan is a grown man. It's about time I started treating him like one."

"But—"

He pressed a finger against her lips. "No buts, Abby.

I love you. That's the way it is and that's the way it's going to stay."

She stared at him with rounded eyes. Then suddenly her lips curved into a smile as big as all outdoors and as bright as the midday sun. "I love you, too," she said. Snuggling against him, she pressed her head next to his shoulder.

"Well?" he murmured into her hair. "Are you going to marry me or aren't you?"

She giggled. "Just try and stop me."

Filled with unspeakable joy, he tilted her head up and kissed her soundly. By the time he released her, they were both breathless.

"There's only one thing that would make me happier, and that's if my uncle could have lived to see this day."

"I know where he's buried."

She inhaled. "Campbell told you?"

Gunnar nodded. "He blurted it out as he prepared to bash my head with that rock. I guess he thought since I was about to die, he had nothing to lose."

"Oh, Gunnar." She pressed her head next to his chest, feeling as if she'd finally come to the end of a very long journey. "Hold me."

# Chapter 41

The grave was shallow, barely three feet deep, and covered with a layer of rocks. The rocks had kept the animals from digging up the remains, and for that Abby was grateful. It was probably the only decent thing Campbell had done in his life.

Gunnar dug another grave, stopping to rest halfway through. According to the doctor, his ribs weren't broken, only bruised, but they still hurt to high heaven. It took a while, but he finally got the hole dug and together he and Abby reburied her uncle.

She took out her knife and cut off a length of her uncle's hair to put in her locket. While Gunnar covered the grave with dirt and rocks, she fashioned a cross out of a tree branch. She etched her uncle's name in the wood with her knife, and thought about Lucy and the child she was carrying. "He gave me a new life. He taught me how to love again, to trust."

Gunnar dropped by her side and helped press the end of the cross into the ground. He brushed her hair away from her damp cheek and kissed her on the forehead. "And you've taught me how to love and to trust, Abby."

"You always knew how to love," she said. "No one could love a brother more than you loved Nathan."

"But it was the wrong kind of love. And it did neither one of us any good." He held her close, enjoying the moment, and wondered about the many quirks of fate that had brought Abby into his life.

\* \* \*

On the day of her wedding, Abby stood in the parlor of Madam Rosie's while Ginger and Ruby fussed over her. She wore a simple white gown trimmed in lace and pearls.

It had been a little over a month since Abby had agreed to be Gunnar's wife. So much had happened since that day. With the coming of the railroad and the increased tension with the labor unions, many miners, fearing violence was about to erupt in Cripple Creek, had already moved their families to Dangling Rope.

Overnight, it seemed, the town's population had increased to over a hundred, and the end wasn't in sight.

Lucy Campbell made it to Raleigh and was living with her family. Abby had written to tell her about her husband's death and Lucy had written back expressing her sadness and grief. Lucy still maintained that her husband had been a kind and loving man when he wasn't drinking.

Otis, threatened by Burt's presence, finally got around to asking for Mom Bull's hand. The day she agreed to marry him, Otis left her restaurant shouting and whooping it up. Mom Bull had finally got her wish; someone had actually left her restaurant jumping for joy.

Nathan had left Dangling Rope and headed for Wyoming. Said he wanted to build another town that was bigger and better than Dangling Rope. Meg surprised the townsfolk by going with him, determined to open her own complexion salon.

Abby suspected Meg pursued yet another dream. It was obvious she had strong feelings for Nathan. Of course, she wouldn't admit it for the world, and had scoffed when Abby suggested it.

"Well, you can deny it all you want, Meg, " Abby muttered to herself as she straightened the delicate white lace at her wrist, "but I know better." And if Nathan had a sensible bone in his body, he was going to know it, too.

Ginger looked up from the floor where she was fixing

Abby's hem. Since giving up dangerous beauty potions, her skin was less pale. She looked almost robust. "Did you say something?"

"I was just thinking aloud. What time do you have?"

Ruby laughed. "Aren't brides supposed to blush and be nervous? I thought only grooms were impatient."

Abby smiled. "Oh, Ruby." She took the young woman's hands and squeezed them tight. "I hope one day you find someone like Gunnar to love."

Ruby bit her lip. "Abby . . . I've been meaning to talk to you. I'm sorry for the way I acted the day you covered my scar."

"I'm the one who should apologize to you," Abby said. She brushed her hand over her friend's head. "I was so eager to try out my products, I didn't take the time to consider your feelings. I'm truly sorry, Ruby."

"There's nothing to be sorry for. Because of you, I was forced to see myself without the scar. It was a frightening moment because with it came the realization that I wasn't crippled or deformed, I was a normal person who just happened to have a scar."

"Everyone has scars," Abby said. "Some of them are inside and I'm afraid those are the hardest to hide. You can't put powder or cream on those."

Ruby nodded. "I guess I'm lucky in that respect. Would you teach me how to cover mine?"

"You know I will. But what made you change your mind?'

Ruby blushed. "You're going to think this is silly of me. But do you remember the day I worked on the railroad? I actually laid some of those rails. I never thought it was possible. I could actually do something useful."

Abby looked up at her in astonishment. "Don't tell me you're thinking of joining the railroad crew!"

Ruby laughed. "Nothing like that. But I've decided to travel to Denver and look for employment. If I can lay railroad track, it only stands to reason that maybe I can do other things. Burt said I was a fast learner."

"Burt?" Abby drew back, noting the pretty red flush on Ruby's cheeks. "Oh, Ruby. I'm so happy for you. This is the best wedding present you could give me."

Mom Bull walked into the parlor, followed by a portly but less pinched-looking Rosie. Rosie had steadfastly refused to wear her corset since shedding it the day she joined the railroad crew. The decision had a disastrous effect on her figure, but did wonders for her disposition.

Mom Bull threw up her hands. "A beautiful bride, handsome groom, and not a blasted preacher in sight."

"Reverend Patcher promised he'd be here no later than Wednesday," Rosie moaned.

"He's only a day late," Ginger said, trying to calm everyone down.

Mom Bull would have none of it. "A day don't mean beans to that scalawag."

That afternoon, Gunnar forced his way into the Opera House and took Abby by the hand. "I've waited long enough for this day." His eyes smoldered with fire as he gazed at his beautiful bride. "I don't intend to wait a moment longer."

He led Abby and the others to Main Street, where they were greeted with applause. Abby was surprised to find Owns Six Horses among the wedding guests. General Macker and his men had ridden through town two weeks earlier looking for the Utes. Gunnar had sent him off in the wrong direction, but Abby knew it was only a matter of time before Owns Six Horses would be captured and hauled back to the reservation he so loathed.

"He's agreed to marry us Indian style," Gunnar explained.

"Oh, dear," Rosie fretted, tugging at her springy curls. "Is that legal?"

Otis laughed aloud. "Since when have you worried about legalities?"

Owns Six Horses stepped in front of the couple. "First paint bodies with paint." He pointed to the clay pots of paint spread across an Indian blanket. Owns Six Horses carefully lifted a pot and dipped the tip of an eagle feather into the shimmering blue paint to demonstrate. "Now sheriff try." He handed the feather to Gunnar. "Know what to say?"

Gunnar gazed at her with so much love, Abby felt as if her heart would burst with happiness. "I know exactly what to say," he said, his voice as soft as midnight velvet. He dipped the end of the feather into the paint and turned back to her.

"Abigail Parker," he began, his voice suddenly hoarse. "If it were within my power to give you the sky and the ocean"—he drew a blue line across each of her soft rounded cheeks—"it couldn't begin to show the full extent of my love for you." Her lips parted as she gazed up at him.

His hand trembled with emotion as he wiped the tip of the feather clean. Taking a steadying breath, he dipped the brush into the yellow paint. "Yellow is the color of the the sun." He zigzagged a line across her lovely smooth forehead. "Few things are meant to last a lifetime. But my dearest, sweet Abby, I vow that my love and devotion to you will burn bright for all eternity." Tears of happiness shimmered on her lashes like tiny diamonds.

Finally he dipped the feather into the third and final color. "Red is the color of my heart." He painted a red circle on her forehead. "This circle represents the endless joy of loving you fully and completely. He drew the brush away and gazed deep into her eyes. "All that I have, and all that I am, I give to you."

He handed her the eagle feather and knelt in front of her so she could reach his face. She brushed her tears away before wiping the feather clean and dipping the tip into the blue paint. "Gunnar Kincaid," she said softly. "My love for you is as deep as the deepest sea and as wide as the whole universe." She ran a blue stripe across his rugged cheekbones and gazed into his gold-flecked eyes.

With the yellow paint, she vowed her undying love. Trembling with happiness and joy, she made a mess of the zigzags on his forehead, but she got the words right and that was all that really mattered.

By the time she uttered her most solemn vow, Mom Bull could be heard sobbing on Otis's shoulder like a newborn babe. "All that I am, and all that I have, I give to you."

Owns Six Horses stepped forward, looking unbearably self-important, and covered Abby and Gunnar with a blanket. "Now you married."

Beneath the blanket, Gunnar whispered in her ear, "Did you hear that? We're married."

"Oh, Gunnar." She looked up at him in wonder. He lowered his head and kissed her.

Clod picked up his fiddle and began playing a lively tune. With the blanket still wrapped around them, Gunnar and Abby led the merry dance that followed.

Much later, Gunnar and Abby walked hand in hand up the hill to his cabin. They'd decided to make the cabin their home until they'd built their own. Ruby and Ginger had snuck up earlier to light the fire and lanterns, and the cabin seemed to radiate a homely warm glow. Gunnar stopped her on the porch and lifted her into the cradle of his arms. "I've wanted to do this since I first met you." Showering her with kisses, he carried her inside.

"Oh, Gunnar." She planted a kiss in the hollow of his neck. "I never thought I could be so happy."

He smiled down at her. Smudges of blue, yellow, and red paint still on his face. "This is just the beginning. I promise you." He carried her into the bedroom and laid her gently, lovingly, upon the bed. "But first we have a little bit of unfinished business to take care of." He kissed her lightly on the lips, then walked to the foot of the bed and pointed to her trunk. "May I?"

He was asking permission to open it. She sat up and nodded, though she couldn't imagine what he wanted in her trunk.

His eyes never leaving her face, he lifted the lid and set the tray and hatbox aside. When she offered no objection, he pulled out a stack of her neatly folded clothes and began placing them in a bureau drawer.

She pressed her fingers against her mouth as she watched him methodically empty her trunk. It had been years since her trunk had been unpacked. After being packed off so many times in haste—and losing some of her precious belongings in the process—she had refused to unpack again.

When he had completed the task, he closed the empty trunk and sat on the bed next to her, sliding his fingers sensuously up her arms. "What do you say, Traveling Lady?"

Her heart sang with happiness and joy as she settled back against the pillow, pulling him with her. "I say my traveling days are over."

He tickled her in an intimate spot and she giggled. She ran her hands down his body and his eyes flared with desire. "My, God, Abby! Don't stop!"

Smiling to herself, she bit his ear and whispered, "Aren't you glad I never learned to *act* like a lady?"

Watch for
Margaret Brownley's
next romance,
*Ribbons on the Wind,*
coming from Topaz
in the winter of 1996

# WE NEED YOUR HELP

To continue to bring you quality romance
that meets your personal expectations,
we at TOPAZ books want to hear from you.
Help us by filling out this questionnaire, and in exchange
we will give you a **free gift** as a token of our gratitude.

- Is this the first TOPAZ book you've purchased? (circle one)

  YES    NO

  The title and author of this book is: _____

- If this was not the first TOPAZ book you've purchased, how many have
  you bought in the past year?

  a: 0 - 5   b 6 - 10   c: more than 10   d: more than 20

- How many romances in total did you buy in the past year?

  a: 0 - 5   b: 6 - 10   c: more than 10   d: more than 20 ____

- How would you rate your overall satisfaction with this book?

  a: Excellent   b: Good   c: Fair   d: Poor

- What was the main reason you bought this book?

  a: It is a TOPAZ novel, and I know that TOPAZ stands
     for quality romance fiction
  b: I liked the cover
  c: The story-line intrigued me
  d: I love this author
  e: I really liked the setting
  f: I love the cover models
  g: Other: _____

- Where did you buy this TOPAZ novel?

  a: Bookstore   b: Airport   c: Warehouse Club
  d: Department Store   e: Supermarket   f: Drugstore
  g: Other: _____

- Did you pay the full cover price for this TOPAZ novel? (circle one)

  YES    NO

  If you did not, what price did you pay? _____

- Who are your favorite TOPAZ authors? (Please list)

- How did you first hear about TOPAZ books?

  a: I saw the books in a bookstore
  b: I saw the TOPAZ Man on TV or at a signing
  c: A friend told me about TOPAZ
  d: I saw an advertisement in_____magazine
  e: Other: _____

- What type of romance do you generally prefer?

  a: Historical   b: Contemporary
  c: Romantic Suspense   d: Paranormal (time travel,
     futuristic, vampires, ghosts, warlocks, etc.)
  d: Regency   e: Other: _____

- What historical settings do you prefer?

  a: England   b: Regency England   c: Scotland
  e: Ireland   f: America   g: Western Americana
  h: American Indian   i: Other: _____

- What type of story do you prefer?
  - a: Very sexy
  - b: Sweet, less explicit
  - c: Light and humorous
  - d: More emotionally intense
  - e: Dealing with darker issues
  - f: Other

- What kind of covers do you prefer?
  - a: Illustrating both hero and heroine
  - b: Hero alone
  - c: No people (art only)
  - d: Other_____

- What other genres do you like to read (circle all that apply)

  Mystery          Medical Thrillers      Science Fiction
  Suspense         Fantasy                Self-help
  Classics         General Fiction        Legal Thrillers
  Historical Fiction

- Who is your favorite author, and why?_____
  _____

- What magazines do you like to read? (circle all that apply)
  - a: *People*
  - b: *Time/Newsweek*
  - c: *Entertainment Weekly*
  - d: *Romantic Times*
  - e: *Star*
  - f: *National Enquirer*
  - g: *Cosmopolitan*
  - h: *Woman's Day*
  - i: *Ladies' Home Journal*
  - j: *Redbook*
  - k: Other:_____

- In which region of the United States do you reside?
  - a: Northeast
  - b: Midatlantic
  - c: South
  - d: Midwest
  - e: Mountain
  - f: Southwest
  - g: Pacific Coast

- What is your age group/sex?     a: Female   b: Male
  - a: under 18
  - b: 19-25
  - c: 26-30
  - d: 31-35
  - e: 56-60
  - f: 41-45
  - g: 46-50
  - h: 51-55
  - i: 56-60
  - j: Over 60

- What is your marital status?
  - a: Married
  - b: Single
  - c: No longer married

- What is your current level of education?
  - a: High school
  - b: College Degree
  - c: Graduate Degree
  - d: Other:_____

- Do you receive the TOPAZ *Romantic Liaisons* newsletter, a quarterly newsletter with the latest information on Topaz books and authors?

  YES          NO

  If not, would you like to?   YES     NO

  Fill in the address where you would like your free gift to be sent:

  Name:_____
  Address:_____
  City:_____ Zip Code:_____

  You should receive your free gift in 6 to 8 weeks.
  Please send the completed survey to:

  Penguin USA•Mass Market
  Dept. TS
  375 Hudson St.
  New York, NY 10014